MW00676579

G.A. HENTY

December 8, 1832 — November 16, 1902

True To The Old Flag
A Tale of the American War of Independence

by

G. A. Henty

ILLUSTRATED BY GORDON BROWNE

PrestonSpeed Publications
Pennsylvania

A note about the name PrestonSpeed Publications:
The name PrestonSpeed Publications was chosen in loving memory of
our fathers, Preston Louis Schmitt and Lester Herbert Maynard
(nicknamed "Speed" for his prowess in baseball).

Originally published by Blackie & Son, Limited,
August 2, 1884
Blackie & Son Title Page Date: 1885

True to the Old Flag: A Tale of the American War of Independence
by G. A. Henty
© 2002 by PrestonSpeed Publications
Published by PrestonSpeed Publications, 51 Ridge Road, Mill Hall,
Pennsylvania 17751.

This book is printed on acid-free paper, and its binding materials have
been chosen for strength and durability.

Heirloom Hardcover Edition ISBN 1-887159-14-2
Popular Softcover Edition ISBN 1-931587-14-0

Printed in the United States of America

PRESTONSPEED PUBLICATIONS
51 RIDGE ROAD
MILL HALL, PENNSYLVANIA 17751
(570) 726-7844
www.prestonspeed.com
November 2002

INTRODUCTION

G. A. Henty's life was filled with exciting adventure. After completing his work at Westminster School, he attended Cambridge University, where he undertook a rigorous course of study and also enjoyed boxing, wrestling, and rowing. The strenuous study and healthy, competitive participation in sports prepared Henty for his adventures. To name just a few, he fought with the British army in the Crimea, served as a war correspondent during Garibaldi's fight for independence in Italy, visited Abyssinia, witnessed the Franco-Prussian war while in Paris, observed the Carlists in Spain, attended the opening of the Suez Canal, toured India with the Prince of Wales (later Edward VII), and visited the California gold fields.

G. A. Henty lived during the reign of Queen Victoria (1837-1901) and began his story-telling career with his own children. After dinner it was his custom to spend an hour or two telling them a story that often continued for days. In fact, some stories lasted for weeks! One evening a friend happened to be present during Henty's "story hour." Watching the children as they sat spell-bound, he urged Henty to write down his stories so others could enjoy them. Happily for us, Henty did so. One of his secretaries reported that he often would pace rapidly back and forth in his study dictating stories as fast as the secretary could record them. He became known to his readers as "The Prince of Story-Tellers" and "The Boy's Own Historian."

Henty's stories revolve around a fictional boy hero during fascinating periods of history. His heroes are diligent, courageous, intelligent, and dedicated to their country and cause in the face of, at times, great peril. Respected historians have acknowledged his histories, particularly the accounts of battles, for their accuracy. His ability to bring his readers action-packed adventure in an accurate historical setting makes the study of history exciting, and removes the drudgery often associated with such study.

Henty's heroes fight wars, sail the seas, discover new lands, conquer evil empires, prospect for gold, and embark upon a host of other exciting adventures. They meet such famous personages as Josephus, Titus, Hannibal, Robert the Bruce, Sir William Wallace, General Marlborough, General Gordon, General Kichner, Robert E. Lee, Frederick the Great, the Duke of Wellington, Huguenot leader Coligny, the explorer Cortez, King Alfred, Napoleon, and Sir Francis Drake, to name just a few. The heroes experience the fall of Jerusalem, the Roman invasion of Britain, the Crusades, the Viking invasion of Europe, the Reign of Terror in France, and the exciting events of the Reformation in various countries, etc. In short, Henty's heroes live during tumultuous times in history and meet many of the most prominent leaders of those times.

PrestonSpeed is delighted to offer the long-out-of-print works of G. A. Henty to a whole new generation of adults and young people. Our Henty titles contain the complete text and all maps and/or illustrations included in the original editions. Although the books have been newly typeset, the original grammar, and spelling remain the same as in the original versions.

Pearson tries the ice

PREFACE

MY DEAR LADS,

You have probably been accustomed to regard the war between England and her Colonies in America as one in which we were not only beaten but to some extent humiliated. Owing to the war having been an unsuccessful one for our arms, British writers have avoided the subject, and it has been left for American historians to describe. These, writing for their own countrymen, and drawing for their facts upon gazettes, letters, and other documents emanating from one side only, have naturally, and no doubt insensibly, given a very strong colour to their own views of the events, and English writers have been too much inclined to accept their account implicitly. There is, however, another and very different side to the story, and this I have endeavoured to show you. The whole of the facts and details connected with the war can be relied upon as accurate. They are drawn from the valuable account of the struggle written by Major Stedman, who served under Howe, Clinton, and Cornwallis, and from other authentic contemporary sources. You will see that although unsuccessful—and success was, under the circumstances, a sheer impossibility—the British troops fought with a bravery which was never exceeded, and that their victories in actual conflict vastly outnumbered their defeats. Indeed it may be doubted whether in any war in which this country has been engaged have our soldiers exhibited the qualities of endurance and courage in a higher degree.

Yours sincerely,

G. A. HENTY.

CONTENTS

ILLUSTRATIONS

TRUE TO THE OLD FLAG
A TALE OF THE AMERICAN WAR OF INDEPENDENCE

CHAPTER I
A FRONTIER FARM

"Concord, March 1, 1774

"MY DEAR COUSIN,—

"I am leaving next week with my husband for England, where we intend to pass some time visiting his friends. John and I have determined to accept the invitation you gave us last summer for Harold to come and spend a few months with you. His father thinks that a great future will ere many years open in the West, and that it is therefore well the boy should learn something of frontier life. For myself, I would rather that he stayed quietly at home, for he is at present over fond of adventure; but as my husband is meditating selling his estate here and moving west, it is perhaps better for him."

"Massachusetts is in a ferment, as indeed are all the Eastern states, and the people talk openly of armed resistance against the government. My husband, being of English birth, and having served in the king's army, cannot brook what he calls the rebellious talk which is common among his neighbours, and is already on bad terms with many around us. I myself am, as it were, a neutral. As an American woman, it seems to me that the colonists have been dealt with somewhat hardly by the English parliament and that the measures of the latter have been high-handed and arbitrary; upon the other hand, I naturally incline toward my husband's views. He maintains that as the king's army has driven out the French and gives protection to the colony, it is only fair that the colonists should contribute to its expenses. The English ask for no contributions towards the expenses of their own country, but demand that at least the expenses of the protection of the colony shall not be charged upon the heavily-taxed people at home. As to the law that the colony shall trade only with the mother country, my husband says that this is the rule in the colonies of Spain, France, Portugal, and the Netherlands, and that the people here, who can obtain what land they choose, and till it without rent, should not grumble at paying this small tax to the mother country. However it be, I fear that troubles will come; and this place being the head and focus of the party hostile to England, my husband, feeling himself out of accord with all his neighbours, saving a few loyal gentlemen like himself, is thinking much and seriously of selling our estate here and of moving away into the new countries of the West, where he will be free from all the disputation and contentious talk which occupies men's time here.

"Indeed, Cousin, times have sadly changed since you were staying with us five years ago. Then, our life was a peaceful and quiet one; now there is nothing but wrangling and strife. The dissenting clergy are, as my husband says was the case in England before the great civil war, the fomenters of this discontent. There are many busybodies who pass their time in stirring up the people by violent harangues and seditious writing; therefore, everyone takes one side or the other, and there is neither peace nor comfort in life.

"Accustomed as I have always been to living in ease and affluence, I dread somewhat the thought of a life on the Indian frontier. One has heard so many dreadful stories of Indian fights and massacres, that I tremble a little at the prospect; but I do not mention this to John, for as other women are, like yourself, brave enough to support these dangers, I would not appear a coward in his eyes. You will see, Cousin, that as this prospect is before us, it is well that Harold should learn the ways of a frontier life. Moreover, John does not like the thought of leaving him here while we are in England, for, as he says, the boy might learn to become a rebel in his absence. Therefore, my dear cousin, we have resolved to send him to you. An opportunity offers in the fact that a gentleman of our acquaintance is, with his family, going this week west, with the intention of settling there; and he will, he tells us, go first to Detroit, whence he will be able to send Harold forward to your farm. The boy himself is delighted at the thought, and promises to return an accomplished backwoodsman. John joins me in kind love to yourself and your husband, and believe me to remain your affectionate cousin,

"MARY WILSON"

Four months after the date of the above letter, a lad some fifteen years old was walking, with a man of middle age, on the shores of Lake Huron. Behind them was a large clearing of about a hundred acres in extent. A comfortable house, with buildings for cattle, stood at a distance of some three hundred yards from the lake; broad fields of yellow corn waved brightly in the sun, and from the edge of the clearing came the sound of a woodman's axe, showing that the proprietor was still enlarging the limits of his farm. Surrounding the house, at a distance of twenty yards, was a strong stockade some seven feet in height, formed of young trees, pointed at the upper end, squared and fixed firmly in the ground. The house itself, although far more spacious and comfortable than the majority of backwood farmhouses, was built in the usual fashion, of solid logs, and was evidently designed to resist attack.

William Welch had settled ten years before on this spot, which was then far removed from the nearest habitation. It would have been a very imprudent act, under ordinary circumstances, to have established himself in so lonely a position, so far removed from the possibility of assistance in case of attack. He settled there, however, just after Pontiac, who was at the head of an alliance of all the Indian tribes of those parts, had, after the long and desperate siege of Fort Pitt, made peace with us upon finding that his friends the French had given up all thought of further resistance to the English, and had entirely abandoned the country. Mr. Welch thought, therefore, that a permanent peace was likely to reign on the frontier, and that he might safely establish himself in the charming location he had pitched upon, far removed from the confines of civilization.

The spot was a natural clearing of some forty acres in extent, sloping down to the water's edge, and a more charming site could hardly have been chosen. Mr. Welch had brought with him three farm-labourers from the East, and as time went on, he extended the clearing by cutting down the forest giants which bordered it.

In spite, however, of the beauty of the position, the fertility of the soil, the abundance of his crops, and the advantages afforded by the lake, both from its plentiful supply of fish and as a highway by which he could convey his produce to market, he had more than once regretted his choice of the location. It was true that there had been no Indian wars on a large scale, but the Indians had several times broken out in sudden incursions. Three times he had been attacked, but fortunately only by small parties, which he had been enabled to beat off. Once, when a more serious danger threatened him, he had been obliged to embark with his wife and child and his more valuable chattels in the great scow in which he carried his produce to market, and had to take refuge in the settlements, to find on his return his buildings destroyed and his farm wasted. At that time he had serious thoughts of abandoning his location altogether, but the settlements were extending rapidly towards him, and, with a prospect of having neighbours before long, and the natural reluctance to give up a place upon which he had expended so much toil, he decided to hold on, hoping that more quiet times would prevail, until other settlers would take up land around him.

The house had been rebuilt more strongly than before. He now employed four men, and had been unmolested since his return to his farm, three years before the date of this story. Already two or three locations had been taken up on the shores of the lake beyond him; a village had grown up thirty-five miles away, and several settlers had established themselves between that place and his home.

"So you are going out fishing this morning, Harold?" Mr. Welch said. "I hope you will bring back a good supply, for the larder is low. I was looking at you yesterday, and I see that you are becoming a first-rate hand at the management of a canoe."

"So I ought to be," the boy said, "considering that for nearly three months I have done nothing but shoot and fish."

"You have a sharp eye, Harold, and will make a first-rate backwoodsman one of these days. You can shoot nearly as well as I can now. It is lucky that I had a good stock of powder and lead on hand; firing away by the hour together as you do consumes a large amount of ammunition. See, there is a canoe on the lake; it is coming this way, too. There is but one man in it; he is a white by his clothes."

For a minute or two they stood watching the boat, and then, seeing that its course was directed towards the shore, they walked down to the edge of the lake to meet it.

"Ah! Pearson, is that you?" Mr. Welch asked. "I thought I knew your long sweeping stroke at a distance. You have been hunting, I see; that is a fine stag you have got there. What is the news?"

"About as bad as can be, Master Welch," the hunter said. "The Irroquois have dug up the tomahawk again, and are out on the war-path. They have massacred John Brent and his family. I heard a talk of it amongst some hunters I met ten days since in the woods. They said that the Irroquois were restless, and that their chief, War Eagle, one of the most troublesome varmint on the whole frontier, had been stirring them up to war. He told them, I heard, that the Pale-faces were pushing farther and farther into the Injun woods, and that, unless they drove them back, the Red-skin hunting-grounds would be gone. I hoped that nothing would come of it, but I might have known better. When the Red-skins begin to stir, there is sure to be mischief before they are quiet again."

The colour had somewhat left Mr. Welch's cheeks as the hunter spoke.

"This is bad news indeed, Pearson," he said gravely. "Are you sure about the attack on the Brents?"

"Sartin sure," the hunter said. "I met their herd; he had been down to Johnson's to fetch a barrel of pork. Just when he got back he heard the Injun yells, and saw smoke rising in the clearing, so he dropped the barrel and made tracks. I met him at Johnson's, where he had just arrived. Johnson was packing up with all haste, and was going to leave; and so I said I would take my canoe and come down the lake, giving you all warning on the way. I stopped at Burns' and Hooper's. Burns said he should clear out at once, but Hooper talked about seeing it through. He has got no wife to be skeary about, and reckoned that with his two hands he could defend his log-hut. I told him I reckoned he would get his har raised if the Injuns came that way; but in course that's his business."

"What do you advise, Pearson? I do not like abandoning this farm again to the mercy of the Red-skins."

"It would be a pity, Master Welch, that's as true as gospel; it's the likeliest clearing within fifty miles round, and you've fixed the place up as snug and comfortable as if it were a farm in the old provinces. In course the question is, what this War Eagle intends to do. His section of the tribe is pretty considerable strong, and although at present I ain't heard that any others have joined, these Injuns are like barrels of gunpowder: when the spark is once struck there is no saying how far the explosion may spread. When one band of them sees as how another is taking scalps, and getting plunder and honour, they all want to be at the same work. I reckon War Eagle has got some two hundred braves who will follow him; but when the news spreads that he has begun his work, all the Irroquois, to say nothing of the Shawnees, Delawares, and other varmint, may dig up the hatchet. The question is, what War Eagle's intentions are. He may make a clean sweep down, attacking all the outlying farms, and waiting till he is joined by a lot more of the red reptiles before attacking the settlements. Then, on the other hand, he may think himself strong enough to strike a blow at Gloucester and some other border villages at once. In that case he might leave the outlying farms alone, as the news of the burning of these would reach the settlements and put them on their guard, and he knows in course that if he succeeds there, he can eat you all up at his leisure."

"The attack upon Brent's place looks as if he meant to make a clean sweep down," Mr. Welch said.

A FRONTIER FARM

"Well," the hunter continued thoughtfully, "I don't know as I sees it in that light. Brent's place was a long way from any other. He might have wished to give his band a taste of blood, and so raise their spirits, and he might reasonably conclude that nout would be known about it for days, perhaps weeks, to come. Then, again, the attack might have been made by some straggling party without orders. It's a dubious question. You have got four hands here, I think, and yourself. I have seen your wife shoot pretty straight with a rifle, so she can count as one; and as this young 'un here has a good idea too with his shooting-iron, that makes six guns. Your place is a strong one, and you could beat off any straggling party. My idea is that War Eagle, who knows pretty well that the place would make a stout fight, won't waste his time by making a regular attack upon it. You might hold out for twenty-four hours; the clearing is open, and there ain't no shelter to be had. He would be safe to lose a sight of men, and this would be a bad beginning, and would discourage his warriors greatly. No, I reckon War Eagle will leave you alone for the present. Maybe he will send a scout to see whether you are prepared; it's as likely as not that one is spying at us somewhere among the trees now. I should lose no time in driving in the animals and getting well in shelter. When they see you are prepared, they will leave you alone, at least for the present; afterwards there's no saying. That will depend on how they gets on at the settlements. If they succeed there and get lots of booty and plenty of scalps, they may march back without touching you; they will be in a hurry to get to their villages and have their feasts and dancings. If they are beaten off at the settlements, I reckon they will pay you a visit for sure; they won't go back without scalps. They will be savage like, and won't mind losing some men for the sake of having something to brag about when they get back. And now, Master Welch, I must be going on, for I want to take the news down to the settlements before War Eagle gets there, and he may be ahead of me now, for aught I know. I don't give you no advice as to what you had best do; you can judge the circumstances as well as I can. When I have been to the settlements and put them on their guard, maybe I shall be coming back again, and in that case you know

7

Jack Pearson's rifle is at your disposal. You may as well tote this stag up to the house; you won't be doing much hunting just for the present, and the meat may come in handy."

The stag was landed, and a minute later the canoe shot away from shore under the steady stroke of the hunter's powerful arms. Mr. Welch at once threw the stag over his shoulders and, accompanied by Harold, strode away towards the house. On reaching it he threw down the stag at the door, seized a rope which hung against the wall, and the sounds of a large bell rung in quick sharp strokes summoned the hands from the fields. The sound of the woodman's axe ceased at once, and the shouts of the men as they drove the cattle towards the house rose on the still air.

"What is the matter, William?" Mrs. Welch asked, as she ran from the house.

"I have bad news, my dear. The Indians are out again, and I fear we have trouble before us. We must hope that they will not come in this direction, but must be prepared for the worst. Wait till I see all the hands and beasts in the stockade, and then we can talk the matter over quietly."

In a few minutes the hands arrived, driving before them the horses and cattle.

"What is it, boss?" they asked. "That was the alarm-bell, sure enough?"

"The Indians are out again," Mr. Welch said, "and in force. They have massacred the Brents, and are making towards the settlements. They may come this way or they may not; at anyrate we must be prepared for them. Get the beasts into the sheds, and then do you all take scythes and set to work to cut down that patch of corn, which is high enough to give them shelter; there's nothing else which will cover them within a hundred yards of the house. Of course you will take your rifles with you and keep a sharp look-out; but they will have heard the bell if they are in the neighbourhood, and will guess that we are on the alert, so they are not likely to attempt a surprise. Shut one of the gates and leave the other ajar, with the bar handy to put up in case you have to make

8

a run for it. Harold will go up to the look-out while you are at work."

Having seen that all was attended to, Mr. Welch went into the house, where his wife was going about her work as usual, pale, but quiet and resolute.

"Now, Jane," he said, "sit down and I will tell you exactly how matters stand, as far as Pearson, who brought the news, has told me. Then you shall decide as to the course we had better take."

After he had told her all that Pearson had said, and the reasons for and against expecting an early attack, he went on, "Now, it remains for you, my dear, to decide whether we shall stay and defend the place till the last against any attack that may be made, or whether we shall at once embark in the scow, and make our way down to the settlements."

"What do you think, William?" his wife asked.

"I scarcely know myself," he answered; "but if I had quite my own way, I should send you and Nelly down to the settlements in the scow, and fight it out here with the hands."

"You certainly will not have your own way in that," his wife said. "If you go, of course I go; if you stay, I stay. I would a thousand times rather go through a siege here and risk the worst, than go down to Gloucester and have the frightful anxiety of not knowing what was happening here. Besides, it is very possible, as you say, that the Indians may attack the settlement itself. Many of the people there have had no experience in Indian war, and the Red-skins are likely to be far more successful in their surprise there than they would be here. If we go, we should have to leave our house, our barns, our stacks, and our animals to the mercy of the savages. Your capital is pretty nearly all embarked here now, and the loss of all this would be ruin to us. At anyrate, William, I am ready to stay here, and to risk what may come, if you are. A life on the frontier is necessarily a life of danger, and if we are to abandon everything, and to have to commence life afresh every time the Indians go on the war-path, we had better give it up at once and return to Massachusetts."

"Very well, my dear," her husband said gravely. "You are a true frontierman's wife; you have chosen as I should have done. It is a choice of evils, but God has blessed and protected us since we came out into the wilderness; we will trust and confide in him now. At anyrate," he went on more cheerfully, "there is no fear of the enemy starving us out. We got in our store of provisions only a fortnight since, and have enough of everything for a three months' siege. There is no fear of our well failing us, and as for ammunition, we have abundance: seeing how Harold was using powder and ball, I had an extra supply when the stores came in the other day. There is plenty of corn in the barn for the animals for months, and I will have the corn which the men are cutting brought in as a supply of food for the cows. It will be useful for another purpose, too: we will keep a heap of it soaked with water, and will cover the shingles with it in case of attack. It will effectually quench their fire-arrows."

The day passed off without the slightest alarm, and by nightfall the patch of corn was cleared away and an uninterrupted view of the ground for the distance of a hundred yards from the house was afforded. When night fell, two out of the four dogs belonging to the farm were fastened out in the open, at a distance of from seventy to eighty yards of the house, the others being retained within the stockade. The garrison was divided into three watches, two men being on the alert at a time, relieving each other every three hours. Mr. Welch took Harold as his companion on the watch. The boy was greatly excited at the prospect of a struggle. He had often read of the desperate fights between the frontier settlers and the Indians, and had longed to take share in the adventurous work. He could scarcely believe that the time had come, and that he was really a sharer in what might be a desperate struggle.

The first watch was set at nine, and at twelve Mr. Welch and Harold came on duty. The men they relieved reported that all was silent in the woods, and that they had heard no suspicious cries of any kind. When the men had retired to their room, Mr. Welch told Harold that he should take a turn round the stockade and visit the dogs. Harold was to keep watch at the gate, to close it after he went out, to put up the bar, and to stand beside it ready to open it instantly if called upon.

Then the farmer stepped out into the darkness, and, treading noiselessly, at once disappeared from Harold's sight. The latter closed the gate, replaced the heavy bar, and stood with one hand on this and the other holding his rifle, listening intently. Once he thought he heard a low growling from one of the dogs, but this presently ceased, and all was quiet again. The gate was a solid one, formed of strong timbers placed at a few inches apart, and bolted to horizontal bars.

Presently he felt the gate upon which his hand rested quiver as if pressure was applied from without. His first impulse was to say "Is that you?" but Mr. Welch had told him that he would give a low whistle as he approached the gate; he therefore stood quiet with his whole attention absorbed in listening. Without making the least stir he peered through the bars, and made out two dark figures behind them. After once or twice shaking the gate, one took his place against it and the other sprang upon his shoulders.

Harold looked up and saw a man's head appear against the sky. Dim as was the light, he could see that it was no European head-gear, a long feather or two projecting from it. In an instant he levelled his rifle and fired. There was a heavy fall, and then all was silent. Harold again peered through the bars. The second figure had disappeared, and a black mass lay at the foot of the gate.

In an instant the men came running from the house, rifles in hand. "What is it?" they exclaimed. "Where is Mr. Welch?"

"He went out to scout round the house, leaving me at the gate," Harold said. "Two men, I think Indians, came up; one was getting over the gate when I shot him. I think he is lying outside—the other has disappeared."

"We must get the master in!" one of the men said. "He is probably keeping away, not knowing what has happened. Mr. Welch," he shouted, "it is all safe here, so far as we know! We are all on the look-out to cover you as you come up."

Immediately a whistle was heard close to the gate; this was cautiously opened a few inches, and was closed and barred directly Mr. Welch entered.

Harold told him what had happened.

"I thought it was something of the sort. I heard Wolf growl, and felt sure that it was not at me. I threw myself down and crept up to him, and found him shot through the heart with an Indian arrow. I was crawling back to the house when I heard Harold's shot. Then I waited to see if it was followed by the war-whoop, which the Red-skins would have raised at once on finding that they were discovered, had they been about to attack in force. Seeing that all was quiet, I conjectured that it was probably an attempt on the part of a spy to discover if we were upon the alert. Then I heard your call and at once came on. I do not expect any attack to-night now, as these fellows must have been alone; but we will all keep watch till the morning. You have done very well, Harold, and have shown yourself a keen watchman. It is fortunate that you had the presence of mind neither to stir nor to call out when you first heard them, for, had you done so, you would probably have got an arrow between your ribs, as poor Wolf has done."

When it was daylight and the gate was opened, the body of an Indian was seen lying without. A small mark on his forehead showed where Harold's bullet had entered, death being instantaneous. His war-paint and the embroidery of his leggings showed him at once to be an Irroquois. Beside him lay his bow, with an arrow which had evidently been fitted to the string for instant work. Harold shuddered when he saw it, and congratulated himself on having stood perfectly quiet. A grave was dug a short distance away, the Indian was buried, and the household proceeded about their work.

The day, as was usual in households in America, was begun with prayer, and the supplications of Mr. Welch for the protection of God over the household were warm and earnest. The men proceeded to feed the animals; these were then turned out of the inclosure, one of the party being always on watch in the little tower which had been erected for that purpose some ten or twelve feet above the roof of the house. From this spot a view was obtainable right over the clearing to the forest which surrounded it on three sides. The other hands proceeded to cut down more of the corn, so as to extend the level space around the house.

CHAPTER II
AN INDIAN RAID

THAT day and the next passed quietly. The first night the man who was on watch up to midnight remarked to Mr. Welch when he relieved him, that it seemed to him that there were noises in the air.

"What sort of noises, Jackson—calls of night-birds or animals? For if so, the Indians are probably around us."

"No," the man said; "all is still round here, but I seem to feel the noise rather than hear it. I should say that it was firing very many miles off."

"The night is perfectly still, and the sound of a gun would be heard a long way."

"I cannot say that I have heard a gun; it is rather a tremble in the air than a sound."

When the man they had relieved had gone down, and all was still again, Mr. Welch and Harold stood listening intently.

"Jackson was right," the farmer said, "there is something in the air. I can feel it rather than hear it. It is a sort of murmur, no louder than a whisper. Do you hear it, Harold?"

"I seem to hear something," Harold said. "It might be the sound of the sea a very long way off, just as one can hear it many miles from the coast, on a still night at home. What do you think it is?"

"If it is not fancy," Mr. Welch replied, "and I do not think that we should all be deceived, it is an attack upon Gloucester."

"But Gloucester is 35 miles away," Harold answered.

"It is," Mr. Welch replied; "but on so still a night as this, sounds can be heard from an immense distance. If it is not this, I cannot say what it is."

14

AN INDIAN RAID

Upon the following night, just as Mr. Welch's watch was at an end, a low whistle was heard near the gate. "Who is there?" Mr. Welch at once challenged.

"Jack Pearson, and the sooner you open the gate the better; there is no saying where these red devils may be lying round."

Harold and the farmer instantly ran down and opened the gate.

"I should advise you to stop down here," the hunter said, as they replaced the bars. "If you did not hear me, you certainly would not hear the Red-skins, and they would all be over the palisade before you had time to fire a shot. I am glad to see you safe, for I was badly scared lest I should find nothing but a heap of ashes here."

The next two men now turned out, and Mr. Welch led his visitor into the house and struck a light. "Hallo, Pearson, you must have been in a skirmish!" he said, seeing that the hunter's head was bound up with a blood-stained bandage.

"It was all that," Pearson said, "and wuss. I went down to Gloucester and told 'em what I had heard, but the darned fools tuk it as quiet as if all King George's troops with fixed bayonets had been camped round 'em. The council got together and palavered for an hour, and concluded that there was no chance whatever of the Irroquois venturing to attack such a powerful place as Gloucester. I told them that the Red-skins would go over their stockade at a squirrel's jump, and that as War Eagle alone had at least 150 braves, while there warn't more than fifty able-bodied men in Gloucester and all the farms around it, things would go bad with 'em if they did not mind. But, bless yer, they knew more than I did about it; most of them had moved from the East, and had never seen an Injun in his war-paint. Gloucester had never been attacked since it was founded nigh ten years ago, and they did not see no reason why it should be attacked now. There was a few old frontiersmen like myself among them, who did their best to stir them up, but it was no manner of good. When the council was over, we put our heads together, and just went through the township a talking to the women, and we had not much difficulty in getting up such a scare among 'em, that before nightfall every one of 'em in the farms around made their husbands move into the stockade of the village.

"When the night passed off quietly, most of the men were just as savage with us as if it had been a false alarm altogether. I pinted out that it was not because War Eagle had left them alone that night that he was bound to do so the next night, or any night after. But in spite of the women they would have started out to their farms the fust thing in the morning if a man had not come in with the news that Carter's farm had been burned, and the whole of the people killed and scalped. As Carter's farm lay only about 15 miles off, this gave them a scare, and they were as ready now to believe in the Injuns, as I had tried to make them the night before. Then they asked us old hands to take the lead, and promised to do what we told them; but when it came to it, their promises were not worth the breath they had spent upon them. There were eight or ten houses outside the stockade, and in course we wanted these pulled down; but they would not hear of it. However, we got them to work to strengthen the stockades, to make loopholes in the houses near them, to put up barricades from house to house, and to prepare generally for a fight. We divided into three watches.

"Well, just as I expected, about eleven o'clock at night the Injuns attacked. Our watch might just as well have been asleep for any good they did, for it was not till the Red-skins had crept up to the stockade all round, and opened fire between the timbers on them, that they knew that they were near. I do them justice to say that they fought stiff enough then, and for four hours they held the line of houses; every Red-skin who climbed the stockade fell dead inside it. Four fires had been lighted directly they attacked to enable us to keep them from scaling the stockade, but they showed us, too, to the enemy, of course.

"The Red-skins took possession of the houses which we had wanted to pull down, and precious hot they made it for us. Then they shot such showers of burning arrows into the village that half of the houses were soon alight. We tried to get our men to sally out and to hold the line of stockade, when we might have beaten them off if all the village had been burned down, but it were no manner of good: each man wanted to stick to his wife and family till the last. As the flames went up, every man who showed himself was shot down, and when at last more than half our number had gone under, the Red-skins brought up fagots, piled them against the stockade outside, and then the hull tribe came bounding over. Our rifles were emptied, for we could not get the men to hold their fire, but some of us chaps as knew what was coming gave the Red-skins a volley as they poured in.

"I don't know much as happened after that. Jack Robins and Bill Shuter, who were old pals of mine, and me, made up our minds what to do, and we made a rush for a small gate that there was in the stockade, just opposite where the Injuns came in. We got through safe enough, but they had left men all round. Jack Robins he was shot dead. Bill and I kept straight on. We had a grapple with some of the Red-skins; two or three on them went down, and Bill and I got through and had a race for it till we got fairly into the forest. Bill had a ball in the shoulder, and I had a clip across the head with a tomahawk. We had a council, and Bill went off to warn some of the other settlements, and I concluded to take to the water and paddle back to you, not knowing whether I should find that the Red-skins had been before me. I thought at anyrate that I might stop your going down to Gloucester, and that if there was a fight, you would be none the worse for an extra rifle."

Mr. Welch told the hunter of the visit of the two Indian spies two nights before.

"Wall," the hunter said, "I reckon for the present you are not likely to be disturbed. The Injuns have taken a pile of booty and something like two hundred scalps, counting the women and children, and they moved off at daybreak this morning in the direction of Tottenham, which I reckon they will attack to-night. Howsomever, Bill has gone on there to warn them, and after the sack of Gloucester, the people of Tottenham won't be caught napping, and there are two or three old frontiersmen who have settled down there, and War Eagle will get a hot reception if he tries it. As far as his band is concerned, you are safe for some days.

The only fear is that some others of the tribe, hurrying up at hearing of his success, may take this place as they go past. And now, I guess that I will take a few hours' sleep. I have not closed an eye for the last two nights."

A week passed quietly. Pearson, after remaining two days, again went down the lake to gather news, and returned a day later with the intelligence that almost all the settlements had been deserted by their inhabitants; the Indians were out in great strength, and had attacked the settlers at many points along the frontier, committing frightful devastations.

Still another week passed, and Mr. Welch began to hope that his little clearing had been overlooked and forgotten by the Indians. The hands now went about their work as usual, but always carried arms with them, while one was constantly stationed on the watch-tower. Harold resumed his fishing, never, however, going out of sight of the house. Sometimes he took with him little Nelly Welch, it being considered that she was as safe in the canoe as she was in the house, especially as the boat was always in sight, and the way up from the landing to the house was under cover of the rifles of the defenders, so that, even in case of an attack, they would probably be able to make their way back.

One afternoon they had been out together for two or three hours. Everything looked as quiet and peaceable as usual; the hands were in the fields near the house; a few of the cows were grazing close to the gate. Harold had been successful in his fishing, and had obtained as many fish as he could carry. He stepped out from the canoe, helped Nelly to land, slung his rifle across his back, and picked up the fish, which were strung on a withy passed through their gills.

He had made but a few steps when a yell arose so loud and terrible that for a moment his heart seemed to stop beating. Then from the corn-fields leaped up a hundred dark figures; then came the sharp crack of rifles, and two of the hands dashed down at full speed towards the house. One had fallen. The fourth man was in the watch-tower. The surprise had been complete. The Indians had made their way like snakes through the long corn, whose waving

18

had been unperceived by the sentinel, who was dozing at his post, half-asleep in the heat of the sun. Harold saw in a moment that it was too late for him to regain the house; the Red-skins were already nearer to it than he was.

"Now, Nelly! Into the boat again! Quick!" he said. "We must keep out of the way till 'tis all over."

Nelly was about twelve years old, and her life in the woods had given her a courage and quickness beyond her years. Without wasting a moment on cries or lamentations she sprang back into the canoe. Harold took his place beside her, and the light craft darted rapidly out into the lake. Not until he was some three or four hundred yards from the shore did Harold pause to look round. Then, when he felt he was out of gunshot distance, he ceased paddling.

The fight was raging now around the house; from loopholes and turret the white puffs of smoke darted angrily out. The fire had not been ineffectual, for several dark forms could be seen lying round the stockade, and the bulk of the Indians, foiled in their attempt to carry the place at a rush, had taken shelter in the corn, and kept up a scattering fire round the house, broken only on the side facing the lake, where there was no growing crop to afford them shelter.

"They are all right now," Harold said cheerfully. "Do not be anxious, Nelly; they will beat them off. Pearson is a host in himself. I expect he must have been lying down when the attack was made. I know he was scouting round the house all night. If he had been on the watch, those fellows would never have succeeded in creeping up so close unobserved."

"I wish we were inside," Nelly said, speaking for the first time. "If I were only with them, I should not mind."

"I am sure I wish we were," Harold agreed. "It is too hard being useless out here when such a splendid fight is going on. Ah! They have their eyes on us!" he exclaimed, as a puff of smoke burst out from some bushes near the shore, and a ball came skipping along on the surface of the water, sinking, however, before it reached it.

"That was a pretty good shot."

AN INDIAN RAID

"Those Indian muskets are no good," Harold said contemptuously, "and the trade powder the Indians get is very poor stuff; but I think that they are well within range of my rifle."

The weapon which Harold carried was an English rifle of very perfect make and finish which his father had given him on parting.

"Now," he said, "do you paddle the canoe a few strokes nearer the shore, Nelly. We shall still be beyond the range of that fellow. He will fire again, and I shall see exactly where he is lying."

Nelly, who was efficient in the management of a canoe, took the paddle, and, dipping it in the water, the boat moved slowly towards the shore. Harold sat with his rifle across his knees, looking intently over the bow of the boat towards the bush from which the shot had come.

"That's near enough, Nelly," he said. The girl stopped paddling, and the hidden foe, seeing that they did not mean to come nearer the shore, again fired.

Harold's rifle was in an instant against his shoulder; he sat immovable for a moment, and then fired.

Instantly a dark figure sprang from the bush, staggered a few steps up the slope, and then fell headlong.

"That was a pretty good shot," Harold said. "Your father told me when I saw a stag's horns above a bush, to fire about two feet behind them and eighteen inches lower. I fired a foot below the flash, and I expect I hit him through the body. I had the sight at 300 yards, and fired a little above it. Now, Nelly, paddle out again. See," he said, "there is a shawl waving from the top of the tower! Put your hat on the paddle and wave it."

"What are you thinking of doing, Harold?" the girl asked presently.

"That is just what I have been asking myself for the last ten minutes," Harold replied. "It is quite clear that as long as the siege is kept up, we cannot get back again, and there is no saying how long it may last. The first thing is, what chance is there of their pursuing us? Are there any other canoes on the lake within a short distance?"

21

"They have one at Braithwaite's," the girl said, "four miles off—but look, there is Pearson's canoe lying by the shore!"

"So there is!" Harold exclaimed. "I never thought of that. I expect the Indians have not noticed it. The bank is rather high where it is lying. They are sure to find it sooner or later. I think, Nelly, the best plan would be to paddle back again so as to be within the range of my rifle while still beyond the reach of theirs. I think I can keep them from using the boat until it is dark."

"But after it is dark, Harold?"

Well, then, we must paddle out into the lake so as to be well out of sight. When it gets quite dark, we can paddle in again, and sleep safely anywhere a mile or two from the house."

An hour passed without change. Then Nelly said, "There is a movement in the bushes near the canoe."

Presently an arm was extended, and proceeded to haul the canoe towards the shore by its head rope. As it touched the bank an Indian rose from the bushes and was about to step in, while a number of flashes of smoke burst out along the shore and the bullets skipped over the water towards the canoe, one of them striking it with sufficient force to penetrate the thin bark a few inches above the water's edge. Harold had not moved, but as the savage stepped into the canoe, he fired, and the Indian fell heavily into the water, upsetting the canoe as he did so.

A yell of rage broke from his comrades.

"I don't think they will try that game again as long as it is daylight," Harold said. "Paddle a little farther out again, Nelly. If that bullet had hit you, it would have given you a nasty blow, though I don't think it would have penetrated. Still, we may as well avoid accidents."

After another hour passed, the fire round the house ceased.

"Do you think the Indians have gone away?" Nelly asked.

"I am afraid there is no chance of that," Harold said. "I expect they are going to wait till night and then try again. They are not fond of losing men, and Pearson and your father are not likely to miss anything that comes within their range as long as daylight lasts."

"But after dark, Harold?"

"Oh, they will try all sorts of tricks, but Pearson is up to them all. Don't you worry about them, dear."

The hours passed slowly away until at last the sun sank and the darkness came on rapidly. So long as he could see the canoe, which just floated above the water's edge, Harold maintained his position; then, taking one paddle, while Nelly handled the other, he sent the boat flying away from the shore out into the lake.

For a quarter of an hour they paddled straight out. By this time the outline of the shore could be but dimly perceived. Harold doubted whether it would be possible to see the boat from shore; but in order to throw the Indians off the scent, should this be the case, he turned the boat's head to the south and paddled swiftly until it was perfectly dark.

"I expect they saw us turn south," he said to Nelly. "The Red-skins have wonderful eyes, so if they pursue at all, they will do it in that direction. At anyrate no human being, unless he borrowed the eyes of an owl, could see us now; so we will turn and paddle the other way."

For two hours they rowed in this direction. "We can go into shore now," Harold said at last. "We must be seven or eight miles beyond the house."

The distance to the shore was longer than they expected, for they had only the light of the stars to guide them, and neither had any experience in night travelling. They had therefore made much further out into the lake than they had intended. At length, however, the dark line of trees rose in front of them, and in a few minutes the canoe lay alongside the bank, and its late occupants were stretched on a soft layer of moss and fallen leaves.

"What are we going to do to-morrow about eating?" Nelly asked.

"There are four or five good-sized fish in the bottom of the canoe," Harold replied. "Fortunately we caught more than I could carry, and I intended to make a second trip from the house for these. I am afraid we shall not be able to cook them, for the Indians can see smoke any distance. If the worse comes to the worst we must eat them raw, but we are sure to find some berries in the wood to-morrow. Now, dear, you had better go to sleep as fast as you can; but first let us kneel down and pray God to protect us and your father and mother."

The boy and girl knelt in the darkness and said their simple prayers. Then they lay down, and Harold was pleased to hear in a few minutes the steady breathing which told him that his cousin was asleep. It was a long time before he followed her example. During the day he had kept up a brave front and had endeavoured to make the best of their position, but now that he was alone he felt the full weight of the responsibility of guiding his companion through the extreme danger which threatened them both. He felt sure that the Indians would prolong the siege for some time, as they would be sure that no reinforcements could possibly arrive in aid of the garrison. Moreover, he by no means felt so sure, as he had pretended to his companion, of the power of the defenders of the house to maintain a successful resistance to so large a number of their savage foes. In the day-light he felt certain they could beat them off, but darkness neutralizes the effect both of superior arms and better marksmanship. It was nearly midnight before he lay down with the determination to sleep, but scarcely had he done so when he was aroused by an outburst of distant firing. Although six or seven miles from the scene of the encounter, the sound of each discharge came distinct to the ear along the smooth surface of the lake, and he could even hear, mingled with the musketry fire, the faint yells of the Indians. For hours, as it seemed to him, he sat listening to the distant contest, and then he, unconsciously to himself, dozed off to sleep, and awoke with a start, to find Nelly sitting up beside him and the sun streaming down through the boughs.

He started to his feet. "Bless me!" he exclaimed. "I did not know that I had been to sleep. It seems but an instant ago that I was listening—" and here he checked himself—"that is, that I was wide awake, and here we are in broad daylight."

Harold's first care was to examine the position of the canoe, and he found that fortunately it had touched the shore at a spot where the boughs of the trees overhead drooped into the water beyond it, so that it could not be seen by anyone passing along the lake. This was the more fortunate, as he saw some three miles away a canoe with three figures on board. For a long distance on either side the boughs of the trees drooped into the water, with only an opening here and there such as that through which the boat had passed the night before.

"We must be moving, Nelly; here are the marks where we scrambled up the banks last night. If the Indians take it into their heads to search the shore both ways, as likely enough they may do, they will be sure to see them. In the first place, let us gather a stock of berries, and then we will get into the boat again, and paddle along under this arcade of boughs till we get to some place where we can land without leaving marks of our feet. If the Indians find the place where we landed here, they will suppose that we went off again before daylight."

For some time they rambled in the wood, and succeeded in gathering a store of berries and wild fruit. Upon these Nelly made her breakfast, but Harold's appetite was sufficiently ravenous to enable him to fall to upon the fish, which, he declared, were not so bad after all. Then they took their places in the canoe again, and paddled on for nearly a mile.

"See, Harold," Nelly exclaimed, as she got a glimpse through the boughs into the lake, "there is another canoe! They must have got the Braithwaite boat. We passed their place coming here, you know. I wonder what has happened there."

"What do you think is best to do, Nelly?" Harold asked. "Your opinion is just as good as mine about it. Shall we leave our canoe behind, land, and take to the woods, or shall we stop quietly in the canoe in shelter here, or shall we take to the lake and trust to our speed to get away—in which case, you know, if they should come up, I could pick them off with my gun before they got within reach?"

"I don't think that would do," the girl said, shaking her head. "You shoot very well, but it is not an easy thing to hit a moving object if you are not accustomed to it, and they paddle so fast that if you miss them once they would be close alongside—at anyrate we should be within reach of their guns—before you could load again. They would be sure to catch us, for although we might paddle nearly as fast for a time, they would certainly tire us out. Then as to waiting here in the canoe, if they come along on foot looking for us, we should be in their power. It is dreadful to think of taking to the woods with Indians all about, but I really think that would be our safest plan."

"I think so too, Nelly, if we can manage to do it without leaving a track. We must not go much farther, for the trees are getting thinner ahead, and we should be seen by the canoes."

Fifty yards farther, Harold stopped paddling. "Here is just the place, Nelly."

At this point a little stream of three or four feet wide emerged into the lake. Harold directed the boat's head towards it. The water in the stream was but a few inches deep.

"Now, Nelly," he said, "we must step out into the water and walk up it as far as we can go—it will puzzle even the sharpest Redskin to find our track then."

They stepped into the water, Harold taking the head-rope of the canoe and towing the light boat—which, when empty, did not draw more than two inches of water—behind him. He directed Nelly to be most careful, as she walked, not to touch any of the bushes, which at times nearly met across the stream.

"A broken twig or withered leaf would be quite enough to tell the Indians that we came along this way," he said. "Where the bushes are thick you must manage to crawl under them. Never mind about getting wet; you will soon dry again."

Slowly and cautiously they made their way up the stream for nearly a mile; it had for some distance been narrowing rapidly, being only fed by little rills from the surrounding swamp land. Harold had so far looked in vain for some spot where they could land without leaving marks of their feet. Presently they came to a place where a great tree had fallen across the stream.

"This will do, Nelly," Harold said. "Now, above all things, you must be careful not to break off any of the moss or bark. You had better take your shoes off; then I will lift you on to the trunk, and you can walk along it without leaving a mark."

It was hard work for Nelly to take off her drenched boots, but she managed at last. Harold lifted her on to the trunk, and said, "Walk along as far as you can, and get down as lightly as possible on to a firm piece of ground. It rises rapidly here, and is, I expect, a dry soil where the upper end of the tree lies."

"How are you going to get out, Harold?"

"I can swing myself up by that projecting root."

Before proceeding to do so, Harold raised one end of the canoe and placed it on the trunk of the tree. Then, having previously taken off his shoes, he swung himself on to the trunk. Hauling up the light bark canoe, and taking especial pains that it did not grate upon the trunk, he placed it on his head, and followed Nelly along the tree. He found, as he had expected, that the ground upon which the upper end lay was firm and dry. He stepped down with great care, and was pleased to see as he walked forward that not the slightest trace of a footmark was left.

"Be careful, Nelly," he exclaimed, when he joined her, "not to tread on a stick or disturb a fallen leaf with your feet, and, above all, to avoid breaking the smallest twig as you pass! Choose the most open ground, as that is the hardest."

In about a hundred yards they came upon a large clump of bushes. "Now, Nelly, raise those lower boughs as gently and as carefully as you can. I will push the canoe under. I don't think the sharpest Indian will be able to take up our track now."

Very carefully the canoe was stowed away, and when the boughs were allowed to fall in their natural position, it was completely hidden from sight to every passer-by. Harold took up the fish, Nelly had filled her apron with the berries, and, carrying their shoes—for they agreed that it would be safer not to put them on—they started on their journey through the deep forest.

CHAPTER III
THE RED-SKIN ATTACK

MR. WELCH was with the men two or three hundred yards away from the house when the Indians suddenly sprang out and opened fire. One of the men fell beside him; the farmer stooped to lift him, but saw that he was shot through the head. Then he ran with full speed towards the house, shouting to the hands to make straight for the gate, disregarding the cattle. Several of these, however, alarmed at the sudden outburst of fire and the yells of the Indians, made of their own accord for the stables, as their master rushed up at full speed. The Indians were but fifty or sixty yards behind when Mr. Welch reached his gate. They had all emptied their pieces, and after the first volley no shots had been fired save one by the watchman on the look-out. Then came the crack of Pearson's rifle, just as Mr. Welch shut the gate and laid the bar in its place. Several spare guns had been placed in the upper chambers, and three reports rang out together, for Mrs. Welch had run upstairs at the first alarm to take her part in the defence.

In another minute the whole party, now six in all, were gathered in the upper room.

"Where are Nelly and Harold?" Mr. Welch exclaimed.

"I saw the canoe close to the shore just before the Indians opened fire," the watchman answered.

"You must have been asleep," Pearson said savagely. "Where were your eyes to let them Red-skins crawl up through the corn without seeing them? With such a crowd of them, the corn must have been waving as if it were blowing a gale. You ought to have a bullet in ye'r ugly carkidge, instead of its being in ye'r mate's out there."

While this conversation was going on, no one had been idle; each took up his station at a loophole, and several shots were fired whenever the movement of a blade of corn showed the lurking-place of an Indian.

The instant the gate had been closed, War Eagle had called his men back to shelter, for he saw that all chance of a surprise was now over, and it was contrary to all Red-skin strategy to remain for one moment unnecessarily exposed to the rifles of the whites. The farmer and his wife had rushed at once up into the look-out as the Indians drew off, and to their joy saw the canoe darting away from shore.

"They are safe for the present, thank God!" Mr. Welch said. "It is providential indeed that they had not come a little farther from the shore when the Red-skins broke out. Nothing could have saved them had they fairly started for the house."

"What will they do, William?" asked his wife anxiously.

"I cannot tell you, my dear; I do not know what I should do myself under the circumstances. However, the boy has got a cool head on his shoulders, and you need not be anxious for the present. Now, let us join the others; our first duty is to take our share in the defence of the house. The young ones are in the hands of God. We can do nothing for them."

"Well?" Pearson asked, looking round from his loop-hole as the farmer and his wife descended into the room, which was a low garret extending over the whole of the house. "Do you see the canoe?"

"Yes, it has got safely away," William Welch said; "but what that lad will do now is more than I can say."

Pearson placed his rifle against the wall. "Now keep your eyes skinned," he said to the three farm hands. "One of yer's done mischief enough this morning already, and you will get your hair raised as sure as you are born unless you look out sharp. Now," he went on, turning to the Welches, "let us go down and talk this matter over. The Injuns may keep on firing, but I don't think they will show in the open again as long as it is light enough for us to draw bead upon them. Yes," he went on, as he looked—through a loophole in the lower story—over the lake, "there they are, just out of range."

"What do you think they will do?" Mrs. Welch asked.

The hunter was silent for a minute.

"It ain't a easy thing to say what they ought to do, much less what they will do; it ain't a good look-out any way, and I don't know what I should do myself. The whole of the woods on this side of the lake are full of the darned red critters. There are a hundred eyes on that canoe now, and go where they will, they will be watched."

"But why should they not cross the lake and land on the other side?" Mr. Welch said.

"If you and I were in that canoe," the hunter answered, "that's about what we should do; but, not to say that it is a long row for them, they two young 'uns would never get across. The Injuns would have them before they had been gone an hour. There is my canoe lying under the bushes; she would carry four, and would go three feet to their two."

"I had forgotten about that," William Welch said; and then added, after a pause, "the Indians may not find it."

"You need not hope that," the hunter answered. "They have found it long before this. I don't want to put you out of heart, but I tell ye, ye will see them on the water before many minutes have passed."

"Then they are lost!" Mrs. Welch said, sinking down in her chair and bursting into tears.

"They air in God's hands, ma'am," the hunter said, "and it is no use trying to deceive you."

"Would it be of any use," William Welch asked, after a pause, "for me to offer the Red-skins that my wife and I will go out and put ourselves in their hands, if they will let the canoe go off without pursuit?"

"Not it," the hunter replied decidedly; "you would be throwing away your own lives without saving theirs, not to mention, although that does not matter a straw, the lives of the rest of us here. It will be as much as we can do, when they attack us in earnest, to hold this place with six guns, and with only four, the chance would be worth nothing. But that is neither here nor there. But you would not save the young ones if you gave up. You cannot trust the word of an Indian on the war-path, and if they went so far as not to kill them, they would carry them off; and after all I ain't sure as death ain't better for them than to be brought up as Indians.

"There!" he said, stopping suddenly as a report of a musket sounded at some little distance off. "The Injuns are trying their range against them; let us go up to the look-out."

The little tower had a thick parapet of logs some three feet high, and, crouching behind this, they watched the canoe.

"He is coming nearer in shore, and the girl has got the paddle," Pearson muttered. "What's he doing now?" A puff of smoke was seen to rise near the border of the lake; then came the sharp crack of Harold's rifle. They saw an Indian spring from the bushes and fall dead.

"Well done, young 'un!" Pearson exclaimed. "I told yer he had got his head screwed on the right way. He is keeping just out of range of their guns, and that piece of his can carry twice as far as theirs. I reckon he has thought of the canoe and means to keep them from using it. I begins to think, Mr. Welch, that there is a chance for them yet. Now let's talk a little to these red devils in the corn."

For some little time Pearson and William Welch turned their attention to the Indians, while the mother sat with her eyes fixed upon the canoe.

"He is coming closer again!" she exclaimed presently.

"He is watching the canoe, sure enough," Pearson said. Then came the volley along the bushes on the shore, and they saw an Indian rise to his feet. "That's just where she lies!" Pearson exclaimed. "He is getting into it. There! Well done, young 'un."

The sudden disappearance of the Indian, and the vengeful yell of the hidden foe, told of the failure of the attempt. "I think they are safe now till nightfall; the Indians won't care about putting themselves within range of that 'ere rifle again."

Gradually the fire of the Indians ceased, and the defenders were able to leave the loopholes. Two of the men went down and fastened up the cattle, which were still standing loose in the yard inside the stockade; the other set to to prepare a meal, for Mrs. Welch could not take her eyes off the canoe.

The afternoon seemed of interminable length. Not a shot was fired; the men, after taking their dinner, were occupied in bringing some great tubs on to the upper storey, and filling them to the brim with water from the well.

This storey projected two feet beyond the one below it, having been so built in order that, in case of attack, the defenders might be able to fire down upon any foe who might cross the stockade and attack the house itself; the floor boards over the projecting portion were all removable. The men also brought a quantity of the newly-cut corn to the top of the house, first drenching it with water.

The sun sank, and as dusk was coming on, the anxious watchers saw the canoe paddle out far into the lake.

"An old frontiersman could not do better!" Pearson exclaimed. "He has kept them out of the canoe as long as daylight lasted. Now he has determined to paddle away, and is making down the lake," he went on presently. "It is a pity he turned so soon, as they can see the course he is taking."

They watched until it was completely dark, but before the light quite faded, they saw another canoe put out from shore and start in the direction taken by the fugitives.

"Will they catch them, do you think?" Mrs. Welch asked.

"No, ma'am," Pearson said confidently; "the boy has got sense enough to have changed his course after it gets dark, though whether he will make for shore or go out towards the other side is more than I can say. You see, they will know that the Injuns are all along this side of the lake, but then, on the other hand, they will be anxious about us, and will want to keep close at hand. Besides, the lad knows nothing of the other side; there may be Injuns there for ought he knows, and besides, it's a skearey thing for a young 'un to take to the forest, especially with a gal in his charge. There ain't no saying what he will do. And now we have got to look after ourselves; don't let us think about them at present. The best thing we can do for them, as well as for ourselves, is to hold this here place. If they live, they will come back to it sooner or later, and it will be better for them to find it standing, and you here to welcome them, than to get back to a heap of ruins and some dead bodies."

"When will the Red-skins attack, do you think?" the farmer asked.

"We may expect them any time now," the hunter answered. "The Injuns' time of attack is generally just before dawn, but they know well enough they ain't likely to catch us asleep any time, and as they know exactly what they have got to do, they will gain nothing by waiting. I wish we had a moon; if we had, we might keep them out of the stockade; but there, it is just as well as 'tis dark after all, for if the moon was up, the young 'uns would have no chance of getting away."

The garrison now all took their places at the loopholes, having first carried the wet fodder to the roof and spread it over the shingles. There was nothing to do now but to wait. The night was so dark that they could not see the outline of the stockade. Presently a little spark shot through the air, followed by a score of others. Mr. Welch had taken his post on the tower, and he saw the arrows whizzing through the air, many of them falling on the roof. The dry grass dipped in the resin, which was tied round their heads, was instantly extinguished as the arrows fell upon the wet corn, and a yell arose from the Indians.

The farmer descended and told the others of the failure of the Indians' first attempt.

"That 'ere dodge is a first-rate 'un," Pearson said. "We are safe from fire, and that's the only thing we have got to be afeard on. You will see them up here in a few minutes."

Everything was perfectly quiet; once or twice the watchers thought that they could hear faint sounds, but could not distinguish their direction. After half an hour's anxious waiting, a terrific yell was heard from below, and at the doors and windows of the lower rooms came the crashing blows of tomahawks.

The boards had already been removed from the flooring above, and the defenders opened a steady fire into the dark mass, that they could faintly make out clustered round the windows and doors.

At Pearson's suggestion, the bullets had been removed from the guns, and heavy charges of buck-shot had been substituted for them, and yells of pain and surprise rose as they fired. A few shots were fired up from below, but a second discharge from the spare guns completed the effect from the first volley. The dark mass broke up, and in a few seconds all was as quiet as before.

Two hours passed and then slight sounds were heard.

"They have got the gate opened, I expect," Pearson said. "Fire occasionally at that; if we don't hit them, the flashes may show us what they are doing."

It was as he had expected; the first discharge was followed by a cry, and by the momentary light they saw a number of dark figures pouring in through the gate. Seeing that concealment was no longer possible, the Indians opened a heavy fire round the house; then came a crashing sound near the door.

"Just as I thought," Pearson said. "They are going to try to burn us out."

For some time the noise continued as bundle after bundle of dried wood was thrown down by the door. The garrison were silent, for, as Pearson said, they could see nothing, and a stray bullet might enter at the loopholes if they placed themselves there, and the flashes of the guns would serve as marks for the Indians.

Presently two or three faint lights were seen approaching.

"Now," Pearson said, "pick them off as they come up. You and I will take the first man, Welch; you fire just to the right of the light, I will fire to the left; he may be carrying the brand in either hand." They fired together, and the brand was seen to drop to the ground. The same thing happened as the other two sparks of light approached; then it was again quiet. Now a score of little lights flashed through the air.

"They are going to light the pile with their flaming arrows," Pearson said. "War Eagle is a good leader."

Three or four of the arrows fell on the pile of dry wood. A moment later the flames crept up, and the smoke of burning wood rolled up into the room above. A yell of triumph burst from the Indians, but this changed into one of wrath as those above emptied the contents of one of the great tubs of water on to the pile of wood below them. The flames were instantly extinguished.

"What will they do next?" Mrs. Welch asked.

"It is like enough," Pearson replied, "that they will give the job up altogether. They have got plenty of plunder and scalps at the settlements, and their attacking us here in such force looks as if the hull of them were on their way back to their villages. If they could have tuk our scalps easy, they would have done it, but War Eagle ain't likely to risk losing a lot of men, when he ain't sartin of winning after all. He has done good work as it is, and has quite enough to boast about when he gits back. If he were to lose a heap of his braves here, it would spoil the success of his expedition. No, I think as he will give it up now."

"He will be all the more anxious to catch the children," Mrs. Welch said despondently.

"It cannot be denied, ma'am, as he will do his best that way," Pearson answered. "It all depends, though, on the boy. I wish I was with him in that canoe. Howsomever, I can't help thinking as he will sarcumvent them somehow."

The night passed without any further attack; by turns half the garrison watched while the other lay down, but there was little sleep taken by any. With the first gleam of daylight, Mrs. Welch and her husband were on the look-out.

"There's two canoes out on the lake," Pearson said. "They are paddling quietly; which is which I can't say."

As the light became brighter, Pearson pronounced positively that there were three men in one canoe and four in the other. "I think they are all Injuns," he said. "They must have got another canoe somewhere along the lake; w'all, they have not caught the young 'uns yet."

"The boats are closing up to each other," Mrs. Welch said.

"They are going to have a talk, I reckon. Yes; one of them is turning and going down the lake, while the other is going up. I would give a heap to know where the young 'uns have got to."

The day passed quietly. An occasional shot towards the house showed that the Indians remained in the vicinity, and indeed, dark

35

forms could be seen moving about in the distant parts of the clearing.

"Will it be possible," the farmer asked Pearson, when night again fell, "to go out and see if we can discover any traces of them?"

"Worse than no use," Pearson said positively. "We should just lose our har without doing no good whatever. If the Injuns in these woods—and I reckon altogether there's a good many hundred of them—can't find them, ye may swear that we can't. That's just what they're hoping, that we shall be fools enough to put ourselves outside the stockade. They will lie close round all night, and a weasel would not creep through them. Ef I thought there was jest a shadow of chance of finding them young 'uns, I would risk it, but there is no chance—not a bit of it."

A vigilant watch was again kept up all night, but all was still and quiet. The next morning the Indians were still round them.

"Don't yer fret, ma'am!" Pearson said, as he saw how pale and wan Mrs. Welch looked in the morning light. "You may bet your last shilling that they have not caught them."

"Why are you so sure?" Mrs. Welch asked. "They may be dead by this time."

"Not they, ma'am. I am as sartin as they are living and free as I am that I am standing here. I know these Injuns' ways. Ef they had caught them they would jest have brought them here and would have fixed up two posts, jest out of rifle range, and would have tied them there, and then would have offered you the choice of giving up this place and your scalps or of seeing them tortured and burnt under your eyes. That's their way. No, they ain't caught them alive, nor they ain't caught them dead neither, for ef they had, they would have brought their scalps to have shown yer. No, they have got away, though it beats me to say how. I have only got one fear, and that is that they might come back before the Injuns have gone. Now I tell ye what we had better do—we had better keep up a dropping fire all night, and all day to-morrow, and so on until the Red-skins have gone. Ef the young 'uns come back across the lake at night and all is quiet, they will think the Injuns have taken themselves off, but if they hear firing still going on, they will know well enough that they are still around the house."

William Welch at once agreed to this plan, and every quarter of an hour or so all through the night a few shots were fired.

The next morning no Indians could be seen, and there was a cessation of the dropping shots which had before been kept up at the house.

"They may be in hiding," Pearson said, in the afternoon, "trying to tempt us out; but I am more inclined to think as how they have gone. I don't see a blade of that corn move; I have had my eyes fixed on it for the last two hours. It are possible, of course, that they are there; but I reckon not. I expect they have been waiting ever since they gave up the attack, in hopes that the young 'uns would come back; but now as they see that we are keeping up a fire to tell them as how they are still round us, they have given it up and gone. When it gets dark to-night, I will go out and scout round."

At ten o'clock at night Pearson dropped lightly from the stockade on the side opposite to the gate, as he knew that if the Indians were there, this would be the point that they would be watching; then, crawling upon his stomach, he made his way slowly down to the lake. Entering the water and stooping low, he waded along by the edge of the bushes for a distance of a mile; then he left the water and struck into the forest. Every few minutes he could hear the discharges of the rifles at the house, but, as before, no answering shots were heard. Treading very cautiously, he made a wide detour and then came down again on the clearing at the end farthest from the lake, where the Indians had been last seen moving about. All was still. Keeping among the trees and moving with great caution, he made his way for a considerable distance along the edge of the clearing; then he dropped on his hands and knees and entered the cornfield, and for two hours he crawled about, quartering the ground like a dog in search of game. Everywhere he found lines where the Indians had crawled along to the edge nearest to the house, but nowhere did he discover a sign of life. Then, still taking great care, he moved down towards the house and made a circuit of it at a short distance outside the stockade; then he rose to his feet.

"Yer may stop shooting!" he shouted. "The pesky rascals are gone." Then he walked openly up to the gate; it was opened at once by William Welch.

"Are you sure they have gone?" he asked.

"Sure as gospel," he answered; "and they have been gone four-and-twenty hours at least."

"How do you know that?"

"Easy enough. I found several of their cooking-places in the woods. The brands were out, and even under the ashes, the ground was cold; so they must have been out for a long time. I could have walked straight on to the house then, but I thought it safer to make quite sure by searching everywhere, for they might have moved deeper into the forest, and left a few men on guard here in case the young 'uns should come back. But it ain't so; they have gone, and there ain't a living soul anywhere nigh the clearing. The young 'uns can come back now, if they will, safely enough."

Before doing anything else the farmer assembled the party together in the living-room, and there solemnly offered up thanks to God for their deliverance from danger, and implored his protection for the absent ones. When this was over, he said to his wife:

"Now, Jane, you had better lie down and get a few hours' sleep. It is already two o'clock, and there is no chance whatever of their returning to-night, but I shall go down to the lake and wait till morning. Place candles in two of the upper windows. Should they be out on the lake, they will see them and know that the Indians have not taken the house."

Morning came without any signs of the absent ones. At daybreak Pearson went out to scout in the woods, and returned late in the afternoon with the news that the Indians had all departed, and that for a distance of ten miles at least the woods were entirely free.

When it became dark, the farmer again went down to the lake and watched until two, when Pearson took his place. Mr. Welch was turning to go back to the house when Pearson placed his hand on his shoulder.

"Listen!" he said, and for a minute the men stood immovable.

"What was it?" the farmer asked.

"I thought I heard the stroke of a paddle," Pearson said. "It might have been the jump of a fish. There! There it is again!" He lay down and put his ear close to the water. "There is a canoe in the lake to the northward; I can hear the strokes of the paddle plainly."

Mr. Welch could hear nothing. Some minutes passed, then Pearson exclaimed:

"There! I saw a break in the water over there! There it is!" he said, straining his eyes in the darkness. "That's a canoe, sure enough, although they have ceased paddling. It is not a mile away."

Then he arose to his feet and shouted "Halloo!" at the top of his voice. An answering shout faintly came back across the water. He again hailed loudly, and this time the answer came in a female voice.

"It's them, sure enough; I can swear to Nelly's voice."

William Welch uncovered his head, and, putting his hand before his face, returned fervent thanks to God for the recovery of his child. Then he dashed off at full speed toward the house. Before he reached it, however, he met his wife running down to meet him, the shouts having informed her that something was seen. Hand in hand they ran down to the water's edge. The canoe was now swiftly approaching. The mother screamed:

"Nelly, is that you?"

"Mamma! Mamma!" came back in the girl's clear tones.

With a low cry of gladness Mrs. Welch fell senseless to the ground. The strain which she had for four days endured had been terrible, and even the assurances of Pearson had failed to awaken any strong feeling of hope in her heart. She had kept up bravely, and had gone about her work in the house with a pale, set face, but the unexpected relief was too much for her.

Two minutes later the bow of the canoe grated on the shore, and Nelly leaped into her father's arms.

"Where is mamma?" she exclaimed.

"She is here, my dear, but she has fainted. The joy of your return has been too much for her."

Nelly knelt beside her mother and raised her head, and the farmer grasped Harold's hand.

"My brave boy," he said, "I have to thank you for saving my child's life. God bless you!"

He dipped his hat in the lake and sprinkled water in his wife's face; she soon recovered, and a few minutes afterwards the happy party walked up to the house, Mrs. Welch being assisted by her husband and Pearson. The two young ones were soon seated at a table ravenously devouring food, and when their hunger was satisfied, they related the story of their adventures, the whole of the garrison being gathered round to listen. After relating what had taken place up to the time of their hiding the canoe, Harold went on:

"We walked about a quarter of a mile until we came to a large clump of underwood. We crept in there, taking great pains not to break a twig or disturb a leaf. The ground was fortunately very dry, and I could not see that our footprints had left the smallest marks. There we have lain hid ever since. We had the fish and the berries, and fortunately the fruit was ripe and juicy, and quenched our thirst well enough, and we could sometimes hear the firing by day and always at night. On the day we took refuge we heard the voices of the Indians down towards the lake quite plainly, but we have heard nothing of them since. Last night we heard the firing up to the middle of the night, and then it suddenly stopped. To-day I crept out and went down to the lake to listen, but it seemed that everything was still. Nelly was in a terrible way, and was afraid that the house had been taken by the Indians, but I told her that could not be, for that there would certainly have been a tremendous lot of firing at last, whereas it stopped after a few shots, just as it had been going on so long. Our provisions were all done, and Nelly was getting very bad for want of water. I of course got a drink at the lake this morning. So we agreed that if everything was still again to-night, we would go back to the place where we had hidden the canoe, launch it, and paddle here. Everything was quiet, so we came along as we had arranged. When I saw the lights in the windows I made sure all was right; still, it was a great relief when I heard the shout from the shore. I knew, of course, that it wasn't a Red-skin's shout. Besides, Indians would have kept quiet till we came alongside."

Very hearty were the commendations bestowed on the boy for his courage and thoughtfulness.

"You behaved like an old frontiersman," Pearson said. "I could not have done better myself. You only made one blunder from the time you set out from shore."

"What was that?" Harold asked.

"You were wrong to pick the berries. The Red-skins, of course, would find where you had landed, they would see the marks where you lay down, and would know that you had paddled away again. Had it not been for their seeing the tracks you made in picking the berries, they might have supposed you had started before day-break, and had gone out of sight across the lake; but those marks would have shown them that you did not take to your canoe until long after the sun was up, and, therefore, that you could not have made across the lake without their seeing you, but must either have landed or be in your canoe under shelter of the trees somewhere along of the shore. It is a marvel to me that they did not find your traces, however careful you were to conceal them. But that's the only error you made, and I tell you, young 'un, that you have a right to be proud of having outwitted a hull tribe of Red-skins."

CHAPTER IV
THE FIGHT AT LEXINGTON

HAROLD remained for four months longer with his cousin. The Indians had made several attacks upon settlements at other points of the frontier, but they had not repeated their incursion in the neighbourhood of the lake. The farming operations had gone on regularly, but the men always worked with their rifles ready to their hand. Pearson had predicted that the Indians were not likely to return to that neighbourhood. Mr. Welch's farm was the only one along the lake that had escaped, and the loss the Indians had sustained in attacking it had been so heavy that they were not likely to make an expedition in that quarter, where the chances of booty were so small and the certainty of a desperate resistance so great.

Other matters occurred which rendered the renewal of the attack improbable. The news was brought by a wandering hunter that a quarrel had arisen between the Shawnees and the Irroquois, and that the latter had recalled their braves from the frontier to defend their own villages in case of hostilities breaking out between them and the rival tribe.

There was no occasion for Harold to wait for news from home, for his father had before starting definitely fixed the day for his return, and when that time approached, Harold started on his eastward journey, in order to be at home about the date of their arrival. Pearson took him in his canoe to the end of the lake, and accompanied him to the settlement, whence he was able to obtain a conveyance to Detroit. Here he took a passage in a trading boat, and made his way by water to Montreal, thence down through Lake Champlain and the Hudson River to New York, and thence to Boston.

The journey had occupied him longer than he expected, and Mr. and Mrs. Wilson were already in their home at Concord when he arrived. The meeting was a joyful one. His parents had upon their return home found letters from Mr. Welch and his wife, describing the events which had happened at the farm, and speaking in the highest terms of the courage and coolness in danger which Harold had displayed, and giving him full credit for the saving of their daughter's life.

Upon the day after Harold's return, two gentlemen called upon Captain Wilson, and asked him to sign the agreement which a number of colonists had entered into, to resist the Mother Country to the last. This Captain Wilson positively refused to do.

"I am an Englishman," he said, "and my sympathies are wholly with my country. I do not say that the whole of the demands of England are justifiable; I think that Parliament has been deceived as to the spirit existing here. But I consider that it has done nothing whatever to justify the attitude of the colonists. The soldiers of England have fought for you against French and Indians, and are still stationed here to protect you. The colonists pay nothing for their land; they pay nothing towards the expenses of the government of the mother country and it appears to me to be perfectly just that people here—free as they are from all the burdens that bear so heavily on those at home—should at least bear the expense of the army stationed here. I grant that it would have been far better had the colonists taxed themselves to pay the extra amount, instead of the mother country taxing them; but this they would not do. Some of the colonists paid their quotum; others refused to do so, and this being the case, it appears to me that England is perfectly justified in laying on a tax. Nothing could have been fairer than the tax that she proposed. The stamp-tax would in no way have affected the poorer classes in the colonies. It would have been borne only by the rich, and by those engaged in such business transactions as required stamped documents. I regard the present rebellion as the work of a clique of ambitious men, who have stirred up the people by incendiary addresses and writing. There are, of course, among them a large number of the men—among them, gentlemen, I place you—who conscientiously believe that they are justified in doing nothing whatever for the land which gave them or their ancestors birth, who would enjoy all the great natural wealth of this vast country without contributing towards the expense of the troops to whom it is due that you enjoy peace and tranquillity. Such, gentlemen, are not my sentiments. You consider it a gross hardship that the colonists are compelled to trade only with the mother country. I grant that it would be more profitable and better for us had we an open trade with the whole world, but in this England only acts as do all other countries towards their colonies. France, Spain, Portugal, and the Netherlands all monopolize the trade of their colonies; all, far more than does England, regard their colonies as sources of revenue. I repeat, I do not think that the course that England has pursued towards us has been always wise, but I am sure that nothing that she has done justifies the spirit of disaffection and rebellion which is ripe throughout these colonies."

"The time will come, sir," one of the gentlemen said, "when you will have reason to regret the line which you have now taken."

"No, sir," Captain Wilson said haughtily. "The time may come when the line that I have taken may cost me my fortune, and even my life, but it will never cause me one moment's regret that I have chosen the part of a loyal English gentleman."

When the deputation had departed, Harold, who had been a wondering listener to the conversation, asked his father to explain to him the exact position in which matters stood.

It was indeed a serious one. The success of England in her struggle with France for the supremacy of North America had cost her a great deal of money. At home the burdens of the people were extremely heavy. The expense of the army and navy was great, and the ministry, in striving to lighten the burdens of the people, turned their eyes to the colonies. They saw in America a population of over 2,000,000 people, subjects of the king, like themselves, living free from rent and taxes on their own land, and paying nothing whatever to the expenses of the country. They were, it is true, forced to trade with England, but this obligation was set wholly at nought. A gigantic system of smuggling was carried on. The custom-house officials had no force at their disposal which would have enabled them to check these operations, and the law enforcing a trade with England was virtually a dead letter.

Their first step was to strengthen the naval force on the American coast, and by additional vigilance to put some sort of check on the wholesale smuggling which prevailed. This step caused extreme discontent among the trading classes of America, and these set to work vigorously to stir up a strong feeling of disaffection against England. The revenue officers were prevented sometimes by force from carrying out their duties.

After great consideration the English government came to the conclusion that a revenue sufficient to pay a considerable proportion of the cost of the army in America might be raised by means of a stamp-tax imposed upon all legal documents, receipts, agreements, and licenses—a tax, in fact, resembling that on stamps now in use in England. The colonists were furious at the imposition of this tax. A Congress, composed of deputies from each State, met, and it was unanimously resolved that the stamp-tax should not be paid. Meetings were everywhere held, at which the strongest and most treasonable language was uttered, and such violent threats were used against the persons employed as stamp-collectors that these, in fear of their lives, resigned their posts.

The stamp-tax remained uncollected, and was treated by the colonists as if it were not in existence.

The whole of the States now began to prepare for war. The Congress was made permanent; the militia drilled, and prepared for fighting, and everywhere the position grew more and more strained. Massachusetts was the head-quarters of disaffection, and here a total break with the mother country was openly spoken of. At times the more moderate spirits attempted to bring about a reconciliation between the two parties. Petitions were sent to the Houses of Parliament, and even at this time, had any spirit of wisdom prevailed in England, the final consequences might have been prevented. Unfortunately, the majority in parliament were unable to recognize that the colonists had any rights upon their side. Taxation was so heavy at home that men felt indignant that they should be called upon to pay for the keeping up of the army in America, to which the untaxed colonists, with their free farms and houses, would contribute nothing. The plea of the colonists that they were taxed by a chamber in which they were unrepresented, was answered by the statement that such was also the case with Manchester, Leeds, and many other large towns which were unrepresented in parliament.

In England neither the spirit nor the strength of the colonists was understood. Men could not bring themselves to believe that these would fight rather than submit, still less that if they did fight it would be successfully. They ignored the fact that the population of the States was one-fourth as large as that of England; that by far the greater proportion of that population were men trained, either in border warfare or in the chase, to the use of the rifle; that the enormous extent of country offered almost insuperable obstacles to the most able army composed of regular troops, and that the vast forests and thinly populated country were all in favour of a population fighting as guerrillas against trained troops. Had they perceived these things, the English people would have hesitated before embarking upon such a struggle, even if convinced, as assuredly the great majority were convinced, of the fairness of their demands. It is true that even had England at this point abandoned altogether her determination to raise taxes in America, the result would probably have been the same. The spirit of disaffection in the colony had gone so far that a retreat would have been considered as a confession of weakness, and a separation of the colonists from the mother country would have happened ere many years had elapsed. As it was, parliament agreed to let the stamp-tax drop, and in its place established some import duties on goods entering the American ports.

The colonists, however, were determined that they would submit to no taxation whatever. The English government, in its desire for peace, abandoned all the duties, with the exception of that on tea, but even this concession was not sufficient to satisfy the colonists. These entered into a bond to use no English goods. A riot took place at Boston, and the revenue officers were forced to withdraw from their posts. Troops were despatched from England,

and the House of Commons declared Massachusetts to be in a state of rebellion.

It must not be supposed that the colonists were by any means unanimous in their resistance to England. There were throughout the country a large number of gentlemen, like Captain Wilson, wholly opposed to the general feeling. New York refused to send members to the Congress, and in many other provinces the adhesion given to the disaffected movement was but lukewarm. It was in the New England provinces that the spirit of rebellion was hottest. These states had been peopled for the most part by Puritans—men who had left England voluntarily, exiling themselves rather than submit to the laws and religion of the country—and among them, as among a portion of the Irish population of America at the present time, the feeling of hatred against the government of England was, in a way, hereditary.

So far but few acts of violence had taken place; nothing could be more virulent than the language of the newspapers of both parties against their opponents, but beyond a few isolated tumults, the peace had not been broken. It was the lull before the storm. The great majority of the New England colonists were bent upon obtaining nothing short of absolute independence; the loyalists and the English were as determined to put down any revolt by force.

The Congress drilled, armed, and organized; the English brought over fresh troops and prepared for the struggle. It was December when Harold returned home to his parents, and for the next three months the lull before the storm continued.

The disaffected of Massachusetts had collected a large quantity of military stores at Concord. These General Gage, who commanded the troops at Boston, determined to seize and destroy, seeing that they could be collected only for use against the government; and on the night of the 19th of April the grenadier and light infantry companies of the various regiments, 800 strong, under command of Lieut.-Col. Smith, of the 10th Regiment, and Major Pitcairne, of the marines, embarked in boats, and were conveyed up Charles River as far as a place called Phipp's Farm. There they landed at midnight, having a day's provisions in their haversacks, and started on their march to Concord, twenty miles distant from Boston.

The design, however, had been discovered by some of the revolutionary party in the town, and two of their number were despatched on horseback to rouse the whole country on the way to Concord, where the news arrived at two o'clock in the morning.

Captain Wilson and his household were startled from sleep by the sudden ringing of the alarm-bells, and a negro servant, Pompey, who had been for many years in their service, was sent down into the town, which lay a quarter of a mile from the house, to find out what was the news. He returned in half an hour.

"Me tink all de people gone mad, massa! Dey swarming out of der houses and filling de streets, all with guns on dem shoulders, all de while shouting and halloing, 'Down with de English! Down with de Red-coats! Dey sha'n't have our guns; dey sha'n't take de cannon and de powder.' Der were ole massa, Bill Emerson, the preacher, with his gun in his hands, shouting to de people to stand firm, and to fight till de last; dey all shout, 'We will!' Dey bery desperate; me fear great fight come on."

"What are you going to do, father?" Harold asked.

"Nothing, my boy; if, as it is only too likely, this is the beginning of a civil war, I have determined to offer my services to the government. Great numbers of loyalists have sent in their names, offering to serve, if necessary, and from my knowledge of drill I shall, of course, be useful. To-day I can take no active part in the fight, but I shall take my horse and ride forward to meet the troops, and warn the commanding officer that resistance will be attempted here."

"May I go with you, father?"

"Yes, if you like, my boy."

"Pompey, saddle two horses at once. You are not afraid of being left alone, Mary?" he said, turning to his wife. "There is no chance of any disturbance here. Our house lies beyond the town, and whatever takes place will be in Concord. When the troops have captured the guns and stores, they will return."

THE FIGHT AT LEXINGTON

Mrs. Wilson said she was not frightened, and had no fear whatever of being left alone. The horses were soon brought round, and Captain Wilson and his son mounted and rode off at full speed. They made a detour to avoid the town, and then, gaining the highroad, went forward at full speed. The alarm had evidently been given all along the line; at every village the bells were ringing, the people were assembling in the streets, all carrying arms, while numbers were flocking in from the farm-houses around. Once or twice Captain Wilson was stopped and asked where he was going.

"I am going to tell the commander of the British force, now marching hither, that if he advances, there will be bloodshed, that it will be the beginning of civil war. If he has orders to come at all hazards, my words will not stop him; if it is left to his discretion, possibly he may pause before he brings on so dire a calamity."

It was just dawn when Captain Wilson and Harold rode into Lexington, where the militia, 130 strong, had assembled. Their guns were loaded and they were ready to defend the place, which numbered about 700 inhabitants.

Just as Captain Wilson rode in, a messenger ran up with the news that the head of the British column was close at hand. Some of the militia had dispersed to lie down until the English arrived. John Parker, who commanded them, ordered the drums to beat and the alarm-guns to be fired, and his men drew up in two ranks across the road.

"It is too late now, Harold," Captain Wilson said. "Let us get out of the line of fire."

The British, hearing the drums and the alarm-guns, loaded, and the advance company came on at the double. Major Pitcairne was at their head, and shouted to the militia to lay down their arms.

It is a matter of dispute, and will always remain one, as to who fired the first shot. The Americans assert that it was the English. The English say that as they advanced, several shots were fired at them from behind a stone wall and from some of the adjoining houses, which wounded one man, and hit Major Pitcairne's horse in two places.

The beginning of the war.

THE FIGHT AT LEXINGTON

The militia disregarded Major Pitcairne's orders to lay down their arms. The English fired; several of the militia were killed, and nine wounded, and the rest dispersed. There was no further fighting, and the English marched on unopposed to Concord.

As they approached the town, the militia retreated from it. The English took possession of a bridge behind the place, and held this while the troops were engaged in destroying the ammunition and gun-carriages. Most of the guns had been removed, and only two 24-pounders were taken. In destroying the stores by fire, the court-house took flames. At the sight of this fire, the militia and armed countrymen advanced down the hill towards the bridge. The English tried to pull up the planks, but the Americans ran forward rapidly. The English guard fired; the colonists returned the fire. Some of the English were killed and wounded, and the party fell back into the town. Half an hour later Colonel Smith, having performed the duty that he was sent to do, resumed the homeward march with the whole of his troops.

Then the militiamen of Concord, with those from many villages around, and every man in the district capable of bearing arms, fell upon the retiring English.

The road led through several defiles, and every tree, every rock, every depression of ground, was taken advantage of by the Americans. Scarcely a man was to be seen, but their deadly fire rained thick upon the tired troops. This they vainly attempted to return, but they could do nothing against an invisible foe, every man of whom possessed a skill with his rifle far beyond that of the British soldier. Very many fell, and the retreat was fast becoming a rout, when, near Lexington, the column met a strong reinforcement which had been sent out from Boston. This was commanded by Lord Percy, who formed his detachment into square, in which Colonel Smith's party, now so utterly exhausted that they were obliged to lie down for some time, took refuge. When they were rested, the whole force moved forward again towards Boston, harassed the whole way by the Americans, who, from behind stone walls and other places of shelter, kept up an incessant fire upon both flanks, as well as in the front and rear, against which the troops could do nothing. At last the retreating column safely arrived at Boston, spent and worn out with fatigue. Their loss was 65 men killed, 136 wounded, 49 missing.

Such was the beginning of the War of Independence. Many American writers have declared that, previous to that battle, there was no desire for independence on the part of the colonists; but this is emphatically contradicted by the language used at the meetings and in the newspapers which have come down to us. The leaders may not have wished to go so far, may not have intended to gain more than an entire immunity from taxation, and an absolute power for the colonists to manage their own affairs. But experience has shown that when the spark of revolution is once lighted, when resistance to the law has once commenced, things are carried to a point far beyond that dreamed of by the first leaders.

Those who commenced the French Revolution were moderate men, who desired only that some slight check should be placed on the arbitrary power of the king, that the people should be relieved in some slight degree from the horrible tyranny of the nobles, from the misery and wretchedness in which they lived. These just demands increased step by step until they culminated in the reign of terror and the most horrible scenes of bloodshed and massacre of modern times.

Men like Washington, and Franklin, and Adams may have desired only that the colonists should be free from imperial taxation, but the popular voice went far beyond this. Three years earlier, wise counsels in the British Parliament might have averted a catastrophe, and delayed for many years the separation of the colonies from their mother country. At the time the march began from Boston to Concord, the American colonists stood virtually in armed rebellion. The militia throughout New England were ready for fight. Arms, ammunition, and military stores were collected in Rhode Island and New Hampshire. The cannon and military stores belonging to the crown had been carried off by the people, 40 cannon being seized in Rhode Island alone. Such being the case, it is nonsense to speak of the fray at Lexington as the cause of the revolutionary war. It was but the spark in the powder. The magazine was ready and primed, the explosion was inevitable, and the fight at Lexington was the accidental incident which set fire to it.

The efforts of American writers, however, to conceal the real facts of the case, to minimize the rebellious language, the violent acts of the colonists, and to make England responsible for the war because a body of troops were sent to seize cannon and military stores intended to be used against them, are so absurd, as well as so untrue, that it is astonishing how wide a credence such statements have received.

From an eminence at some distance from the line of retreat Captain Wilson and his son watched sorrowfully the attack upon the British troops. When at last the combatants disappeared from sight through one of the defiles, Captain Wilson turned his horse's head homewards.

"The die is cast," he said to his wife, as she met him at the door. "The war has begun, and I fear it can have but one termination. The colonists can place forces in the field twenty times as numerous as any army that England can spare. They are inferior in drill and in discipline; but these things, which are of such vast consequence in a European battlefield, matter but little in such a country as this. Skill with the rifle and knowledge of forest warfare are far more important. In these points the colonists are as superior to the English soldiers as they are in point of numbers. Nevertheless, my dear, my duty is plain. I am an Englishman, and have borne His Majesty's commission, and I must fight for the king. Harold has spoken to me as we rode home together, and he wishes to fight by my side. I have pointed out to him that as he was born here, he can without dishonour remain neutral in the struggle. He, however, insists that, as a loyal subject of the king, he is entitled to fight for him. He saw to-day many lads not older than himself in the rebel ranks, and he has pleaded strongly for permission to go with me. To this I have agreed. Which would you prefer, Mary—to stay quietly here, where I imagine you would not be molested on account of the part I take, or will you move into Boston and stop with your relations there until the struggle has ended one way or the other?"

TRUE TO THE OLD FLAG

As Mrs. Wilson had frequently talked over with her husband the course that he would take in the event of civil war actually breaking out, the news that he would at once offer his services to the British authorities did not come as a shock upon her. Even the question of Harold accompanying his father had been talked over; and although her heart bled at the thought of husband and son being both engaged in such a struggle, she agreed to acquiesce in any decision that Harold might arrive at. He was now nearly sixteen, and in the colonies a lad of this age is, in point of independence and self-reliance, older than an English boy. Harold, too, had already shown that he possessed discretion and coolness as well as courage; and although, now that the moment had come, Mrs. Wilson wept passionately at the thought of their leaving her, she abstained from saying any word to dissuade them from the course they had determined upon. When she recovered from her fit of crying, she said that she would accompany them at once to Boston as, in the first place, their duties might for some time lie in that city, and that in any case she would obtain far more speedy news there of what was going on throughout the country than she would at Concord. She would, too, be living among her friends, and would meet with many of the same convictions and opinions as her husband's, whereas in Concord the whole population would be hostile.

Captain Wilson said that there was no time to be lost, as the whole town was in a tumult. He therefore advised her to pack up such necessary articles as could be carried in the valises on the horses' backs.

Pompey and the other servants were to pack up the most valuable effects, and to forward them to a relation of Mrs. Wilson's, who lived about three miles from Boston. There they would be in safety, and could be brought into the town if necessary. Pompey and two other old servants were to remain in charge of the house and its contents. Jake, an active young negro some twenty-three or twenty-four years old, who was much attached to Harold, whose personal attendant and companion he had always been, was to accompany them on horseback, as was Judy, Mrs. Wilson's negro maid.

As evening fell, the five horses were brought round, and the party started by a long and circuitous route, by which, after riding for nearly forty miles, they reached Boston at two o'clock next morning.

CHAPTER V
BUNKER'S HILL

THE excitement caused by the news of the fight at Concord was intense, and as it spread through the colonies, the men everywhere rushed to arms. The fray at Lexington was represented as a wanton outrage, and the facts wholly ignored that the colonists concerned in it were drawn up in arms to oppose the passage of the king's troops, who were marching on their legitimate duty of seizing arms and ammunition collected for the purpose of warring against the king. The colonial orators and newspaper writers affirmed then, as they have affirmed since, that up to the day of Lexington no one had a thought of firing a shot against the government. A more barefaced misstatement was never made. Men do not carry off cannon by scores and accumulate everywhere great stores of warlike ammunition without a thought of fighting. The colonists commenced the war by assembling in arms to oppose the progress of British troops obeying the orders of the government. It matters not a whit on which side the first shot was fired. American troops have many times since that event fired upon rioters in the streets, under circumstances no stronger than those which brought on the fight at Lexington.

From all parts of New England the militia and volunteers poured in, and in three days after the fight, 20,000 armed men were encamped between the rivers Mystic and Roxburgh, thus besieging Boston. They at once set to work throwing up formidable earthworks, the English troops remaining within their intrenchments across the neck of land joining Boston with the mainland.

The streets of Boston were crowded with an excited populace when Captain Wilson and his party rode into it at two in the morning. No one thought of going to bed, and all were excited to the last degree at the news of the battle. All sorts of reports prevailed. On the colonial side it was affirmed that the British in their retreat had shot down the women and children, while the soldiers affirmed that the colonists had scalped many of their number who fell in the fight. The latter statement was officially made by Lord Percy in his report of the engagement.

Captain Wilson rode direct to the house of his wife's friends. They were still up, and were delighted to see Mary Wilson, for such exaggerated reports had been received of the fight that they were alarmed for her safety. They belonged to the moderate party, who saw that there were faults on both sides, and regretted bitterly both the obstinacy of the English parliament in attempting to coerce the colonists, and the determination of the latter to oppose by force of arms the legitimate rights of the mother country.

Until the morning the events of the preceding day were talked over; a few hours' repose were then taken, after which Captain Wilson went to the headquarters of General Gage and offered his services. Although Boston was the headquarters of the disaffected party, no less than 200 men came forward as volunteers in the king's service, and Captain Wilson was at once appointed to the command of a company of 50 men. He had, before leaving the army, taken part in several expeditions against the Indians, and his knowledge of forest warfare rendered him a valuable acquisition. Boston was but poorly provisioned; and as, upon the day when the news of Lexington reached New York, two vessels laden with flour for the use of the troops at Boston were seized by the colonists, and many other supplies cut off, the danger of the place being starved out was considerable. General Gage therefore offered no opposition to the exit from the city of those who wished to avoid the horror of a siege, and a considerable portion of the population made their way through to the rebel lines. Every day brought news of fresh risings throughout the country; the governors of the various provinces were powerless; small garrisons of English troops were disarmed and made prisoners; and the fortress of Ticonderoga, held only by fifty men, was captured by the Americans without resistance.

In one month after the first shot was fired, the whole of the American colonies were in rebellion.

The news was received in England with astonishment and sorrow. Great concessions had been made by parliament, but the news had reached America too late to avoid hostilities. Public opinion was divided; many were in favour of granting at once all that the colonists demanded, and many officers of rank and position resigned their commissions rather than fight against the Americans. The division, indeed, was almost as general and complete as it had been in the time of our own civil war. In London the feeling in favour of the colonists was strong, but in the country generally the determination to repress the rising was in the ascendant. The colonists had with great shrewdness despatched a fast-sailing ship to Europe upon the day following the battle of Lexington, giving their account of the affair and representing it as a massacre of defenceless colonists by British troops; and the story thus told excited a sympathy which would not, perhaps, have been extended to them had the real facts of the case been known. Representatives from all the colonists met at Philadelphia to organize the national resistance; but as yet, although many of the bolder spirits spoke of altogether throwing off allegiance to England, no resolution was proposed to that effect.

For the first six weeks after his arrival at Boston, Captain Wilson was engaged in drilling his company. Harold was, of course, attached to it, and entered with ardour upon his duties. Captain Wilson did not attempt to form his men into a band of regular soldiers; accuracy of movement and regularity of drill would be of little avail in the warfare in which they were likely to be engaged. Accuracy in shooting, quickness in taking cover, and steadiness in carrying out any general orders were the principal objects to be attained. Most of the men had already taken part in frontier warfare; the majority of them were gentlemen—Englishmen who, like their captain, had come out from home and purchased small estates in the country. The discipline, therefore, was not strict, and off duty all were on terms of equality.

BUNKER'S HILL

Towards the end of May and beginning of June considerable reinforcements arrived from England; and, as a step preparatory to offensive measures, General Gage, on the 12th of June, issued a proclamation offering in His Majesty's name a free pardon to all who should forthwith lay down their arms, John Hancock and General Adams only excepted, and threatening with punishment all who should delay to avail themselves of the offer. This proclamation had no effect whatever.

Near the peninsula of Boston, on the north, and separated from it by the Charles river, which is navigable and about the breadth of the Thames at London Bridge, is another neck of land called the "Peninsula of Charlestown." On the north bank, opposite Boston, lies the town of Charlestown, behind which in the centre of the peninsula rises an eminence called "Bunker's Hill." Bunker's Hill is sufficiently high to overlook any part of Boston, and near enough to be within cannon-shot. This hill was unoccupied by either party; and about this time the Americans, hearing that General Gage had come to a determination to fortify it, resolved to defeat his resolution by being the first to occupy it.

About 9 in the evening of the 16th of June, a detachment from the colonial army, 1000 strong, under the command of Colonel Prescott, moved along the Charlestown road and took up a position on a shoulder of Bunker's Hill, which was known as "Breed's Hill," just above the town of Charlestown. They reached this position at midnight. Each man carried a pick and shovel, and all night they worked vigorously in intrenching the position. Not a word was spoken, and the watch on board the men-of-war in the harbour were ignorant of what was going on so near at hand. At daybreak the alarm was given, and the *Lively* opened a cannonade upon the redoubt. A battery of guns was placed on "Copp's Hill," behind Boston, distant 1200 yards from the works, and this also opened fire. The Americans continued their work, throwing up fresh intrenchments, and singularly, only one man was killed by the fire from the ships and redoubt. A breastwork was carried down the hill to the flat ground, which, intersected by fences, stretched

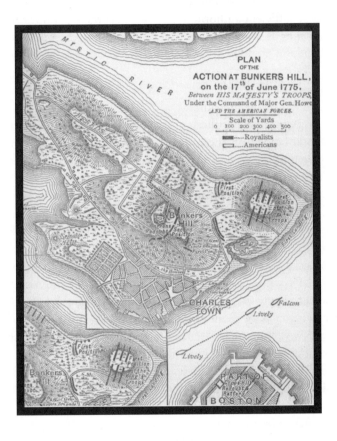

away to the Mystic. By 9 o'clock they had completed their intrenchments.

Prescott sent off for reinforcements, but there was little harmony among the colonial troops. Disputes between the contingents of the various provinces were common; there was no head of sufficient authority to enforce his orders upon the whole; and a long delay took place before the reinforcements were sent forward.

In the meantime the English had been preparing to attack the position. The 5th, 38th, 43d, and 52d Regiments, with ten companies of the grenadiers and ten of the light infantry, with a proportion of field artillery, embarked in boats, and, crossing the harbour, landed on the outward side of the peninsula near the Mystic, with a view of outflanking the American position and surrounding them. The force was under the command of Major-General Howe, under whom was Brigadier-General Pigott.

Upon seeing the strength of the American position, General Howe halted and sent back for further reinforcements. The Americans improved the time thus given them by forming a breast-work in front of an old ditch. Here there was a post and a rail-fence. They ran up another by the side of this and filled the space between the two with the new-mown hay, which, cut only the day before, lay thickly over the meadows.

Two battalions were sent across to reinforce Howe, while large reinforcements, with six guns, arrived to the assistance of Prescott. The English had now a force consisting, according to different authorities, of between 2000 and 2500 men. The colonial force is also variously estimated, and had the advantage both in position and in the protection of their intrenchments, while the British had to march across open ground. As individual shots the colonists were immensely superior, but the British had the advantages given by drill and discipline.

The English lines advanced in good order, steadily and slowly, the artillery covering them by their fire. Presently the troops opened fire, but the distance was too great and they did but little execution. Encumbered with their knapsacks, they ascended the steep hill towards the redoubt with difficulty, covered as it was by grass reaching to their knees. The colonists did not fire a shot until the English line had reached a point about 150 yards from the intrenchments. Then Prescott gave the order, and from the redoubt and the long line of intrenchments flanking it flashed a line of fire. Each man had taken a steady aim with his rifle resting on the earthwork before him, and so deadly was the fire that nearly the whole front line of the British fell. For ten minutes the rest stood with dogged courage firing at the hidden foe; but these, sheltered while they loaded, and only exposing themselves momentarily while they raised their heads above the parapets to fire, did such deadly execution that the remnant of the British fell back to the foot of the hill.

While this force, which was under the command of General Pigott, had been engaged, another division under Howe himself moved against the rail-fence. The combat was a repetition of that which had taken place on the hill. Here the Americans reserved their fire until the enemy were close; then, with their muskets resting on the rails, they poured in a deadly fire; and after in vain trying to stand their ground, the troops fell back to the shore.

Captain Wilson was standing with Harold on Copp's Hill watching the engagement.

"What beautiful order they go in!" Harold said, looking admiringly at the long lines of red-coated soldiers.

"It is very pretty," Captain Wilson said, sadly, "and may do in regular warfare; but I tell you, Harold, that sort of thing won't do here. There is scarce a man carrying a gun behind those intrenchments who cannot with certainty hit a bull's-eye at 150 yards. It is simply murder, taking the men up in regular order against such a foe sheltered by earthworks."

At this moment the long line of fire darted out from the American intrenchments.

"Look there!" Captain Wilson cried in a pained voice. "The front line is nearly swept away! Do you see them lying almost in an unbroken line on the hillside? I tell you, Harold, it is hopeless to

The second advance at Bunker's Hill.

look for success if we fight in this way. The bravest men in the world could not stand such a fire as that."

"What will be done now?" Harold asked, as the men stood huddled upon the shore.

"They will try again," Captain Wilson said. "Look at the officers running about among them and getting them into order."

In a quarter of an hour the British again advanced both towards the redoubt and the grass fence. As before, the Americans withheld their fire, and this time until the troops were far closer than before, and the result was even more disastrous. Some of the grenadier and light infantry companies who led lost three-fourths, others nine-tenths, of their men. Again the British troops recoiled from that terrible fire. General Howe and his officers exerted themselves to the utmost to restore order when the troops again reached the shore, and the men gallantly replied to their exhortations. Almost impossible as the task appeared, they prepared to undertake it for the third time. This time a small force only were directed to move against the grass fence, while the main body, under Howe, were to attack the redoubt on the hill.

Knapsacks were taken off and thrown down, and each man nerved himself to conquer or die. The ships in the harbour prepared the way by opening a heavy cannonade. General Clinton, who was watching the battle from Copp's Hill, ran down to the shore, rowed across the harbour, and put himself at the head of two battalions. Then, with loud cheers, the troops again sprang up the ascent. The American ammunition was running short, many of the men not having more than three or four rounds left, and this time they held their fire until the British troops were within twenty yards. These had not fired a shot, the order being that there was to be no pause, but that the redoubt was to be carried with the bayonet. For a moment they wavered when the deadly volley was poured in upon them. Then with a cheer they rushed at the intrenchments. All those who first mounted were shot down by the defenders, but the troops would not be denied, and, pouring over the earthworks, leaped down upon the enemy.

For a few minutes there was a hand-to-hand fight, the Americans using the butt-ends of their muskets, the English their bayonets. The soldiers were exhausted with the climb up the hill and their exertions under a blazing sun, and the great majority of the defenders of the redoubt were therefore enabled to retreat unharmed, as, fresh and active, they were able to outrun their tired opponents, and as the balls served out for the English field-pieces were too large, the artillery were unable to come into action.

The colonists at the rail-fence maintained their position against the small force sent against them till the main body at the redoubt had made their escape. The British were unable to continue the pursuit beyond the isthmus.

In the whole history of the British army there is no record of a more gallant feat than the capture of Bunker's Hill; and few troops in the world would, after two bloody repulses, have moved up the third time to assail such a position, defended by men so trained to the use of the rifle. A thousand and fifty-four men, or nearly half their number, were killed and wounded, among whom were eighty-three officers. In few battles ever fought was the proportion of casualties to the number engaged so great. The Americans fought bravely, but the extraordinary praise bestowed upon them for their valour appears misplaced. Their position was one of great strength, and the absence of drill was of no consequence whatever in such an engagement. They were perfectly sheltered from their enemy's fire while engaged in calmly shooting him down, and their loss up to the moment when the British rushed among them was altogether insignificant. Their casualties took place after the position was stormed and on their retreat along the peninsula, and amounted in all to 145 killed and captured and 304 wounded. It may be said that both sides fought well, but from the circumstances under which they fought, the highest credit is due to the victors.

The battle, however, though won by the English, was a moral triumph for the Americans, and the British parliament should at once have given up the contest. It was from the first absolutely certain that the Americans, with their immense superiority in numbers, could, if they were only willing to fight, hold their vast country against the British troops, fighting with a base thousands of miles away. The battle of Bunker's Hill showed that they were so willing, that they could fight sternly and bravely; and this point once established, it was little short of madness for the English government to continue the contest. They had not even the excuse of desiring to wipe out the dishonour of a defeat. Their soldiers had won a brilliant victory, and had fought with a determination and valour never exceeded, and England could have afforded to say, "We will fight no more; if you, the inhabitants of a vast continent, are determined to go alone, are ready to give your lives rather than remain in connection with us, go and prosper. We acknowledge we cannot subdue a nation in arms."

From the height of Copp's Hill it could be seen that the British had suffered terribly. Captain Wilson was full of enthusiasm when he saw the success of the last gallant charge of the English soldiers, but he said to Harold:

"It is a disastrous victory. A few such battles as these and the English army in America would cease to exist."

But although they were aware that the losses were heavy, they were not prepared for the truth. The long grass had hidden from view many of those who fell, and when it was known that nearly half of those engaged were killed or wounded, the feeling among the English was akin to consternation.

The generalship of the British was wholly unworthy of the valour of the troops. There would have been no difficulty in placing some of the vessels of light draught so far up the Mystic as to outflank the intrenchments held by the colonists; indeed, the British troops might have been landed farther up the Mystic, in which case the Americans must have retreated instantly to avoid capture. Lastly, the troops, although fighting within a mile of their quarters, were encumbered with three days' provisions, and their knapsacks, constituting, with their muskets and ammunition, a load of 125 lbs. This was indeed heavily handicapping men who had, under a blazing sun, to climb a steep hill, with grass reaching to their knees, and intersected by walls and fences.

American writers describe the defenders of the position as inferior in numbers to the assailants; but it is due to the English to say that their estimate of the number of the defenders of the intrenchments differs very widely from this. General Gage estimated them as being fully three times as numerous as the British troops. It is probable that the truth lies between the two accounts.

Captain Wilson returned with Harold greatly dispirited to his house.

"The look-out is dreadfully bad," he said to his wife, after describing the events of the day. "So far as I can see, there are but two alternatives—either peace, or a long and destructive war, with failure at its end. It is even more hopeless trying to conquer a vast country like this, defended by irregulars, than if we had a trained and disciplined army to deal with. In that case, two or three signal victories might bring the war to a conclusion but, fighting with the irregulars, a victory means nothing beyond so many of the enemy killed. There are scarcely any cannon to take, no stores or magazines to capture. When the enemy is beaten, he disperses, moves off, and in a couple of days gathers again in a fresh position. The work has no end. There are no fortresses to take, no strategical positions to occupy, no great roads to cut. The enemy can march anywhere, attack and disperse as he chooses, scatter, and reform when you have passed by. It is like fighting the wind."

"Well, John, since it seems so hopeless, cannot you give it up? Is it too late?"

"Altogether too late, Mary; and if I were free to-morrow, I would volunteer my services again next day. It is not any the less my duty to fight in my country's cause because I believe the cause to be a losing one. You must see that yourself, dear. If England had been sure to win without my aid I might have stood aloof. It is because everyone's help is needed that such services as I can render are due to her. A country would be in a bad way, indeed, whose sons were only ready to fight when their success was a certainty."

The Congress determined now to detach Canada from the English side, and prepared a force for the invasion of that state, where the British had but a few regular troops.

Captain Wilson was one morning summoned to head-quarters. On his return he called together four or five of the men best acquainted with the country. These had been in their early days hunters or border scouts, and knew every foot of the forest and lakes.

"I have just seen the general," Captain Wilson said. "A royalist brought in news last night that the rebels are raising a force intended to act against Montreal. They reckon upon being joined by a considerable portion of the Canadians, among whom there is, unfortunately, a good deal of discontent. We have but two regiments in the whole colony. One of these is at Quebec. The rebels, therefore, will get the advantage of surprise, and may raise the colony before we are in a condition to resist. General Howe asked me to take my company through the woods straight to Montreal. We should be landed a few miles up the coast at night. I suppose some of you know the country well enough to be able to guide us."

Several of the men expressed their ability to act as guides.

"I have fought the Indians through them woods over and over again," said one of them, a sinewy, weather-beaten man of some sixty years old, who was known as Peter Lambton. He had for many years been a scout attached to the army, and was one of the most experienced hunters on the frontier. He was a tall angular man, except that he stooped slightly, the result of a habit of walking with the head bent forward in the attitude of listening. The years which had passed over him had had no effect upon his figure. He walked with a long noiseless tread, like that of an Indian, and was one of the men attached to his company, in whom, wisely, Captain Wilson had made no attempt to instil the very rudiments of drill. It was, the captain thought, well that the younger men should have such a knowledge of drill as would enable them to perform simple manœuvres, but the old hunters would fight in their own way, a way infinitely better adapted for forest warfare than any that he could teach them. Peter and some of his companions were in receipt of small pensions, which had been bestowed upon them for their services with the troops. Men of this kind were not likely to take any lively interest in the squabbles as to questions of taxation; but when they found that it was coming to fighting, they again offered their services to government, as a matter of course. Some were attached to the regular troops as scouts, while others were divided among the newly-raised companies of loyalists.

Peter Lambton had for the last four years been settled at Concord. He had, during the war with the French, served as a scout with the regiment to which Captain Wilson belonged, and had saved that officer's life when, with a portion of his company, he was surrounded and cut off by hostile Indians. A strong feeling of friendship had sprung up between them, and when, four years before, there had been a lull in the English fighting on the frontier, Peter had retired on his pension and the savings which he had made during his many years' work as a hunter, and had located himself in a cottage on Captain Wilson's estate. It was the many tales told him by the hunter of his experiences in Indian warfare that had fired Harold with a desire for the life of a frontier hunter, and had given him such a knowledge of forest life as had enabled him to throw off the Indians from his trail. On Harold's return, the old hunter had listened with extreme interest to the story of his adventures, and had taken great pride in the manner in which he had utilized his teachings. Peter made his appearance in the city three days after the arrival of Captain Wilson there.

"I look upon this here affair as a favourable occurrence for Harold," he said to Captain Wilson. "The boy has lots of spirits, but if it had not been for this he might have grown up a regular town greenhorn, fit for nothing but to walk about in a long coat, and to talk pleasant to women; but this will just be the making of him. With your permission, Cap., I shall take him under my charge and teach him to use his eyes and his ears, and I reckon he will turn out as good an Indian fighter as you will see on the frontier."

"But it is not Indians that we are going to fight, Peter," Captain Wilson said. "I heartily wish it was."

"It will be the same thing," Peter said; "not here, in course; there will be battles between the regulars and the colonists, regular battles like that at Quebec, where both parties was fools enough to march about in the open and get shot down by hundreds. I don't call that fighting; that's just killing, and there ain't no more sense in it than in two herd of buffalo charging each other on the prairie. But there will be plenty of real fighting—expeditions in the woods and Indian skirmishes, for you will be sure that the Indians will join in, some on one side and some on the other. It ain't in their nature to sit still in their villages while powder is being burnt. A few months of this work will make a man of him, and he might have a worse teacher than Peter Lambton. You just hand him over to my care, Cap., and I will teach him all I know of the ways of the woods, and I tell yer there ain't no better kind of edication for a young fellow. He larns to use the senses God has given him, to keep his head when another man would lose his presence of mind, to have the eye of a hawk and the ear of a hound to get so that he scarcely knows what it is to be tired or hungry, to be able to live while other men would starve, to read the signs of the woods like a printed book, and to be in every way a man and not a tailor's figure."

"There is a great deal in what you say, old friend," Captain Wilson answered; "and such a training cannot but do a man good. I wish with all my heart that it had been entirely with red foes that the fighting was to be done. However, that cannot be helped, and as he is to fight, he could not be in better hands than yours. So long as we remain here, I shall teach him what drill I can with the rest of the company, but when we leave this town and the work really begins, I shall put him in your charge to learn the duties of a scout."

The young negro, Jake, had also enlisted, for throughout the war the negroes fought on both sides, according to the politics of their masters. There were only two other negroes in the company, and Captain Wilson had some hesitation in enlisting them, but they made good soldiers. In the case of Jake, Captain Wilson knew that he was influenced in his wish to join solely by his affection for Harold, and the lad's father felt that in the moment of danger the negro would be ready to lay down his life for him.

There was great satisfaction in the band when they received news that they were at last about to take the field. The long inaction had been most wearisome to them, and they knew that any fighting that would take place round Boston would be done by the regular troops. Food too was very scarce in town, and they were heartily weary of the regular drill and discipline. They were then in high spirits as they embarked on board the *Thetis* sloop of war and sailed from Boston harbour.

It was a pitiful parting between Mrs. Wilson and her husband and son. It had been arranged that she should sail for England in a ship that was leaving on the following week, and should there stay with her husband's family, from whom she had a warm invitation to make their home her own until the war was over.

The *Thetis* ran out to sea. As soon as night fell, her bow was turned to land again, and about midnight the anchor was let fall near the shore some twenty miles north of Boston. The landing was quickly effected, and with three days' provisions in their knapsacks, the little party started on their march. One of the scouts had come from that neighbourhood and led them by paths avoiding all villages and farms. At daybreak they bivouacked in a wood, and at nightfall resumed the march. By the next morning they had left the settlements behind and entered a belt of swamp and forest extending west to the St. Lawrence.

CHAPTER VI
SCOUTING

A PARTY of six men were seated around a fire in the forest which covered the slopes of the northern shore of Lake Champlain. The spot had been chosen because a great tree had fallen, bringing down several others in its course, and opening a vista through which a view could be obtained of the surface of the lake. The party consisted of Peter Lambton, Harold, Jake, Ephraim Potter, another old frontiersman, and two Indians.

The company under Captain Wilson had made its way safely to the St. Lawrence, after undergoing considerable hardships in the forest. They had been obliged to depend entirely on what game they could shoot, and such fish as they could catch in the rivers whose course they followed. They had, however, reached Montreal without loss, and there they found that General Carleton had in all about 500 regulars, and about 200 volunteers who had recently been engaged.

It was clear that if the people of Canada were as hostile to the connection with England as were those of the other colonies, the little force at the disposal of the English general could do nothing to defend the colony against the strong force which the Americans were collecting for its invasion. Fortunately this was not the case. Although the Canadians were of French descent, and the province had been wrested by arms from France, they for the most part preferred being under English rule to joining the insurgent colonies. They had been in no way oppressed by England; their property had been respected, and above all things no attempt had ever been made to interfere with their religion. In the New England provinces the hard puritan spirit of the early fathers had never ceased to prevail. Those who had fled from England to obtain freedom of worship had been intolerant persecutors of all religion different from their

72

own. The consequence was that the priests of Canada were wholly opposed to any idea of union with the insurgent colonists. Their influence over the people was great, and although these still objected to the English rule, and would have readily taken up arms against it under other circumstances, they had too little sympathy with the New Englanders to join in their movement, which, if successful, would have placed Canada under the rule of the United States instead of that of England.

The upper classes of Canadians were almost to a man loyal to the English connection. They had been well treated, and enjoyed indeed a greater state of independence than had been the case under French rule. Moreover, they were for the most part descended from old French families, and their sympathies were entirely opposed to popular insurrection. Thus, when Captain Wilson and his party reached Montreal, they found that, in spite of the paucity of English troops under the command of General Carleton, the position was not so bad as had been feared by General Gage. It was possible, and indeed probable, that Upper Canada might fall into the hands of the Americans, and that even Quebec itself might be captured; but unless the people joined the Americans, the success of the latter would be but temporary. With the spring the navigation of the river would be open, and reinforcements would arrive from England. The invaders would then be at a disadvantage. Separated from home by a wide tract of forest-covered country, they would have the greatest difficulty in transporting artillery, ammunition, and stores, and fighting as an army in invasion they would be placed in a very different position to that occupied by the colonists fighting on their own ground. It was probable, however, that for a time the tide of invasion would succeed.

The Indians of the Five Nations, as those dwelling near the British frontier at this point were called, had offered their services to the general, and volunteered to cross the frontier to recapture Ticonderoga and Cowpoint, which had been seized by the Americans, and to carry the war into the colonies. General Carleton, however, an exceedingly humane and kind-hearted man, shrank from the horrors that such a warfare would entail upon the colonists.

He accepted the services of the Indians as far as the absolute defence of Canada from invasion, but refused to allow them to cross the frontier.

On the arrival of Captain Wilson with his little force, he was ordered to march at once to the fort of St. John's, which was held by a party of regular troops.

On arriving at that place, the two scouts had been sent down towards Lake Champlain to watch the proceedings of the enemy. Harold had obtained leave from his father to accompany the scouts, and Jake had been permitted to form one of the party. Peter Lambton had grumbled a little at this last addition to the number; he knew Jake's affection for his young master, and the great strength of the negro would have rendered him useful in a hand-to-hand fight, but he was altogether unaccustomed to forest work and his habit of bursting into fits of laughter on the smallest provocation, as is the manner of his race, enraged the scout to the last degree; indeed, he had not left the fort above an hour when he turned savagely on the negro.

"Look-ee here," he said, "if that's the way ye'r agoing on, the sooner yer turns yer face and tramps back to the fort the better. When you were at Concord, it did no harm to make as much noise as a jackass braying whenever you opened that mouth of yours, but it won't do in the forests; it would cost us our har, and you your wool, ef yer were to make that noise with the enemy anywhere within fifteen miles of yer. I ain't agoing, if I knows it, to risk my sculp on such a venture as this, still less I ain't agoing to see this young chap's life thrown away. His father hez put him in my charge, and I ain't agoing to see him sacrificed in no such way. So ye've got to make up yer mind; yer have got to keep that mouth of yours shut tight, or yer 'ave got to tramp back to the fort."

Jake gave many promises of silence, and although at first he often raised his voice to a point far exceeding that considered by the hunters safe in the woods, he was each time checked by such a savage growl on the part of Peter, or by a punch in the ribs from Harold, that he quickly fell into the ways of the others, and never spoke above a loud whisper.

SCOUTING

At a short distance from the fort they were joined by the two Indians, who were also out on a scouting expedition on their own account. They had previously been well known both to Peter and Ephraim. They were warriors of the Seneca tribe, one of the Five Nations.

They had now been for two days on the north shore of Lake Champlain. They were sitting round a fire eating a portion of a deer which had been shot by Harold that morning. So far they had seen nothing of the enemy. They knew that three thousand men, under Schuyler and Montgomery, had marched to the other end of the lake. The colonists had been sending proclamations across the frontier to the inhabitants, saying that they were coming as friends to free them from the yoke of England, and calling upon them to arise and strike for freedom. They were also in negotiation with some of the chiefs of the Five Nations, and with other Indian tribes, to induce them to join with them.

"I propose," Peter said, when the meal was finished and he had lighted his pipe, "to go down the lake and see what they are doing. Deer-Tail here tells me that he knows where there is a canoe. He, Harold, and me will go and reconnoitre a bit; the other three had best wait here till we comes back with news. In course, chief," he continued to the other Indian, after explaining to him in his own language what he intended to do, "you will be guided by circumstances—you can see a long way down the lake, and ef anything should lead you to think that we are in trouble, you can take such steps as may seem best to you. It's mighty little I should think of the crowd of colonists; but ef, as you say, a number of the warriors of the Five Nations, indignant at the rejection of their offers by the English general, have gone down and joined the colonists, it will be a different affair altogether."

The "Elk," as the second Seneca chief was called, nodded his assent. In a few words Peter told Harold what had been arranged. Jake looked downcast when he heard that he was not to accompany his master, but as he saw the latter had, since leaving the fort, obeyed without questioning every suggestion of the scout, he offered no remonstrance.

75

A quarter of an hour later Peter rose, Deer-Tail followed his example, and Harold at once took up his rifle and fell in in their steps. There was but little talk in the woods, and the matter having been settled, it did not enter the mind either of Peter or of the Indian to say a word of adieu to their comrades. Harold imitated their example, but gave a nod and a smile to Jake as he started.

Half an hour's tramp took them to the shore of the lake. Here they halted for a minute, while the Indians closely examined the locality. With the wonderful power of making their way straight through the forest to the required spot, which seems to be almost an instinct among Indians, Deer-Tail had struck the lake within two hundred yards of the point which he aimed at. He led the way along the shore until he came to a spot where a great maple had fallen into the lake; here he turned into the forest again, and in fifty yards came to a clump of bushes; these he pushed aside and pointed to a canoe which was lying hidden among them. Peter joined him, the two lifted the boat out, placed it on their shoulders, and carried it to the lake. There were three paddles in it. Peter motioned Harold to take his place in the stern and steer, while he and the Indian knelt forward and put their paddles in the water.

"Keep her along on the right shore of the lake, about fifty yards from the trees; there is no fear of anyone being lurking about near this end."

The canoe was light and well made, and darted quickly over the water under the strokes of the three paddlers. It was late in the afternoon when they started, and before they had gone many miles, darkness had fallen. The canoe was run in close to shore, where she lay in the shadow of the trees until morning. Just as the sun rose, the Red-skin and Peter simultaneously dipped their paddles in the water and sent the canoe under the arches of the trees; they had at the same instant caught sight of four canoes making their way along the lake.

"Thems Injuns," Peter whispered. "They are scouting to see if the lake's free. If the general could have got a couple of gun-boats up the Sorrel, the enemy could never have crossed the lake, and it would have given them a month's work to take their guns round it.

It's lucky we were well under the trees, or we should have been seen."

"What had we best do, Deer-Tail?"

For two or three minutes the scouts conversed together in the Indian tongue.

"The Seneca agrees with me," Peter said. "It is like enough there are Injuns scouting along both shores; we must lay up here till nightfall; ef we are seen they would signal by smoke, and we should have them canoes back again in no time. By their coming, I expect the expedition is starting, but it won't do to go back without being sure of it."

The canoe was paddled to a spot where the bushes grew thickly by the bank. It was pushed among these, and the three, after eating some cooked deer's flesh which they had brought with them, prepared to pass the day.

"The Seneca and I will keep watch by turns," the scout said. "We will wake you if we want ye."

Harold was by this time sufficiently accustomed to the ways of the woods to obey orders at once without offering to take his turn at watching, as his inclination led him to do, and he was soon sound asleep. It was late in the afternoon when he was awoke by the scout touching him.

"There are some critters coming along the bank," he said in a whisper. "They ain't likely to see us, but 'tis best to be ready." Harold sat up in the canoe, rifle in hand, and, listening intently, heard a slight sound such as would be produced by the snapping of a twig. Presently he heard upon the other side of the bushes, about a few yards distant, a few low words in an Indian tongue. He looked at his companions. They were sitting immovable, each with his rifle directed towards the sound, and Harold thought it would fare badly with any of the passers if they happened to take a fancy to peer through the bushes. The Indians had, however, no reason for supposing that there were any enemies upon the lake, and they consequently passed on without examining more closely the thicket by the shore. Not until it was perfectly dark did Peter give the sign for the continuance of the journey. This time, instead of skirting the lake, the canoe was steered out toward its centre. For some time they paddled, and then several lights were seen from ahead.

"I thought so," the scout said. "They have crossed to the Isle La Motte, and they are making as many fires as if they war having a sort of picnic at home. We must wait till they burns out, for we darn't go near the place with the water lit up for two or three hundred yards round. It won't be long, for I reckon it must be past eleven o'clock now."

The fires were soon seen to burn down. The paddles were dipped in the water, and the canoe approached the island.

"I would give something," Peter said, "to know whether there are any Red-skins there. Ef there are, our chance of landing without being seen ain't worth talking of; ef they are not, we might land a hull fleet; at anyrate we must risk it. Now, Harold, the chief and me will land and find out how many men there are here, and, ef we can, how long they are likely to stop. You keep the canoe about ten yards from shore, in the shadow of the trees, and be ready to move close the instant you hear my call. I shall just give the croak of a frog. The instant we get in, you paddle off without a word. Ef ye hears any shouts, and judges as how we have been seen, ye must just act upon the best of yer judgment."

The boat glided noiselessly up to the shore. All was still there, the encampment being at the other side of the island. The two scouts, red and white, stepped noiselessly on to the land. Harold backed the canoe a few paces with a quick stroke upon the paddle, and seeing close to him a spot where a long branch of a tree dipped into the water, he guided the canoe among the foliage, and there sat without movement, listening almost breathlessly.

Ere many minutes had elapsed, he heard footsteps coming along the shore. They stopped when near him. Three or four minutes passed without the slightest sound, and then a voice said, in tones which the speaker had evidently tried to lower, but which were distinctly audible in the canoe:

"I tell yer, Red-skin, it seems to me as how you have brought us here on a fool's errand. I don't see no signs of a canoe, and it ain't likely that the British would be along the lake here, seeing as how there is a score of canoes with your people in them, scouting ahead."

"I heard canoe," another voice said, "first at other end of the island, and then coming along here."

"And ef yer did," the first speaker said, "likely enough it was one of the canoes of your people."

"No," the Indian answered; "if canoe come back with news, would have come straight to fires."

"Well, it ain't here, anyway," the first speaker said, "and I don't believe yer ever heard a canoe at all. It is enough to make a man swear, to be called up just as we were making ourselves comfortable for the night, on account of an Indian's fancies. I wonder at the general's listening to them. However, we have got our orders to go round the island and see ef there is any canoe on either shore, so we had better be moving, else we shall not get to sleep before morning."

Harold held his breath as the group passed opposite to him. Fortunately, the trunk of the tree grew from the very edge of the water, and there were several bushes growing round it, so that at this point the men had to make a slight detour inland. Harold felt thankful indeed that he had taken the precaution of laying his canoe among the thick foliage, for although the night was dark, it would have been instantly seen had it been lying on the surface of the lake. Even as it was, a close inspection might have detected it, but the eyes of the party were fixed on the shore, as it was there, if at all, that they expected to find an empty canoe lying.

Harold was uneasy at the discovery that there were still some Red-skins on the island. It was possible, of course, that the one he had heard might be alone as a scout, but it was more likely that others of the tribe were also there.

After landing, Peter and the Seneca made their way across the island to the side facing the American shore. Creeping cautiously along, they found a large number of flat-bottomed boats, in which the Americans had crossed from the mainland, and which were, Peter thought, capable of carrying two thousand men. They now made their way towards the spot where the forces were encamped.

The fires had burned low, but round a few of them men were still sitting and talking. Motioning to the Seneca to remain quiet, Peter sauntered cautiously out on to the clearing where the camp was formed. He had little fear of detection, for he wore no uniform, and his hunter's dress afforded no index to the party to which he was attached.

A great portion of the Americans were still in their ordinary attire, it having been impossible to furnish uniforms for so great a number of men as had been suddenly called to arms throughout the colonies.

From the arbours of boughs which had been erected in all directions, he judged that the force had been already some days upon the island. Large numbers of men, however, were sleeping in the open air; and picking his way cautiously among them, he threw himself down at a short distance from one of the fires, by which three or four men were sitting.

For some time they talked of camp matters, the shortness of food, and want of provisions.

"It is bad here," one said presently; "it will be worse when we move forward. Schuyler will be here to-morrow with the rest of the army, and we are to move down to Isle-aux-Noix, at the end of the lake, and I suppose we shall land at once and march against St. John's. There are only a couple of hundred Britishers there, and we shall make short work of them."

"The sooner the better, I say," another speaker remarked. "I am ready enough to fight, but I hate all this waiting about. I want to get back to my farm again."

"You are in a hurry, you are," the other said. "You don't suppose we are going to take Canada in a week's time, do you? Even if the Canadians join us, and by what I hear, that ain't so sartin after all, we shall have to march down to Quebec, and that's no child's play. I know the country there. It is now the 4th of September; another month and the winter will be upon us, and a Canadian winter is no joke, I can tell you."

"The more reason for not wasting any more time," the other one grumbled. "If Montgomery had his way, we should go at them quickly enough, but Schuyler is always delaying. He has kept us waiting now since 17th of last month; we might have been half-way to Quebec by this time."

"Yes," the other said, "if the Britishers had run away as we came; but we have got St. John's and Fort Chamblée to deal with, and they may hold out some time. However, the sooner we begin the job, the sooner it will be over, and I am heartily glad that we move to-morrow."

Peter had now obtained the information he required, and rising to his feet again, with a grumbling remark as to the hardness of the ground, he sauntered away towards the spot where he had left the Indian. Just as he did so, a tall figure came out from an arbour close by. A fire was burning just in front, and Peter saw that he was a tall and handsome man of about forty years of age. He guessed at once that he was in the presence of the colonial leader.

"You are, like myself," the new-comer said, "unable to sleep, I suppose?"

"Yes, general," Peter answered; "I found I could not get off, and so I thought I would stretch my legs in the wood a bit. They are lying so tarnal thick down there, by the fires, one can't move without treading on them."

"Which regiment do you belong to?"

"The Connecticut," Peter replied, for he knew by report that a regiment from this province formed part of the expedition.

"As good men as any I have," the general said cordially. "Their only fault is that they are in too great a hurry to attack the enemy."

"I agree with the rest, general," Peter said; "it's dull work wasting our time here when we are wanted at home. I enlisted for six months, and the sooner the time's up, the better, say I."

"You have heard nothing moving?" the general asked. "One of the Chippewas told me that he heard a canoe out in the lake. Ah, here he is!"

At that moment five or six men, headed by an Indian, issued from the wood close by. It was too late for Peter to try to withdraw, but he stepped aside a pace or two as the party approached.

"Well! Have you found anything?" the general asked.

"No find," the Chippewa said shortly.

"I don't believe as there ever was a canoe there," the man who followed him said. "It was just a fancy of the Indian's."

"No fancy," the Indian asserted angrily. "Canoe there. No find."

"It might have been one of our own canoes," Montgomery said in a conciliatory tone. "The Indians are seldom mistaken. However, if no one has landed, it matters not either way."

"Only as we have had a tramp for nothing," the colonist said. "However, there is time for a sleep yet. Hallo!" he exclaimed, as his eye fell on Peter Lambton. "What, Peter! Why, how did you get here? Why, I thought as how—General," he exclaimed, sharply turning to Montgomery, "this man lives close to me at Concord! He is a royalist, he is, and went into Boston and joined the corps they got up there!"

"Seize him!" Montgomery shouted, but it was too late.

As the man had turned to speak to the general, Peter darted into the wood. The Chippewa, without waiting to hear the statement of the colonist, at once divined the state of things, and, uttering his war-whoop, dashed after the fugitive. Two or three of the colonists instantly followed, and a moment later three or four Indians who had been lying on the ground leaped up and darted like phantoms into the wood.

The general no sooner grasped the facts, than he shouted an order for pursuit, and a number of the men most accustomed to frontier work at once followed the first party of pursuers. Others would have done the same, but Montgomery shouted that no more should go, as they would only be in the others' way, and there could not be more than two or three spies on the island.

After the Chippewa's first war-cry, there was silence for the space of a minute in the forest. Then came a wild scream, mingled with another Indian yell. A moment later the leading pursuers came upon the body of the Chippewa. His skull had been cleft with a tomahawk, and the scalp was gone.

As they were clustered round the body, two or three of the Indians ran up; they raised the Indian wail as they saw their comrade, and with the rest took up pursuit.

Peter and the Seneca were now, however, far among the trees, and, as their pursuers had nothing to guide them, they reached the spot where they had left the canoe, unmolested.

On the signal being given, Harold instantly paddled to the shore. Not a word was spoken until the canoe was well out in the lake. Occasional shots were heard on shore as the pursuers fired at objects which they thought were men. Presently a loud Indian cry rose from the shore.

"They see us," Peter said. "However, we are out of shot, and can take it easy." The Red-skin said a few words. "You are right, chief."

"The chief says," he explained to Harold, "that as there are Red-skins on the island, they have probably some canoes. The moon is just getting up beyond that hill, and it will be light enough to see us half across the lake. It would not matter if the water was free, but what with Injuns prowling along the shores and out on the lake, we shall have to use our wits to save our har."

"Look!" he exclaimed two or three minutes later, as two columns of bright flame at a short distance from them shot up at the end of the island.

"They are Injun signals. As far as they can be seen, Injuns will know that there are enemies on the lake. Now, paddle your hardest, Harold; and do you, chief, keep your eyes and your ears open for sights and sounds."

Under the steady strokes of the three paddles, the bark canoe sped rapidly over the water. When the moon was fairly above the edge of the hill, they halted for a moment and looked back. The two columns of fire still blazed brightly on the island, which was now three miles astern, and two dark spots could be seen on the water about half-way between them and it.

"You can paddle, my lads," Peter Lambton said to the distant foes, "but you will never catch us. I would not heed you, if it were not for the other varmint ahead." He stood up in the canoe and looked anxiously over the lake.

"It is all clear as far as I can see at present," he said.

"Can't we land, Peter, and make our way back on foot?"

"Bless you," Peter said, "there ain't a native along the shore there but has got his eye on this canoe. We might as well take her straight back to the island as try to land. Better; for we should get a few hours before they tried and shot us there, while the Injuns would not give us a minute. No, we must just keep to the water; and now paddle on again, but take it quietly. It is no odds to let those varmints behind gain on us a little. You need not think about them. When the danger comes we shall want every ounce of our strength."

For half an hour they paddled steadily on. The pursuing canoes were now less than a mile behind them.

"I would give a good deal," muttered the scout, "for a few black clouds over the moon. We would make for shore then, and risk it; it will be getting daylight before long. Ah!" he exclaimed, pausing suddenly, as the chief stopped rowing. "A canoe on each side is rowing out to cut us off."

Harold was now paddling forward, while the scout had the place at the stern. The former was surprised to feel the canoe shooting off from its former course at right angles towards the shore; then, curving still more round, they began to paddle back along the lake.

The canoes which had been pursuing them were nearly abreast of each other. They had embarked from opposite sides of the island, but they had been gradually drawing together, although still some distance apart, when Peter turned his canoe. Seeing his manœuvre, both turned to head him off, but by so doing they occupied an entirely different position in relation to each other, one canoe being nearly half a mile nearer to them than the other.

"Take it easy," Peter said; "these varmint will cut us off, and we have got to fight, but we can cripple the one nearest to us before the other comes up."

The boats were now darting over the water in a line which promised to bring the leading canoe almost in collision with that of Peter. When within two hundred yards of each other, Peter ceased rowing.

"Now," he said, "Harold, see if you can pick one of those fellows off. It's no easy matter, travelling at the pace they are. You fire first."

Harold took a steady aim and fired.

A yell of derision told that he had missed. The Indians stopped paddling. There was a flash, and a ball struck the canoe. At the same moment Peter fired.

"There is one down!" he exclaimed. The Seneca fired, but without result, and the three unwounded Indians in the canoe— for it had contained four men—replied with a volley.

Harold felt a burning sensation, as if a hot iron passed across his arm.

"Hit, boy?" Peter asked anxiously, as he gave a short exclamation.

"Nothing to speak of," Harold replied.

"The varmint are lying by, waiting for the other canoe. Paddle straight at them."

The Indians at once turned the boat and paddled to meet their companions, who were fast approaching.

"Now," Peter exclaimed, "we have got 'em in a line—a steady aim this time!" The three rifles spoke out, one of the Indians fell into the boat, and the paddle of another was struck from his grasp.

"Now," the scout shouted, "paddle away! We have got them all fairly behind us!"

Day broke just as they were again abreast of the island; one canoe was following closely, two others were a mile and a half behind, while the one with which they had been engaged had made for the shore.

"What do you mean to do?" Harold asked Peter.

"I mean to run as close as I can round the end of the island, and then make for the place where they must have embarked on the mainland. They may have seen the signal fires there, but will not know what has been going on. So now row your best. We must leave the others as far behind as possible."

For the first time since they started the three paddlers exerted themselves to the utmost. They had little fear that there were any more canoes on the island, for had there been they would have joined in the chase. It was only necessary to keep so far from the end of the island as would take them out of reach of fire. Several shots were discharged as they passed, but these fell short as the canoe shot along at its highest rate of speed, every stroke taking it farther from its nearest pursuer.

At the end of an hour's paddling, this canoe was a mile and a half behind. Its rowers had apparently somewhat abated their speed in order to allow the other two boats to draw up to them, for the result of the encounter between their comrades and the fugitives had not been of a nature to encourage them to undertake a single-handed contest with them.

CHAPTER VII
IN THE FOREST

SEE, Peter!" Harold exclaimed. "There is a whole fleet of boats ahead!"

"I sees 'em," Peter said, "and have seed 'em for the last quarter of an hour. It is Schuyler with the rest of what they calls their army. Steer a little out of the course; we must pass close by them. They won't suspect nothing wrong, and will suppose we are merely carrying a message."

In half an hour they were abreast of the flotilla, consisting of flat boats laden with troops. With them were two or three Indian canoes. Peter steered so as to pass at a distance of a hundred and fifty yards. They rowed less strongly now, but still vigorously. There was a shout from the boat.

"All well on the island!"

"All well!" Peter shouted back, waving his hand, and without further word the canoe passed on.

"There! Do you hear that?" Peter exclaimed. "They are firing shots from the canoes to call their attention. The chances are they won't hear them, for the rattle of their oars, and the talking, and the row they are making are enough to drown the sound of a cannon. Now put it on again as hard as you can. Another hour will take us to the landing-place."

They could see when the flotilla came up to the pursuing boats that the canoes which accompanied it turned their heads and joined in the pursuit, but they were now near three miles ahead, and there was no chance whatever of their being overtaken. They slackened their speed slightly as they approached the land, and rowed up to the landing-place without any signs of extraordinary haste.

A few men were loitering about. "What is the news from the island?" one asked, as they landed.

"All well there," Peter said.

"Did you see anything of Schuyler?"

"Yes, we met him about half-way across."

"What have you come for?"

"General Montgomery says that no spare flints have been sent over for the firelocks."

"I'll swear that some went," one of the men exclaimed, "for I packed a sack of them myself in one of the boats!"

"I suppose they have been mislaid," Peter said. "Perhaps some of the stores have got heaped over them. Ef you are quite sartin, we have had our journey for nothing."

"As sartin as life," the man replied. "I'll swear to the sackful of flints; and tarnation heavy they was, too."

"Well, then, I need not trouble about it farther," Peter said. "We will take a rest, and paddle back in an hour or two. Was there any marking on the sack, so as I may tell the general how to look for it?"

"Marks!" the man repeated "Why, it had FLINTS written on it in big black letters six inches long. It must turn up anyhow. They will find it when they come to shift the stores."

Then, accompanied by his two companions, Peter strolled quietly through the little village. Stopping at a small store, he purchased some flour and tea; then he followed the road inland, and was soon out of sight of the village. He stopped for a moment and then shook his head.

"It's no use trying to hide our trail here," he said. "The road's an inch thick in dust, and, do what we will, they will be able to see where we turn off. It is our legs as we have got to trust to for a bit. We've got a good half-hour's start of the canoes; they were a long three miles behind when we struck the shore."

Leaving the road, he led the way with a long swinging stride across the cultivated land. Twenty minutes' walk took them into the forest, which extended from the shore of the lake many miles inland.

IN THE FOREST

"Take off your boots, Harold," he said, as he entered the wood. "Those heels will leave marks that a Red-skin could pick up at a run. Now tread, as near as you can, in the exact spot where the Seneca has trodden before you. He will follow in my track, and you may be sure that I shall choose the hardest bits of ground I can come across. There, the varmint are on shore!"

As he spoke, an angry yell rose from the distant village. At a long steady pace, which taxed to the utmost Harold's powers as a walker, they kept their way through the woods, not pursuing a straight course, but turning, winding, and zigzagging every few minutes. Harold could not but feel impatient at what seemed to him such a loss of time, especially when a yell from the edge of the wood told that the Indians had traced them thus far—showed, too, that they were far nearer than before. But, as Peter afterwards explained to him, all this turning and winding made it necessary for the Indians to follow every step, as they would an animal, to guess the direction they had taken. The weather had been dry and the ground was hard; therefore, the most experienced trapper would be obliged to proceed very slowly on the trail, and would frequently be for a time at fault; whereas, had they continued in a straight line, the Indians could have followed at a run, contenting themselves with seeing the trail here and there. They came across two or three little streams running down toward the lake; these they followed, in some cases up, in others down, for a considerable distance, leaving the bed where the bushes grew thick, and hid the marks of their feet as they stepped out from the water. Harold would gladly have gone at a run, but Peter never quickened his pace; he knew that the Indians could not pick up the trail at a rate faster than that at which they were going, and that great delay would be caused at each of the little streams, as it would be uncertain whether they had passed up or down.

As the time passed, the Indian yells, which had, when they first entered the wood, sounded so alarmingly near, died away, and a perfect stillness reigned in the forest. It was late in the afternoon, however, before Peter halted.

"We can rest now," he said. "It will be hours before the critters can be here. Now let us have some tea."

He began to look for some dried sticks. Harold offered to assist.

"You sit down," the scout said. "A nice sort of fire we should get with sticks of your picking up! Why, we should have a smoke that would bring all the Injuns in the woods on to us. No, the sticks as the Seneca and me will pick up won't give as much smoke as you can put in a tea-cup; but I would not risk even that if we was nigh the lake, for it might be seen by any Red-skins out in a canoe. But we are miles back from the lake, and there ain't no other open space where they could get a view over the tree-tops."

Harold watched the Indian and the scout collecting dry leaves and sticks, and took particular notice, for future use, of the kinds which they selected. A light was struck with a flint and steel, and soon a bright blaze sprang up, without, so far as Harold could see, the slightest smoke being given off. Then the hunter produced some food from his wallet and a tin pot. He had at the last spring they passed filled a skin which hung on his shoulder with water, and this was soon boiling over the fire. A handful of tea was thrown in, and the pot removed. Some flour, mixed with water, was placed on a small iron plate, which was put on the red-hot ashes. A few cakes were baked, and with these, the cold venison and the tea, an ample meal was made.

After nearly an hour's halt, they again proceeded on their way. A consultation had taken place between Peter and the Seneca as to the best course to be pursued. They could, without much difficulty or risk, have continued the way through the woods beyond the lake, but it was important that they should reach the other side by the evening of the following day, to give warning of the intended attack by the Americans. There were, they knew, other Red-skins in the woods besides those on their trail, and the nearer they approached the shore, the greater the danger. They had, however, determined that they would, at all hazards, endeavour to obtain another canoe and cross the lake. Until nightfall they continued their course, and then, knowing that their trail could no longer be followed, they made down to the lake. They were many miles distant from it, and Harold was completely worn out when at last he saw a gleam of water through the trees. He was not yet to rest. Entering the lake, they began wading through it, at a few feet from the edge.

After an hour's walking thus, they entered the bushes, which thickly covered the shore, made their way through these until they came to a spot sufficiently open for them to lie down, and Harold, wrapping himself in the blanket which he carried over his shoulder, was sound asleep in less than a minute. When he woke the sun was shining brightly.

"Get up, youngster; we are in luck," the scout said. "Here's a canoe with two of the varmint making towards the shore. By the way they are going, they will land not far off."

The scout led the way, crawling on his hands and knees to the water's edge, to where the Seneca was sitting watching the canoe through a cover of green leaves. The course that the boat was taking would lead it to a point some three hundred yards from where they were sitting.

"We shall have no difficulty in managing them," Harold said, and grasped his rifle eagerly.

"Not too fast," Peter said; "the chances are that the varmint have friends on shore. Like enough they have been out fishing."

The shore formed a slight sweep at this point, and the bushes in which they were hidden occupied the point at one extremity. In the centre of the little bay there was a spot clear from bushes; to this the canoe was directed. As it approached the shore, two other Indians appeared at the water's edge. One of them asked a question, and in reply a paddler held up a large bunch of fish.

"Just as I thought; like enough there are a dozen of them there," said Peter.

On reaching the shore, the men sprang out, taking their fish with them. The canoe was fastened by its head-rope to the bushes, and the Indians moved a short distance inland.

"There is their smoke," Peter said, indicating a point some thirty feet from the lake, but so slight was it, that, even when it was pointed out to him, Harold could hardly make out the light mist rising from among the bushes. Presently he looked round for the Seneca, but the Indian had disappeared.

"He has gone scouting," Peter said, in answer to Harold's question. "If there are only four of them, it would be an easy job, but I expect there is more of the red varmint there."

In ten minutes the Seneca returned as noiselessly as he had gone; he opened his hand and all the fingers twice, the third time he showed only three fingers.

"Thirteen," Peter said; "too many of them even for a sudden onslaught."

The Indian said a few words to Peter; the latter nodded, and Deer-Tail again quietly stole away.

"He is going to steal the boat," Peter said. "It is a risky job, for where it lies it can be seen by them as they sit. Now you and me must be ready with our shooting-irons to cover him if need be. Ef he is found out before he gets the boat, he will take to the woods and lead them away from us; but ef he is fairly in the boat, then we must do our best for him. If the wust comes to the wust, I reckon we can hold these bushes agin 'em for some time; but in the end, I don't disguise from ye, youngster, they will beat us."

Harold now sat intently watching the canoe. It seemed an age to him before he saw a hand emerge from the bushes and take hold of the head-rope.

The motion given to the canoe was so slight as to be almost imperceptible; it seemed as if it was only drifting gently before the slight breeze which was creeping over the surface of the lake. Half its length had disappeared from the open space, when an Indian appeared by the edge of the water. He looked at the canoe, looked over the lake, and withdrew again. The hand had disappeared in the bushes on his approach. The movement of the canoe, slight as it was, had caught his eye; but, satisfied that it was caused only by the wind, he had returned to his fire again. The hand appeared again through the bushes, and the canoe was drawn along until hidden from the sight of those sitting by the fire. Again the watchful Indian appeared, but the boat was lying quietly by the bushes at the full length of its head-rope. He stooped down to see that this was securely fastened, and again retired. Harold held his breath, expecting that every moment the presence of the Seneca would be discovered. Scarcely had the Indian disappeared than the Seneca crawled out from the bushes. With a sweep of his knife he cut the rope of the canoe, and noiselessly entered it, and as he did so, gave a shove with his foot, which sent it dancing along the shore towards the spot where Harold and his companion were hidden. Then he seized the paddle, and in half a dozen strokes brought it within reach of them. Harold and Peter stepped into it; as they did so, there was a sudden shout. The Indian had again strolled down to look at the canoe, whose movements, slight as they had been, had appeared suspicious to him. He now, to his astonishment, saw it at the point with two white men and an Indian on board. He had left his gun behind him, and, uttering his war-cry, bounded back for it.

"Round the point—quick!" Peter exclaimed. "They will riddle us in the open."

Two strokes took the canoe round the projecting point of bushes, and she then darted along the shore, driven by the greatest efforts of which the three paddlers were capable. Had the shore been open, the Indians would have gained upon them, but they were unable to force their way through the thick bushes at anything like the rate at which the canoe was flying over the water. The first start was upwards of a hundred yards, and this was increased by fifty before the Indians, arriving at the point, opened fire. This distance is beyond anything like an accurate range with Indian guns. Several bullets struck the water round the canoe.

"Now, steer out," Peter said, as the firing suddenly ceased. "They are making a detour among the bushes, and will come down ahead of us if we keep near the shore."

Two or three more shots were fired, but without effect, and the canoe soon left the shore far behind.

"Now," Peter said, "I think we are safe. It is not likely they have another canoe anywhere near on this side, as most of them would have gone with the expedition. Ef the firing has been heard, it will not attract much attention, being on this side, and I see nothing in the way of a boat out in the lake. Still, these Red-skins' eyes can see most any distance. Now, chief," he went on to the Indian in his native language, "the young 'un and I will lie down at the bottom of the boat. Do you paddle quietly and easily, as ef you were fishing. The canoe with a single Indian in it will excite no suspicion, and even if you see other canoes, you had better keep on in that way, unless you see that any of them are intending to overhaul you."

The chief nodded assent. Peter and Harold stretched themselves at full length in the canoe, and the Indian paddled quietly and steadily on. For an hour not a word was spoken in the canoe. Harold several times dozed off to sleep. At last the Seneca spoke:

"Many boats out on water—American army."

Harold was about to raise his head to look out when Peter exclaimed: "Lie close, Harold! If a head were shown now, it would be wuss than ef we had sat up all the time. We know there are Injun canoes with the flats, and they may be watching us now. We may be a long way off, but there is no saying how far a Red-skin's eyes can carry. Can you see where they are going to, chief?" he asked the Seneca. "Are they heading for Isle-aux-Noix, as we heard them say they were going to do?"

The Seneca nodded, "Going to island."

"Then," Peter said, "the sooner we are across the lake, the better." The Seneca again spoke, and, after a consultation with Peter, laid in his paddle.

"What is he doing now?" Harold asked.

"Our course lies pretty near the same way as theirs," Peter said. "The island is but a short distance from the shore, near the mouth of the Sorrel, so where we are going would take us right across their line. We fooled them yesterday, but are not likely to do it again to-day. So the chief has stopped paddling, and makes as if he were fishing. I doubt whether it will succeed, for he would hardly be fishing so far out. However, we shall soon see. It is better so than to turn and paddle in any other direction, as that would be sure to excite their suspicions."

IN THE FOREST

The fleet of boats had already passed the spot where the canoe would have crossed had she been going directly across the lake when she was first seen, and was therefore now ahead of it. The great flotilla kept on as if the canoe with its single occupant in its rear had not excited suspicion. The Seneca, however, knew that sharp eyes must be upon him. The manner in which the canoe had baffled pursuit the day before must have inflicted a severe blow upon the pride of the Indians; and although, having driven them off the lake, they could have no reason for suspecting that their foes could have obtained a fresh canoe, the Seneca knew that their vigilance would not sleep for a moment. Therefore, although bending over the side of the canoe as if watching his lines, his eyes were never off the boats.

"There are canoes making for the shore both ways," he said at last. "It is time that my white brother should take the paddle."

Peter and Harold at once sat up in the boat and looked round the lake, which at this point was about ten miles wide. The canoe was four from the eastern side, the flotilla was a mile farther up the lake, and the same distance nearer to the western shore. Four or five canoes were detaching themselves from the flotilla, apparently rowing direct for the shore. It would have been easy for the canoe to have regained the eastern side long before she could have been cut off, but here they might find the Chippewas. The Indians whose boat they had taken would assuredly follow along the shores of the lake in hopes that something might occur to drive them back. Besides, had they landed there, they would be unable to carry in time the news of the approaching attack upon St. John's. For the same reason it was important to land up the lake near the Canadian end.

Peter rapidly took in the situation. He saw that it was possible, and only just possible, to reach the shore, at a point opposite to that at which they now were, before the hostile canoes could cut them off from it. If they headed them there, they would be obliged to run down to the other end of the lake before effecting a landing, while he could not calculate on being able to beat all the canoes,

95

most of which carried four paddlers, who would strain every nerve to retrieve their failure of the previous day.

Not a word was spoken as the boat darted through the water. Harold, unaccustomed to judge distances, could form no idea whether the distant canoes would or would not intercept them. At present both seemed to him to be running towards the shore on nearly parallel courses, and the shorter distance that the Indians would have to row seemed to place them far ahead. The courses, however, were not parallel, as the Indians were gradually turning their canoes to intercept the course of that which they were pursuing. As the minutes went by, and the boats converged more and more towards the same point, Harold saw how close the race would be. After twenty minutes' hard paddling, the boats were within a quarter of a mile of each other, and the courses which they were respectively taking seemed likely to bring them together at about a quarter of a mile from the shore. There were three Indian canoes, and these kept well together. So close did the race appear that Harold expected every moment to see Peter sweep the head of the canoe round and make a stern chase of it by running down on the lake. This, however, Peter had no intention of doing. The canoes, he saw, travelled as fast as his own, and could each spare a man to fire occasionally, while he and his companions would all be obliged to continue paddling. Better accustomed to judge distances than Harold, he was sure, at the speed at which they were going, he would be able to pass somewhat ahead of his foes.

"Row all you know, Harold," he said. "Now, chief, send her along."

Harold had been rowing to the utmost of his strength, but he felt, by the way the canoe quivered at every stroke, that his companions were only now putting out their extreme strength. The boat seemed to fly through the water, and he began to think for the first time that the canoe would pass ahead of their pursuers. The latter were clearly also conscious of the fact, for they now turned their boats' heads more towards the shore, so that the spot where the lines would meet would be close to the shore itself. The canoes were now within two hundred yards of each other. The Indians were nearer to the shore, but the oblique line that they were following would give them about an equal distance to row to the point for which both were making. Harold could not see that there was the slightest difference in the rate at which they were travelling. It seemed to him that the four canoes would all arrive precisely at the same moment at the land, which was now some five or six hundred yards distant.

Another two minutes' paddling, and when the canoes were but seventy or eighty yards apart, Peter, with a sweep with his paddle, turned the boat's head nearly half round, and made obliquely for the shore, so throwing his pursuers almost astern of him. The shore was but three hundred yards distant; they were but fifty ahead of their pursuers. The latter gave a loud yell at seeing the change in the position in the chase. They had, of course, foreseen the possibility of such a movement, but had been powerless to prevent it. They were, however, prepared, for on the instant one man in each canoe dropped his paddle and, standing up, fired. It is, however, a difficult thing to take aim when standing in a canoe dancing under the vigorous strokes of three paddlers. It was the more difficult since the canoes were at the moment sweeping round to follow the movement of the chase. The three balls whistled closely round the canoe, but no one was hit.

The loss of three paddlers for even so short a time checked the pace of the canoes. The Indians saw that they could not hope to overtake their foes, whose canoe was now but a few lengths from shore. They dropped their paddles, and each man seized his rifle. Another moment, and the nine pieces would have poured their fire into the canoe about fifty yards ahead of them, when from the bushes on the shore three puffs of smoke shot out, and three of the Indians fell, one of them upsetting his boat in his fall. A yell of surprise and dismay broke from them, the guns were thrown down, the paddles grasped again, and the heads of the canoes turned from the shore. The Indians in the overturned boat did not wait to right it, but scrambled into the other canoes, and both were soon paddling at the top of their speed from the shore, not, however, without further damage, for the guns in the bushes again spoke out and

Peter and the Seneca added their fire the instant they leaped from the boat to shore, and another of the Indians was seen to fall. Harold was too breathless when he reached the bank to be able to fire. He raised his gun, but his hands trembled with the exertion that he had undergone, and the beating of his heart and his short panting breath rendered it impossible for him to take a steady aim. A minute later Jake burst his way through the bushes.

"Ah! Massa Harold!" he exclaimed. "Bress the Lord dat we was here. What a fright you hab giben me! To be sure we hab been watching you for a long time. Ephraim and de Red-skin dey say dey saw little spot far out on lake, behind all dose boats; den dey say other boats set off in chase. For a long time Jake see nothing about dat, but at last he see dem; den we hurry along de shore, so as to get near de place to where de boats row. Ebery moment me tink dat dey catch you up. Ephraim say, no, berry close thing, but he tink you come along first, but dat we must shoot when dey come close. We stand watch for some time, den Ephraim say dat you no able to get to dat point. You hab to turn along de shore, so we change our place and run along, and sure nough de boat's head turns, and you come along in front of us. Den we all shoot, and the Red-skins dey tumble over."

"Well, Jake, it is fortunate indeed that you were on the spot, for they could scarcely have missed all of us. Besides, even if we had got to shore safely, they would have followed us, and the odds against us would have been heavy."

"That ar war a close shave, Peter," Ephraim said; "all-fired close shave I call it."

"It war, Ephraim, and no mistake."

"Why didn't yer head down along the lake?"

"Because I got news that the colonists air going to attack St. John's to-morrow, and I want to get to the fort in time to put 'em on their guard; besides, both sides of the lake are sure to be full of hostile Injuns. Those canoes paddled as fast as we did, and in the long run might have worn us out."

"Did you have a fight on the lake two nights ago? Me and the Red-skin thought we heard firing."

IN THE FOREST

"We had a skirmish with them," Peter said. "A pretty sharp shave it war, too, but we managed to slip away from them. Altogether, we have had some mighty close work, I can tell yer, and I thought more than once as we were going to be wiped out."

While they were speaking, the men had already started at a steady pace through the woods, away from the lake, having first drawn up the canoe and carefully concealed it.

It was late at night when they reached Fort St. John. A message was at once despatched to a party of the Senecas, who were at their village, about sixteen miles away. They arrived in the morning, and, together with a portion of the garrison, moved out and took their place in the wooded and marshy ground between the fort and the river. Scouts were sent along the Sorrel, and these returned about one o'clock, saying that a large number of boats were coming down the lake, from Isle-aux-Noix. It had been determined to allow the colonists to land without resistance, as the commander of the fort felt no doubt of his ability, with the assistance of his Indian allies, to repulse their attack. Some twelve hundred men were landed, and these at once began to advance towards the fort, led by their two generals, Schuyler and Montgomery. Scarcely had they entered the swamp, when from every bush a fire was opened upon them. The invaders were staggered, but pushed forward, in a weak and undecided way, as far as a creek which intercepted their path. In vain General Montgomery endeavoured to encourage them to advance. They wavered and soon began to fall back, and in an hour from the time of their landing, they were again gathered on the bank of the river. Here they threw up a breastwork, and as his numbers were greatly inferior, the British officer in command thought it unadvisable to attack them. After nightfall the colonists took to their boats and returned to Isle-aux-Noix, their loss, in this their first attempt at the invasion of Canada, being nine men.

A day or two later the Indians again attempted to induce General Carleton to permit them to cross the frontier and carry the war into the American settlements, and upon the general's renewed refusal they left the camp in anger and remained from that time altogether aloof from the contest.

St. John's was now left with only its own small garrison. Captain Wilson was ordered to fall back with his company to Montreal, it being considered that the garrison of St. John's was sufficient to defend that place for a considerable time. As soon as the Indians had marched away, having sent word to the colonists that they should take no further part in the fight, Montgomery, who was now in command, Schuyler having fallen sick, landed the whole of the force and invested the fort. An American officer, Ethan Allen, had been sent with a party to try to raise the colonists in rebellion in the neighbourbood of Chamblée. He had with him thirty Americans, and was joined by eighty Canadians. Dazzled by the success which had attended the surprise of Ticonderoga, he thought to repeat the stroke by the conquest of Montreal. He crossed the river in the night about three miles below the city. Peter and some other scouts who had been watching his movements crossed higher up, and brought the news; and thirty-six men of the 26th Regiment, Captain Wilson's company, and two or three hundred loyal Canadians, the whole under the command of Major Campbell, attacked Ethan Allen. He was speedily routed, and with thirty-eight of his men taken prisoners. The siege of St. John's made but little progress; the place was well provisioned, and the Americans encamped in the low swampy ground around it suffered much from ill health. The men were mutinous and insolent, the officers incapable and disobedient. So far the invasion of Canada, of which such great things had been hoped by the Americans, appeared likely to turn out a complete failure.

CHAPTER VIII
QUEBEC

GENERAL CARLETON, seeing that Montgomery's whole force was retained idle before St. John's, began to hope that the winter would come to his assistance before the invaders had made any serious progress. Unfortunately he had not reckoned on the utter incapacity of the officer in command of Fort Chamblée. Major Stopford of the 7th Regiment had a hundred and sixty men and a few artillerymen, and the fort was strong and well provided with provisions. American spies had found the inhabitants around the place favourable to the Americans. Major Brown was sent down, therefore, by Montgomery, with a small detachment and, being joined by the inhabitants, sat down before the fort. They had only two six-pounders, and could have effected nothing had the fort been commanded by a man of bravery and resources. Such was not the character of its commander, who, after a siege of only a day and a half, surrendered the place with all its stores, which were of inestimable value to the invaders, who, indeed, were upon the edge of giving up the siege of the fort, their ammunition being entirely exhausted; but the six tons of gunpowder, the seventeen cannon, mortars, and muskets, which fell into their hands, enabled them to carry on the siege of St. John's with renewed vigour. There was no excuse whatever for the conduct of Major Stopford in allowing these stores to fall into the hands of the Americans, as even had he not possessed courage to defend the fort, he might, before surrendering, have thrown the whole of the ammunition into the river, upon which there was a safe sally-port, where he could have carried on the operation entirely unmolested by the enemy. The colours of the 7th Regiment were captured and sent to Congress as the first trophy of the war.

The siege of St. John's was now pushed on by Montgomery with vigour. Colonel Maclean, with eight hundred Indians and Canadians, attempted to relieve it, crossing the St. Lawrence in small boats. On nearing the other bank they were, however, received with so heavy a fire by the Americans posted there that they were obliged to retire without effecting a landing. Provisions and ammunition were now running short in St. John's; there was no hope whatever of relief from the outside, and the officer commanding was therefore obliged to surrender on the 14th of November after a gallant defence.

As there were only some fifty or sixty regulars in Montreal, General Carleton was unable to defend that town, and upon the news of the fall of St. John's, he at once retired to Quebec, and Montreal was occupied by the Americans. In the meantime another expedition had been despatched by the Americans under Arnold. This officer, with fifteen hundred men, had started for Quebec from a point one hundred and thirty miles north of Boston. Suffering enormous fatigue and hardship, the force made its way up the river; past rapids, cataracts, and through swamps they dragged and carried their boats and stores. They followed the bed of the river up to its source, and then crossing the watershed, descended the Chaudiere and Duloup rivers on to the St. Lawrence, within a few miles of Quebec.

This was a wonderful march—one scarcely equalled in the annals of military history. Crossing the St. Lawrence in canoes, Arnold encamped with his little force upon the heights of Abraham. Such a daring attempt could not have been undertaken had not the Americans been aware of the extreme weakness of the garrison at Quebec; it consisted only of fifty men of the 7th Regiment, two hundred and forty of the Canadian militia, a battalion of seamen from the ships of war under the command of Captain Hamilton of the Lizard, two hundred and fifty strong, and the colonial volunteers under Colonel Maclean.

The fortifications were in a ruinous condition. It was fortunate that Colonel Maclean, who had come from the Sorrel upon the surrender of St. John's by forced marches, arrived on the very day on which Arnold appeared before the city. Directly he arrived, Arnold attacked the city at the gate of St. Louis, but was sharply repulsed. He then desisted from active operations, and awaited the arrival of Montgomery, who was marching down from Montreal. The flotilla in which Carleton was descending the river was attacked by the Americans, who came down the Sorrel, and was captured, with all the troops and military stores which it was bringing down. General Carleton himself escaped in a small boat under cover of night, and reached Quebec.

Captain Wilson's company had been attached to the command of Colonel Maclean, and with it arrived in Quebec in safety.

Upon the arrival of Montgomery with his army the city was summoned to surrender. A strong party in the town were favourable to the invaders, but General Carleton treated the summons with contempt, and turned all the inhabitants who refused to join in the defence of the city outside the town.

The winter had now set in in earnest, and the difficulties of the besiegers were great. Arnold's force had been much weakened by the hardships that they had undergone, Montgomery's by desertions; the batteries which they erected were overpowered by the fire of the defenders, and the siege made no progress whatever. The men became more and more disaffected and mutinous; many of them had nearly served the time for which they had enlisted, and Montgomery feared that they would leave him when their engagement came to an end. He in vain tempted the besieged to make a sally. Carleton was so certain that success would come by waiting that he refused to allow himself to hazard it by a sortie.

The weather was fighting for him, and the besiegers had before them only the alternatives of taking the place by storm or of abandoning the siege altogether. They resolved upon a storm. It was to take place at day-break on the thirty-first of December. Montgomery determined to make four attacks—two false and two real ones. Colonel James Livingstone with two hundred Canadians was to appear before St. John's gate, and a party under Colonel Brown were to feign a movement against the upper town, and from high ground there were to send up rockets as the signal for the real attacks to commence—that led by Montgomery from the south, and that under Arnold from the north-west—both against the lower town.

The false attacks were made too soon, the rockets being fired half an hour before the main columns reached their place of attack. The British were not deceived, but judging these attacks to be feints, left but a small party to oppose them, and marched the bulk of their forces down towards the lower town; their assistance, however, came too late, for before they arrived the fate of the attack was already decided. The Americans advanced under circumstances of great difficulty. A furious wind with cutting hail blew in their faces; the ground was slippery and covered with snow.

Half an hour before the English supports arrived on the spot, Montgomery, with his leading company, reached the first barricade, which was undefended. Passing through this, they pressed on towards the next. The road leading to it was only wide enough for five or six persons abreast. On one side was the river, on the other a steep cliff; in front was a log-hut with loopholes for musketry, and a battery of two three-pounders. It was held by a party of thirty Canadians and eight militiamen under John Coffin, with nine sailors under Bairnsfeather, the captain of a transport, to work the guns. Montgomery with sixty men pushed on at a run to carry the battery, but when within fifty yards, Bairnsfeather discharged his pieces, which were loaded with grape-shot, with deadly aim. Montgomery, his aide-de-camp Macpherson, Lieutenant Cheeseman, and ten others fell dead at the first discharge, and with them the soul of the expedition fled. The remaining officers endeavoured to get the men to advance, but none would do so, and they fell back without losing another man. So completely cowed were they that they would not even carry off the bodies of their general and his companions. These were brought into Quebec next day and buried with the honours of war by the garrison.

The force under Arnold was far stronger than that under Montgomery. The Canadian guard appointed to defend the first barrier fled at the approach, but the small body of sailors fought bravely, and were all killed or wounded. Arnold was shot through

John Coffin and Bairnsfeather in the battery.

the leg and disabled. Morgan, who commanded the advanced companies, led his men on and carried the second barrier after an obstinate resistance. They were attacking the third when Maclean with his men from the upper town arrived. The British then took the offensive and drove the enemy back, and a party going round fell upon their rear. Fifty were killed in Arnold's column, four hundred taken prisoners, and the rest retreated in extreme disorder.

Thus ended the assault upon Quebec—an assault which was all but hopeless from the first, but in which the Americans showed but little valour and determination. In fact, throughout the war it may be said that the Americans, when fighting on the defensive behind trees and entrenchments, fought stubbornly, but that they were feeble in attack, and wholly incapable of standing against British troops in the open.

It would now have been easy for Carleton to have sallied out and taken the offensive, but he preferred holding Quebec quietly. He might have easily driven the Americans from their position before the walls, but with the handful of troops under his orders, he could have done nothing towards carrying on a serious campaign in the open.

Until spring came, and the rivers were opened, no reinforcements could reach him from England, while the Americans could send any number of troops into Canada. Carleton therefore preferred to wait quietly within the walls of Quebec, allowing the winter, hardships, and disunion to work their natural effects upon the invaders.

Arnold sent to Washington to demand ten thousand more troops, with siege artillery. Several regiments were sent forward, but artillery could not be spared. Eight regiments entered Canada, but they found that instead of meeting, as they had expected, an enthusiastic reception from the inhabitants, the population were now hostile to them. The exactions of the invading army had been great, and the feeling in favour of the English was now all but universal.

On the 5th of May two frigates and a sloop of war made their way up the river to Quebec. The Americans endeavoured to embark their sick and artillery above the town. Reinforced by the marines, the garrison sallied out and attacked the enemy, who fled with precipitation, leaving their provisions, cannon, five hundred muskets, and two hundred sick behind them. The British pursued them until they reached the mouth of the Sorrel.

The arrival of the fleet from England brought news of what had taken place since Captain Wilson's company had marched from Boston, a short time after the battle of Bunker's Hill. Immediately after the battle the colonists had sent two deputies, Penn and Lee, with a petition to parliament for the restoration of peace. This petition was supported by a strong body in parliament. The majority, however, argued that, from the conduct of the Americans, it was clear that they aimed at unconditional, unqualified, and total independence. In all their proceedings they had behaved as if entirely separated from Great Britain. Their professions and petition breathed peace and moderation; their actions and preparations denoted war and defiance; every attempt that could be made to soften their hostility had been in vain; their obstinacy was inflexible; and the more England had given in to their wishes, the more insolent and overbearing had their demands become. The stamp-tax had been repealed, but their ill-will had grown rather than abated. The taxations on imports had been entirely taken off, save on one small item; but rather than pay this, they had accumulated arms and ammunition, seized cannon belonging to the king, and everywhere prepared for armed resistance. Only two alternatives remained for the British nation to adopt—either to coerce the colonists to submission or to grant them their entire independence.

These arguments were well founded; the concessions which had been made had but encouraged the colonists to demand more. No good whatever would have come from entering into negotiation; there remained but the two alternatives. It would, however, have been far better had parliament, instead of deciding on coercion, withdrawn altogether from the colonies; for although hitherto the Americans had shown no great fighting qualities, it was clear that so small an army as England could spare could not permanently keep down so vast a country, if the people were determined upon independence. They might win every battle—might overpower every considerable force gathered against them; but they could only enforce the king's authority over a mere fractional portion of so great an area. England, however, was unaccustomed to defeat. Her spirit in those days was proud and high, and by a large majority parliament voted for the continuance of the war. The next step taken was one unworthy of the country; it tended still farther to embitter the war, and it added to the strength of the party in favour of the colonists at home. Attempts were made by the government to obtain the services of large numbers of foreign troops. Negotiations were entered into with Russia, Holland, Hesse, and other states. Most of these proved ineffectual, but a considerable number of troops were obtained from Hesse.

The news of these proceedings excited the Americans to renewed efforts. The force under Washington was strengthened, and he took possession of Dorchester Height, commanding the town of Boston. A heavy cannonade was opened on the city. The British guns answered it, but the American position gave them an immense advantage. General Howe, who was in command, at first thought of attempting to storm the heights, but the tremendous loss sustained at the battle of Bunker's Hill deterred him from the undertaking. His supineness during the past four months had virtually lost the American colonies to England. He had under his command eight thousand troops, who could have routed with ease the undisciplined levies of Washington. Instead, however, of leading his men out against the enemy, he had suffered them to be cooped up for months in the city, and had failed to take! possession of the various heights commanding the town. Had he done this, Boston might have resisted a force many times as strong as that which advanced against it; and there was now nothing left for the English but to storm the heights with enormous loss, or to evacuate the city.

The first was the alternative which had been chosen when the Americans seized Bunker's Hill, the second was that which was now adopted.

Having adopted this resolution, Howe carried it out in a manner which would in itself be sufficient to condemn him as a military leader. Nothing was done to destroy the vast stores of arms and ammunition, and two hundred and fifty pieces of cannon were left for the colonists to use against England. No steps were taken to warn ships arriving from England of the surrender of the town. The consequence was, that in addition to the vast amount of stores captured in the town, numbers of the British store-ships fell into the hands of the Americans—among them a vessel which, in addition to carbines, bayonets, gun-carriages, and other stores, had on board more than seventy tons of powder, while Washington's whole stock was all but exhausted.

But worse even than this hurried and unnecessary abandonment of vast munitions of war, was the desertion of the loyalist population. Boston was full of loyalists, among whom were many of the wealthier and better-born persons in the colony, who from the commencement of the troubles had left their homes, their fortunes, and their families to rally round the standard of their sovereign. The very least that Howe could have done for these loyal men would have been to have entered into some terms of capitulation with Washington, whereby they might have been permitted to depart to their homes and to the enjoyment of their property. Nothing of the sort was attempted, and the only choice offered to a loyalist was to remain in the town, exposed to certain insult and ill-treatment, perhaps to death, at the hands of the rebels, or to leave in the transports for England or Halifax, and to be landed here penniless and starving.

Howe's conduct in this was on a piece with his behaviour throughout the campaign; he was, however, little if at all inferior to the other generals, who vied with each other in incapacity and folly. Never, indeed, in the whole history of England were her troops led by men so inefficient, so sluggish, and so incapable as those who commanded her armies in the American revolutionary war.

The first ships from England which arrived at Quebec were followed a few days later by the *Niger* and *Triton*, convoy transports, with troops. The British now took the offensive in earnest. From the west Captain Forster marched from Detroit with forty men of the 8th Regiment, a hundred Canadians and some Indians, against a pass called the "Cedars," situated fifteen leagues above Montreal. This was held by four hundred men, with two cannon. As soon as the British force opened fire, the Americans surrendered. The following day Forster's force, advancing, came upon a hundred and forty men under Major Sherbourne, who were marching to reinforce the garrison at the Cedars. These were forced to retreat, and a hundred of them taken prisoners.

Arnold, with seven hundred men, advanced against the British force. The British officer, fearing that in case of an attack, the Indians with him might massacre the prisoners, released the whole of them, four hundred and seventy-four in number, under the promise that an equal number of British prisoners should be returned. This engagement was shamefully broken by the Americans, who raised a number of frivolous excuses, among others that prisoners taken by the British were ill-treated—an accusation which excited the indignation of the prisoners themselves, some of whom wrote to members of Congress stating that nothing could be kinder or more courteous than the treatment which they received.

While Forster was advancing towards Montreal from the west, Carleton was moving up against the Americans at Sorrel from Quebec. At the death of Montgomery, Wooster had taken the command of the main American force. He had been succeeded by Thompson; but the latter dying of smallpox, Sullivan took his place. The new commander determined to take the offensive against the English, and despatched a force of about two thousand men to attack General Fraser, who held a post at a place called the Three Rivers.

A Canadian peasant brought news to General Fraser of the approach of the Americans, and, as he had received reinforcements from below, he determined to anticipate their attack. His movements were completely successful. Some of the Americans fought well, but the rest dispersed with but little resistance. Two hundred were killed and a hundred and fifty taken prisoners. The rest succeeded in returning to Sorrel.

QUEBEC

The main body of the British army now came up the river in their ships, and as they approached Sorrel, Sullivan broke up his camp and retreated, and at the same time, Arnold, who commanded at Montreal, evacuated the town and joined Sullivan's army at St. John's.

Had the English pushed forward with any energy, the whole of the American army of invasion would have fallen into their hands. They were completely broken in spirits, and suffering terribly from sickness, and were wholly incapable of making any defence. Burgoyne, however, who commanded the advance of the English army, moved forward very slowly, and the Americans were enabled to take to their boats and cross, first to Isle-aux-Noix, and then to Crown Point. An American historian, who saw them after they landed, says: "At the sight of so much privation and distress I wept until I had no more power to weep. I did not look into a tent or hut in which I did not find either a dead or dying man. Of about 5000 men, full half were invalids. In little more than two months they had lost by desertion and death more than 5000 men."

Captain Wilson and his company were not present with the advance of the British troops. General Howe, after evacuating Boston, had sailed with his army to Halifax, there to wait until a large body of reinforcements should be sent in the spring from England. General Carleton had in his despatches mentioned favourably the services which the little company of loyalists from Boston had performed, and Lord Howe wrote requesting that the company should be sent down by ship to Halifax, as he was about to sail from New York to undertake operations on a large scale, and should be glad to have with him a body of men accustomed to scouting and acquainted with the country. Accordingly, the company was embarked in a transport, and reached Halifax early in June. On the 11th they sailed with the army, and arrived at Sandy Hook on the 29th. On the 3d of July the army landed on Staten Island, opposite Long Island, and soon afterwards Lord Howe, brother of General Howe, arrived with the main army from England, raising the total force to nearly 30,000 men. It consisted of two battalions of light infantry, two of grenadiers, the 4th, 5th,

10th, 17th, 22d, 23d, 27th, 35th, 38th, 40th, 42d, 43d, 44th, 45th, 49th, 52d, 55th, 63d, and 64th Regiments of foot, part of the 46th and 71st Regiments, and the 17th Regiment of light dragoons. There were besides two battalions of volunteers from New York, each a thousand strong. Had this force arrived, as it should have done, three months earlier, they might have achieved great things, but the delay had enabled the Americans to make extensive preparations to meet the coming storm.

Lord Howe brought with him a communication from parliament, giving to him and his brother full power to treat with the Americans on any terms which they might think fit. Upon his arrival, Lord Howe addressed a letter to Dr. Franklin, informing him of the nature of his communication, expressing hopes that he would find in America the same disposition for peace that he brought with him, and requesting his aid to accomplish the desired end. Dr. Franklin, in answer, informed Lord Howe that "prior to the consideration of any proposition for friendship or peace, it would be required that Great Britain should acknowledge the independence of America, should defray the expense of the war, and indemnify the colonists for all damages committed."

After such a reply as this, Lord Howe had no alternative but to commence hostilities, which he did by landing the army in Gravesend Bay, Long Island. The enemy offered no opposition to the landing, but retreated at once, setting fire to all the houses and granaries, and taking up a position on the wooded heights which commanded the line by which the English must advance.

The American main force, 15,000 strong, were posted on a peninsula between Mill Creek and Wallabout Bay, and had constructed a strong line of intrenchments across the end of the peninsula. The intrenchments were strengthened by abattis, and flanked with strong redoubts. 5000 remained to guard this post, and 10,000, under General Puttenham, advanced to hold the line of wooded hills which run across the island.

In the centre of the plain, at the foot of these hills, stood the village of "Flat-bush."

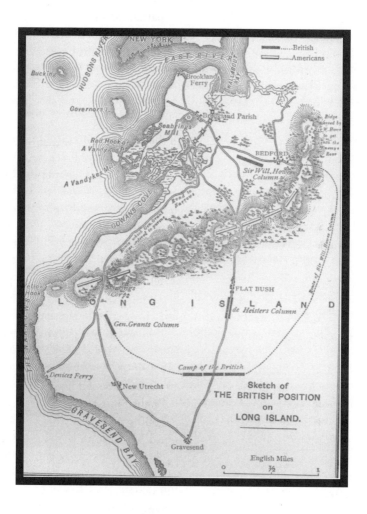

The Hessian division of the British army, under General De Heister, advanced against this, while General Clinton, with the right wing of the English army, moved forward to attack the enemy's left.

This force marched at 9 o'clock at night on the 26th of August; General Sir William Howe himself accompanied it. The line of hills trended away greatly to the left, and the enemy had neglected to secure the passes over the hills on this flank; consequently at 9 o'clock in the morning the British passed the range of hills without resistance, and occupied Bedford in its rear. Had Sir William Howe now pushed on vigorously, the whole of Puttenham's force must have been captured.

In the meantime the Hessians from Flat-bush attacked the centre of the Americans, and after a warm engagement routed them, and drove them into the woods with a loss of three pieces of cannon.

On the British left General Grant also advanced, and at midnight carried a strong pass on the enemy's left. Retiring, they held a still stronger position farther back, and offered a fierce resistance until the fires at Bedford showed that the English had obtained a position almost in their rear, when they retreated precipitately.

The victory was a complete one, but it had none of the consequences which would have attended it had the English pushed forward with energy after turning the American left. Six pieces of cannon were captured, and 2000 men killed or taken prisoners. The English lost 70 killed and 230 wounded.

So impetuously did the English attack, that even Sir William Howe admitted that they could have carried the intrenchments. He alleges he did not permit them to do so, because he intended to take the position by regular approaches, and wished therefore to avoid the loss of life which an immediate assault would have occasioned. On the 27th and 28th regular approaches were commenced, but on the 29th, under cover of a fog, the Americans embarked in boats, and succeeded in carrying the whole of their force, without the loss of a man, across to the mainland.

The escape of this body of men was disgraceful in the extreme to the English commanders. They had a great fleet at their disposal, and had they placed a couple of frigates in the East River, between Long Island and New York, the escape would have been impossible, and General Washington and his army of 15,000 men must have been taken prisoners. Whether this misfortune would have proved conclusive of the war, it is now too late to speculate, but so splendid an opportunity was never before let slip by an English general, and the negligence was the more inexcusable inasmuch as the fleet of boats could be seen lying alongside of the American position. Their purpose must have been known, and they could at any moment have been destroyed by the guns of a ship of war taking up its position outside them.

Lord Howe despatched the American General Sullivan, who had been taken prisoner on Long Island, to Congress, repeating his desire to treat. A committee of three members accordingly waited on Lord Howe, who informed them that it was the most ardent wish of the king and government of Great Britain to put an end to the dissatisfaction between the mother country and the colonists. To accomplish this desire, every act of parliament which was considered obnoxious to the colonists should undergo a revisal, and every just cause of complaint should be removed, if the colonists would declare their willingness to submit to the authority of the British government. The committee replied that it was not America which had separated herself from Great Britain, but Great Britain had separated herself from America. The latter had never declared herself independent until the former had made war upon her, and that even if Congress were willing to place America in her former situation, it could not do so, as the declaration of independence had been made in consequence of the congregated voice of the whole people, by whom alone it could be abolished. The country was determined not to return under the domination of England.

The negotiations were therefore broken off. Lord Howe published a declaration to the people of America, giving the answer of the committee to his offer of reconciliation. He acquainted them with the fact that the parent state was willing to receive into its bosom and protection all who might be willing to return to their former obedience. In taking this step, Lord Howe was convinced that a majority of the inhabitants of America were still willing to enter into an accommodation of the differences between the two powers, and the conviction was not ill founded. The declaration, however, produced but little effect, for the dominant section, that resolved to break off all connection with England, had acquired the sole management of affairs, and no offers which could possibly have been made would have been accepted by them.

Convinced that all further negotiations would be ineffectual, Lord Howe prepared to carry his army across from Long Island to New York, where the American army had taken up their post after the retreat from Long Island. The armies were separated by the East River, with a breadth of about 1300 yards. A cannonade was kept up for several days. On the 13th of September some ships of war were brought up to cover the passage. Washington, seeing the preparations, began to evacuate the city and to abandon the strong intrenchments which he had thrown up. At 11 o'clock on the morning of the 15th, the men-of-war opened a heavy fire, and Clinton's division, consisting of 4000 men in 84 boats, sailed up the river, landed on New York Island at a place called Kipp's Bay, and occupied the heights of Inclenberg, the enemy abandoning their intrenchments at their approach. General Washington rode towards Kipp's Bay to take the command of the troops stationed there, but found the men who had been posted at the lines running away, and the brigades who should have supported them flying in every direction, heedless of the exertions of their generals.

Puttenham's division, of 4000 men, was still in the lower city, and would be cut off unless the British advance should be checked. Washington therefore made the greatest efforts to rally the fugitives, and to get them to make a stand to check the advancing enemy, but in vain, for as soon as even small bodies of Red-coats were seen advancing, they broke and fled in panic.

Howe as usual delayed giving orders for an advance, and thus permitted the whole of Puttenham's brigade, who were cut off and must have been taken prisoners, to escape unharmed. And thus, with comparatively little loss, the Americans drew off, leaving behind them only a few heavy cannon and some bayonets and stores.

So rapid had been their flight at the approach of the English, that only fifteen were killed, two men falling on the English side.

CHAPTER IX
THE SURPRISE OF TRENTON

THE Americans, finding that they were not pursued, rallied from their panic, and took up a position at Harlington and Kingsbridge. So great was the disorganization among them, that, had the British advanced at once, they would have taken the place with scarcely any loss, strong as it was by nature and by the intrenchments which Washington had prepared. Great numbers deserted, disputes broke out between the troops of the various states, insubordination prevailed, and the whole army was utterly disheartened by the easy victories which the British had obtained over them. Washington reported the cowardice of his troops to Congress, who passed a law inflicting the punishment of death for cowardice.

Before leaving New York, the Americans had made preparations for burning the whole town, but the speediness of their retreat prevented the preparations being carried into effect. However, fire was set to it in several places, and a third of the town was destroyed.

The position taken up by the enemy was so strong that it was determined to operate in the rear. Some redoubts were thrown up to cover New York during the absence of the main part of the British force.

A portion of the British army was landed at a point threatening the retreat of the Americans, and a series of skirmishes of no great importance took place. The enemy fell back from their most advanced works, but no general move was undertaken, although, as the numbers on both sides were about even, and the superior fighting powers of the English had been amply demonstrated, there could have been no doubt as to the result of a general battle. Lord Howe, however, wasted the time in a series of petty movements, which, although generally successful, had no influence upon the result, and served only to enable the Americans to recover from the utter depression which had fallen upon them after the evacuation of Long Island and the loss of New York.

Gradually the Americans fell back across a country so swampy and difficult that it was now no longer possible to bring on a general action. Their retreat, however, had the effect of isolating the important positions of Kingsbridge and Fort Washington. The latter post was of the utmost importance, inasmuch as it secured the American intercourse with the Jersey shore. The fortifications were very strong, and stood upon rising and open ground. It was garrisoned by 3000 of the best American troops, under the command of Colonel Magaw. Washington was gradually withdrawing his army, and had already given orders that Fort Washington should be evacuated; but General Lee, who was second in command, so strongly urged that it should be retained, that, greatly against his own judgment, he was obliged to consent to its being defended, especially as Colonel Magaw insisted that the fort could stand a siege. On the night of the 14th of November the British passed some troops across the creek, and Lord Howe summoned the place to surrender on pain of the garrison being put to the sword. Magaw had, upon the previous day, received large numbers of reinforcements, and replied that he should defend the fort. Soon after daybreak on the 16th, the artillery opened on both sides. Five thousand Hessians, under the command of General Knyphausen, moved up the hill, penetrated some of the advanced works of the enemy, and took post within a hundred yards of the fort. The second division, consisting of the guards and light infantry, with two battalions of Hessians and the 33d Regiment, landed at Island Creek, and after some stiff fighting, forced the enemy from the rocks and trees up the steep and rugged mountain. The third and fourth divisions fought their way up through similar defences. So steep was the hill that the assailants could only climb it by grasping the trees and bushes, and so obstinate was the defence that the troops were sometimes mixed up together.

The bravery and superior numbers of the British troops bore down all resistance, and the whole of the four divisions reached their places round the fort. They then summoned it to surrender, and its commander, after half an hour's consideration, seeing the impossibility of resisting the assault which was threatened, opened the gates.

Upon the English side about 800 men were killed and wounded, of whom the majority were Hessians. These troops fought with extreme bravery. The American loss, owing to their superior position, was about 150 killed and wounded, but the prisoners taken amounted to over 3000.

On the 18th Lord Howe landed a strong body on the Jersey shore under Lord Cornwallis, who marched to Fort Lee and surprised it. A deserter, however, had informed the enemy of his approach, and the garrison had fled in disorder, leaving their tents, provisions, and military stores behind them. Lord Cornwallis, pushing forward with great energy, drove the Americans out of New Jersey. Another expedition occupied Rhode Island.

Cold weather now set in, and the English went into winter quarters. Their success had been complete, without a single check, and had they been led vigorously, the army of Washington might on two occasions have been wholly destroyed. In such a case the moderate portion of the population of the colonies would have obtained a hearing, and a peace honourable to both parties might have been arrived at.

The advantage gained by the gallantry of the British troops was, however, entirely neutralized by the lethargy and inactivity of their general; and the colonists had time given them to recover from the alarm which the defeat of their troops had given them, to put another army in the field, and to prepare on a great scale for the following campaign.

The conduct of General Howe in allowing Washington's army to retire almost unmolested was to the officers who served under him unaccountable. His arrangements for the winter were even more singularly defective. Instead of concentrating his troops, he scattered them over a wide extent of country at a distance too great to support each other, and thus left it open to the enemy to crush them in detail.

General Howe now issued a proclamation offering a free pardon to all who surrendered, and great numbers of colonists came in and made their submission. Even in Philadelphia the longing for peace was so strong that General Washington was obliged to send a force there to prevent the town from declaring for England.

During the operations which had taken place since the landing of the British troops on Long Island, Captain Wilson's company had taken but little part in the operations. All had been straightforward work, and conducted on the principles of European warfare. The services of the volunteers as scouts had not therefore been called into requisition. The success which at first attended the expedition had encouraged Captain Wilson to hope for the first time since the outbreak of the revolution that the English might obtain such decisive successes that the colonists would be willing to accept some propositions of peace such as those indicated by Lord Howe—a repeal of all obnoxious laws, freedom from any taxation except that imposed by themselves, and a recognition of the British authority. When, however, he saw that Lord Howe, instead of actively utilizing the splendid force at his disposal, frittered it away in minor movements, and allowed Washington to withdraw with his beaten army unmolested, his hopes again faded, and he felt that the colonists would in the long run succeed in gaining all that they contended for.

When the army went into winter quarters, the company was ordered to take post on the Delaware. There were four frontier posts at Trenton, Bordenton, White-horse, and Burlington. Trenton, opposite to which lay Washington with the main body of his army, was held by only 1200 Hessians; and Bordenton, which was also on the Delaware, was, like Trenton, garrisoned by these troops. No worse choice could have been made. The Hessians were brave soldiers, but their ignorance of the language and of the country made them peculiarly unsuitable troops for outpost work, as they were unable to obtain any information. As foreigners, too, they were greatly disliked by the country people.

Nothing was done to strengthen these frontier posts, which were left wholly without redoubts, or intrenchments, into which the garrison could withdraw in case of attack.

Captain Wilson's little company were to act as scouts along the line of frontier. Their headquarters were fixed at Bordenton, where Captain Wilson obtained a large house for their use. Most of the men were at home at work of this kind, and Peter Lambton, Ephraim, and the other frontiersmen were despatched from time to time in different directions to ascertain the movements and intentions of the enemy. Harold asked his father to allow him, as before, to accompany Peter. The inactivity of a life at a quiet little station was wearisome, and with Peter he was sure of plenty of work, with a chance of adventure. The life of exercise and activity which he had led for more than a year had strengthened his muscles and widened his frame, and he was now able to keep up with Peter, however long and tiresome the day's work might be. Jake, too, was of the party. He had developed into an active soldier, and although he was but of little use for scouting purposes, even Peter did not object to his accompanying him, for the negro's unfailing good temper and willingness to make himself useful had made him a favourite with the scout.

The weather was now setting in exceedingly cold. The three men had more than once crossed the Delaware in a canoe and scouted in the very heart of the enemy's country. They were now sitting by the bank watching some drifting ice upon the river.

"There won't be many more passages of the river by water," Peter remarked; "another ten days, and it will be frozen right across."

"Then we can cross on foot, Peter."

"Yes, we can do that," the scout said; "and so can the enemy. Ef their general has got any interprise with him, and ef he can get those chaps as he calls soldiers to fight, he will be crossing over one of these nights and capturing the hull of those Hessians at Trenton; what General Howe means by leaving them there is more nor I can think. He might as well have sent so many babies! The critters can fight, and fight well too, and they are good soldiers, but what's the good of them in a frontier post? They know nothing of the country, they can't speak to the people, nor ask no questions, nor find out nothing about what's doing the other side of the river. They air no more than mere machines. What was wanted was two or three battalions of light troops, who would make friends with the country people, and larn all that is doing opposite. If the Americans are sharp, they will give us lots of trouble this winter, and you will find there won't be much sitting quiet for us at Bordenton. Fortunately, Bordenton and Trenton ain't far apart, and one garrison ought to be able to arrive to the assistance of the other before it is overpowered; however, we shall see. Now, I propose that we cross again to-night, and try and find out what the enemy are doing. Then we can come back and manage for you to eat your Christmas dinner with yer father, as you seem to have bent yer mind upon that, though why it matters about dinner one day more than another is more nor I can see."

That night the three scouts crossed the river in the canoe. Avoiding all houses, they kept many miles straight on beyond the river, and lay down for a few hours before morning dawned; then they turned their faces the other way, and walked up to the first farm-house they saw.

"Can we have a drink of milk?" the hunter asked.

"You can," the farmer replied, "and some breakfast, if you like to pay for it. At first I was glad to give the best I had to those who came along, but there have been such numbers going one way and the other, either marching to join the army or running away to return to their homes, that I should be ruined if I gave to all comers."

"We are ready to pay," Peter said, drawing some money from his pocket.

"Then come in and sit down."

In a few minutes an excellent breakfast was put before them.

"You are on your way to join the army, of course?" the farmer asked.

"Just that," Peter replied. "We think it's about our time to do a little shooting, though I don't suppose there will be much done till the spring."

"I don't know," the farmer said; "I should not be surprised if the general wakes up them Germans when the Delaware gets frozen. I heard some talk about it from some men who came past yesterday. Their time was expired, they said, and they were going home. I hear, too, that they are gathering a force down near Mount Holly, and I reckon that they are going to attack Bordenton."

"Is that so?" Peter asked. "In that case we might as well tramp in that direction; it don't matter a corn shuck to us where we fight, so as it's soon. We've came to help lick these British, and we means to do it."

"Ah!" the farmer said. "I have heard that sentiment a good many times, but I have not seen much come of it yet. So far it seems to me as the licking has been all the other way."

"That is so," Peter agreed. "But every one knows that the Americans are just the bravest people on the face of the habitable arth. I reckon that their dander is not fairly up yet; but when they begin in arnest you will see what they will do."

The farmer gave a grunt which might mean anything. He had no strong sympathies either way, and the conduct of the numerous deserters and disbanded men who had passed through his neighbourbood had been far from impressing him favourably. "I don't pretend to be strong either for the Congress or the King. I don't want to be taxed, but I don't see why the colonists should not pay something towards the expenses of the government; and now that parliament seems willing to give all we ask for, I don't see what we want to go on fighting for."

"Wall!" Peter exclaimed, in a tone of disgust. "You are one of the half-hearted ones."

"I am like the great majority of the people of this country. We are of English stock, and we don't want to break with the old country; but the affairs have got into the hands of the preachers, and the newspaper men, and the chaps that wants to push themselves forward and make their pile out of the war. As I read it, it's just the civil war in England over again. We were all united at the first against what we considered as tyranny on the part of the parliament, and now we have gone setting up demands which no one dreamed of at first, and which most of us object to now, only we have no longer the control of our own affairs."

"The great heart of this country beats for freedom," Peter Lambton said.

"Pooh!" said the farmer contemptuously. "The great heart of the country wants to work its farms and do its business quietly. The English general has made fair offers which might well be accepted, and as for freedom, there was no tyranny greater than that of the New England States. As long as they managed their own affairs, there was neither freedom of speech nor religion. No, sir, what they called freedom was simply the freedom to make every one else do and think like the majority."

"Wall, we won't argue it out," Peter said, "for I am not good at argument, and I came here to fight and not to talk. Besides, I want to get to Mount Holly in time to join in this battle, so I guess we'll be moving."

Paying for the breakfast, they started at once in the direction of Mount Holly, which lay some twenty-five miles away. As they approached the place early in the afternoon, they overtook several men going in the same direction. They entered into conversation with them, but could only learn that some four hundred and fifty of the militia from Philadelphia, and the counties of Gloucester and Sailing, had arrived on the spot. The men whom they had overtaken were armed countrymen who were going to take a share in the fight on their own account.

Entering the place with the others, Peter found that the information given him was correct.

"We better be out of this at once," he said to Harold, "and make to Bordenton."

"You don't think that there is much importance in the movement," Harold said, as they tramped along.

"There ain't no importance whatever," Peter said, "and that's what I want to tell them. They're never thinking of attacking the two thousand Hessians at Bordenton with that ragged lot."

"But what can they have assembled them for, within twelve miles of the place?" Harold asked.

"It seems to me," the hunter replied, "that it's just a trick to draw the Germans out from Bordenton and so away from Trenton. At anyrate it is well that the true account of the force here should be known; these things gets magnified, and they may think that there is a hull army here."

It was getting dusk when they entered Bordenton, and Harold was glad when he saw the little town, for since sunset on the evening before, they had tramped nearly sixty miles. The place seemed singularly quiet. They asked the first person they met what had become of the troops, and they were told that Col. Donop, who commanded, had marched, an hour before, with his whole force of two thousand men towards Mount Holly, leaving only eighty men in garrison at Bordenton.

"We are too late," Harold said. "They have gone by the road, and we kept straight through the woods, and so missed them."

"Wall, I hope no harm will come of it. I suppose they mean to attack at daybreak, and in course that rabble will run without fighting. I hope when the colonel sees as how thar is no enemy there worth speaking of, he will march straight back again."

Unfortunately this was not the case. The militia, according to their orders, at once dispersed when their outposts told them of the approach of the British; but the German officer, instead of returning instantly, remained for two days near Mount Holly, and so gave time to Washington to carry out his plans.

Captain Wilson's company had gone out with the force, and Peter and his companions had the house to themselves that night. Harold slept late, being thoroughly fatigued by his long march the day before, carrying his rifle, blanket, and provisions. Peter woke him at last.

"Now, young 'un, you've had a good sleep; it's eleven o'clock. I am off to Trenton to see what is doing there. Will you go with me, or will you stop here on the chance of eating your dinner with your father?"

"Oh, it's Christmas-day," Harold said, stretching. "Well, what do you think, Peter? Are they likely to come back or not?"

THE SURPRISE OF TRENTON

"They ought to be back, there is no doubt about that, but whether they will or not is a different affair altogether. I have never seed them hurry themselves yet, not since the war began. Things would have gone a good deal better if they had, but time never seems of no consequence to them. They marched twelve miles last night, and I reckon it's likely that they will halt to-day, and won't be back till to-morrow. I feel oneasy in my mind about the whole affair, for I can't see a single reason for the enemy sending that weak force to Mount Holly, unless it was to draw away the troops from here, and the only motive there could be for that would be because they intended to attack Trenton."

"Very well, Peter, I will go with you."'

Accompanied by Jake, they set out at once for Trenton. On arriving there they found no particular signs of vigilance. Since the Hessians had reached Trenton, their discipline had much relaxed; a broad river separated them from the enemy, who were known to be extremely discontented and disorganized. They had received instruction on no account to cross the river to attack the colonials, and the natural consequence of this forced inactivity had manifested itself. Discipline was lax, and but a slight watch was kept on the movements of the enemy across the stream. Ignorant of the language of the people, they were incapable of distinguishing between those who were friendly and those who were hostile to the crown and they behaved as if in a conquered country, taking such necessaries as they required without payment, and even sending parties to a considerable distance on plundering expeditions.

Peter, on his arrival, proceeded to the headquarters of Col. Rhalle, who was in command—an officer of great bravery and energy. One of his officers was able to speak English, and to him Peter reported the departure of the force from Bordenton, of which Col. Rhalle was already aware, and the weakness of the American force at Mount Holly. He stated also his own belief that it was merely a feint to draw off Col. Donop, and that preparatory to an attack on Trenton. The officer treated the information lightly, and pointing to the mass of ice floating down the river, asked whether it would be possible for boats to cross. "When the river freezes," he said, "there may be some chance of attack; till then we are absolutely safe." Peter, shaking his head, rejoined his companions, and told them of the manner in which his advice had been received.

"But it would be difficult to cross the river," Harold said. "Look at the masses of ice on the water."

"It would be difficult," the hunter admitted, "but not by no manner of means impossible; determined men could do it. Wall, I have done my duty, and can do no more. Ef the night passes off quietly, we will cross again before daybreak, and go right into the Yankee camp and see what they are up to. Now, Harold, you can take it easy till nightfall. There is nought to be learnt till then, and as we shall be on foot all night, ye may as well sleep to-day."

Returning to a spot on the bank of the river at a short distance from the town, they made a fire, on which Jake cooked some steaks of venison they had procured. After smoking a pipe, the hunter set the example by stretching himself on the ground near the fire, and going off to sleep. Used as he was to night marches, he had acquired the faculty of going to sleep at any hour at will. Jake and Harold were some time before they followed his example, but they too were at last asleep. At sunset they were on their feet again, and after taking supper, proceeded along the river.

The night passed off quietly, and Harold became convinced that his companion's fears were unfounded. Towards morning he suggested that it was time to be crossing the river.

"I am not going yet," the hunter said. "Before I start we will go down to Trenton Ferry, a mile below the town; ef they come over at all, it's likely enough to be there. There will be time then to get back and cross before it is light. It's six o'clock now."

They kept along the road by the river until they were within a quarter of a mile of the ferry. Presently they saw a dark mass ahead.

"Jerusalem!" Peter exclaimed. "There they are!" They immediately discharged their rifles and ran back at full speed to the outposts, which were but a quarter of a mile from the town. The Americans had also pressed forward at full speed, and the outposts, who had been alarmed by the discharge of the rifles, were forced at once to abandon the post and to run into the town, whither they had, on hearing the rifles, already sent in one of their number with the news. Here all was in confusion. The Hessian leader was trying to collect his troops, who were hurrying in from their quarters; but many of them thought more of storing their plunder away in the waggons, than of taking their places in the ranks.

Washington had crossed with 2500 men, with a few field-pieces, and upon gaining the Jersey side had divided his troops into two detachments, one of which marched by the riverside, the other by an upper road. Hurrying forward, they surrounded the town, and placing their field-pieces in the road, opened fire on the astonished Hessians. Rhalle had by this time succeeded in assembling the greater part of his force, and charged the Americans with his usual courage. He received, however, a mortal wound as he advanced. His troops immediately lost heart and, finding their retreat cut off, at once surrendered. A body of Hessian light horse succeeded in making their escape. The casualties were few on either side, but a thousand prisoners were taken. Two other divisions of the Americans had attempted to cross, the one at Bordenton, the other at Mackenzie's Ferry, but both had failed, owing to the quantity of floating ice. Washington retired across the Delaware the same afternoon.

The consequences of this success were great. The spirits of the Americans, which had fallen to the lowest ebb in consequence of the uninterrupted series of defeats, rose greatly. They found that the British were not invincible; and that if unable to oppose them in great battles, they might at least inflict heavy losses on them and weary them out with skirmishes and surprises. The greatest joy reigned throughout the various states; fresh levies were ordered; the voices of the moderate party, which had been gaining strength, were silenced, and the determination to continue the war vigorously was in the ascendency.

The lesson given at Trenton was wholly lost upon the English commander-in-chief. Instead of at once ordering General Leslie to advance from Princetown and to hold the enemy in check by reoccupying and fortifying Trenton, he allowed Colonel Donop to abandon Bordenton and to fall back to Princetown—thus laying it open to Washington to cross the Delaware again and carry the war into New Jersey. Washington, after waiting eight days, seeing the indecision and ineptitude of the British general, again crossed with 4000 men and occupied Trenton.

Peter Lambton and his two companions were not among the prisoners taken at Trenton. On entering the town, Harold was about to join the Hessians assembling under Colonel Rhalle, but Peter gave a violent tug to his coat.

"Come along, young 'un," he said. "The darned fools have let themselves be caught in a trap, and they will find there is no way out of it. In ten minutes the Americans will be all round the place; and as I don't wish to spend a year or two in a Yankee prison at present, I am going to make tracks at once. Fighting aren't no good now. Men who will let themselves be caught in a trap like this will never be able to cut their way out of it. Come on."

Much against his will, Harold yielded to Peter's wishes, and the three kept straight on through the town by the river-side and issued into the country beyond before the Americans had surrounded it. A minute or two after leaving the town the light horse galloped past.

"There are some more out of the hole, and I reckon that's about all. There, do yer hear the guns? The Yanks have brought their artillery over—I reckon the fight won't last long."

For two or three minutes there was a roar of musketry; then this suddenly ceased.

"I thought as much," Peter said. "They have surrendered. If they had only kept together and fought well, they should have cut their way through the enemy. Lord! What poor things regular soldiers are in the dark! A frontiersman would just as soon fight in the dark as in the light; but here are the men who climbed up the hill to Fort Washington—and that was no child's play—no better nor a pack of women when they are attacked half-asleep and half-awake just as day is breaking."

The three comrades walked to Bordenton, which, they were relieved to find, had not been attacked. A few miles beyond this place they met Colonel Donop marching back at full speed with his corps, having received the news of the disaster at Trenton from the horsemen who had fled. They joined their company and marched with the whole to Princetown.

A fortnight later, Lord Cornwallis, with the forces at Brunswick, under General Grant, advanced to Princetown, and then moved forward to attack the army at Trenton. General Washington, on his approach, retired from the town, and, crossing a rivulet at the back of it, took post on some high ground there, with the apparent intention of defending himself against an attack. It was late in the afternoon, and a heavy cannonade was kept up till night-time. Lord Cornwallis determined to attack next morning. At two in the morning, however, Washington retired suddenly, leaving his fires burning. Quitting the main road, he made a long circuit through Allenstown, and marched with all speed toward Princetown, which place he intended to surprise. When Lord Cornwallis advanced, he had left the 17th, 40th, and 55th Regiments there.

On arriving at Trenton, however, he had sent word back for the 17th and 55th to advance to Maidenhead, a village half-way between Princetown and Trenton. Colonel Mawhood, who commanded, marched at daylight, but scarcely had he started when he met Washington advancing with his army. The morning was foggy and it was at first supposed that the enemy were a body of British troops marching back to Princetown; it was soon, however, found that the force was a hostile one. Its strength could not be seen on account of the fog, and he determined to engage it. Possessing himself of some high ground, he sent his waggons back to Princetown, and ordered the 40th Regiment to come out to his assistance.

As the Americans advanced, the artillery on both sides opened fire. The leading columns of the colonists soon showed signs of disorder. The 17th Regiment fixed bayonets and with great gallantry charged the enemy in front of them, driving them back with considerable slaughter; and so far did they advance that they were separated from the other battalions, and cutting their way through the American force, the regiment pursued its march to Maidenhead. The 40th and 55th fought stoutly, but were unable to make their way through the American force, and fell back to Brunswick, while the Americans occupied Princetown. At daybreak Lord Cornwallis discovered the retreat of the American army, and, being apprehensive for the safety of Brunswick, where great stores of the army were accumulated, marched with all haste towards that town.

Brigadier Matthew, the officer commanding there, on hearing of the approach of the enemy, at once despatched the store waggons towards the rear, and drew up his small command to defend the place to the last. The gallant resistance before Princetown had, however, delayed the Americans so long that the van of the army of Cornwallis was already close to their rear as they approached Brunswick. Seeing this, Washington abandoned his design on that town, and crossed the Millstone River, breaking down the bridge at Kingstown to stop pursuit.

Washington now overran East and West Jersey, penetrated into Essex county, and, making himself master of the country opposite to Staten Island, thus regained almost all the district which the English had taken from him in the autumn.

All this greatly heightened the spirit and courage of the Americans, while the loyalists and the English troops were disheartened and disgusted at seeing an army of 30,000 fine troops kept inactive, while the enemy, with but 4000 men, who were wholly incapable of opposing an equal number of English troops, were allowed to wander unchecked, to attack and harass the English pickets, and to utilize the whole of the resources of their country. Had General Howe entertained a fixed desire to see English authority overthrown in America, he could not have acted in a manner more calculated to carry those wishes into effect.

CHAPTER X
A TREACHEROUS PLANTER

IT must not be supposed that the whole of the time was spent in scouting and fighting. Between the armies lay a band of no man's land. Here, as elsewhere, the people of the country were divided in their opinions, but generally made very little display of these, whatever they might be. It is true that, as a rule, non-combatants were but little interfered with; still, a warm and open display of sympathy with one side or the other was likely to be attended by the loss of cattle and damage to crops when the other party got the upper hand. In some other states feeling ran much higher. In the Carolinas the royalists were most cruelly persecuted. Their property was destroyed, and they were in many cases shot down without mercy; but as a rule, throughout the colonies a considerable latitude of opinion was allowed. This was especially so in the zone between the armies in the Jerseys. None could tell what the positions of the armies a week hence might be, and any persecution inflicted by the one party might lead to retaliation upon a shift of positions a few weeks later. A general toleration therefore reigned.

Next to Peter Lambton, Harold's greatest friend in the corps was a young man named Harvey. He was of good family, and belonged to New York. Being a strong loyalist, he had, like many other gentlemen, enlisted for service under the old flag. He had naturally many acquaintances among the county families, and Harold often accompanied him in his visits to one or other of them.

During the winter, when things were quiet, the duties of the scouts were light, and it was the habit among them that one-third should be on outpost duty at a time, the rest being free to move about as they liked. The scouts had no fixed order or position; they went out alone, or in twos or threes, as it pleased them, their duty simply being to watch everything that was going on along the enemy's line of outposts, to bring in the earliest news of any intended movements, and to prevent dashing parties of the enemy's horsemen from making raids into or behind the British lines. They were not, of course, expected to check bodies of cavalry starting on a raid, but simply to obtain information of their having left their lines and of the direction taken, and then to hurry back to the British posts, whence a force of cavalry would be sent out to intercept or check the invaders. Many dashing exploits were performed by the cavalry on both sides in the way of getting behind their opponents' quarters, cutting off provision trains, attacking small posts, and carrying off straggling parties.

One of the houses to which Harold used most frequently to accompany his friend Harvey was situated nearly half-way between the rival armies, and was about eight miles from either. The owner— Mr. Jackson—was a man of considerable wealth, and the house was large and well appointed. He had—before the troubles—begun a fine business as a lawyer in New York, but when the outbreak of hostilities put a stop to all business of a legal kind in that city, he had retired to his country house. Although himself born in England, he professed to be entirely neutral; but his family were undisguisedly loyal. It consisted of his wife and two daughters, girls of seventeen and eighteen years old.

When the English army advanced to the neighbourbood of his property, Mr. Jackson was always ready to offer his hospitality to the officers of corps which might be stationed near him, and he similarly opened his house to the Americans when they in turn advanced as the British turned back. Being, as he always made a point of saying, perfectly neutral in the struggle, he was glad to meet gentlemen, irrespective of the opinions they held. The line taken by Mr. Jackson was one which was very largely pursued among the inhabitants of the country houses and farms scattered over what was throughout the war a debatable land. So frequent were the changes of the position of the armies that none could say who might be in possession in a week's time, and it was therefore an absolute necessity for those who wished to live unmolested to abstain from any strong show of partisanship.

A TREACHEROUS PLANTER

As is always the case in struggles of this kind, the female population were more enthusiastic in their partisanship and more pronounced in their opinions than the men; and although, upon the arrival of a troop of cavalry or a detachment of foot belonging to the other side, the master of the house would offer what hospitality he was capable of, impartially, it was not difficult to perceive, by the warmth or coldness of the female welcome, what were the private sentiments of the family.

Harold was not long in discovering, from the frequency with which Harvey proposed an excursion to the Jacksons', and from his conduct there, that Isabelle, the eldest daughter, was the object which mainly attracted him. The families had long been friends; and Harvey, although now serving as a simple scout, was of a position equal to her own. The friends were always cordially received by Mr. Jackson, and Harold was soon as intimate there as his comrade. They usually left their quarters a little before dusk, and started back late at night. Often as Mr. Jackson pressed them to stay, they never accepted his invitation.

The scouts, from their activity and ubiquitousness, were the *bêtes-noirs* of the Americans, whose most secret plans were constantly detected and foiled by the sagacity and watchfulness of these men, whose unerring rifles made frequent gaps in the ranks of the officers. They therefore spared no pains, whenever there was a chance of killing or capturing any of these most troublesome foes, and Harvey and Harold knew that a report of their presence at the Jacksons' would suffice to bring a party of horsemen from the American lines. Their visits, therefore, were always made after dark and at irregular intervals; and in spite of their inclination to the contrary, they made a point of returning at night to their quarters.

Other visitors were often present at the Jacksons'—the sons and daughters of neighbours—and there was generally music and singing, and sometimes the young people stood up for a dance.

The scouts wore no regular uniform, although there was a general similarity in their attire, which was that of an ordinary backwoods hunter. When off duty they were allowed to dress as they pleased, and at Mr. Jackson's the two friends were attired in the ordinary dress of colonists of position. At these little gatherings political subjects were never discussed, and a stranger spending an evening there would not have dreamt that the house stood between two hostile armies, that at any moment a party of horsemen belonging to one side or other might dash into the courtyard, and that even those laughing and talking pleasantly together might be of opinions diametrically opposed.

Harvey and Harold were introduced to visitors simply as friends from New York; and although the suspicions as to their character and position might be strong, no one thought of asking questions.

"I do not like that fellow Chermside," Harvey said one night as he and his friend were returning to their quarters.

They were mounted; for although when on duty the scouts worked on foot, many of them who were men of property kept horses which they used when not so engaged. Harvey had two horses, and one of these was always at Harold's service.

"I am not surprised you don't like him," Harold replied, with a laugh; "and I imagine the dislike is mutual. When two gentlemen are paying attentions to one lady they seldom appreciate each other's merits very cordially."

"I don't think it is entirely that," Harvey laughed. "Isabelle and I understand each other, and I have no fear of his rivalry, but I do not like him."

"I do not think I like him myself," Harold said, more seriously; "and yet I do not know why I should not. When he has been there alone with us and the family he has frequently used expressions showing his strong leaning towards the loyalists' side."

"I don't put much faith in that," Harvey said. "He knows how strongly Mr. Jackson and the girls lean towards the crown, and would say anything that he thought would please Isabelle. I have spoken to her, and she thinks that he is sincere; in fact she has rather a good opinion of him. However, we shall see. It was rather curious that that party of Morgan's cavalry should have ridden up the other night and searched the house two hours after we left. You see, we had agreed to sleep there that night, and only changed our minds after the others had all left, when we remembered that we were both for duty early next morning. It might have been a coincidence, of course, but it had an ugly look. I think Mr. Jackson thought so, too, for he did not ask us to stop to-night. Anyhow, I wish Chermside's plantation was not so near this and that he did not drop in so often."

A week later they paid another visit. When dinner was over Harold was chatting with Mr. and Mrs. Jackson. Harvey was sitting at the piano where the eldest girl was playing, and the younger was looking out of window.

"We are going to have another fall of snow," she said. "There is not a star to be seen. Oh!" she exclaimed suddenly.

"What is it, my dear?" Mr. Jackson asked.

"There is a rocket gone up from the woods."

"A rocket!" Mr. Jackson repeated.

"Yes, papa; there are the stars falling now."

"That is a curious thing," Mr. Jackson said, while the others went to the window. They stood watching for some minutes, but nothing was to be seen.

"I do not like that rocket," Mr. Jackson said, as they left the window. "It means something. It can only be a signal. People don't let off rockets for amusement nowadays. Did you meet anyone on the road?"

"No, sir," Harvey said; "not a soul."

"I do not like it," their host repeated. "It means mischief of some sort or other. I do not wish to seem inhospitable, but my advice to you is, get on your horses at once and ride to your quarters. You are on duty to-morrow, and you told me you would pass near here on your way towards the enemy's lines. You might look in as you go past and hear whether anything came of it. If I mistake not, we shall have another visit from Morgan's horse this evening."

Much against their inclination the young men followed Mr. Jackson's advice.

The next day they, with Peter and Jake, stopped at the house as they passed.

"I was right," their host said, as the two young men entered. "An hour after you left, twenty of Morgan's horse rode up here. They would not take my word that we were alone, but searched the house from top to bottom, and were evidently greatly disappointed at finding no one. I have been making inquiries this morning and find that all the servants were in the house at the time my daughter saw the rocket, so I hope that I have no traitor here; still, it is clear that someone must be keeping watch over your movements."

"Have you asked, sir," Harvey said, after a pause, "whether anyone came after we had arrived?"

"I do not see how anyone could come; but I will ask."

He rang the bell, and a negro servant appeared.

"Did anyone come to the house yesterday, Cæsar, after these gentlemen came—any beggar or pedlar, or anyone of that sort?"

"No, sir, no one came except Massa Chermside. He get off his horse and ask if you hab any visitors. I said that Massa Harvey and Massa Wilson were here. He say he call again another night when the family alone, and rode off."

"Just what I expected, sir," Harvey said, when the servant left the room. "I have always doubted that fellow's honesty."

"Oh, nonsense!" Mr. Jackson replied. "You must be mad, Harvey. Chermside's father was an old friend of mine, and I have known the young fellow since he was a child. I should as soon suspect one of my own daughters of being capable of such an act of gross treachery as laying a plot to bring the American cavalry down upon guests of mine. The idea is preposterous! Bless me, how amused the girls will be at your suspecting their old playfellow!"

"I hope I may be mistaken, sir," Harvey said, "but Harold's opinion of him agrees with mine, and in talking it over last night, we both put our finger on him as the man who fired the rocket. Well, now we must be pushing on. We are bound for the ford where Morgan's horse must have come over, and shall hear from our fellows there whether they rode straight here after crossing, as, if so, there can be no doubt whatever that the rocket was a signal."

Mr. Jackson's suspicions aroused.

Upon arriving at the ford they found that Morgan's horse had only crossed an hour before the time at which they arrived at Mr. Jackson's. One of the scouts had instantly taken word to the nearest cavalry outpost, but the enemy had recrossed the river before these had arrived on the spot.

After three days on duty at the front the party returned to their lines, and the next time that the young men rode out to their friends, they took with them Jake and Peter, to whom they related the circumstances.

The scouts proceeded on foot, and separated from the others a mile before reaching the house, having arranged that Peter should scout round it, while Jake should proceed to the plantation of Mr. Chermside and keep a sharp look-out there.

They had arranged with Mr. Jackson that no mention of the rocket should be made to anyone, however intimate with the family.

"I am glad to see you again," the host said, as they entered the room where the family were assembled; "although I own that these two raids of Morgan's horse have made me uneasy. The girls have been immensely amused at your suspicions of young Chermside."

"How could you think such a thing?" Isabelle said. "He was here on the following evening and was as indignant as we were at the thought of treachery being at work. He quite agreed with us that the coming of the Yankees could hardly have been accidental."

"You said nothing about the rocket, I hope?" Harvey asked.

"No, we kept quite silent about that, as you made such a point of it; but it seemed ridiculous with him. But I shall be in a fright now every time you come."

"We have brought two of our men with us," Harvey said, "and they are scouting round, so we shall hear if another rocket goes up; and even if the person who let it up suspects that the last was seen—as he might do from our having left so suddenly—and tries some other plan to warn the enemy, we can trust our men to fire a shot and so give us warning in time. We have told the groom not to take the saddles off the horses, as we may stop but a short time."

A treacherous friend caught.

At eight o'clock a disturbance was heard outside, and Jake entered the room, dragging with him by main force the young planter.

"What is the meaning of this?" Mr. Jackson asked, as they rose from their seats in surprise.

"Me tell you, sar," Jake answered. "Me had orders from Massa Harold to watch outside ob de house ob dis fellow and see what going on dere. About half an hour after me got dere a nigger come along running from dis direction. Dat no business of Jake's, so he stood in de trees and let him pass. He go into the house; five minutes afterwards dis feller he come out and he walk away. Jake follow him bery quiet to see what him after. He walk more dan a mile, then he get on to de oder side of dat big hill; den me see him stop, and Jake think it time to interfere, so he ran up and catch him. He had put dis ting against a stump of a tree, and had him pistol in him hand, and was on de point of firing it close to dis ting, so as to light him."

As Jake spoke, he held out a rocket. Several times while Jake had been speaking, the planter had tried to interrupt him, but each time, Jake, who had not released his hold of him, gave him so violent a shake that he was fain to be silent.

"This is a scandalous indignity!" he exclaimed furiously, when Jake finished. "What do you mean, sir," he demanded of Harvey, "by setting this nigger to watch my abode? I will have satisfaction for this treatment."

"It seems, sir," Mr. Jackson said, signing to Harvey to be silent, "that you have been detected in a gross act of treachery. My friends have suspected you of it, but I indignantly denied it. Could we believe, I and my family, that you, whom we have known as a child, would betray our guests to the Americans? Loyalists and republicans are alike welcome here. I do not ask my friends their opinions. My house is neutral ground, and I did not think that any who used it would have had the treachery to turn it into a trap; still less did I imagine you would do so. These gentlemen would be perfectly within their right did they take you out and hang you from the nearest tree, but for my sake I trust that they will not do so; but should the American cavalry ever again visit this house, under circumstances which may lead it to be supposed that they have been brought here to capture my guests, I shall let them punish you as you deserve. No word of mine will be raised in your favour. Now, sir, go, and never again enter this house, where the loathing and contempt that I feel for you will, I know, be shared by the ladies of my family."

At a nod from Harold, Jake released his hold of the captive, who, without a word, turned and left the room.

Not a word was spoken for a minute or two after he had left. The youngest girl was the first to speak.

"The wretch!" she exclaimed. "To think that Herbert Chermside should turn out such a mean traitor! Papa, I would have let them hang him at once. It would have served him right. Now he may do us all harm."

"I do not know that you are not right, Ada," Mr. Jackson replied gravely. "I am far from saying that I acted wisely; young Chermside has many friends among the Americans, and it is possible that he may work us harm. However, my position as a neutral is well established. Officers on both sides have at times been welcomed here, and his report, therefore, that our friends here are often with us can do us no harm. However, henceforth he must be regarded as an enemy, and there will always be danger in these visits. So long as the American outposts are within an hour's ride, he can have the road watched, and although he is not likely to venture upon signalling with rockets, he may send or take word on horseback. A bonfire too might be lit at the other side of the hill to call them over. Altogether you will never be safe from home except when you have a strong body of your own troops between this and the river."

"I am glad to say," Harvey answered, "that in consequence of the news of Morgan's raids on this side, a body of 200 infantry and a troop of cavalry are to move to-morrow and take up their position by the ford, so we shall be safe from any surprise from that direction."

"I am very glad to hear it," Mr. Jackson said. "It will relieve me of a great anxiety. But pray be watchful when you are in this neighbourhood. You have made a bitter enemy, and after what he has proved himself capable of, we cannot doubt that he would hesitate at nothing. I understand," he went on, with a smile towards his eldest daughter, "what is at the bottom of his conduct, and as I have long suspected his hopes in that quarter, I am not surprised that he is somewhat hostile to you; still, I never for a moment deemed him capable of this."

The next day Mr. Jackson learned that his neighbour had left his plantation, and had told his servants that he was not likely to return for some time.

Shortly after this a series of bad luck attended the doings of the British scouts: several parties were killed or captured by the enemy, and they were constantly baffled by false reports, while the Americans appeared to forestall all their movements. It was only when enterprises were set on foot and carried out by small bodies that they were ever successful, anything like combined action by the orders of the officers constantly turning out ill.

"There must be a traitor somewhere," Peter said, upon the return of a party from an attempt which, although it promised well, had been frustrated—to carry off a number of cattle from one of the American depots. "It ain't possible that this can be all sheer bad luck. It ain't no one in our company, I will be bound. We ain't had any new recruits lately, and there ain't a man among us whom I could not answer for. There must be a black sheep in Gregory's or Vincent's corps. The enemy seem up to every move, and between us we have lost more than thirty men in the last few weeks. There ain't no doubt about it: there is a traitor somewhere, and he must be a clever one, and he must have pals with him, or he could not send news of what we are doing so quickly. It beats me altogether, and the men are all furious."

"I have been talking with some of our men," Peter said, a few days afterwards, "and we agree that we are bound to get to the bottom of this matter. We are sartin sure that the traitor don't belong to us. What we propose is this, that the hull of us shall go up together without saying a word to a soul, and scatter ourselves along the river at all the points where a chap going with a message to the enemy would be likely to cross. The night we go out, we will get the three captains all to give orders to their men for an expedition, so that whoever it is that sends messages from here would be sure to send over word to the Yankees; and it will be hard if we do not catch him—what do you say?"

"I think the plan is a very good one," Harold answered. "If you like, I will go with my father and ask Gregory and Vincent to send their men."

Captain Wilson at once went to these officers. They were as much irritated and puzzled as were their men by the failures which had taken place, and agreed that next evening an order should be issued for the men of the three corps to act in combination, and to allow it to leak out that they intended to surprise an American post situated near the river, 21 miles distant. Captain Wilson's scouts, instead of going with the others, were to act on their own account.

On the day arranged, as soon as it became dark, the forty scouts quietly left their quarters in small parties and made their way towards the river, striking it at the point where a messenger would be likely to cross upon his way to give warning to the American post of the attack intended to be made upon it. They took post along the river at a distance of 50 or 60 yards apart, and silently awaited the result. Several hours passed and no sound broke the stillness of the woods. An hour before dawn Peter Lambton heard a slight crack, as that of a breaking twig. It was some distance back in the woods, but it seemed to him by the direction that the man who caused it would strike the river between himself and Jake, who was stationed next to him. He noiselessly stole along toward the point. Another slight sound afforded him a sure indication of the direction in which the man, whoever he might be, was approaching. He hastened his steps, and a minute later a negro issued from the wood close to him; he stood for an instant on the river-bank and was about to plunge in when Peter threw his arms around him.

Although taken by surprise, the negro struggled desperately, and would have freed himself from the grip of the old scout had not Jake run up instantly to his comrade's assistance. In a minute the negro was bound, and two shots were then fired, the concerted signal by which it would be known along the line that a capture had been effected. In a few minutes the whole body was assembled. The negro, who refused to answer any questions, was carried far back into the woods, and a fire was lighted.

"Now, nigger," Peter said, taking as captor the lead in the matter, "just tell us right away where you was going and who sent you."

The negro was silent.

"Now, look ye here, darky, you are in the hands of men who are no jokers. Ef you tell us at once who put ye on to this trick, no harm will happen to you; but ef ye don't, we will just burn the skin off your body bit by bit."

Still the negro was silent.

"Half-a-dozen of yez," Peter said, "as have got iron ramrods, shove them into the fire. We will soon find this nigger's tongue."

Not a word was spoken until the ramrods were heated red-hot.

"Now," Peter said, "two of yez clap your ramrods against this darky's flanks."

The negro struggled as the men approached him, and gave a terrific yell as the hot iron was applied to his sides.

"I will tell you, sars—oh, have mercy upon me, and I will tell you eberyting!"

"I thought," Peter said grimly, "that you would find a tongue soon enough. Now, then, who sent you?"

"My massa," the negro answered.

"And who is your master?"

The negro was again silent, but as, at a nod from Peter, the men again raised the ramrods, he blurted out, "Massa Chermside."

The name was known to many of the scouts, and a cry of anger broke from them.

A TREACHEROUS PLANTER

"I thought as much," Harvey said. "I suspected that scoundrel was at the bottom of it all along."

"Where is he?" he asked the negro.

"Me not know, sar."

"You mean you won't say," Peter said. "Try the vartue of them ramrods again."

"No, no!" the negro screamed. "Me swear me do not know where him be! You may burn me to death if you will, but I could not tell you."

"I think he is speaking the truth," Harvey said. "Wait a minute. Have you done this before?" he asked the negro.

"Yes, sar; eight or ten times me swim de river at night."

"With messages to the Americans?"

"Yes, sar; messages to American officers."

"Have you any written message—any letter?"

"No, sar, me never take no letter. Me only carry this." And he took out from his hair a tiny ball of paper smaller than a pea.

It was smoothed out, and upon it were the words, "Gen. Washington." "Where I go, sar, I show dem this, and dey know then dat de message can be believed."

"But how do you get the message? How do you see your master?"

"Massa's orders were dat me and two oders were to meet him ebery night after it got dark at a tree a mile from de place where de soldiers are. Sometime he no come; when he come he gibes each of us a piece of money, and tell us to carry a message across the river. We start by different ways, swim across de water in different places, take de message, and come back to de plantation."

"A pretty business!" Peter said. "Now you must come back with us to the post, and tell your story to the commanding officer. Then we must see if we cannot lay hands on this rascally master of yours."

Upon the news being told, the general in command sent a party out, who, after searching the house and out-buildings of the plantation in vain, set fire to them and burned them to the ground. The negroes were all carried away, and employed to labour for the army. The town and all the surrounding villages were searched, but no trace could be obtained of the missing man. One of the men of Gregory's corps of scouts disappeared. He had recently joined, but his appearance as a man with beard and whiskers in no way agreed with that of the planter. He might, however, have been disguised, and his disappearance was in itself no proof against him, for the scouts were under no great discipline, and when tired of the service, often left without giving notice of their intention of doing so. It was, moreover, possible that he might have fallen by an enemy's bullet.

The strongest proof in favour of the deserter being Chermside was that henceforth the scouts were again as successful as before, often surprising the enemy successfully.

Now that the ford nearest to Mr. Jackson's was strongly guarded, the young men had no apprehension of any surprise, although such an event was just possible, as the cavalry on both sides often made great circuits in their raids upon each other's country. That Chermside was somewhere in the neighbourhood they believed, having indeed strong reason for doing so, as a rifle was one evening fired at them from the wood as they rode over, the ball passing between their heads. Pursuit at the time was impossible, but the next day a number of scouts searched the woods without success. Soon after they heard that Chermside had joined the Americans, and obtained a commission in a body of their irregular horse.

Harvey was now formally engaged to Isabelle Jackson, and it was settled that the wedding should take place in the early spring at New York. When not on duty he naturally spent a good deal of his time there, and Harold was often over with him. Since he had been fired at in the woods, Isabelle had been in the highest state of nervous anxiety lest her lover's enemy should again try to assassinate him, and she begged Harold always to come over with him if possible, as the thought of his riding alone through the wood filled her with anxiety.

Although he had no order to do so, Jake, whenever he saw Harold and his friend canter off towards the Jacksons', shouldered his rifle and went out after them to the house, where, so long as they stayed, he scouted round and round with the utmost vigilance. Very often Harold was ignorant of his presence there; but when, after his return, he found by questioning him how he had been employed, he remonstrated with him on such excessive caution.

"Can't be too cautious, massa," Jake said. "You see dat fellow come one of dese days."

Jake's presentiment turned out correct. One evening when with several friends the young men were at Mr. Jackson's, the sound of the report of a rifle was heard at a short distance.

"That must be Jake's rifle!" Harold exclaimed. "Quick, Harvey, to your horse!"

It was too late. As they reached the door, a strong party of American cavalry dashed up to it.

"Surround the house!" an officer shouted. "Do not let a soul escape."

The young men ran upstairs again.

"We are caught," Harvey said. "Escape is cut off. The Yankee cavalry are all round the house. Good-bye, Isabelle; we shall meet one of these days again, dear."

The girl threw herself into his arms.

"Be calm, love," he said. "Do not let this scoundrel have the satisfaction of triumphing over you."

A moment later Chermside, accompanied by several soldiers, entered the room.

"I am sorry to disturb so pleasant a party," he said in a sneering voice; "but if Americans choose to entertain the enemies of their country, they must expect these little disagreeables."

Mr. Jackson abruptly turned his back upon him, and no one else spoke, although he was personally well known to all.

"These are the two men," he said to the soldiers; "two of the most notorious scouts and spies on the frontier. We will take them to headquarters, where a short shrift and two strong ropes will be their lot."

"The less the word spy is in the mouth of such a pitiful traitor as yourself, the better, I should say," Harvey said quietly, and, walking forward with Harold, he placed himself in the hands of the soldiers.

No one else spoke. Isabelle had fainted when she heard the threat of execution against her lover. Ada stood before her with a look of such anger and contempt on her young face that Chermside fairly winced under it.

"To horse!" he said sullenly, and turning, followed his men and prisoners downstairs.

The troop, Harold saw, numbered some two hundred sabres. They had with them a number of riderless horses, whose accoutrements showed that they belonged to an English regiment; most of the men, too, had sacks of plunder upon their horses. They had evidently made a successful raid, and had probably attacked a post, and surprised and driven off the horses of a squadron of cavalry, and were now on their return towards lines.

"This is an awkward business, Harold," Harvey said, as, in the midst of their captors, they galloped off from the Jacksons'. "Of course it's all nonsense about our being hung; still, I have no wish to see the inside of a prison, where we may pass years before we are exchanged. Once handed over to the authorities, we shall be safe, but I shall not feel that we are out of danger so long as we are in this scoundrel's hands. Fortunately, there are officers of superior rank to himself with the squadron; otherwise, I have no doubt at all that he would hang us at once."

Such was indeed the case, and Chermside was at that moment fuming intensely at the chance which had thrown his rival in his hands, at a time when he was powerless to carry out his vengeance. He had, indeed, ventured to suggest that it would be less trouble to hang the prisoners at once, but the major in command had so strongly rebuked him for the suggestion that he had at once been silenced.

"I blush that I should have heard such words from the mouth of an American officer. It is by such deeds, sir, that our cause is too often disgraced. We are soldiers fighting for the independence of our country, not lawless marauders. Had these men been taken in their civilian dress over on our side of the river, they would have been tried and hung as spies; but they were on neutral ground, and in fact in the rear of their own posts. There is no shadow of defence for such an accusation. Should I ever hear a similar suggestion, I shall at once report your conduct to General Washington, who will know how to deal with you."

"I wonder what has become of Jake," Harold said to his comrade. "I trust he was not shot down."

"Not he," Harvey said. "He made off after firing his rifle, you may be sure, when he saw that there was nothing to be done. The fellow can run like a hare, and I have no doubt that by this time he has either got back to the village and given the alarm there, or has made for the ford. There are 100 cavalry there now, as well as the infantry. Jake will be there in an hour from the time he started. The dragoons will be in the saddle five minutes later, and it is just possible they may cut off our retreat before we have crossed the river. Peter is on duty there, and if he happens to be at the post when Jake arrives, he will hurry up with all the scouts he can collect."

Jake had taken flight as Harvey supposed. He had, after firing his rifle, taken to the wood, and had remained near the house long enough to see which way the cavalry rode when they started. Then he made for the post at the ford at the top of his speed. It was less than an hour from starting when he arrived there, and three minutes later the cavalry trumpets were blowing "To horse!" After giving his message to the officer in command, Jake went into the village, where the sounds of the trumpet brought all the soldiers into the little street.

"Hullo, Jake! Is that you?" a familiar voice asked. "What the tarnel is up now?"

Jake hastily related what had taken place.

"Tarnation!" Peter exclaimed. "This is a bad job. They are making, no doubt, for Finchley's Ford, 15 miles down the river. With an hour's start they are sure to be there before us."

"What are you going to do, Peter; are you tinking of running wid de cavalry?"

"Thinking of running to the moon!" the scout said contemptuously. "You can run well, I don't deny, Jake, but you

151

could not run 15 miles with the dragoons, and if you could, you would get there too late. Yer bellows are going pretty fast already. Now don't stand staring there, but hurry through the camp and get all our boys together. Tell them to meet by the waterside. Get Gregory and Vincent's men as well as our own. There are twenty or thirty altogether in the place."

Without asking a question, Jake ran off to carry out the orders, and in a few minutes twenty-four men were collected together on the bank.

"Now, you fellows," Peter said, "we've got to rescue these two young chaps out of the hands of the Yankees. Those who don't want to join, and mind you the venture is a risky one, had better say so at once and stop behind."

No one moved.

"What I propose is this: we will take the ferry-boat, which ain't no good to no one, seeing as how the Yankees are one side of the river and we the other, and we'll drop down the stream about 10 mile. Then we will land on their side of the river and strike inland, hiding the boat under the bushes somewhere. They will halt for the night when they are safe across the river. There are 500 or 600 of their infantry camped on the ford. There are 200 on our side, but the Yankees will ride through in the dark, and get across before the Red-coats are awake. Now, I propose that after we have landed, we make a detour until we get near the Yanks' camp. Then the rest will wait and two or three of us will go in and see if we cannot get the young fellows out of wharever they have put them. Then we will join you and make a running fight of it back to the boat."

The others assented. The boat was amply large enough for all, and pulling her out into the stream, they dropped down, keeping under shelter of the trees on the British side. Half an hour after they had started, they heard the faint sound of distant musketry.

"There," Peter said; "the Yanks are riding through the British camp, close to the ford." A few more shots were heard, and then all was silent. The stream was swift, for it was swollen by recent rains, and at three in the morning the boat touched the bank about a mile above the ford. The party disembarked noiselessly, and, fastening the boat to a tree, moved along towards the camp.

When they were within 400 or 500 yards of the village, Peter chose Jake and two others of his band, and telling the rest to remain where they were, ready for action, he struck inland. He made a wide sweep and came in at the back of the camp.

Here there were no sentries, as the only danger to be apprehended was upon the side of the river. Peter therefore entered boldly. In front of the principal house a sentry was walking up and down, and he, in the free-and-easy manner usual in the American army, gladly entered into conversation with the new-comers.

"All pretty quiet about here?" Peter asked. "We are from the West, and have just come down to do a little fighting with the Britishers. I reckon they ain't far off now."

"They are just across the river," the sentry said. "Have you come far?"

"We have made something like 200 miles this week, and mean to have a day or two's rest before we begin. We have done some Indian fighting, my mates and me in our time, and we says to ourselves it was about time we burned a little powder against the Red-coats. Things seem quiet enough about here; nothing doing, eh?"

"Not much," the sentry said; "just skirmishes. Some of our cavalry came across through the Red-coats late to-night. I hear they have got a quantity of plunder and some fine horses, and they have brought in a couple of the British scouts."

"And what have they done with them?" Peter asked. "Strung them up, I suppose."

"No, no; we ain't fighting Indians now; we don't hang our prisoners. No, they are safe under guard over there in the cavalry camp, and will be taken to head-quarters to-morrow."

"Wall," Peter said, stretching himself, "I feel mighty tired, and shall jest look for a soft place for an hour's sleep before morning."

So saying, he sauntered away, and the sentry resumed his walk.

Peter and his three companions now moved off towards the spot where, as the sentry had indicated, the cavalry were encamped. They were not in tents, but were sleeping wrapped up in their blankets. Two tents, however, had been erected, lent probably by the infantry on the spot. One was much larger than the other, and sentries were placed before each. They had some difficulty in making their way, for the night was dark, and the cavalry had picketed their horses without order or regularity. In their search they had to use great caution to avoid stumbling over the sleeping men; but at last they saw the tents faintly against the sky. They crawled cautiously up. There were two sentries on the smaller tent.

"Now, Jake," Peter whispered, "you are the blackest, and so had better do the trick. Don't cut a hole in the tent, for they would be safe to hear the canvas tear. Crawl under. It's been put up in haste, and ain't likely to be pinned down very tight. They are safe to be bound, and when you have cut the cords, and given them time to get the use of their feet, then crawl along and join us."

Jake did as he was instructed. One of the sentries was pacing up and down before the entrance, the other making a circuit round the tent. The circle was a somewhat large one to avoid stumbling over the tent ropes. Jake, therefore, watching his opportunity, had no difficulty in crawling up and squeezing himself under the canvas before the sentry returned.

"Hush!" he whispered, as he let the canvas fall behind him. "It's Jake."

Both the captives were fast asleep. Jake, feeling about in the darkness, found them one after the other, and, putting his hands on their mouths to prevent them making an exclamation, he woke them, and soon cut the cords with which they were bound hand and foot. Then in whispers he told them what had happened. They chafed their limbs to produce circulation, for they had been tightly tied, and then one by one they crawled out of the tent.

Harvey went first, and was safely across before the sentry returned. Harold followed, but, as he went, in his hurry he struck a tent rope.

A TREACHEROUS PLANTER

"What's that?" the sentry in front asked sharply. "Bill, was that you?"

"No," his comrade replied. "Something's up; look into the tent."

And so saying, he ran round behind, whilst the sentry in front rushed into the tent, and, kicking about with his feet, soon found that it was empty.

Jake, on hearing the exclamation, at once crawled from the tent, but, as he did so, the sentry, running round, saw him and levelled his rifle. Before he could fire, a shot was heard, and the man fell dead.

Jake started to his feet and joined his friends. The other sentry also discharged his rifle, and the whole camp awoke and sprang to their feet. The horses, alarmed at the sudden tumult, plunged and kicked; men shouted and swore, every one asking what was the matter. Then loud cries were heard that the sentry was shot and the prisoners had escaped.

Running closely together, and knocking down all who stood in their way, the fugitives hurried in the darkness until at the edge of the camp, and then started at full speed.

The trumpets were now sounding to horse, and several shots were fired after them. Many of the horses had not been unsaddled, and mounted men at once dashed off. Several had seen the little party rush away, and the horsemen were speedily on their track. The six men ran at the top of their speed, and were soon close to their hidden friends.

"This way, this way, I see them!" shouted a voice, which Harold and Harvey recognized as that of their enemy, who a minute later galloped up with half a dozen troopers. It was not until he was within a few yards that his figure was clearly discernible; then Peter Lambton's rifle flashed out, and the planter fell from his horse with a bullet in his brain.

Jake and the other two men also fired, and the horsemen, astonished at their number, reined in their horses to await the coming up of more of their comrades.

In another minute the fugitives were with their friends, and at a rapid trot the whole ran up the river bank towards the spot where they had hidden their boat.

The country was covered with brushwood and forest, and as the cavalry, now swollen to a considerable force, advanced, they were greeted by so heavy a fire, that, astonished at this strong force of foes upon their side of the river, and not knowing how numerous they might be, they halted and waited for the infantry to come up. Long before the enemy were prepared to advance against the unknown foe, the scouts reached their boat and crossed in safety to the other side.

Shortly after this adventure Mr. Jackson and his family moved for the winter into New York, where, soon after their arrival, the wedding between Harvey and Isabelle took place, the former retiring from the corps of scouts.

CHAPTER XI
THE CAPTURE OF PHILADELPHIA

DURING the course of the spring of 1777, a large number of loyal colonists had volunteered their services. They had been embodied into battalions, and when the army prepared to take the field, they were placed in garrisons in New York and other places, thus permitting the employment of the whole of the British force in the field. The Americans had occupied themselves in strongly fortifying the more defensible positions, especially those in a mountain tract of country called the Manor of Courland. This was converted into a sort of citadel, where large quantities of provisions, forage, and stores of all kinds were collected. About fifty miles from New York, up the North River, was a place called Peeks Hill, which served as a port to the Manor of Courland. The country was so difficult and mountainous that General Howe shrank from engaging his army in it. He determined, however, to attack and destroy Peeks Hill, and a party of five hundred men, under the command of Col. Bird of the 15th Regiment, were sent up the river in two transports to destroy it. The garrison, consisting of 800 men, set fire to the place and withdrew without firing a shot. The British completed the destruction of the stores and returned to New York.

A little later 2000 men were sent on a similar expedition against the town of Danbury, another place on the confines of Courland Manor, where great stores had also been collected. They proceeded up the East River and landed at Camp's Point. They started on foot at ten o'clock at night, and after a ten hours' march arrived at eight o'clock at Danbury. The enemy evacuated the place on their approach, and the English set fire to the great magazines filled with stores of all kinds.

The news of the march of the English had spread rapidly, and the enemy assembled from all quarters and posted themselves under the command of General Arnold, at a town called Ridgefield, through which the English would have to pass on their return. Here they threw up intrenchments. It was late in the afternoon when the English, fatigued with the long march, arrived at this spot. They did not hesitate, however, but when the Americans opened fire, they boldly assailed the intrenchments and carried them with the bayonet. They were unable to march further, and, lying down so as to form an oblong square, slept till morning. All night the Americans continued to come up in great force, and in the morning, as the troops advanced, a terrible fire was opened upon them from the houses and stone walls in which the country abounded. The British had to fight every foot of their way. General Wooster had brought up some field-artillery on the side of the Americans. Gradually, however, the column fought its way forwards until it arrived within half a mile of Camp's Point. Here two strong bodies of the enemy barred their way. The column were by this time greatly exhausted; the men had had no real rest for three days and two nights, and several dropped on the road with fatigue. Brigadier-general Erskine, however, picked out 400 of those who were in the best condition, and attacked the two bodies of the enemy with such vigour that he put them utterly to flight, and the column, again advancing, reached their destination without further molestation. Nearly 200 men, including 10 officers, were killed and wounded on the part of the British; the loss of the Americans was still greater, and General Wooster and some field-officers were among the slain.

Many other skirmishes took place with varied success. The Americans at Bondwick, seven miles from Brunswick, 1200 in number, were surprised and routed by Cornwallis; while on the other hand, the American Col. Meigs carried out a most dashing expedition by crossing to Long Island and destroying a quantity of stores at a place called Saggy Harbour, burning a dozen brigs and sloops which lay there, taking ninety prisoners, and returning safely across the sound.

In June, Washington, with 8000 men, was encamped in a strong position at Middlebrook. General Howe, although he had

THE CAPTURE OF PHILADELPHIA

30,000 men, hesitated to attack him here; by a feigned retreat, however, he succeeded in drawing General Washington from his stronghold, and inflicted a decisive defeat on 3000 of his men. Washington fell back to his position in the mountains, and General Howe retired altogether from Jersey and withdrew his troops to Staten Island. A dashing feat was executed at this time by Col. Barton of the American army. Learning that General Prescott, who commanded at Rhode Island, had his headquarters at a distance of a mile from his troops, he crossed from the mainland in two boats, seized the general in his bed, and carried him off through the British fleet. The object of this dashing enterprise was to obtain a general to exchange for the American General Lee, who had been captured by the British.

General Howe, in June, again marched against Washington, and again fell back without doing anything. Had he, instead of thus frittering away his strength, marched to the Delaware, crossed that river, and advanced against Philadelphia, Washington would have been forced to leave his stronghold and either fight in the open or allow that important city to fall into the hands of the English.

General Howe now embarked his army in transports. Had he sailed up the North River to Albany, he would have effected a junction with General Burgoyne's army, which was advancing from Canada, and with the united force could have marched through America from end to end as he chose. Instead of doing so, he sailed down to Chesapeake Bay and there disembarked the whole army, which had been pent up in transports from the 3d of July to the 24th August. Not till the 11th of September did they advance in earnest towards Philadelphia. The Americans, therefore, had ample time to take up a strong position and fortify it. This they did on the other side of the Brandywine Creek. Under cover of a cannonade, the British advanced, mastered the fort, and carried the entrenchments. General Sullivan, with a considerable force, had now arrived, accompanied by General Washington himself. He took up his position a short distance from the Brandywine, his artillery well placed and his flanks covered with woods.

The following afternoon the British attacked. The Americans fought well, but the British were not to be denied, and, rushing forward, drove the enemy from their position into the woods in their rear. Here they made a stand and were only dislodged after a desperate resistance. The greater portion of them fled in all directions. Washington himself, with his guns and a small force, retreated eight miles from Chester, and then marched by Derby to Philadelphia. Here he waited three days, rallying his troops, and then, having recruited his stores from the magazines, marched away.

All this time the British remained inactive on the ground they had won. In the battle, the Americans lost 300 killed, 600 wounded, and 400 prisoners. Several guns were also taken. The British lost 100 killed and 400 wounded.

On the 20th of September they advanced towards Philadelphia. The American General Wayne had concealed himself in the woods with 1500 men, with the intention of harassing the rear of the British army. News of this having been obtained, Major-general Grey was despatched at once to surprise him; he ordered his men not to load but to rely wholly on the bayonet. The success of the expedition was complete. General Wayne's outpost was surprised, and the British troops rushed into his encampment. 300 of the Americans were killed or wounded, and 100 taken prisoners. The rest escaped through the woods. On the English side 1 officer was killed, 7 privates killed and wounded.

The capture of Philadelphia was an important advantage to the British, but it could not be thoroughly utilized until the fleet could come up the river to the town. The American Congress, which had sat at Philadelphia until General Howe approached the town, had taken extensive measures for rendering the passage impracticable. Three rows of chevaux-de-frise, composed of immense beams of timber bolted and fastened together and stuck with iron spikes, were sunk across the channel, and these lines were protected by batteries. At these forts were fourteen large row-boats, each carrying a heavy cannon, two floating batteries carrying nine guns each, and a number of fire-ships and rafts.

THE CAPTURE OF PHILADELPHIA

The forts commanding the chevaux-de-frise were abandoned on the approach of the British, and Captain Hamond, of the *Roebuck*, succeeded, in spite of the opposition of the enemy's boats and batteries, in making an opening through the chevaux-de-frise sufficiently wide for the fleet to pass.

Large numbers of troops having been sent away from "German Town," a place seven miles from Philadelphia, where the main body of the British army were posted, General Washington determined to attempt the surprise of that position. For this purpose he reinforced his army by drawing 1500 troops from Peek's Hill, and 1000 from Virginia; and at daybreak on the 4th of October, under cover of a thick fog, he made an attack on the troops posted at the head of the village.

Half of the British force lay on one side of the village and half on the other, and had the attack upon the place succeeded, the British army would have been cut in sunder. The village was held by the 40th Regiment, who, fighting obstinately, were driven back among the houses. The Americans were pushing forward in five heavy columns, when Lieutenant-colonel Musgrave, who commanded the 40th, threw himself into a large stone house. Here he offered a desperate resistance, and so impeded the advance of the enemy that time was given for the rest of the British troops to get under arms.

General Washington ordered a whole brigade of infantry to attack the house, and turned four guns against it. Colonel Musgrave and his men, however, resisted desperately, and held the post until Major-general Grey with the 3d Brigade, and Brigadier-general Agnew with the 4th Brigade, came up and attacked the enemy with great spirit. The engagement was for some time very hot. At length a part of the right wing fell upon the enemy's flank, and the Americans retired with great precipitation. The fog was so dense that no pursuit could be attempted.

On the part of the English 600 were killed and wounded. The loss of the Americans amounted to between 200 and 300 killed, 600 wounded, and 400 taken prisoners. General Howe had, on the previous night, been acquainted with the intention of General

Washington to attack the place, and had he taken the proper measures to have received them, the American army would have been destroyed. He took no measures whatever, gave no warning to the army, and suffered the camp to be taken by surprise.

After this battle the fleet and army united, cleared away the chevaux-de-frise across the Delaware, and took the forts commanding them after some hard fighting.

The passage of the Delaware being thus opened and the water communication secured, the army went to their winter quarters at Philadelphia.

Captain Wilson and his son had taken no part in any of these operations, as, a short time after the capture of Harold and Harvey by the American cavalry, the company had been disbanded. The men, when they entered the service, had volunteered for a year. This time already had been greatly exceeded—twenty months had passed since the battle of Bunker's Hill—and although the men were willing to continue to give their services so long as it appeared to them that there was a prospect of a favourable termination of the war, no such hope any longer remained in their minds. The great army which England had sent over had done nothing towards restoring the king's authority in the colonies; and if, after a year's fighting, its outposts were still within a few miles of New York, how could it be expected or even hoped that it could ever subdue a country containing hundreds of thousands of square miles? The retreat from the Delaware and the virtual handing over of New Jersey again to Washington was the finishing stroke which decided the volunteers to demand their discharge, according to the terms of their engagement. Except during the Canadian campaign they had had but little fighting, nor in such a warfare as that which General Howe was carrying on was there much scope for their services. Many of the gentlemen who formed the majority of the company, and who for the most part had friends and connections in England, sailed for that country. Some had left wives and families on their estates when they took up arms; and most of them, despairing of the final success of the war, had instructed their agents to sell these estates for any sum that they would fetch. Others—

among them Captain Wilson—now followed their example. It was but a mere tithe of the value of the property that was obtained, for money was scarce in the colonies, and so many had sold out and gone to England, rather than take part on one side or the other of the fratricidal strife, that land and houses fetched but nominal prices.

Mrs. Wilson had long since gone to England, and her husband, having made arrangements for the disposal of his property, now determined to join her. Fortunately he possessed means irrespective of his estate in America. This, indeed, had come to him through his wife, and his own fortune and the money obtained by the sale of his commission had remained invested in English securities. While determined on this course for himself, he left it to his son to choose his own career. Harold was now nearly eighteen, and his life of adventure and responsibility had made a man of him. His father would have preferred that he should have returned with him to England, but Harold finally decided upon remaining. In war men's passions become heated, the original cause of quarrel sinks into comparative insignificance, and the desire for victory, the determination to resist, and a feeling of something like individual hatred for the enemy become predominant motives of the strife.

This was especially the case in the American war; on both sides there were many circumstances which heightened the passions of the combatants. The loyalists in the English ranks had been ruined by the action of their opponents—many had been reduced from wealth to poverty, and each man felt a deep passion of resentment at what he regarded his personal grievance. Then, too, the persistent misrepresentations both of facts and motives on the part of the American writers and speakers added to the irritation. The loyalists felt that there were vast numbers throughout the colonies who agreed with them, and regarded Congress as a tyrannical faction rather than the expression of the general will. In this, no doubt, they were to some extent mistaken, for by this time the vast majority of the people had joined heart and soul in the conflict. Men's passions had become so stirred up that it was difficult for any to remain neutral; and although there were still large numbers of loyalists throughout the States, the vast bulk of the people had resolved that the only issue of the contest was complete and entire separation from the mother country.

Harold had now entered passionately into the struggle. He was in constant contact with men who had been ruined by the war; he heard only one side of the question, and he was determined, so long as England continued the struggle, to fight on for a cause which he considered sacred. He was unable to regard the prospects of success as hopeless. He saw the fine army which England had collected, he had been a witness of the defeat of the Americans whenever they ventured to stand the shock of the British battalions, and in spite of the unsatisfactory nature of the first campaign, he could not bring himself to believe that such an army could fail.

When the company was disbanded, he decided to continue to serve as a scout; but, sharing in the general disgust in the army at the incapacity of General Howe, he determined to take ship again for Canada and take service under General Burgoyne, who was preparing with a well-appointed army to invade the States from that side.

When he communicated his determination to Peter Lambton, the latter at once agreed to accompany him.

"I have gone into this business," the hunter said, "and I mean to see it through. Settling down don't suit me. I ain't got any friends at New York, and I shud be miserable just loafing about all day doing nothing. No, I shall see this business out to the end, and I would much rather go with you than any one else."

Jake was of the same opinion. Accustomed all his life to obey orders, and to the life on his master's plantation, he would not have known what to do if left to his own devices. Captain Wilson pointed out to him that he could easily obtain work on the wharves of New York, or as a labourer on a farm, but Jake would not listen to the proposal, and was, indeed, hurt at the thought that he could leave his young master's side as long as Harold continued in the war.

Accordingly, the day after Captain Wilson sailed for England, the three comrades embarked in a ship for Halifax, whence another vessel took them to Quebec. They then sailed up the river to Montreal, and took service as scouts in General Burgoyne's army.

For political reasons General Burgoyne had been appointed to the command of the expedition which had been prepared, and General Carleton, naturally offended at being passed over, at once resigned the governorship. His long residence in Canada, his knowledge of the country, of the manners of its inhabitants, and the extent of its resources, and his acquaintance with the character of the Indians, rendered him far more fit for command than was General Burgoyne. In military knowledge and experience, too, he was his superior, and had he retained a command the fate of the expedition would probably have been very different.

The army under General Burgoyne consisted of 7173 men, exclusive of artillerymen. Of these about half were Germans. The Canadians were called upon to furnish men sufficient to occupy the woods on the frontier and to provide men for the completion of the fortifications at Sorrel, St. John's, Chamblée, and Isle-aux-Noix, to furnish horses and carts for carriage, and to make roads when necessary. A naval force was to go forward with him on the lake. The Indian question had again to be decided. Several tribes volunteered to join the British. General Burgoyne hesitated, as General Carleton had done before, to accept their services, and only did so finally on the certainty that if he refused their offers they would join the Americans. He resolved, however, to use them as little as possible. He knew that their object in all wars was murder and destruction, and although he wished to conquer the Americans, he did not desire to exterminate them.

On the 16th of June, 1777, General Burgoyne advanced from St. John's. The naval force had preceded the army and opened a way for its advance. The troops were carried in a flotilla of boats, and, under the protection of the fleet, passed Lake Champlain and landed at Crown Point.

Harold and his companions had joined the army a fortnight previously, and as they crossed the lake with the fleet, they could not but remember their last expedition there. At Crown Point, they were joined by 1000 Indians, who marched round the lake, and at this place General Burgoyne gave them a great feast, and afterwards made a speech to them, exhorting them to abstain from all cruelty, to avoid any ill-treatment of unarmed combatants, and to take as prisoners all combatants who fell into their hands.

But while thus exhorting the Indians to behave with humanity and moderation, the general took a most ill-judged step, which not only did the English cause great harm, but was used by the Americans with much effect as a proof of the cruel way in which England warred against the colonists. He issued a proclamation threatening to punish with the utmost severity all who refused to attach themselves to the British cause, and at the same time he magnified the ferocity of the Indians, pointing out with great emphasis their eagerness to butcher those who continued hostile to the mother country, whose interests they had espoused.

This proclamation was naturally construed by the Americans as a threat to deliver over to the tender mercies of the Indians to slay, scalp, and destroy all who ventured to resist the authority of the king.

The Americans had fallen back on the approach of the British, and upon the landing being effected, the scouts were instantly sent forward.

Among the Indians who had joined at Crown Point were the Senecas—among them their old friend Deer-Tail.

The scouts received no particular orders, and were free to regulate their own movements. Their duty was to reconnoitre the country ahead, and to bring in any information they might gather as to numbers and position of the enemy.

Finding that Peter and his companions were about to start, Deer-Tail said that instead of waiting for the feast he would take five of his warriors and accompany them.

It was at Ticonderoga that the Americans had prepared to make their first stand. The place lies on the western shore of the lake a few miles to the northward of the narrow inlet uniting Lake Champlain to Lake George. It was to reconnoitre the fort that the party now set out. News had been brought that the Americans had been executing great additional works, and the British general was anxious to learn the nature of these before he advanced.

It was certain that the enemy would on their side have sent out scouts to ascertain the movements of the royal army, and the party proceeded with the greatest care. They marched in the usual fashion in Indian file; the Seneca chief led the way, followed by one of his braves; then came Peter, Harold, and Jake; the other Senecas marched in the rear.

When they came within a few miles of the fort, their progress was marked with profound caution. Not a word was spoken, their tread was noiseless, and the greatest pains were taken to avoid stepping on a twig or dried stick. The three scouts, when they left St. John's, had abandoned their boots, and had taken to Indian moccasins. Several times slight murmurs were heard in the forest, and once a party of four American frontiersmen were seen in the wood. The party halted and crouched in the bushes. The Senecas turned towards Peter as if asking if an attack should be made, but the latter shook his head. A single shot would have been heard far away in the woods, and their further progress would have been arrested. Their object now was not to fight, but to penetrate close to the American intrenchments.

When the enemy had passed on, the party continued its way. As they neared the fort, the caution observed increased. Several times they halted while the Seneca, with one of his braves, crawled forward ahead to see that all was clear. At last they stood on the edge of a great clearing; before them, just within gun-shot range, stood the fort of Ticonderoga. Peter Lambton was well acquainted with it, and beyond the fact that the space around had been cleared of all trees, and the stockades and earthworks repaired, little change could be seen.

As he was gazing, the Indian touched his shoulder, and pointed to a high hill on the opposite side of the narrow straits. This had been cleared of trees, and on the top a strong fort had been erected. Many cannon were to be seen along its crest, the roofs of huts, and a large number of men. Half-way up the hill was another battery, and a third still lower down, to sweep the landing.

"They have been working hard," the hunter said, "and the army will have a mighty tough job before it. What do you think of that, Harold?"

"It is a very strong position," Harold said, "and will cost us a tremendous number of men to take it. The fort cannot be attacked till that hill has been carried, for its guns completely command all this clearing."

For some time they stood gazing at the works, standing well back among the trees so as to be screened from all observation. At last Harold said, "Look at that other hill behind; it is a good bit higher than that which they have fortified, and must be within easy range both of it and the fort. I don't see any works there; do you?"

Peter and the Seneca chief both gazed long and earnestly at the hill, and agreed that they could see no fortification there.

"It won't do to have any doubt about it," Peter said; "we must go round and have a look at it."

"We shall have to cross the river," Harold remarked.

"Ay, cross it we must," Peter said. "That hill's got to be inspected."

They withdrew into the wood again, and made a wide sweep till they came down upon the river, two miles above Ticonderoga. They could not reach the water itself, as a road ran along parallel with it, and the forest was cleared away for some distance. A number of men could be seen going backward and forward on the road.

Having made their observations, the scouts retired again into a thick part of the forest and waited till nightfall.

"How are we to get across?" Harold asked Peter. "It's a good long swim, and we could not carry our muskets and ammunition across."

"Easy enough," the scout said. "Did you not notice down by the road a pile of planks? I suppose a waggon has broken down there, and the planks have been turned out, and nobody has thought anything more about them. We shall each take a plank, fasten our rifle and ammunition upon it, and swim across; there won't be any difficulty about that. Then when we have seen what there is on the top of that ere hill, we will tramp round to the other end of the lake. I heard that the army was to advance half on each side, so we shall meet them coming."

When it was perfectly dark they left their hiding-place and crossed the clearing to the spot where Peter had seen the planks. Each took one of them and proceeded to the river-side. Peter, Harold, and Jake divested themselves of some of their clothes, and fastened these with their rifles and ammunition to the planks. To the Indians the question of getting wet was one of entire indifference, and they did not even take off their hunting shirts. Entering the water the party swam noiselessly across to the other side, pushing their planks before them. On getting out, they carried the planks for some distance, as their appearance by the water's edge might excite a suspicion on the part of the Americans that the works had been reconnoitred.

After hiding the planks in the bushes, they made their way to Sugar Hill, as the eminence was called. The ascent was made with great circumspection, the Indians going on first. No signs of the enemy were met with, and at last the party stood on the summit of the hill. It was entirely unoccupied by the Americans.

"Well, my fine fellows," laughed the scout, "I reckon yer have been doing a grist of work, and that yer might just as well have been sitting down quietly smoking your pipes. What on arth possessed ye to leave this hill unguarded?"

In point of fact General St. Clair, who commanded the Americans, had perceived that his position was commanded from this spot. He had, however, only 3000 men under him, and he considered this number too small to hold Ticonderoga, Mount Independence, and Sugar Hill. The two former posts could afford no assistance to the garrison of a fort placed on Sugar Hill, and that place must therefore fall if attacked by the British. On the other hand, he hoped that should the attention of the English not be called to the importance of the position by the erection of works upon it, it might be overlooked, and that General Burgoyne on his arrival might at once attack the position which he had prepared with so much care.

Having ascertained that the hill was unoccupied, Peter proposed at once to continue the march. Harold, however, suggested to him that it would be better to wait until morning, as, from their lofty position, they would be able to overlook the whole of the enemy's lines of defence, and might therefore obtain information of vital importance to the general. Peter saw the advantage of the suggestion; two of the Indians were placed on watch, and the rest of the party lay down to sleep. At daybreak they saw that the delay had been fully justified, for they had now a view of the water which separated Ticonderoga from Mount Independence, and perceived that the Americans had made a strong bridge of communication between these posts. Twenty-two piers had been sunk at equal distances, and between them boats were placed, fastened with chains to the piers. A strong bridge of planks connected the whole. On the Lake Champlain side of the bridge, a boom, composed of great trees fastened together with double chains, had been placed. Thus not only had a communication been established across the stream, but an effectual barrier erected to the passage of the fleet. Fully satisfied with the result of their investigations, the party set out on their return.

CHAPTER XII
THE SETTLER'S HUT

BEFORE starting they stood for a minute or two looking over the forest which they were to traverse. To Harold's eye, all appeared quiet and still; here and there were clearings where settlers had established themselves, but, with these exceptions, the forest stretched away like a green sea.

"Tarnation!" Peter exclaimed. "We shall have all our work to get through safely, eh, chief?"

The Seneca nodded.

"What makes you say so?" Harold asked in surprise. "I see nothing."

Peter looked at him reproachfully. "I am downright ashamed of yer, lad. You should have been long enough in the woods this time to know smoke when you see it. Why, there it is curling up from the trees in a dozen, ay, in a score of places. There must be hundreds of men out scouting or camping in them woods."

Harold looked fixedly again at the forests, but even now he could not detect the signs which were so plain to the scout. "You may call me as blind as a bat, Peter," he said, with a laugh; "but I can see nothing. Looking hard, I imagine I can see a light mist here and there, but I believe it is nothing but fancy."

"It is clear enough to me, lad, and to the Red-skins. What do you say, chief?"

"Too much men," the Seneca replied sententiously.

For another minute or two he and Peter stood watching the forest, and then in a few words consulted together as to the best line to follow to avoid meeting the foe who, to their eyes, swarmed in the forest.

"It's mighty lucky," the hunter said, as they turned to descend the hill, which was covered with trees to its very summit, "that they are white men, and not Red-skins, who are out in the woods there. I don't say that there are not many frontiersmen who know the way of the woods as well as the Red-skins. I do myself, and when it comes to fighting, we can lick them on their own ground; but in scouting we ain't nowhere, not the best of us. The Red-skins seem to have an instinct more like that of an animal than a man. I don't say as he can smell a man a mile off as a dog can do, but he seems to know when the enemy is about. His ears can hear noises which we can't; his eyes can see marks on the ground when the keenest-sighted white man can see nothing. If that wood was as full of Red-skins as it is of whites to-day, our sculps would not be worth a charge of powder."

"You are not going to follow the shores of the lake, I suppose?" Harold asked.

"No," Peter said; "they will be as thick as peas down there, watching for the first sight of our fleet. No, we must just keep through the woods and be as still and as silent as ef the trees had ears. You had best look to the priming of yer piece before we goes farther, for it's likely enough you will have to use it before the day's done, and a miss-fire might cost you yer life. Tell that nigger of yours that he is not to open his mouth again till I gives him leave."

With a long stealthy tread the party descended the mountain and took their way through the woods. Every hundred yards or so they stopped and listened intently. When any noise, even of the slightest kind, was heard, all dropped to the ground until the chief had scouted round and discovered the way was clear. Once or twice they heard the sound of men's voices and a distant laugh, but they passed on without seeing those who uttered them.

Presently they again heard voices, this time raised as if in angry dispute. The Seneca would, as before, have made a long detour to avoid them, but Peter said, "Let us have a squint at what's going on, chief."

With redoubled caution, they again advanced, until they stood at the edge of the clearing. It was a patch of land some hundred yards wide, and extending from the shore of the lake nearly a quarter of a mile inland. In the centre stood a log-hut, neatly and carefully built. A few flowers grew around the house, and the whole bore signs of greater neatness and comfort than was usual in the cabins of the backwood settlers.

The point where the party had reached the edge of the wood was immediately opposite the house. Near it stood a group of some twenty men, one of whom, apparently their leader, was gesticulating angrily as he addressed a man who stood facing him.

"I tell yer, ye are a darned royalist; ye are a traitor to the country, and I have a mind to hang yer and all belonging to yer to the nearest bough."

"I tell you," the man answered calmly, but in the still air every word he said could be heard by those at the edge of the forest, "I hae naething to do with the trouble ane way or the ither. I am a quiet settler, whose business only is to mak a hame for my wife and bairn; but if you ask me to drink success to the Congress and confusion to the king's troops, I tell you I will na' do it, not even if you are brutal enough, but this I canna believe possible, to carry your threats into execution. I hae served my time in a king's regiment. With the bounty I received instead o' pension on my discharge I settled here wi' my wife and bairn, and no one shall say that Duncan Cameron was a traitor to his king. We do no harm to anyone; we tak no part for or against you; we only ask to be allowed to live in peace."

"That ye shall not," the man said. "The king's troops have got Indians with them, and they are going to burn and kill all those who will not take part with them. It's time we should show them as we can play at that game too. Now, ye have either got to swear to be faithful to the States of America, or up ye go."

"I canna' swear," the settler said firmly; "you may kill me if you will, but if you are men, you will nae harm my wife and girl."

"We will just do to you as the Red-skins will do to our people," the man said. "We will make a sweep of the hull lot of you. Here, you fellows, fetch the woman and girl out of the house and then set a light to it."

Four or five of the men entered the house. A minute later screams were heard, and a woman and child dragged out. The settler sprang towards them, but three or four men seized him.

"Now," the man said, stepping towards the house, "we will show them a bonfire."

As he neared the door a crack of a rifle was heard and the ruffian fell dead in his tracks. A yell of astonishment and rage broke from his followers.

"Jeerusalem! Youngster, you have got us into a nice fix! However, since you have begun it, here goes."

And the rifle of the hunter brought down another of the Americans. These, following the first impulse of a frontiersman when attacked, fled for shelter to the house, leaving the settler with his wife and daughter standing alone.

"Yer had best get out of the way," Peter shouted, "or ye may get a bit of lead that wasn't intended for yer!"

Catching up his child, Cameron ran towards the forest, making for the side on which his unknown friends were placed, but keeping down towards the lake so as to be out of their line of fire.

"Do yer make down to them, Harold," Peter said. "Tell them that they had best go to some neighbour's, and stop there for a day or two. The army will be here to-morrow or next day. Be quick about it, and come back as fast as yer can. I tell yer we are in a hornet's nest, and it will be as much as we can do to get out of it."

A scattering fire was now being exchanged between the Redskins behind the shelter of the trees and the Americans firing from the windows of the log-house. Harold was but two or three minutes absent.

"All right, Peter!" he exclaimed, as he rejoined them.

"Come along then," the hunter said. "Now, chief, let us make up round the top of this clearing and then foot it."

The chief at once put himself at the head of the party and the nine men strode away again through the forest. It was no longer silent. Behind them the occupants of the hut were still keeping up a brisk fire towards the trees, while from several quarters shouts could be heard, and more than once the Indian war-whoop rose in the forest.

"That's just what I was afeard of," Peter muttered. "There are some of those darned varmint with them. We might have found our way through the Whites, but the Red-skins will pick up our trail as sartin as if we were driving a waggon through the woods."

Going along at a swinging noiseless trot, the party made their way through the forest. Presently a prolonged Indian whoop was heard in the direction from which they had come. Then there were loud shouts and the firing ceased.

"One of the red reptiles has found our trail," Peter said. "He is with a party of Whites, and they have shouted the news to the gang in the clearing. Wall, we may calculate we have got thirty on our trail, and as we can hear them all round, it will be a sarcumstance if we get out with our sculps."

As they ran, they heard shouts from those behind, answered by others on both flanks. Shots too were fired as signals to call the attention of other parties. Several times the Seneca chief stopped and listened attentively, and then changed his course as he heard suspicious noises ahead. Those behind them were coming up, although still at some distance in the rear. They could hear the sound of breaking trees and bushes as their pursuers followed them in a body.

"Ef it was only the fellows behind," Peter said, "we could leave them easy enough, but the wood seems alive with the varmint."

It was evident the alarm had spread through the forest, and that the bands scattered here and there were aware that an enemy was in their midst. The dropping fire which the pursuers kept up afforded an indication as to the direction in which they were making, and the ringing war-whoop of the hostile Indians conveyed the intelligence still more surely.

Presently there was a shout a short distance ahead, followed by the sound of a rifle-ball as it whizzed close to Harold's head and buried itself in a tree that he was passing. In a moment each of the party had sheltered behind a tree.

"It is of no use, chief," Peter said. "We shall have the hull pack from behind upon us in five minutes. We must run for it, and take our chances of being hit."

Swerving somewhat from their former line, they again ran on. Bullets whisked round them, but they did not pause to fire a shot in return.

"Tarnation!" Peter exclaimed, as the trees in front of them opened and they found themselves on the edge of another clearing. It was considerably larger than that which they had lately left, being 300 yards across, and extending back from the lake fully half a mile. As in the previous case, a log-hut stood in the centre some 200 yards back from the lake.

"There is nothing for it, chief," Peter said. "We must take to the house and fight it out there. There are a hull gang of fellows in the forest ahead, and they will shoot us down if we cross the clearing."

Without a moment's hesitation the party rushed across the clearing to the hut. Several shots were fired as they dashed across the open, but they gained the place of refuge in safety. The hut was deserted; it had probably belonged to royalists, for its rough furniture lay broken on the ground, boxes and cupboards had been forced open, and the floor was strewn with broken crockery and portions of wearing apparel.

Harold looked round; several of the party were bleeding from slight wounds.

"Now to the windows," Peter said, as he barred the door. "Pile up bedding and anything else that yer can find against the shutters, and keep yerselves well under cover. Don't throw away a shot. We shall want all our powder, I can tell yer. Quickly now, there ain't no time to be lost."

While some began carrying out his instructions below, others bounded upstairs and scattered themselves through the upper rooms. There were two windows on each side of the house—one at each end. Disregarding the latter, Peter and Harold took post at the windows looking towards the forest, from which they had just come. The chief and another Indian posted themselves to watch the other side. At first no one was to be seen. The party who had fired at them as they ran across the open had waited for the coming up of the strong band who were following before venturing to show themselves. The arrival of the pursuers was heralded by the opening of a heavy fire towards the house. As the assailants kept themselves behind trees, no reply was made, and the defenders occupied themselves by piling the bedding against the shutters that they had hastily closed. Loopholes had been left in the walls when the hut was first built; the moss with which they were filled up was torn out, and each man took his post at one of these. As no answering shot came from the house, the assailants became bolder, and one or two ventured to show themselves from behind shelter. In a moment Harold and Peter, whose rifles would carry more truly and much farther than those of the Indians, fired.

"Two wiped out!" Peter said, as the men fell and shouts of anger arose from the woods. "That will make them careful."

This proof of the accuracy of the aim of the besieged checked their assailants, and for some time they were very careful not to expose themselves. From both sides of the forest, a steady fire was maintained. Occasionally, answering shot flashed out from the house—when one of the enemy incautiously showed an arm or a part of his body from behind the trees—and it was seldom the rifles were fired in vain. Four or five of the Americans were shot through the head as they leaned forward to fire, and after an hour's exchange of bullets, the attack ceased.

"What are they going to do now?" Harold asked.

"I expect they are going to wait till nightfall," Peter said. "There is no moon, and they will be able to work up all round the house. Then they'll make a rush together at the door and lower windows. We shall shoot down a good many on them; and then they'll burst their way in, or will set fire to the hut, and there'll be an end of it. That's what will happen."

"And you think there is no way of making our way out?" Harold asked.

"It's a mighty poor chance, if there is one at all," the hunter replied. "I should say by the fire there must be nigh a hundred of them now, and it is likely that by nightfall there will be three times as many. As soon as it gets dusk, they will creep out from the woods and form a circle round the house, and gradually work up to it. Now let us cook some vittals; we have had nothing to eat this morning yet, and it must be nigh eleven o'clock. I don't see why we should be starved, even if we have got to be killed to-night."

One of the party was left on watch on each side of the house, and the others gathered in the room below, where a fire was lit and the strips of dried deer-flesh which they carried were soon frying over it. Harold admired the air of indifference with which his companions set about preparing the meat. Every one was aware of the desperate nature of the position, but no allusion was made to it. The negro had caught the spirit of his companions, but his natural loquacity prevented his imitating their habitual silence.

"Dis bad affair, Master Harold," he said. "We just like so many coons up in tree, with a whole pack of dogs round us, and de hunters in de distance coming up with de guns. However, dis child reckon dat some ob dem hunters will get hit hard before dey get us. Jake don't care one bit for himself, massa, but he bery sorry to see you in such a fix."

"It can't be helped, Jake," Harold said, as cheerfully as he could. "It was my firing that shot which got us into it, and yet I cannot blame myself. We could not stand by and see those ruffians murder a woman and child."

"Dat's so, Massa Harold; der was no possinbility of seeing dat. I reckon dat when dose rascals come to climb de stairs, dey will find dat it are bery hard work."

"I don't think they will try, Jake; they are more likely to heap brushwood against the door and windows and set it alight, and then shoot us down as we rush out. This hut is not like the one I had to defend against the Irroquois. That was built to repel Indians' attacks; this is a mere squatter's hut."

After the meal was over, Peter and the Seneca chief went upstairs, looked through the loopholes, and talked long and earnestly together; then they rejoined the party below.

The defence of the hut.

"The chief and I are of opinion," Peter said to Harold, "that it are of no manner of use our waiting to be attacked here. They would burn us out to a sartinty; we should have no show of a fight at all. Anything is better than that. Now, what we propose is that directly it gets fairly dark, we should all creep out and make for the lake. Even ef they have formed their circle round us, they ain't likely to be as thick there as they are on the other side. What they will try to do, of course, is to prevent our taking to the forest; and there will be such a grist of them that I don't believe one of us would get through alive if we tried it. Now they will not be so strong towards the lake, and we might break through to the water. I don't say as there's much chance of our gitting away, for I tell you fairly that I don't believe that there's any chance at all; but the chief here and his braves don't want their scalps to hang in the wigwams of the Chippewas, and I myself, ef I had the choice, would rather be drowned than shot down. It don't make much difference, but of the two I had rather. Ef we can reach the lake, we can swim out of gunshot range. I know you can swim like a fish, and so can Jake, and the Indians swim as a matter of course. Ef we dive at first, we may get off; it will be so dark they won't see us with any sartinty beyond fifty yards. When we are once fairly out in the lake, we can take our chance."

"And is there a chance, Peter? Although, if there is none, I quite agree with you that I would rather be drowned than shot down. If one were sure of being killed by the first shot, that would be the easiest death; but if we were only wounded they would probably hang us in the morning."

"That's so," the hunter said. "Wall, I can hardly say that there is a chance; and yet I cannot say as how there ain't. In the first place, they may have some canoes and come out after us; there are pretty safe to be some along the shore here. The settlers would have had them for fishing."

"But what chance will that give us?" Harold asked.

"Wall," the hunter replied, "I reckon in that case as our chance is a fair one. Ef we dive and come up close alongside we may manage to upset one of them, and in that case we might get off. Wall, that's one chance. Then ef they don't come out in canoes we might swim three or four miles down the lake and take to land. They could not tell which way we should go, and would have to scatter over a long line; it's just possible as we might land without being seen. Once in the woods and we should be safe. So you see we have two chances. In course we must throw away our rifles and ammunition before we come to the water."

"At anyrate," Harold said, "the plan is a hopeful one; and I agree with you that it is a thousand times better to try it than it is to stop here with the certainty of being shot down before morning."

The afternoon passed quietly; a few shots were fired occasionally from the wood, and taunting shouts were heard of the fate which awaited them when night approached.

A vigilant watch was kept from the upper windows, but Peter thought that it was certain the enemy would make no move until it became perfectly dark, although they would establish a strong cordon all round the clearing in case the besieged should try and break out. Harold trembled with impatience to be off as the night grew darker and darker. It seemed to him that at any moment the assailants might be narrowing the circle round the house, and had he been the leader, he would have given the word long before the scout made a move.

At last Peter signalled that the time had come. It was perfectly dark when the bars were noiselessly removed from the door and the party stole out. Everything seemed silent, but the very stillness made the danger appear more terrible. Peter had impressed upon Harold and Jake the necessity for moving without making the slightest noise. As soon as they left the house, the whole party dropped on their hands and knees. Peter and the Seneca chief led the way; two of the braves came next. Harold and Jake followed; the remaining Indians crawled in the rear. Peter had told his comrades to keep as close as possible to the Indians in front of them, and, grasping their rifles, they crept along the ground. As they led the way, Peter and the Seneca carefully removed from before them every dried twig and threw it on one side.

The distance to be traversed from the hut to the water was about two hundred yards, and half of this was passed over before they encountered any obstacle. Then suddenly there was an exclamation, and Peter and the Seneca sprang to their feet as they came in contact with two men crawling in the opposite direction. They were too close to use their rifles, but a crushing blow from the Seneca's tomahawk cleft down the man in front of him, while Peter drew his long knife from the sheath and buried it in the body of his opponent.

The others had also leapt to their feet, and each as he did so fired at the dark figures which rose around them. They had the advantage of the surprise. Several scattered shots answered their volley; then, with their rifles clubbed, they rushed forward. For a moment there was a hand-to-hand fight. Harold had just struck down a man opposite to him when another sprang upon him; so sudden was the attack that he fell from the shock. But in an instant Jake buried his knife between his opponent's shoulders and dragged Harold to his feet.

"Run for your life, Massa Harold! De whole gang is upon us!"

And indeed the instant the first shot broke the silence of the woods, a babel of sounds arose from the whole circuit of the clearing; shouts and yells burst out from hundreds of throats. There was no further use for concealment, and from all sides the men who had been advancing to the attack rushed in the direction where the conflict was taking place. This, however, lasted but a few seconds. As Peter had expected, the line was thinner towards the lake than upon the other sides, and the rush of nine men had broken through it. Shouts were heard from the woods on either side extending down to the water, showing that the precaution had been taken by the assailants of leaving a portion of their force to guard the line of forest should the defenders break through the circle.

At headlong speed the little band rushed down to the water's edge, dropped their ammunition pouches by its edge, threw their rifles a few yards into the water, to be recovered, perhaps, on some future occasion, and then dived in. The nearest of the pursuers were some 30 yards behind when they neared the water's edge. Swimming as far under water as they could hold their breath, each came to the surface for an instant, and then again dived. Momentarily as they showed themselves they heard the rattle of musketry behind, and the bullets splashed thickly on the water. The night, however, was so dark that the fire could only be a random one. Until far out from the shore they continued diving, and then gathered together.

"We are pretty well out of range now," Peter said, "and quite out of sight of the varmint. Now we can wait a bit and see what they do next."

The enemy were still keeping up a heavy fire from the shore, hallooing and shouting to each other as they fancied they caught a glimpse of their enemies.

"There must be two or three hundred of them," Peter said. "We have fooled them nicely so far."

By the crashing of the bushes, the fugitives could hear strong parties making their way along the shore in either direction. An hour passed, during which the fugitives floated nearly opposite the clearing.

"Hallo!" Peter exclaimed presently. "There is a canoe coming along the lake. I expect they got it from Cameron's."

As he spoke, a canoe appeared round the point. Two men were standing up holding blazing torches. Two others paddled, while two, rifle in hand, sat by them. Almost at the same moment another canoe, similarly manned, pushed out from the shore immediately opposite.

"I wish we had known of that canoe," Peter said. "It would have saved us a lot of trouble; but we had no time for looking about. I suspected those settlers must have had one laid up somewheres. Now," he went on, "let's make our plans. The canoes are sure to keep pretty nigh each other. They will most likely think as we have gone down the lake, and will not be looking very sharply after us at present. It will never do to let them pass us. Now Jake and I, and two of the Injuns, will take one canoe, and the chief and three of his braves the other. We must move round so as to get between them and the shore, and then dive and come up close to them. Now, Harold, do you swim out a bit further and then make a splash so as to call their attention. Do it once or twice till you see that they have got their eyes turned that way. Then lie very quiet, so as to keep them watching for another sound. That will be our moment for attacking them."

They waited till the two canoes joined each other and paddled slowly out from shore. Then the eight swimmers started off to make their detour, while Harold swam quietly further out into the lake. The canoes were about 300 yards from shore, and were paddling very slowly, the occupants keeping a fixed look along the lake. There was perfect quiet on the shore now, and when Harold made a slight splash with his hand upon the water, he saw it was heard. Both canoes stopped rowing, the steerers in each case giving them a steer so that they lay broad-side to the land, giving each man a view over the lake. They sat as quiet as if carved in stone. Again Harold made a splash, but this time a very slight one, so slight that it could hardly reach the ears of the listeners.

A word or two was exchanged by the occupants of the boats.

"They are farther out on the lake, Bill," one said.

"I am not sure," another answered. "I rather think the sound was farther down. Listen again."

Again they sat motionless. Harold swam with his eyes fixed upon them. Every face was turned his way, and none were looking shoreward. Then, almost at the same instant, there was a shout from both boats. The men with torches seemed to lose their balance. The lights described a half circle through the air and were extinguished. A shout of astonishment broke from the occupants, mingled with the wild Seneca war-yell, and he knew that both canoes were upset.

There was the sound of a desperate struggle going on. Oaths and wild cries rose from the water. Heavy blows were struck, while from the shore arose loud shouts of dismay and rage. In two minutes all was quiet on the water. Then came Peter's shout—

"This way, Harold. We shall have the canoes righted and bailed in a minute. The varmin are all wiped out." With a lightened heart,

Harold swam toward the spot. The surprise had been a complete success. The occupants of the canoes, intent only upon the pursuit, and having no fear of attack—for they knew that the fugitives must have thrown away their rifles—were all gazing intently out on the lake, when, close to each canoe on the shore side, four heads rose from out of the water. In an instant eight hands had seized the gunwale, and before the occupants were aware of their danger, the canoes were upset.

Taken wholly by surprise, the Americans were no match for their assailants; the knives of the latter did their work before the frontiersmen had thoroughly grasped what had happened. Two or three, indeed, had made a desperate fight, but they were no match for their opponents, and the struggle was quickly over.

On Harold reaching the canoes, he found them already righted and half emptied of water. The paddles were picked up, and in a few minutes, with a derisive shout of adieu to their furious enemy on the shore, the two canoes paddled out into the lake. When they had attained a distance of about half a mile from the shore, they turned the boats' heads and paddled north. In three hours they saw lights in the wood.

"There are the troops," Peter said. "Soldiers are never content unless they are making fires big enough to warn every Red-skin within fifty miles that they are coming."

As they approached the shore, the challenge from the English sentinel came over the water:

"Who comes there?"

"Friends," Peter replied.

"Give the pass-word."

"How on arth am I to give the pass-word," Peter shouted back, "when we have been three days away from the camp?"

"If you approach without the pass-word, I fire," the sentinel said.

"I tell ye," Peter shouted, "we are scouts with news for the general!"

"I can't help who you are," the sentinel said. "I have got my orders."

185

"Pass the word along for an officer!" Harold shouted. "We have important news!"

The sentry called to the one next him, and so the word was passed along the line. In a few minutes an officer appeared on the shore, and after a short parley, the party were allowed to land, and Peter and Harold were at once conducted to the headquarters of General Burgoyne.

CHAPTER XIII
SARATOGA

WHAT is your report?" asked General Burgoyne, as the scouts were conducted into his tent.

"We have discovered, sir, that the Americans have strongly fortified Mount Independence, which faces Ticonderoga, and have connected the two places by a bridge across the river, which is protected by a strong boom. Both positions are, however, overlooked by Sugar Hill, and this they have entirely neglected to fortify. If you were to seize this, they would have to retire at once."

The general expressed his satisfaction at the news, and gave orders that steps should be taken to seize Sugar Hill immediately. He then questioned the scouts as to their adventures, and praised them highly for their conduct.

The next day the army advanced, and at nightfall both divisions were in their places, having arrived within an hour or two of each other from the opposite sides of the lake. Sugar Hill was seized the same night, and a strong party were set to work cutting a road through the trees. The next morning the enemy discovered the British at work erecting a battery on the hill, and their general decided to evacuate both Ticonderoga and Mount Independence instantly. Their baggage, provisions, and stores were embarked in 200 boats and sent up the river. The army started to march by the road.

The next morning the English discovered that the Americans had disappeared. Captain Lutwych immediately set to work to destroy the bridge and boom, whose construction had taken the Americans nearly twelve months' labour. By nine in the morning a passage was effected, and some gun-boats passed through in pursuit of the enemy's convoy. They overtook them near Skenesborough, engaged and captured many of their largest craft, and obliged them to set several others on fire, together with a large number of their boats and barges.

A few hours afterwards a detachment of British troops in gunboats came up the river to Skenesborough. The cannon on the works which the Americans had erected there opened fire, but the troops were landed, and the enemy at once evacuated their works, setting fire to their store-houses and mills. While these operations had been going on by water, Brigadier-general Fraser, at the head of the advance corps of grenadiers and light infantry, pressed hard upon the division of the enemy which had retired by the Hubberton Road, and overtook them at five o'clock in the morning.

The division consisted of 1500 of the best colonial troops under the command of Colonel Francis. They were posted on strong ground, and sheltered by breast-works composed of logs and old trees. General Fraser's detachment was inferior in point of numbers to that of the defenders of the position, but as he expected a body of the German troops under General Reidesel to arrive immediately, he at once attacked the breastworks. The Americans defended their post with great resolution and bravery. The reinforcements did not arrive so soon as was expected, and for some time the British made no way.

General Reidesel, hearing the fire in front, pushed forward at full speed with a small body of troops. Among these was the band, which he ordered to play.

The enemy, hearing the music, and supposing that the whole of the German troops had come up, evacuated the position, and fell back with precipitation. Colonel Francis and many others were killed, and 200 taken prisoners. On the English side 120 men were killed and wounded.

The enemy from Skenesborough were pursued by Col. Hill, with the 9th Regiment, and were overtaken near Fort Anne. Finding how small was the force that pursued them in comparison to their own, they took the offensive. A hot engagement took place, and after three hours' fighting, the Americans were repulsed with great slaughter and forced to retreat after setting fire to Fort Anne and Fort Edward.

In these operations the British captured 148 guns, with large quantities of stores. At Fort Edward, General Schuyler was joined by General St. Clair, but even with this addition the total American strength did not exceed 4400.

Instead of returning from Skenesborough to Ticonderoga, whence he might have sailed with his army up to Lake George, General Burgoyne proceeded to cut his way through the woods to the lake. The difficulties of the passage were immense: swamps and morasses had to be passed; bridges had to be constructed over creeks, ravines, and gulleys. The troops worked with great vigour and spirit. Major-general Phillips had returned to Lake George and transported the artillery, provisions, and baggage to Fort George, and thence by land to a point on the Hudson river, together with a large number of boats for the use of the army in their intended descent to Albany.

So great was the labour entailed by this work that it was not until the 30th of July that the army arrived on the Hudson river. The delay of three weeks had afforded the enemy time to recover their spirits and recruit their strength. General Arnold arrived with a strong reinforcement, and a force was detached to check the progress of Col. St. Leger, who was coming down from Montreal by way of Lake Ontario and the Mohawk river, to effect a junction with General Burgoyne.

General Burgoyne determined to advance at once. The army was already suffering from want of transport, and he decided to send a body of troops to Bennington, a place twenty-four miles to the eastward of the Hudson river, where the Americans had large supplies collected. Instead of sending light infantry, he despatched 600 Germans—the worst troops he could have selected for this purpose, as they were very heavily armed and marched exceedingly slowly. Several of the officers remonstrated with him, but with his usual infatuated obstinacy he maintained his disposition.

On approaching Bennington, Col. Baum, who commanded the Germans, found that a very strong force was gathered there. He sent back for reinforcements, and 500 more Germans, under Lieut.-col. Breyman, were despatched to his assistance. Long, however, before these slowly-moving troops could arrive, Col. Baum was attacked by the enemy in vastly superior numbers. The Germans fought with great bravery, and several times charged the Americans and drove them back. Fresh troops continued to come up on the enemy's side, and the Germans having lost a large number of men, including their colonel, were forced to retreat into the woods. The enemy then advanced against Col. Breyman, who was ignorant of the disaster that had befallen Baum, and with his detachment had occupied twenty-four hours in marching sixteen miles. The Germans again fought well, but, after a gallant resistance, were obliged to fall back. In these two affairs they lost 600 men.

In the meantime Col. St. Leger had commenced his attack upon Fort Stanwix, which was defended by 700 men. The American General Harkemar advanced with 1000 men to its relief. Col. St. Leger detached Sir John Johnson with a party of regulars and a number of Indians, who had accompanied him, to meet them. The enemy advanced incautiously and fell into an ambush. A terrible fire was poured into them, and the Indians then rushed down and attacked them hand to hand. The Americans, although taken by surprise, fought bravely, and succeeded in making their retreat, leaving 400 killed and wounded behind them.

Col. St. Leger had no artillery which was capable of making any impression on the defences of the fort. Its commander sent out a man, who, pretending to be a deserter, entered the British camp and informed Col. St. Leger that General Burgoyne had been defeated and his army cut to pieces, and that General Arnold, with 2000 men, was advancing to raise the siege. Col. St. Leger did not credit the news, but it created a panic among the Indians, the greater portion of whom at once retired without orders, and St. Leger, having but a small British force with him, was compelled to follow their example, leaving his artillery and stores behind him.

On the 13th of September General Burgoyne, having with immense labour collected thirty days' provisions on the Hudson, crossed the river by a bridge of boats and encamped on the heights of Saratoga. His movements had been immensely hampered by the vast train of artillery which he took with him. In an open country a powerful force of artillery is of the greatest service to an army, but

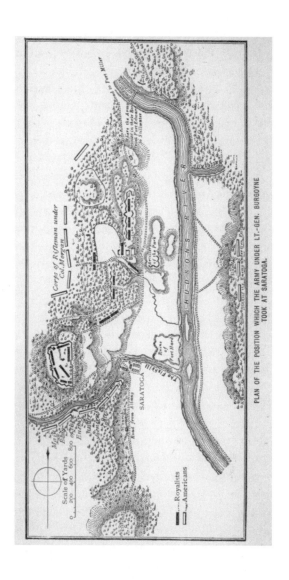

PLAN OF THE POSITION WHICH THE ARMY UNDER LT.-GEN. BURGOYNE TOOK AT SARATOGA.

in a campaign in a wooded and roadless country it is of little utility and enormously hampers the operations of an army. Had General Burgoyne, after the capture of Ticonderoga, pressed forward in light order without artillery, he could unquestionably have marched to New York without meeting with any serious opposition, but the six weeks' delay had enabled the Americans to collect a great force to oppose him.

On the 19th, as the army were advancing to Stillwater, 5000 of the enemy attacked the British right. They were led by General Arnold, and fought with great bravery and determination. The brunt of the battle fell on the 20th, 24th, and 62d Regiments. For four hours the fight continued without any advantage on either side, and at night-fall the Americans drew off, each side having lost about 600 men. After the battle of Stillwater the whole of the Indians with General Burgoyne left him and returned to Canada.

Hampered with his great train of artillery, unprovided with transport, in the face of a powerful enemy posted in an exceedingly strong position, General Burgoyne could neither advance nor retreat. The forage was exhausted, and the artillery horses were dying in great numbers. He had hoped that Sir William Howe would have sailed up the Hudson and joined him, but the English commander-in-chief had taken his army down to Philadelphia. Sir Henry Clinton, who commanded at New York, endeavoured with a small force at his command to make a diversion by operating against the American posts on the river Hudson, but this was of no utility.

Burgoyne's army was now reduced to little more than 5000 men, and he determined to fall back upon the lakes. Before doing this, however, it would be necessary to dislodge the Americans from their posts on his left. Leaving the camp under the command of General Hamilton, he advanced with 1500 men against them. Scarce had the detachment started when the enemy made a furious attack on the British left. Major Ackland, with the grenadiers, was posted here, and for a time defended himself with great bravery. The light infantry and 24th were sent to their assistance, but, overpowered by numbers, the left wing was forced to retreat into their intrenchments. These the enemy, led by General Arnold, at once attacked with great impetuosity. For a long time the result was doubtful, and it was not until the American leader was wounded that the attack ceased. In the meantime the intrenchments defended by the German troops under Colonel Breyman had also been attacked. Here the fight was obstinate, but the German intrenchments were carried, Colonel Breyman killed, and his troops retreated with the loss of all their baggage and artillery. Two hundred prisoners fell into the hands of the Americans.

That night the British army was concentrated on the heights above the hospital. General Gates, who commanded the Americans, moved his army so as to entirely inclose the British; and the latter, on the night of the 8th of October, retired to Saratoga, being obliged, however, to leave all their sick and wounded in hospital. These were treated with the greatest kindness by the Americans. An attempt was now made to retreat to Fort George or Fort Edward, but the Americans had taken up positions on each road and fortified them with cannon.

Only about 3500 fighting men now remained, of whom but one-half were British, and scarce eight days' provisions were left. The enemy, four times superior in point of numbers, held every line of retreat, and eluded every attempt of the British to force them to a general engagement.

The position was hopeless, and on the 13th of October a council of war was held, and it was determined to open negotiations for a surrender. Two days were spent in negotiations, and it was finally agreed that the army should lay down its arms, that it should be marched to Boston and there allowed to sail for England on condition of not serving again in North America during the contest. The Canadians were to be allowed to return at once to their own country. On the 16th the army laid down its arms. It consisted of 3500 fighting men and 600 sick, and nearly 2000 boatmen, teamsters, and other non-effectives.

Never did a general behave with greater incompetence than that manifested by General Burgoyne from the day of his leaving Ticonderoga; and the disaster which befell his army was entirely the result of mismanagement, procrastination, and faulty generalship.

Had Harold remained with the army until its surrender, his share in the war would have been at an end, for the Canadians, as well as all others who laid down their arms, gave their word of honour not to serve again during the war. He had, however, with Peter Lambton and Jake, accompanied Colonel Baum's detachment on its march to Bennington. Scouting in front of the column, they had ascertained the presence of large numbers of the enemy, and had, by hastening back with the news, enabled the German colonel to make some preparations for resistance before the attack burst upon him. During the fight that ensued, the scouts, posted behind trees on the German left, had assisted them to repel the attack from that quarter, and they had, when the Germans gave way, effected their escape into the woods, and managed to rejoin the army.

They had continued with it until it moved to the hospital heights after the disastrous attack by the Americans on their camp. General Burgoyne then sent for Peter Lambton, who was, he knew, one of his most active and intelligent scouts.

"Could you make your way through the enemy's lines down to Ticonderoga?" he asked.

"I could try, colonel," Peter said. "Me and the party who work with me could get through, if anyone could; but more nor that I can't say. The Yanks are swarming around pretty thick, I reckon; but if we have luck, we might make a shift to get through."

"I have hopes," the general said, "that another regiment, for which I asked General Carleton, has arrived there. Here is a letter to General Powell, who is in command, to beg him to march with all his available force, to fall upon the enemy posted on our line of communication. Unless the new regiment has reached him, he will not have a sufficient force to attempt this, but if this has come up, he may be enabled to do so. He is to march in the lightest order and at full speed, so as to take the enemy by surprise. Twelve hours before he starts, you will bring me back news of his coming, and I will move out to meet him. His operations in their rear will confuse the enemy, and enable me to operate with a greater chance of success. I tell you this because, if you are surrounded and in difficulties, you may have to destroy my despatch. You can then convey my instructions by word of mouth to General Powell, if you succeed in getting through."

Upon leaving headquarters Peter joined his friends.

"It's a risksome business," he went on, after informing them of the instructions he had received. "But I don't know as it is much more risksome than stopping here. It don't seem to me that this army is like to get out of the trap into which their general has led them. Whatever he wanted to leave the lakes for is more nor I can tell. However, generaling ain't my business, and I would not change places with the old man to-day, not for a big sum of money. Now, chief, what do you say? How is this 'ere business to be carried out?"

The Seneca, with the five braves who had from the first accompanied them, were now the only Indians with the British army. The rest of the Red-skins, disgusted with the dilatory progress of the army, and foreseeing inevitable disaster, had all betaken themselves to their homes. They were, moreover, angered at the severity with which the English general endeavoured to suppress their tendency to acts of cruelty on the defenceless settlers. The Red-skin has no idea of civilized warfare. His sole notion of fighting is to kill, burn, and destroy, and the prohibition of all irregular operations, and of the infliction of unnecessary suffering, was in his eyes an act of incomprehensible weakness. The Seneca chief remained with the army simply because his old comrade did so. He saw that there was little chance of plunder, but he and his braves had succeeded, in fair fight, in obtaining many scalps, and would, at least, be received with high honour on their return to their tribe.

A long discussion took place between the chief and Peter before they finally decided upon the best course to be pursued. They were ignorant of the country, and of the disposition of the enemy's force, and could therefore only decide to act upon general principles. They thought it probable that the Americans would be most thickly posted upon the line between the British army and the lakes, and their best chance of success would therefore be to make their way straight ahead for some distance, and then, when they had penetrated the American lines, to make a long detour round to the lakes.

Taking four days' provisions with them, they started when nightfall had fairly set in. It was intensely dark, and in the shadows of the woods, Harold was unable to see his hand before him. The Indians, however, appeared to have a faculty of seeing in the dark, for they advanced without the slightest pause or hesitation, and were soon in the open country. The greatest vigilance was now necessary. Everywhere they could hear the low hum which betokens the presence of many men gathered together. Sometimes a faint shout came to their ears, and for a long distance around, the glow in the sky told of many fires. The party now advanced with the greatest caution, frequently halting while the Indians went on ahead to scout, and more than once they were obliged to alter their direction as they came upon bodies of men posted across their front. At last they passed through the line of sentinels and, avoiding all the camps, gained the country in the Americans' rear.

They now struck off to the right, and by daybreak were far round beyond the American army, on their way to Ticonderoga. They had walked for fifteen hours when they halted, and it was not until late in the afternoon that they continued their journey. They presently struck the road which the army had cut in its advance and, keeping parallel with this through the forest, they arrived the next morning at Fort Edward. A few hours' rest here and they continued their march to Ticonderoga. This place had been attacked by the Americans a few days previously, but the garrison had beaten off the assailants.

On the march they had seen many bodies of the enemy moving along the road, but their approach had in every case been detected in time to take refuge in the forest. On entering the fort, Peter at once proceeded to General Powell's quarters, and delivered the despatch with which he had been intrusted. The general read it.

"No reinforcements have arrived," the general said, "and the force here is barely sufficient to defend the place; and it would be madness for me to set out on such a march with the handful of troops at my disposal."

He then questioned Peter concerning the exact position of the army, and the latter had no hesitation in saying that he thought the whole force would be forced to lay down their arms, unless some reinforcements reached them from below.

This, however, was not to be. General Clinton captured Forts Montgomery and Clinton, the latter a very strong position, defended with great resolution by 400 Americans. The 7th and 26th Regiments, and a company of grenadiers, attacked on one side, the 63d Regiment on the other. They had no cannon to cover their advance, and had to cross ground swept by ten pieces of artillery. In no event during the war did the British fight with more resolution. Without firing a shot they pressed forward to the foot of the works, climbed over each others' shoulders on to the walls, and drove the enemy back. The latter discharged one last volley into the troops and then laid down their arms. Notwithstanding the slaughter effected by this wanton fire after all possibility of continuing a resistance was over, quarter was given, and not one of the enemy was killed after the fort was taken. The British loss was 140 killed and wounded; 300 Americans were killed, wounded, and taken prisoners. The fleet attacked the American squadron on the river and entirely destroyed it. Beyond sending a flying squadron up the river to destroy the enemy's boats and stores of provisions, nothing further could be done to effect a diversion in favour of General Burgoyne.

Four days after Harold's arrival at Ticonderoga, the news of the surrender of General Burgoyne reached the place. Upon the following day he suggested to Peter Lambton that they should visit the clearing of the ex-soldier Cameron, and see whether their interference had saved him and his family. Upon arriving at the spot whence Harold had fired the shot which had brought discovery upon them, they saw a few charred stumps alone remaining of the snug house which had stood there. In front of it, upon the stump of a tree, Cameron himself was sitting, in an attitude of utter depression.

They walked across the clearing to the spot, but although the sound of their footsteps must have reached his ear, the man did not look up until Harold touched him on the shoulder.

"What has happened?" he asked. "Who has done this ruin?"

The man still remained with his head bent down, as if he had not heard the question.

"We had hoped that you had escaped," Harold went on. "We were hidden in the wood when we saw those ruffians drive your wife and daughter out, and it was the shot from my rifle that killed their leader and brought them down on us—and a narrow escape we had of it—but we hoped that we had diverted them from their determination to kill you and your family."

Cameron looked up now. "I thank ye, sir," he said. "I thank ye wi' a' my hairt for your interference on our behalf. I heerd how closely ye were beset that night, and how ye escaped. They thought na' mair o' us, and when the royal army arrived the next day, we were safe; but ye might as weel ha' let the matter gang on—better, indeed, for then I should be deed instead o' suffering. This wark"— and he pointed towards the remains of the house—"is Red-skin devilry. A fortnight sin' a band o' Indians fell upon us. I was awa'. They killed my wife and burned my house, and ha' carried off my bairn."

"Who were they?" Harold asked.

"I dinna ken," Cameron replied; "but a neebour o' mine whose place they attacked, and whom they had scalped and left for deed, told me that they were a band o' the Irroquois who had come down from Lake Michigan and advanced wi' the British. He said that they, with the other Red-skins, desairted when their hopes o' plunder were disappointed, and that on their way back to their tribes they burnt and ravaged every settlement they came across. My neebour was an old frontiersman; he had fought against the tribe, and knew their war-cry. He deed the next day. He was mair lucky than I am."

"The tarnal ruffians!" Peter exclaimed. "The murdering varmint! And to think of them carrying off that purty little gal of yours! I suppose by this time they are at their old game of plundering

Donald Cameron's despair.

and slaying on the frontier. It's nought to them which side they fight on. Scalps and plunder is all that they care for."

The unfortunate settler had sat down again on the log, the picture of a broken-hearted man. Harold drew Peter a short distance away.

"Look here, Peter," he said. "Now Burgoyne's army has surrendered and winter is close at hand, it is certain that there will be no further operations here, except perhaps that the Americans will recapture the place. What do you say to our undertaking an expedition on our own account to try and get back this poor fellow's daughter? I do not know whether the Seneca would join us; but we three—of course I count Jake—and the settler might do something. I have an old grudge against these Irroquois myself, as you have heard; and, for ought I know, they may long ere this have murdered my cousins."

"The Seneca will join," Peter said, "willing enough. There is an old feud between his tribe and the Irroquois. He will join fast enough. But mind, youngster, this ain't no child's play; it ain't like fighting those American clodhoppers. We shall have to deal with men as sharp as ourselves, who can shoot as well, hear as well, see as well, who are in their own country, and who are a hundred to one against us. We have got hundreds and hundreds of miles to travel afore we gets near them. It's a big job; but if, when ye thinks it all over, you are ready to go, Peter Lambton ain't the man to hold back. As you say, there is nought to do this winter, and we might as well be doing this as anything else."

The two men then went back to the settler.

"Cameron," Harold said, "it is of no use sitting here grieving. Why not be up in pursuit of those who carried off your daughter?"

The man sprang to his feet. "In pursuit!" he cried fiercely. "In pursuit! Do ye think Donald Cameron wad be sitting here quietly if he kenned where to look for his daughter—where to find the murderers o' his wife? But what can I do? For three days after I cam' back and found what had happened, I was just mad. I could na think nor rest, nor do ought but throw mysel on the ground and pray to God to tak' me. When at last I could think, it was too late. It wad ha'e mattered naething to me that they were a hundred to one. If I could ha' killed but one o' them I wad ha' died happy; but they were gone, and how could I follow them—how could I find them? Tell me where to look, mon—show me the way, and if it be to the ends o' the airth, I will go after them."

"We will do more than that," Harold said. "My friends and myself have still with us the six men who were with us when we were here before. Five are Senecas, the other a faithful negro, who would go through fire and water for me. There is little chance of our services being required during the winter with the British army. We are interested in you and in the pretty child we saw here, and if you will, will accompany you in the search for her. Peter Lambton knows the country well, and if anyone could lead you to your child and rescue her from those who carried her off, he is the man."

"Truly!" gasped the Scotchman. "And will ye truly gang wi' me to find my bairn? May the guid God o' heaven bless you!" and the tears ran down his cheeks.

"Gather your traps together at once, man," Peter said. "Let us go straight back to the fort; then I will set the matter before the chief, who will, I warrant me, be glad enough to join in the expedition. It's too late to follow the track of the red varmint. Our best plan will be to make straight for the St. Lawrence, to take a boat if we can get one—if not, two canoes—and to make up the river and along Ontario. Then we must sell our boat, cross to Erie, and then get fresh canoes and go on by Detroit into Lake Huron, and so up in the country of these reptiles. We shall have no difficulty, I reckon, in discovering the whereabouts of the tribe which has been away on this expedition."

The Scotchman took up the rifle. "I am ready," he said, and without another word the party started for the fort.

Upon their arrival there a consultation was held with the Seneca. The prospect of an expedition against his hereditary foes filled him with delight, and three of his braves also agreed to accompany them. Jake received the news with the remark: "All right, Massa Harold; it make no odds to dis chile war he goes. You have said de word; Jake ready."

Half an hour sufficed for making the preparations, and they at once proceeded to the point where they had hidden the two canoes on the night when they joined General Burgoyne before his advance upon Ticonderoga. These were soon floating on the lake, and they started to paddle to the mouth of the Sorrel and down this river into the St. Lawrence, and thence to Montreal. Their rifles they had recovered from the lake upon the day following that on which Ticonderoga was first captured, Deer-Tail having despatched to the spot two of his braves, who recovered them without difficulty by diving, and brought them back to the fort.

At Montreal they stayed but a few hours. An ample supply of ammunition was purchased, and provisions sufficient for the voyage; and then, embarking in the two canoes, they started up the St. Lawrence. It was three weeks later when they arrived at Detroit, which was garrisoned by a British force. Here they heard that there had been continuous troubles with the Indians on the frontier, that a great many farms and settlements had been destroyed, and numbers of persons murdered.

Their stay at Detroit was a short one. Harold obtained no news of his cousins, but there were so many tales told of Indian massacres that he was filled with apprehension on their account. His worst apprehensions were justified when the canoes at length came within sight of the well-remembered clearing. Harold gave a cry as he saw that the farm house no longer existed. The two canoes were headed towards shore, and their occupants disembarked and walked towards the spot where the house had stood. The site was marked by a heap of charred embers. The outhouses had been destroyed, and a few fowls were the only living things to be seen in the fields.

"This here business must have taken place some time ago," Peter said, breaking the silence. "A month, I should say, or perhaps more."

For a time Harold was too moved to speak. The thought of his kind cousins and their brave girl all murdered by the Indians filled him with deep grief. At last, however, he said, "What makes you think so, Peter?"

"It is easy enough to see as it was after the harvest, for ye see the fields is all clear. On the other hand, there is long grass shooting up through the ashes. It would take a full month, perhaps six weeks, afore it would do that. Don't you think so, chief?"

The Seneca nodded. "A moon," he said.

"Yes, about a month," replied Peter. "The grass grows quick after the rains."

"Do you think that it was a surprise, Peter?

"No man can tell," the hunter answered. "If we had seen the place soon afterwards, we might have told. There would have been marks of blood. Or if the house had stood, we could have told by the bullet holes and the colour of the splintered wood, how it happened, and how long back. As it is, not even the chief can give yer an idea."

"Not an attack," the Seneca said; "a surprise."

"How on arth do you know that, chief?" the hunter exclaimed in surprise, and he looked round in search of some sign which would have enabled the Seneca to have given so confident an opinion. "You must be a witch surely."

"A chief's eyes are not blind," the Red-skin answered, with a slight smile of satisfaction at having for once succeeded when his white comrade was at fault. "Let my friend look up the hill: two dead men there."

Harold looked in the direction in which the chief pointed, but could see nothing. The hunter, however, exclaimed:

"There is something there, chief, but even my eyes could not tell they were bodies!"

The party proceeded to the spot and found two skeletons; a few remnants of clothes lay around, but the birds had stripped every particle of flesh from the bones. There was a bullet in the forehead of one skull, the other was cleft with a sharp instrument.

"It is clear enough," the hunter said; "there has been a surprise. Likely enough the hull lot were killed without a shot being fired in defence."

203

CHAPTER XIV
RESCUED

HAROLD was deeply touched at the evidences of the fate which had befallen the occupants of his cousin's plantation.

"If there are any more of these to be found," pointing to their remains, "we might find out for a certainty whether the same fate befell them all."

The Seneca spoke a word to his followers and the four Indians spread themselves over the clearing. One more body was found: it was lying down near the water as if killed in the act of making for the canoe.

"The others are probably there," Peter said, pointing to the ruins. "The three hands were killed in the fields, and most likely the attack was made at the same moment on the house. Indeed, I am pretty sure that it was so, for the body by the water lies face downwards with his head towards the lake. He was no doubt shot from behind as he was running. There must have been Injuns round the house then, or he would have made for that instead of the water."

The Seneca touched Peter on the shoulder and pointed towards the farm. A figure was seen approaching. As it came nearer they could see that he was a tall man dressed in the deer-skin shirt and leggings usually worn by hunters. As he came near, Harold gave an exclamation: "It is Jack Pearson!"

"It are Jack Pearson," the hunter said, "though for the moment I can't recollect yer—though yer face seems known. Why," he exclaimed in changed tones, "it's that boy Harold growed into a man!"

"It is," Harold replied, grasping the frontiersman's hand.

"And ye may know me too," Peter Lambton said, "though it's twenty years since we fought side by side against the Mohawks."

"Why, old hoss, are you above ground still?" the hunter exclaimed heartily. "I am glad to see you again, old friend. And what are you doing here, you and Harold and these Senecas? For they is Senecas, sure enough. I have been in the woods for the last hour, and have been puzzling myself nigh to death. I seed them Injuns going about over the clearing sarching, and for the life of me I could not think what they were adoing. Then I seed them gathered down here, with two white men among them, so I guessed it was right to show myself."

"They were searching to see how many had fallen in this terrible business," Harold said, pointing to the ruins.

The hunter shook his head. "I am feared they have all gone under. I were here a week afterwards; it were just as it is now. I found the three hands lying killed and sculped in the fields; the others, I reckon, is there. I has no doubt at all about Bill Welch and his wife, but it may be that the gal has been carried off."

"Do you think so?" Harold exclaimed eagerly. "If so, we may find her too with the other."

"What other?" Pearson asked.

Harold gave briefly an account of the reason which had brought them to the spot, and of the object they had in view.

"You can count me in," Pearson said. "There is just a chance that Nelly Welch may be in their hands still; and in any case I am longing to draw a lead on some of the varment to pay 'em for this," and he looked round him, "and a hundred other massacres round this frontier."

"I am glad to hear ye say so," Peter replied. "I expected as much of ye, Jack. I don't know much of this country, having only hunted here for a few weeks, and with a party of Delawares, twenty years afore the Irroquois moved so far west."

"I know pretty nigh every foot of it," Jack Pearson said. "When the Irroquois were quiet, I used to do a deal of hunting in their country. It are good country for game."

"Well, shall we set out at once?" Harold asked, impatient to be off.

"We cannot move to-night," Pearson answered, and Harold saw that Peter and the Indians agreed with him.

"Why not?" he asked. "Every hour is of importance."

"That is so," Peter said; "but there is no going out on the lake to-night. In half an hour we shall have our first snow-storm, and by morning it will be two foot deep."

Harold turned his eyes towards the lake and saw what his companions had noticed long before. The sky was overcast, and a thick bank of hidden clouds was rolling up across the lake, and the thick mist seemed to hang between the clouds and the water. "That's snow," Peter said. "It is late this year, and I would give my pension if it were a month later."

"That is so," Pearson said. "Snow ain't never pleasant in the woods, but when you are scouting round among Indians it are a caution. We'd best make a shelter before it comes on."

The two canoes were lifted from the water, unloaded, and turned bottom upward; a few charred planks which had formed part of the roof of the outhouses were brought and put up to form a sort of shelter. A fire was lit and a meal prepared. By this time the snow had begun to fall. After the meal was over, pipes were lit, and the two hunters earnestly talked over their plans, the Seneca chief throwing in a few words occasionally; the others listened quietly. The Indians left the matter in the hands of their chief, while Harold and Cameron knew that the two frontiersmen did not need any suggestion from them. As to Jake, the thought of asking questions never entered his mind. He was just at present less happy than usual, for the negro, like most of his race, hated cold, and the prospect of wandering through the woods in deep snow made him shudder, as he crouched close to the great fire that they had built.

Peter and Jack Pearson were of opinion that it was exceedingly probable that the Welches had been destroyed by the very band which had carried off little Janet Cameron. The bodies of Indians who had been on the war-path with the army had retired some six weeks before, and it was about that time Pearson said that the attack on the settlements had been made.

RESCUED

"I heard some parties of Red-skins who had been with the British troops had passed through the neighbourhood, and there were reports that they were greatly dissatisfied with the results of the campaign. As likely as not some of that band may have been consarned in the attack on this place three years ago, and passing nigh it, may have determined to wipe out that defeat. An Injun never forgives. Many of their braves fell here, and they could scarcely bring a more welcome trophy back to their villages than the scalps of Welch and his men."

"Now, the first thing to do," Peter said, "is to find out what particular chief took his braves with him to the wars. Then we have got to find his village, and there, likely enough, we shall find Cameron's daughter, and maybe the girl from here. How old was she?"

"About fifteen," Pearson said; "and a fine girl, and a pretty girl too. I dun know," he went on, after a pause, "which of the chiefs took part in the war across the lakes, but I suspect it were War Eagle. There are three great chiefs, and the other two were trading on the frontier. It was War Eagle who attacked the place afore, and would be the more likely to attack it again if he came anywhere near it. He made a mess of it before, and would be burning to wipe out his failure if he had a chance."

"Where is his place?"

"His village is the furthest of them all from here. He lives up near the falls of Sault Ste Marie, between Lake Superior and Huron. It is a village with nigh three hundred wigwams."

"It ain't easy to see how it's to be done. We must make to the north shore of the lake. There will be no working down here through the woods; but it's a pesky difficult job, about as hard a one as ever I took part in."

"It is that," Pearson said; "it can't be denied. To steal two white girls out of a big Indian village ain't a easy job at no time, but with the snow on the ground it comes as nigh to an impossibility as anything can do."

For another hour or two they talked over the route they should take, and their best mode of proceeding. Duncan Cameron sat and listened with an intent face to every word. Since he had joined them he had spoken but seldom; his whole soul was taken up with the thought of his little daughter. He was ever ready to do his share, and more than his share, of the work of paddling and at the portages, but he never joined in conversation; and of an evening, when the others sat round the fire, he would move away and pace backwards and forwards in anxious thought until the fire burned low and the party wrapped themselves in their blankets and went off to sleep.

All the time the conversation had been going on, the snow had fallen heavily, and before it was concluded, the clearing was covered deep with the white mantle. There was little wind, and the snow fell quietly and noiselessly. At night the Indians lay down round the fire, while the white men crept under the canoes, and were soon fast asleep. In the morning it was still snowing, but about noon it cleared up. It was freezing hard, and the snow glistened as the sun burst through the clouds. The stillness of the forest was broken now by sharp cracking sounds, as boughs of trees gave way under the weight of snow; in the open it lay more than two feet deep.

"Now," Peter said, "the sooner we are off the better."

"I will come in my own canoe," Pearson said. "One of the Injuns can come with me, and we shall keep up with the rest."

"There is room for you in the other canoes," Harold said.

"Plenty of room," the hunter answered. "But you see, Harold, the more canoes the better. There ain't no saying how closely we may be chased, and by hiding up the canoes at different places, we give ourselves so much more chance of being able to get to one or the other. They are all large canoes, and at a pinch any one of them might hold the hull party, with the two gals thrown in. But," he added to Harold, in a low voice, "don't you build too much on these gals, Harold. I would not say so while that poor fellow is listening, but the chance is a desperate poor one, and I shall think we are mighty lucky ef we don't leave all our scalps in that ere Red-skin village."

The traps were soon placed in the canoes, and just as the sun burst out, the three boats started. It was a long and toilsome journey.

RESCUED

Stormy weather set in, and they were obliged to wait for days by the lake till its surface calmed. On these occasions they devoted themselves to hunting, and killed several deer. They knew that there were no Indian villages near, and in such weather it would be impossible that any Red-skins would be in the woods. They were enabled, therefore, to fire without fear of the reports betraying their presence. The Senecas took the opportunity of fabricating snow-shoes for the whole party, as these would be absolutely necessary for walking in the woods. Harold, Jake, and Duncan Cameron at once began to practise their use. The negro was comical in the extreme in his first attempts, and shouted so loudly with laughter each time that he fell head-foremost into the snow that Peter said to him angrily, "Look ye here, Jake, it's dangerous enough letting off a rifle at a deer in these woods, but it has to be done because we must lay in a supply of food, but a musket-shot is a mere whisper to yer shouting. Thunder ain't much louder than you laughing—it shakes the hull place, and might be heard from here well nigh to Montreal. Ef you can't keep that mouth of yours shut, ye must give up the idee of learning to use them shoes, and must stop in the canoe while we are scouting on shore."

Jake promised to amend, and from this time, when he fell in the soft snow-wreaths, he gave no audible vent to his amusement, but a pair of great feet, with the snow-shoes attached, could be seen waving above the surface, until he was picked up and righted again.

Harold soon learned, and Cameron went at the work with grim earnestness. No smile ever crossed his face at his own accidents or at the wild vagaries of Jake, which excited silent amusement even among the Indians. In a short time the falls were less frequent, and by the time they reached the spot where they were determined to cross the lake—at the point where Huron and Michigan join— the three novices were able to make fair progress in the snow-shoes.

The spot fixed upon was about twelve miles from the village of War Eagle, and the canoes were hidden at distances of three miles apart. First Pearson, Harold, and Cameron disembarked; Jake, Peter, and one of the Indians alighted at the next point; and the

Seneca chief and two of his followers proceeded to the spot nearer to the Indian village. Each party as they landed struck straight into the woods, to unite at a point eight miles from the lake and as many from the village. The hunters had agreed that should any Indians come across the tracks, less suspicion would be excited than would have been the case were they found skirting the river, as it might be thought that they were made by Indians out hunting.

Harold wondered how the other parties would find the spot to which Pearson had directed them, but in due time all arrived at the rendezvous. After some search a spot was found where the underwood grew thickly, and there was an open place in the centre of the clump. In this the camp was established. It was composed solely of a low tent of about two feet high, made of deers' hides sewed together, and large enough to shelter them all. The snow was cleared away, sticks were driven into the frozen ground, and strong poles laid across them; the deer-skin was then laid flat upon these. The top was little higher than the general level of the snow, an inch or two of snow was scattered over it, and to anyone passing outside the bushes the tent was completely invisible.

The Indians now went outside the thicket and with great care obliterated, as far as possible, the marks upon the snow. This could not be wholly done, but it was so far complete that the slightest wind which would send a drift over the surface would wholly conceal all traces of passage.

They had before crossing the lake cooked a supply of food sufficient for some days. Intense as was the cold outside, it was perfectly warm in the tent. The entrance as they crept into it was closed with a blanket, and in the centre a lamp, composed of deer's fat in a calabash with a cotton wick, gave a sufficient light.

"What is the next move?" Harold asked.

"The chief will start, when it comes dusk, with Pearson," Peter said. "When they get close to the village he will go in alone. He will paint Irroquois before he goes."

"Cannot we be near at hand to help them in case of a necessity?" Harold asked.

"No," Peter said. "It would be no good at all. If it comes to fighting they are fifty to one, and the lot of us would have no more chance than two. If they are found out, which ain't likely, they must run for it, and they can get over the snow a deal faster than you could, to say nothing of Cameron and Jake. They must shift for themselves and will make straight for the nearest canoe. In the forest they must be run down sooner or later, for their tracks would be plain. No, they must go alone."

When night came on, the Seneca produced his paints, and one of his followers marked his face and arms with the lines and flourishes in use by the Irroquois; then, without a word of adieu, he took his rifle and glided out from the tent, followed by Pearson. Peter also put on his snow-shoes and prepared to follow.

"I thought you were going to stay here, Peter."

"No, I am going half-way with them. I shall be able to hear the sound of a gun. Then, in case they are trapped, we must make tracks for the canoes at once, for after following them to the lake, they are safe to take up their back track to see where they have come from; so ef I hear a gun I shall make back here as quick as I can come."

When the three men had started, silence fell on the tent. The Red-skins at once lay down to sleep, and Jake followed their example. Harold lay quiet, thinking over the events which had happened to him in the last three years, while Cameron lay with his face turned towards the lamp with a set anxious look on his face. Several times he crawled to the entrance and listened when the crack made by some breaking bough came to his ear. Hours passed, and at last Harold dozed off, but Cameron's eyes never closed until about midnight the blanket at the entrance moved and Peter entered.

"Hae ye seen the others?" Cameron exclaimed.

"No, and were not likely to," Peter answered. "It was all still to the time I came away, and afore I moved I was sure they must have left the village. They won't come straight back, bless yer; they will go away in the opposite direction and make a sweep miles round. They may not be here for hours yet; not that there is much chance of their tracks being traced. It has not snowed for over a week, and the snow round the village must be trampled thick for a mile and more—with the squaws coming and going for wood, and the hunters going out on the chase. I have crossed a dozen tracks or more on my way back. If it were not for that, we darn't have gone at all, for if the snow was new fallen the sight of fresh tracks would have set the first Injun that came along a wondering; and when a Red-skin begins to wonder, he sets to, to ease his mind at once by finding out all about it, ef it takes him a couple of days' sarch to do so. No, you can lie down now for some hours; they won't be here till morning."

So saying, the scout set the example by wrapping himself up and going to sleep, but Cameron's eyes never closed until the blanket was drawn on one side again, and in the gray light of the winter morning, the Seneca and Pearson crawled into the tent.

"What news?" Harold asked, for Cameron was too agitated to speak.

"Both gals are there," Pearson answered.

An exclamation of thankfulness broke from Harold and a sob of joy issued from the heart of the Scotchman, and for a few minutes his lips moved, as he poured forth his silent thankfulness to God.

"Wall, tell us all about it," Peter said. "I can ask the chief any questions afterwards."

"We went on straight enough to the village," the hunter began. "It are larger than when I saw it last, and War Eagle's influence in the tribe must have increased. I didn't expect to find no watch, the Red-skins having, so far as they knew, no enemies within 500 miles of them. There were a lot of fires burning and plenty of Red-skins moving about among them. We kept on till we could get quite close, and then we lay up for a time below a tree at the edge of the clearing. There were a sight too many of them about for the Seneca to go in yet a while. About half an hour arter we got there we saw two white gals come out of one of the wigwams and stand for a while to warm theirselves by one of the fires. The tallest of the two, well nigh a woman, was Nelly Welch; I knew her, in course. The other was three or four years younger, with yaller hair over her shoulders. Nelly seemed quiet and sad like, but the other seemed more at home—she laughed with some of the Red-skin gals, and even joined in their play. You see," he said, turning to Cameron, "she had been captured longer, and children's spirits soon rise again. Arter a while they went back to the wigwam. When the fires burned down, and the crowd thinned, and there was only a few left sitting in groups round the embers, the Seneca started. For a long time I saw nothing of him, but once or twice I thought I saw a figure moving among the wigwams. Presently the fires burnt quite down and the last Indian went off. I had begun to wonder what the chief was doing, when he stood beside me. We made tracks at once, and have been tramping in a long circle all night. The chief can tell you his part of the business hisself."

"Well, chief, what have you found out?" Peter asked.

The Indian answered in his native tongue, which Peter interpreted from time to time for the benefit of his white companions:

"When Deer-Tail left the white hunter he went into the village. It was no use going among the men, and he went round by the wigwams and listened to the chattering of the squaws. The tribe were all well contented, for the band brought back a great deal of plunder which they had picked up on their way back from the army. They had lost no braves, and every one was pleased. The destruction of the settlement of the white man who had repulsed them before was a special matter for rejoicing. The scalps of the white man and his wife are in the village. War Eagle's son, the Young Elk, is going to marry the white girl. There are several of the braves whose heads have been turned by her white skin and by her bright eyes, but the Young Elk is going to have her. There have been great feastings and rejoicings since the return of the warriors, but they are to be joined to-morrow by the Beaver's band, and then they will feast again. When all was quiet I went to the wigwam where the white girls are confined. An old squaw and two of War Eagle's daughters are with them. Deer-Tail had listened while they prepared for rest, and knew on which side of the wigwam the tall white maiden slept. He thought that she would be awake. Her heart would be sad, and sleep would not come to her soon, so he crept round there and cut a slit in the skin close to where she lay. He put his head in at the hole, and whispered, 'Do not let the white girl be afraid; it is a friend. Does she hear him?' She whispered, 'Yes.' 'Friends are near,' he said. 'The young warrior Harold, whom she knows, and others, are at hand to take her away. The Irroquois will be feasting to-morrow night. When she hears the cry of a night-owl, let her steal away with her little white sister and she will find her friends waiting.' Then Deer-Tail closed the slit and stole away to his friend the white hunter. I have spoken."

"Just what I expected of you, chief," Peter said warmly. "I thought as how you would manage to get speech to them somehow. If there is a feast to-night it is hard ef we don't manage to get them off."

"I suppose we must lie still all day, Peter."

"You must so," the hunter said. "Not a soul must show his nose outside the tent except that one of the Red-skins will keep watch to be sure that no straggler has come across our tracks and followed them up. Ef he were to do that he might bring the hull gang down upon us. Yer had best get as much sleep as yer can, for yer don't know when yer may get another chance."

At nightfall the whole party issued from the tent and started towards the Indian village. All arrangements had already been made. It was agreed that Pearson and the Seneca should go up to the village, the former being chosen because he was known to Nelly. Peter and one of the Red-skins were to take post a hundred yards farther back, ready to give assistance in case of alarm, while the rest were to remain about half a mile distant. Cameron had asked that he might go with the advance party, but upon Peter pointing out to him that his comparatively slow rate of progression in snow-shoes would, in case of discovery, lead to the recapture of the girls, he at once agreed to the decision. If the flight of the girls was discovered soon after leaving the camp, it was arranged that the Seneca and Peter should hurry at once with them to the main body, while the other two Indians should draw off their pursuers in another direction. In the event of anything occurring to excite the suspicion of the Indians before there was a chance of the girls being brought safely to the main body, they were to be left to walk quietly back to camp, as they had nothing to fear from the Indians. Peter and the Seneca were then to work round by a circuitous route to the boat, where they were to be joined by the main body, and to draw off until another opportunity offered for repeating the attempt.

It was eight o'clock in the evening when Pearson and the Seneca approached the village. The fires were burning high, and seated round them were all the warriors of the tribe; a party were engaged in a dance representing the pursuit and defeat of an enemy. The women were standing in an outer circle clapping their hands and raising their voices in loud cries of applause and excitement as the dance became faster and faster. The warriors bounded high, brandishing their tomahawks. A better time could not have been chosen for the evasion of the fugitives. Nelly Welch stood close to a number of Indian girls, but slightly behind them. She held the hand of little Janet Cameron.

Although she appeared to share in the interest of the Indians in the dance, a close observer would have had no difficulty in perceiving that Nelly was preoccupied. She was, indeed, intently listening for the signal. She was afraid to move from among the others lest her absence should be at once detected, but so long as the noise was going on, she despaired of being able to hear the signal agreed upon. Presently an Indian brave passed close to her, and as he did so whispered in her ear in English, "Behind your wigwam—friends there." Then he passed on and moved round the circle as if intending to take his seat at another point.

The excitement of the dance was momentarily increasing, and the attention of the spectators was riveted to the movements of the performers. Holding Janet's hand, Nelly moved noiselessly away from the place where she had been standing. The movement was unnoticed, as she was no longer closely watched—a flight in the depth of winter appearing impossible. She kept round the circle till no longer visible from the spot she had left. Then, leaving the crowd, she made her way towards the nearest wigwams. Once behind these, the girl stole rapidly along under their shelter until they stood behind that which they usually habited. Two figures were standing there. They hesitated for a moment, but one of them advanced.

"Jack Pearson!" Nelly exclaimed, with a low cry of gladness.

"Just that same, Nelly, and right glad to see you. But we have no time for greeting now; the hull tribe may be after us in another five minutes. Come along, pretty," he said, turning to Janet, "you will find somebody yer know close at hand."

Two minutes later the child was in her father's arms, and after a moment's rapturous greeting between father and child, and a very delighted one between Nelly Welch and her cousin Harold, the flight was continued.

"How long a start do you think we may have?"

"Half an hour maybe. The women may be some time afore they miss her, and they will sarch for her everywhere afore they give the alarm, as they will be greatly blamed for their carelessness."

There had been a pause in the flight for a few seconds when the Seneca and Pearson arrived with the girls at the point where Peter and the other Indians were posted, two hundred yards from the camp. Up to this point the snow was everywhere thickly trampled, but as the camp was left farther behind, the footprints would naturally become more scarce. Here Pearson fastened to the girls' feet two pairs of large moccasins; inside these, wooden soles had been placed. They therefore acted to some extent like snow-shoes, and prevented the girls' feet from sinking deeply, while the prints which they left bore no resemblance to their own. They were strapped on the wrong way, so that the marks would seem to point towards the village rather than away from it. Both girls protested that they should not be able to get along fast in these encumbrances, but one of the men posted himself on either side of each, and assisted them along; and as the moccasins were very light, even with the wooden soles inside, they were soon able to move with them at a considerable pace.

Once united, the whole party kept along at the top of their speed. Peter Lambton assisted Cameron with Janet, and the girl, half lifted from the ground, skimmed over the surface like a bird, only touching the snow here and there with the moccasins. Nelly Welch needed no assistance from Harold and Pearson. During the long winters she had often practised on snow-shoes, and was, consequently, but little encumbered with the huge moccasins, which to some extent served the same purpose.

They had been nearly half an hour on their way when they heard a tremendous yell burst from the village.

"They have missed you," Peter said. "Now it is a fair race. We have got a good start, and shall get more, for they will have to hunt up the traces very carefully, and may be an hour, perhaps more, before they strike upon the right one. If the snow had been new fallen, we should have had them after us in five minutes; but even a Red-skin's eye will be puzzled to find out at night one track among such hundreds.

"I have but one fear," Pearson said to Harold.

"What is that?"

"I am afeard that, without waiting to find the tracks, they may send off half-a-dozen parties to the lake. They will be sure that friends have taken the gals away, and will know that their only chance of escape is by the water. On land we should be hunted down to a certainty, and the Red-skins, knowing that the gals could not travel fast, will not hurry in following up the trail. So I think that they will at once send off parties to watch the lake, and will like enough make no effort to take up the trail till morning."

This was said in a low whisper, for although they were more than two miles from the village, it was necessary to move as silently as possible.

"You had best tell the others what you think, Pearson; it may make a difference in our movements."

A short halt was called, and the Seneca and Peter quite agreed with Pearson's idea.

"We had best make for the canoe that is farthest off. When the Red-skins find the others, which they are pretty sure to do, for they will hunt every bush, they are likely to be satisfied, and to make sure that they will catch us at one or the other."

Thus much decided upon, they continued their flight, now less rapidly, but in perfect silence. Speed was less an object than concealment. The Indians might spread, and a party might come across them by accident. If they could avoid this, they were sure to reach their canoe before morning, and unlikely to find the Indians there before them.

It was about twelve miles to the spot where they had hidden the canoe, and although they heard distant shouts and whoops ringing through the forest, no sound was heard near them.

CHAPTER XV
THE ISLAND REFUGE

THE night was intensely cold and still, and the stars shone brightly through the bare boughs overhead.

"Are you sure you are going all right?" Nelly asked Harold. "It is so dark here that it seems impossible to know which way we are going."

"You can trust the Indians," Harold said. "Even if there was not a star to be seen, they could find their way by some mysterious instinct. How you are grown, Nelly! Your voice does not seem much changed, and I am longing to see your face."

"I expect you are more changed than I am, Harold," the girl answered. "You have been going through so much since we last met, and you seem to have grown so tall and big. Your voice has changed very much too; it is the voice of a man. How in the world did you find us here?"

Pearson had gone on ahead to speak to the Seneca, but he now joined them again.

"You must not talk," he said. "I hope there are no Red-skins within five miles of us now; but there is never any saying where they may be."

There was, Harold thought, a certain sharpness in the hunter's voice, which told of a greater anxiety than would be caused by the very slight risk of the quietly spoken words being heard by passing Red-skins, and he wondered what it could be.

They were now, he calculated, within a mile of the hiding-place where they had left the boat, and they had every reason for believing that none of the Indians would be likely to have followed the shore so far. That they would be pursued, and that in so heavily-laden a canoe they would have great difficulty in escaping, he was well aware, but he relied on the craft of the hunters and Senecas for throwing their pursuers off the trail.

All at once the trees seemed to open in front, and in a few minutes the party reached the river. A cry of astonishment, and of something akin to terror broke from Harold. As far as the eye could reach, the lake was frozen. Their escape was cut off.

"That's just what I have been expecting," Pearson said. "The ice had begun to form at the edge when we landed, and three days and nights of such frost as we have had since were enough to freeze Ontario. What on arth is to be done?"

No one answered. Peter and the Red-skins had shared Pearson's anxiety, but to Harold and Cameron the disappointment was a terrible one; as to Jake, he left all the thinking to be done by the others. Harold stood gazing helplessly on the expanse of ice which covered the water. It was not a black smooth sheet, but was rough and broken, as if, while it had been forming, the wind had broken the ice up into cakes again and again, while the frost as often had bound them together.

They had struck the river within a few hundred yards of the place where the canoe was hidden, and, after a short consultation between the Seneca chief, Peter Lambton, and Pearson, moved down towards that spot.

"What are you thinking of doing?" Harold asked, when they gathered round the canoe.

"We are going to load ourselves with the ammunition and deer's flesh," Peter said, "and to make for a rocky island which lies about a mile off here; I noticed it as we landed. There is nothing to do but to fight it out to the last there; it are a good place for defence, for the Red-skins won't like to come out across the open, and even covered by a dark night, they would show on this white surface."

"Perhaps they won't trace us."

"Not trace us!" the trapper repeated scornfully. "Why, when daylight comes they will pick up our track and follow it as easy as you could that of a waggon across the snow."

They were just starting when Harold gave a little exclamation.

"What is it, lad?"

THE ISLAND REFUGE

"A flake of snow fell on my face."

All looked up. The stars had disappeared; another flake and another fell on the faces of the upturned party.

"Let us thank the good God," Peter said quietly. "There is a chance for our lives yet; half an hour's snow and the trail will be lost."

Faster and faster the snow-flakes came down. Again the leaders consulted.

"We must change our plans now," Peter said, turning to the others. "So long as they could easily follow our tracks, it mattered nothing that they should find the canoe here; but now it is altogether different. We must take it along with us."

The weight of the canoe was very small. The greater part of its contents had already been removed. There was a careful look round to see that nothing remained on the bank; then four of the men lifted it on their shoulders, and the whole party stepped out upon the ice. The snow was now falling heavily, and to Harold's eyes there was nothing to guide them in the direction that they were following. Even the Indians would have been at a loss had not the Seneca, the instant the snow began to fall, sent on one of his followers at full speed toward the island. Harold wondered at the time what his object could be as the Indian darted off across the ice, but he now understood. Every minute or two the low hoot of an owl was heard, and towards this sound the party directed their way through the darkness and snow.

So heavy was the fall that the island rose white before them as they reached it. It was of no great extent—some twenty or thirty yards across, and perhaps twice that length. It rose steeply from the water to a height of from ten to fifteen feet. The ground was rough and broken, and several trees and much brushwood grew in the crevices of the rock.

The Seneca and the hunters made a rapid examination of the island, and soon fixed upon the spot for their camp. Towards one end the island was split in two, and an indentation ran some distance up into it. Here a clear spot was found some three or four feet above the level of the water. It was completely hidden from the

221

sight of anyone approaching by water, by thick bushes. There the canoe was turned over, and the girls, who were both suffering from the intense cold, were wrapped up in blankets and placed under its shelter. The camp was at the lower end of the island, and would therefore be entirely hidden from view of Indians gathered upon the shore. In such a snow-storm, light would be invisible at a very short distance, and Peter did not hesitate to light a fire in front of the canoe.

For three hours the snow continued to fall. The fire had been sheltered by blankets stretched at some distance above it. Long before the snow ceased it had sunk down to a pile of red embers. A small tent had now been formed of blankets for the use of the girls; brushwood had been heaped over this, and upon the brushwood snow had been thrown, the whole making a shelter which would be warm and comfortable even in the bitterest weather. A pile of hot embers was placed in this little tent until it was thoroughly heated; blankets were then spread, and the girls were asked to leave the shelter of the canoe and take their place there.

The canoe itself was now raised on four sticks three feet from the ground; bushes were laid round it, and snow piled on, thus forming the walls of which the canoe was the roof. All this was finished long before the snow had ceased falling, and this added a smooth white surface all over, so that to a casual eye both tent and hut looked like two natural ridges of the ground. They were a cheerful party which assembled in the little hut. The remainder of the embers of the fire had been brought in, and intense as was the cold outside, it was warm and comfortable within. Tea was made and the pipes filled, and they chatted for some time before going off to sleep.

Duncan Cameron was like a man transfigured. His joy and thankfulness for the recovery of his daughter were unbounded. Harold's pleasure too at the rescue of his cousin was very great; and the others were all gratified at the success of their expedition. It was true that the Indians had as yet gained no scalps, but Harold had promised them before starting that should the expedition be successful, they should be handsomely rewarded.

"The Indian darted off across the ice."

"We must not reckon as we are safe yet," Peter said in answer to one of Harold's remarks. "The Red-skins ain't going to let us slip through their fingers so easy as all that. They have lost our trail and have nothing but their senses to guide them, but an Indian's senses ain't easily deceived in these woods. Ef this snow begins again and keeps on for two or three days, they may be puzzled; but ef it stops, they will cast a circle round their camp at a distance beyond where we could have got before the snow ceased, and ef they find no new trails they will know that we must be within that circle. Then as to the boats, when they find as we don't come down to the two as they have discovered, and that we have not made off by land, they will guess as there was another canoe hidden somewhere, and they will sarch high and low for it. Well, they won't find it; and then they will suppose that we may have taken to the ice, and they will sarch that. Either they will get to open water or to the other side. Ef there is open water anywhere within a few miles they may conclude that we have carried a canoe, launched it there, and made off. In that case, when they have sarched everywhere, they may give it up. Ef there ain't no such open water they will sarch till they find us. It ain't likely that this island will escape them. With nine good rifles here we can hold the place against the hull tribe, and as they would show up against the snow they can no more attack by night than by day."

"I don't think our food will hold out beyond seven or eight days," Harold said.

"Jest about that," Peter answered; "but we can cut a hole in the ice and fish, and can hold out that way, if need be, for weeks. The wust of it is that the ice ain't likely to break up now until the spring. I reckon that our only chance is to wait till we get another big snow-storm, and then to make off; the snow will cover our trail as fast as we make it, and once across to the other shore, we may get away from the varmint. But I don't disguise from you, Harold, that we are in a very awkard trouble, and that it will need all the craft of the chief here, and all the experience of Pearson and me to get us all out of it."

THE ISLAND REFUGE

"The guid God has been vera merciful to us sae far," Duncan Cameron said; "he will surely protect us to the end. Had he na sent the snow just when he did, the savages could ha'e followed our trail at once; it was a miracle wrought in our favour. He has aided us to rescue the twa bairns frae the hands of the Indians, and we may surely trust in his protection to the end. My daughter and her friend ha'e, I am vera sure, before lying down to sleep, entreated his protection; let us a' do the same." And the old soldier, taking off his cap, prayed aloud to God to heed and protect them.

Harold and the frontiersmen also removed their caps and joined in the prayer, and the Senecas looked on silent and reverent at an act of worship which was rare among their white companions.

As Peter was of opinion that there was no chance whatever of any search on the part of the Indians that night, and therefore was no need to set a watch, the whole party wrapped themselves up in their blankets and were soon asleep.

When Harold woke next morning, it was broad day-light. The Senecas had already been out, and had brought news that a strong party of Indians could be seen moving along the edge of the forest, evidently searching for a canoe. One of the Indians was placed on watch, and two or three hours later he reported that the Indians were now entirely out of sight, and were, when last seen, scouting along the edge of the forest.

"Now," Peter said, "the sooner we get another snow-storm, the better. Ef we had been alone we could have pushed on last night, but the gals was exhausted and would soon have died of the cold. Now with a fresh start they would do. If we can't cross the lake I calculate that we are about thirty miles from a point on the north shore below the falls of St. Marie, and we could land there, and strike across through the woods for the settlement. It would be a terrible long journey round the north of Huron, but we must try it if we can't get across."

"But we could go off by night, surely," Harold said, "even if there is no fresh snow."

"We could do that," Peter replied; "no doubt of it. But ef they were to find our tracks the next day, aye, or within three days, they would follow us and overtake us before we got to the settlements. Ef we were alone it would be one thing, but with the gals it would be another altogether. No, we must stop here till a snow-storm comes, even if we have to stop for a month. There is no saying how soon some of those Indians may be loafing round, and we daren't leave a trail for them to take up."

They had scarcely ceased speaking when a low call from the Indian placed on watch summoned the chief to his side. A minute later the latter rejoined the group below and said a few words to Peter.

"Jest as I thought!" the latter grumbled, rising with his rifle across his arm. "Here are some of the varmint coming out this er' way. Likely enough it's a party of young braves just scouting about on their own account to try and get honour by discovering us when their elders have failed. It would have been better for them to have stopped at home."

The party now crept up to the top of the rock, keeping carefully below its crest.

"Ef you show as much as a hair above the top line," Peter said, "they will see you sartin."

"Would it not be as well," Harold asked, "for one of us to show himself? There is no possibility of further concealment; and if they go off without any of them being killed, the others might be less bitter against us than they would if they had lost some of their tribe."

Peter laughed scornfully.

"Yer haven't had much to do with the Injuns, lad, but I should have thought you would have had better sense nor that. Have not these Injuns been a murdering and a slaying along the frontier all the summer, falling on defenceless women and children? Marcy and pity ain't in their nature, and fight or no fight, our scalps will dry in their wigwams if they get us into their power. They know that we can shoot, and mean to, and that will make them careful of attacking us, and every hour is important. Now," he said to the others, "do you each cover a man and fire straight through your sights when I gives the word. There's others watching them, you may be sure, and ef the whole five go down together it will make em think twice afore they attack us again."

Peering between some loose rocks so that he could see without exposing his head above the line, Harold watched the five Indians approaching. They had evidently some doubts as to the wisdom of the course they were pursuing, and were well aware that they ran a terrible risk standing there in the open before the rifles of those concealed, should the fugitives be really there. Nevertheless, the hope of gaining distinction, and the fear of ridicule from those watching them on shore, should they turn back with their mission unaccomplished, inspired them with resolution. When within three hundred yards of the island they halted for a long time. They stood gazing fixedly; but although no sign of life could be perceived, they were too well versed in Indian warfare to gain any confidence from the apparent stillness. Throwing themselves flat on the snow and following each other in single line, by which means their bodies were nearly concealed from sight in the track which their leader made through the light yielding snow, they made a complete circuit of the island. They paused for some time opposite the little forked entrance in which the camp was situated, but apparently saw nothing, for they kept round until they completed the circuit.

When they reached the point from which they had started, there was apparently a short consultation among them. Then they continued their course in the track that they had before made until they reached a spot facing the camp. Then they changed order, and still prone in the snow, advanced abreast towards the island.

"The varmint have guessed that ef we are here, this is the place where we should be hidden," Peter whispered in Harold's ear.

As the Indians had made their circuit, the party in the island had changed their position so as always to keep out of sight. They were now on the top of the island, which was a sort of rough plateau. The girls had been warned when they left them to remain perfectly quiet in their shelter, whatever noise they might hear. Peter and the Seneca watched the Indians through holes which they had made with their ramrods through a bank of snow. The others remained flat in the slight depression behind it. At the distance of one hundred and fifty yards, the Indians stopped.

"The varmint see something!" Peter said. "Maybe they can make out the two snow heaps through the bushes; maybe they can see some of our footsteps in the snow."

"They are going to fire!" he exclaimed. "Up, lads! They may send a bullet into the hut whar the gals are hidden."

In an instant the line of men sprang to their feet. The Indians, taken by surprise at the sudden appearance of a larger number of enemies than they expected, fired a hasty volley, and then sprang to their feet and dashed towards the shore. But they were deadly rifles which covered them. Peter, Harold, and Pearson could be trusted not to miss even a rapidly moving object at that distance, and the men were all good shots. Not in regular order but as each covered his man the rifles were discharged. Four out of the five Indians fell, and an arm of the fifth dropped useless by his side; however, he still kept on. The whites reloaded rapidly, and Harold was about to fire again when Pearson put his hand on his shoulder. "Don't fire; we have shown them that we can shoot straight. It is just as well at present that they should not know how far our rifles will carry."

The four Senecas dashed out across the snow and speedily returned each with a scalp hanging at his belt.

A loud yell of anger and lamentation had risen from the woods skirting the shore as the Indians fell, but after this died away, a deep silence reigned.

"What will be their next move?" Cameron asked Peter as they gathered again in their low hut, having placed one of the Indians on watch.

"We shall hear nothing of them till nightfall," Peter said. "Their first move, now they know as we are here, will be to send off to fetch up all the tribe who are in search of us. When it comes on dark they will send scouts outside of us on the ice to see as we don't escape, not that they would much mind ef we did, for they could track us through the snow and come up with us whenever they chose. No, they may be sure we shall stay where we are. It may

Watching the Indians' approach.

be they will attack us to-night, maybe not; it would be a thing more risksome than Red-skins often undertake, to cross the snow under the fire of nine rifles. I ain't no doubt they would try and starve us out, for they must know well enough that we can have no great store of provisions. But they know as well as we do that ef another snow-storm come on, we might slip away from them without leaving a foot-mark behind. It's jest that thought as may make them attack."

"Well, we can beat them off if they do," Harold said confidently.

"Wall, we may and we may not," the scout answered. "Anyhow, we can kill a grist of them afore they turn us out on this here island."

"That's sartin enough," Pearson put in; "but they are a strong tribe and ef they can harden their hearts and make a rush it's all up with us. I allow that it's contrary to their custom, but when they see no other way to do with, they may try."

"I suppose if they do try a rush," Harold said, "they will do it against this end of the island?"

"Yes, you may bet your money on that," the scout answered. "In other places the rock goes pretty nigh straight up from the water, but here it's an easy landing. Being so close to them, they are sure to know all about it; but even ef they didn't, the chap that got away would tell them. I don't much expect an attack to-night; the bands won't be back yet. They will have a grand palaver to-night, and there will be a big talk afore they decide what is best to be done, so I think we are safe for to-night. To-morrow we will set to work and build a shelter for the pretty ones up above, where they will be safe from stray shots. Then we will throw up a breast-work with loose rocks on the top of the slope round this cove, so as to give it them hot when they land."

"You have plenty of powder?" Harold asked.

"Dollops," Peter replied; "more than we could fire away if we were besieged here for a month."

"Then you could spare me twenty pounds or so?"

"We could spare you a whole keg, if you like; we have got three full. But what are you thinking of now, young 'un?"

"I was thinking," Harold answered, "of forming a line of holes, say three feet apart, in the ice, across the mouth of the cove. If we were to charge them with powder and lay a train between them, we could, when the first dozen or so have passed the line, fire the train and break up the ice; this would prevent the others following and give them such a bad scare that they would probably make off, and we could easily deal with those who had passed the line before we fired it."

"That's a good idea of yours, lad. A fust-rate idea. The ice must be a foot thick by this time, and ef you put in your charges eight inches and tamp them well down you will shiver the ice for a long way round. The idea is a fust-rate one."

Pearson and Cameron assisted in the work, and the Indians, when Peter had explained the plan to them, gave deep guttural exclamations of surprise and approval. The process of blasting was one wholly unknown to them.

"I will mak' the holes," Cameron said; "I ha'e seen a deal of blasting when I was in the army. I can heat the end of a ramrod in a fire and hammer it to the shape of a borer."

"A better way than that, Cameron," Harold said, "will be to heat the end of a ramrod white hot. You will melt holes in the ice in half the time it would take you to bore them. That was what I was thinking of doing."

"Right you are, lad!" Pearson said. "Let's set about it at once."

A large fire was now lighted outside the huts, for there was no longer any occasion for secrecy. The ends of three or four of the ramrods were placed in the fire, and two lines of holes were bored in the ice across the mouth of the little cove. These lines were twelve feet apart, and they calculated that the ice between them would be completely broken up, even if the fractures did not extend a good way beyond the lines. The holes were of rather larger diameter than the interior of a gun barrel. It was found that the ice was about fifteen inches thick, and the holes were taken down ten inches. Three or four charges of powder were placed in each; a stick of a quarter of an inch in diameter was then placed in each hole, and pounded ice was rammed tightly in around it until the holes were filled up, a few drops of water being poured in on the top so as to freeze the whole into a solid mass. There was no fear of the powder being wetted, for the frost was intense. Then the sticks were withdrawn and the holes left filled with powder. With the heated ramrods little troughs were sunk half an inch deep, connecting the tops of the holes; lines of powder were placed in these trenches; narrow strips of skin were laid over them, and the snow was then thrown on again. The two lines of trenches were connected at the ends at the shore, so that they could be fired simultaneously.

While the men were occupied with this work, the girls had cooked some venison steaks and made some cakes.

It was just nightfall when they had finished, and all sat down and enjoyed a hearty meal. Peter and one of the Senecas undertook the watch for half the night, when they were to be relieved by Pearson and the chief. The early part of the night passed off quietly, but an hour before morning, the party were aroused by the sharp crack of two rifles. Seizing their arms, all rushed out.

"What is it, Pearson?"

"Two of their scouts," Pearson answered, pointing to two dark bodies on the snow at a distance of about one hundred yards. "I suppose they wanted to see if we was on the watch. We made them out almost as soon as they left the shore, but we let them come on until we was sartin of our aim. There ain't no more about as we can see, so yer can all turn in again for another hour or two."

There was no fresh alarm before morning, and when the sun rose, it shone over a wide expanse of snow, unbroken save where lay the bodies of the two Indians—whose scalps already hung at the belt of the Seneca—and those of their four comrades who had fallen in the first attack.

The day passed quietly; towards the afternoon two Indians were seen approaching from the shore. They were unarmed, and held their hands aloft as a sign of amity. Peter and Pearson at once laid down their guns, left the island, and advanced to meet them. They were Indian chiefs of importance.

THE ISLAND REFUGE

"Why have my white brothers stolen in at night upon the village of the War-Eagle and slain his young men?"

"It is what you have been doing all last year, chief," Pearson, who spoke the dialect better than Peter, replied. "But we injured no one; we did not kill women and children, as your warriors have done in the white villages. We only came to take what you had stolen from us, and ef your young men have been killed, it is only because they tried to attack us."

"The white men must see," the chief said, "that they cannot get away. The water is hard and their canoe will not swim in it. The snow is deep, and the tender feet cannot walk through it; my warriors are very numerous, and the white men cannot fight their way through them. The white settlements are very far away and their friends cannot reach them; and it will be many months before the water softens, and long before that the white men will have eaten their moccasins."

"Wall, chief," Pearson said, "we are in a tight hole, I grant you; but I am far from allowing that we ain't no chances left to us yet. What do you propose? I suppose you have some proposition to make."

"Let the white man leave behind them their guns and their powder and the maidens they have taken from War-Eagle's camp; then let them go in peace. They shall not be harmed."

Pearson gave a short laugh. "War-Eagle must think that the white men are foolish. What is to prevent the red warriors from taking all our scalps when our arms are in their hands?"

"The word of a great chief," War-Eagle said. "War-Eagle never lies."

"You may not lie, chief," Pearson said bluntly, "but I have known many a treaty broken afore now. You and your people may not touch us, but there are other Red-skins about, and I would not give a beaver's skin for our scalps ef we were to take the back trail to the settlements, without arms in our hands. Besides that, we have among us the father of the gal who was stole far away off from Lake Champlain, and a relative of hers whose parents you have killed down on the lake. If we were to agree to give up our arms, it stands to reason it ain't likely they would agree to give up the gals. No, no, chief; your terms are not reasonable. But I tell you what we will do: if you will give us your word that neither you or your tribe shall molest us in our retreat, we will go back to the settlements, and will engage that when we get back there we will send you nine of the best rifles money can buy, with plenty of powder and ball, and blankets, and such like."

The chief waved his hand in contemptuous refusal of the terms. "There are six of my young men's scalps at your girdles, and their places are empty. War-Eagle has spoken."

"Very well, chief," Pearson said. "If nothing but sculps will content you, to fighting it must come; but I warn you that your tribe will lose a good many more afore they get ours."

So saying, without another word they separated, each party making their way back to their friends.

"What on earth can he have proposed such terms as these for?" Harold asked, when Pearson had related what had taken place between him and the chief. "He must have known we should not accept them."

"I expect," Pearson said, "he wanted to see who we were, and to judge what sort of spirit we had. It may be, too, that there was a party among the tribe who had no stomachs for the job of attacking this place, and so he was obliged to make a show of offering terms to please them, but he never meant as they should be accepted. No, I take it they will wait a few days to see what hunger will do. They must be pretty sure that we have not a very large supply of food."

CHAPTER XVI
THE GREAT STORM

LET us overhaul our packages," Harold said, "and see what provisions we have left. It would be as well to know how we stand."

It was found that they had a sufficient supply of flour to last with care for a fortnight. The meal was nearly exhausted. Of tea they had an abundance. The sugar was nearly out, and they had three bottles of spirits. "Could we not make the flour last more than the fourteen days by putting ourselves on half rations?" Harold asked.

"We might do that," Peter said; "but I tell you the rations would be small even for fourteen days. We have calkilated according to how much we eat when we have plenty of meat, but without meat it would be only a starvation ration to each. Fortunately we have fish-hooks and lines, and by making holes in the ice, we can get as many fish as we like. Wall, we can live on them alone, if need be, and an ounce or two of flour, made into cakes, will be enough to go with them. That way the flour would last us pretty nigh two months. I don't say that if the wust comes to the wust, that we might not hold on, on fish, right to the spring. The lake is full of them, and some of them have so much oil in them that they are nigh as good as meat."

"Do you think, Peter, that if the Indians make one great attack and are beaten off, they will try again?"

"No one can say," Peter answered. "Indian nature can never be calkilated upon. I should say if they got a thundering beating, they ain't likely to try again, but there is never no saying."

"The sooner they attack and get it o'er, the better," Cameron said. "I ha'e na slept a wink the last twa nights. If I doze off for a moment, I wake up thinking that I hear their yells. I am as ready to fight as ony o' you when the time comes, but the thought o' my daughter here makes me nervous and anxious. What do you say, Jake?"

"It all de same to Jake, Massa Cameron; Jake sleeps bery sound, but he no like de tought ob eating noting but fish for five or six months. Jake nebber bery fond of fish."

"You will like it well enough when you get accustomed to it, Jake," Pearson said. "It is not bad eating on a pinch, only you want to eat a sight of it to satisfy you. Well, let us see how the fish will bite."

Four holes were cut in the ice at a short distance apart. The hooks were attached to strong lines and baited with deer's flesh, and soon the fishing began. The girls took great interest in the proceeding. Nelly was an adept at the sport, having generally caught the fish for the consumption of the household at home. She took charge of one of the lines, Harold of another, while Jake and one of the Senecas squatted themselves by the other holes. There had been some discussion as to whether the fishing should take place on the side of the island facing the shore, or behind the rocks, but the former was decided upon. This was done because all were anxious that the expected attack should take place as soon as possible, and the event was likely to be hastened when the Indians saw that they were provided with lines, and were therefore able to procure food for a considerable time.

It was soon manifest that if they could live upon fish they need feel no uneasiness as to its supply. Scarcely had the lines been let down than fish were fast to them. Harold and the other men soon had trout, from three to six pounds, lying on the ice beside them, but Nelly was obliged to call Pearson to her assistance, and the fish when brought to the surface was found to be over twenty pounds in weight. An hour's fishing procured them a sufficient supply for a week's consumption. There was no fear as to the fish keeping, for in a very short time after being drawn from the water, they were frozen stiff and hard. They were hung up to some boughs near the huts, and the party were glad enough to get into shelter again, for the cold was intense.

THE GREAT STORM

As before, the early part of the night passed quietly; but towards morning, Peter, who was on watch, ran down and awakened the others. "Get your shooting-irons and hurry up," he said. "The varmint are coming this time in arnest."

In a minute every one was at the post assigned to him. A number of dark figures could be seen coming over the ice.

"There are nigh two hundred of them," Peter said. "War-Eagle has brought the hull strength of his tribe."

Contrary to their usual practice, the Indians did not attempt to crawl up to the place they were about to attack, but advanced at a run across the ice. The defenders lost not a moment in opening fire, for some of their rifles would carry as far as the shore.

"Shoot steady," Peter said; "don't throw away a shot."

Each man loaded and fired as quickly as he could, taking a steady aim, and the dark figures which dotted the ice behind the advancing Indians showed that the fire was an effectual one. The Indians did not return a shot. Their chief had no doubt impressed upon them the uselessness of firing against men lying in shelter, and had urged them to hurry at the top of their speed to the island and crush the whites in a hand-to-hand fight.

It was but three or four minutes from the time the first shot was fired before they were close to the island. They made, as Peter had expected, towards the little cove, which was indeed the only place at which a landing could well be effected. Harold ran down and hid himself in a bush at the spot where the train terminated, carrying with him a glowing brand from the fire.

"War-Eagle means to have our sculps this time," Peter said to Pearson. "I never seed an uglier rush. White men could not have done better."

The Indians had run in scattered order across the ice, but they closed up as they neared the cove. As they rushed towards it, four fell beneath the shots of half the defenders, and another four a few seconds later from a volley by the other section.

In a wonderfully short time the first were ready again, and the Indians wavered at the slaughter and opened fire upon the breastwork, behind which the defenders were crouching. Those

237

behind, however, pressed on, and with terrific yells the mass of Indians bounded forward.

Harold had remained inactive, crouching behind the bush. He saw the head of the dark mass rush past him, and then applied the brand to the train.

There was a tremendous explosion. Yells and screams rent the air, and in an instant a dark line of water twenty feet wide stretched across the mouth of the cove. In this were pieces of floating ice, and numbers of Indians struggling and yelling. Some made only a faint struggle before they sank, while others struck out for the side farthest from the island.

The main body of Indians, appalled by the explosion, checked themselves in their course, and at once took to flight; some, unable to check their impetus, fell into the water upon the wounded wretches who were struggling there. Those who had crossed stood irresolute, and then turning, leapt into the water. As they struggled to get out on the opposite side, the defenders maintained a deadly fire upon them, but in two or three minutes the last survivor had scrambled out and all were in full flight towards the shore.

"I think we have seen the last of the attacks," Peter said, as they came down from their breastwork and joined Harold in the cove. "That was a fust-rate notion of yours, lad. Ef it had not been for that, we should have been rubbed out sure enough; another minute and we should have gone down. They were in arnest and no mistake; they had got the steam up, and was determined to finish with us at once, whatever it cost them."

The instant the attack had ceased, Cameron had hastened to the hut where the girls were lying, to assure them that all danger was over, and that the Indians were entirely defeated. In an hour a fresh skin of ice had formed across the streak of water, but as through its clear surface many of the bodies of the Indians could be seen, the men threw snow over it, to spare the girls the unpleasantness of such a sight every time they went out from the cove. The bodies of all the Indians who had fallen near the island were also covered with snow. Those nearer the shore were carried off by the Irroquois in their retreat.

THE GREAT STORM

"I suppose, Peter," Harold said, as they sat round the fire that evening, "you have been in quite as awkward scrapes as this before, and have got out all right?"

"Why, this business ain't as nothing to that affair we had by Lake Champlain. That war as bad a business, when we was surrounded in that log-hut, as ever I went through—and I have been through a good many. Pearson and me nigh got our hair raised more nor once in that business of Pontiac's. He were a great chief, and managed to get up the biggest confederation agin us that's ever been known. It were well for us that that business didn't begin a few years earlier, when we were fighting the French; but you see, so long as we and they was at war, the Indians hoped as we might pretty well exterminate each other, and then they intended to come in and finish off whoever got the best of it. Well, the English, they drove the French back, and finally a treaty was made in Europe by which the French agreed to clear out.

"It was just about this time as Pontiac worked upon the tribes to lay aside their own quarrels and to join the French in fighting agin us. He got the Senecas, and the Delawares, and the Shawnees, the Wyandots, and a lot of other tribes from the lakes, and the hull country between the Niagara River and the Mississippi.

"Jack Pearson and me, we happened to be with the Miamis when the bloody belt which Pontiac was sending round as a signal for war arrived at the fort there. Jack and me knew the Red-skins pretty well, and saw by their manner as something unusual had happened. I went to the commandant of the fort and told him as much. He didn't think much of my news. The soldier chaps always despise the Red-skins till they see them come yelling along with their tomahawks, and then as often as not it's jest the other way. Howsumdever, he agreed at last to pay any amount of trade goods I might promise to the Miamis if the news turned out worth finding out. I discovered that a great palaver was to be held that evening at the chief's village, which was a mile away from the fort.

"I had seen a good deal of the Miamis, and had fought with them against the Shawnees, so I could do as much with them as most. Off Pearson and I goes to the chief, and I says to him, 'Look

239

ye here, chief, I have good reasons to believe that you have got a message from Pontiac, and that it means trouble. Now don't you go and let yourself be led away by him. I have heard rumours that he is getting up a great confederation agin the English. But I tell you, chief, if all the Red-skins on this continent was to join together, they could do nothing agin the English. I don't say as you mightn't wipe out a number of little border forts, for no doubt you might; but what would come of it? England would send out as many men as there are leaves in the forest, who would scorch up the Red-skin nations as a fire on the prairie scorches up the grass. I tell yer, chief, no good can come on it. Don't build yer hopes on the French; they have acknowledged that they are beaten, and are all going out of the country. It would be best for you and for your people to stick to the English. They can reward their friends handsomely, and ef you jine with Pontiac, sooner or later trouble and ruin will come upon you. Now I can promise you, in the name of the officer of the fort, a good English rifle for yerself, and fifty guns for your braves, and ten bales of blankets, ef yer will make a clean breast on it and first tell us what devilry Pontiac is up to, and next jine us freely—or at anyrate hold aloof altogether from this conspiracy till yer see how things is going.'

"Wall, the chief he thought the matter over, and said he would do his best at the palaver that night, but that till that was over and he knew what the council decided upon, he could not tell me what the message was. I was pretty well satisfied, for the 'Prairie Dog' was a great chief in his tribe, and, I felt pretty sartin, he would get the council to go the way he wanted. I told him I should be at the fort, and that the governor would expect a message after the council was over.

"It was past midnight when the chief come with four of his braves. He told us that the tribe had received a bloody belt from Pontiac and a message that the Mingoes and Delawares, the Wyandots and Shawnees, were going to dig up the hatchet against the Whites, and calling upon him and his people to massacre the garrison of the fort, and then to march to join Pontiac, who was about to fall upon Detroit and Fort Pitt. They were directed to send the belt on to the tribes on the Wabash, but they loved the English and were determined to take no part against them; therefore they delivered the belt to their friend the white commander, and hoped that he would tell the great king in England that the Miamis were faithful to him. The governor highly applauded their conduct, and said that he would send the news to the English governor at New York, and at once ordered the presents which I had promised to be delivered to the chief for himself and his braves. When they had gone, he said:

"'You were right, Peter. This news is important indeed, and it is clear that a terrible storm is about to burst upon the frontier. Whether the Miamis will keep true is doubtful, but now I am on my guard, they will find it difficult to take the fort. But the great thing is to carry the news of what has happened to Detroit, to put them on their guard. Will you and Pearson start at once?'

"In course we agreed, though it was clear that the job was a risksome one, for it would be no easy matter to journey through the woods with the hull Red-skin tribes out on the war-path.

"The commander wanted me to carry the belt with me, but I said, 'I might jest as well carry my death warrant to the first Red-skins as I come across!' Major Gladwin, who commanded at Detroit, knew me, and I didn't need to carry any proof of my story. So afore the Miamis had been gone half an hour, Jack and me took the trail for Detroit. We had got a canoe hidden on the lake a few miles away, and we was soon on board. The next morning we seed a hull fleet of canoes coming down the lake. We might have made a race with 'em, but, being fully manned, the chances was as they would have cut us off, and seeing that at present war had not been declared, we judged it best to seem as if we weren't afeard. So we paddles up to them, and found as they were a lot of Wyandots whose hunting-grounds lay up by Lake Superior. In course I did not ask no questions as to whar they was going, but jest mentioned as we was on our way down to Detroit. 'We are going that way too,' the chief said, 'and shall be glad to have our white brothers with us.' So we paddled along together until, about noon, they landed. Nothing was said to us as how we were prisoners, but we could see as how we was just as much captives as ef we had been tied with buckskin ropes.

"Jack and me talked it over, and agreed as it was no manner o' use trying to make our escape, but that as long as they chose to treat us as guests, we had best seem perfectly contented, and make no show of considering as they were on the war-path; although, seeing as they had no women or children with them, a baby could have known as they were up to no good.

"The next morning they started again at daybreak and, after paddling some hours, landed and hid away their canoes and started on foot. Nothing was said to us, but we saw as we was expected to do as they did. We went on till we was within ten miles of Detroit and then we halted. I thought it was best to find out exactly how we stood, so Jack and I goes up to the chief and says that as we was near Detroit we would jest say good-bye to him and tramp in.

"'Why should my white brothers hurry?' he said. 'It is not good for them to go on alone, for the woods are very full of Indians.' 'But,' I said, 'the hatchet is buried between the Whites and the Red-skins, so there is no danger in the woods.' The chief waved his hand, 'My white brothers have joined the Wyandots, and they will tarry with them until they go into Detroit. There are many Red-skins there, and there will be a grand palaver; the Wyandots will be present.'

"Jack and me made no signs of being dissatisfied, but the position was not a pleasant one, I can tell you. Here was the Red-skins a clustering like bees around Detroit, ready to fall upon the garrison and massacre them, and we, who was the only men as knew of the danger, was prisoners among the Red-skins. It was sartin, too, that though they might not take our lives till they had attacked the garrison, they was only keeping us for the pleasure of torturing us quietly arterwards. The situation was plain enough; the question was, what war to be done? There was about sixty of the varmint around us sitting by their fires and looking as if they didn't even know as we was there, but we knew as sharp eyes was watching us, and that afore we had gone five yards, the hull lot would be on our track.

THE GREAT STORM

"Jack and me did not say much to each other, for we knew how closely we were watched, and didn't want them to think as we were planning our escape, so after a few words we sat down by one of the fires till it got time to lie down for the night; but we had both been a thinking. We saw when we lay down that the Indians lay pretty well around us, while two on them, with their rifles ready to hand, sat down by a fire close by, and threw on some logs as if they intended to watch all night.

"It was a goodish-size clearing as they had chosen for a camping-ground, and we should have had to run some distance afore we got to the shelter of the trees. The moon too was up, and it war well-nigh as light as day, and anxious as we was to get away, we agreed that there war no chance of sliding off, but that it would be better to wait till next day.

"When we woke our guns was gone. We complained to the chief, who said coldly that his young men would carry the guns, and would give them back to us when we got to Detroit. It were no use saying more, for he might at any moment have ordered us to be bound, and it were better to keep the use of our legs as long as we could.

"For two days we stayed there, not seeing the shadow of a chance of getting away. Several Red-skin runners came in and spoke to the chief, and we got more and more anxious to be off. We were still allowed to walk about, provided we did not go near the edge of the clearing. Whenever we went that way, two Indians who kept guard by turns over us, shouted to us to go no further.

"The third morning, after a runner had come in, the chief gave the word for a move, and we set out. We saw that they was not taking the direct line to Detroit, although still going in that direction, and after two hours' marching through the woods, we got down on to the Detroit river. Here was a big encampment, and some three or four hundred Shawnees and Delawares was gathered here. A chief came up to us as we entered the open. He gave an order to the Wyandots, and in a minute we was bound hand and foot, carried to a small wigwam, and chucked down inside like two logs of wood.

"After a little talk Jack and I agreed as after all we had a better chance of escaping now, than when we was watched by a hull tribe, and we concluded that there weren't no time to be lost. The Wyandots had no doubt been brought up in readiness to strike the blow, and even if we had known nothing about the belt, we should have been sure that mischief was intended when these three bands of red varmint had gathered so close to the fort. It was sartin we could do nothing till night, but we both strained our cords as much as possible to get them to stretch a bit, and give us a better chance of slipping out of them. No one came near us for some time, and as we could hear the sound of voices, we guessed that a great council was taking place, and we agreed at once to loosen the knots, so as to be in readiness for work, as like enough they would put a sentry over us at night.

"It was a risky thing to try, fur we might be disturbed at any minute. Still we thought it were our only chance, so Jack set to work with his teeth at my knots, and in a quarter of an hour had loosened them; then I undid his. We unbound our thongs and then fastened them up again so that to the eye they looked just the same as before, but really with a jerk they would fall off us.

"I must teach you how to do that, Harold; some time yer may find it of use. The knots was tied up as tightly as before, and it would have needed a close examination to see that we was not tied as tight as ever. Not a word was spoken and we was as quiet as mice, fur we could hear two Red-skins talking outside. You may guess we was pretty slick about it; and I don't know as ever I felt so thankful as when we laid ourselves down again, just as we had been throwed, without the slit in the tent having opened and a red face peered in.

"A quarter of an hour later, a Red-skin came in and looked at us. Seeing, as it seemed to him, as we hadn't moved, he went out again. Just before nightfall two on them came in together, rolled us over and looked at the knots. They found as these was all right; then one sat down just in the door of the tent, and the other took his place outside. We waited some hours.

244

THE GREAT STORM

"At last the fires burnt low and the camp got quiet. We knew it was well-nigh hopeless to wait for them all to be asleep, for Red-skin nature is a restless one, and especially when there is anything on hand, they will turn out two or three times in the night to smoke their pipes by the fires, and they would be the more restless since, as we had seen, there was only four or five wigwams erected and all would be sleeping on the ground. At last I thought the time was come, and gave Jack a nudge and we both sat up.

"It were a ticklish moment, young 'un, I can tell yer, for we knew that it were scarce possible to get off without the alarm being raised. Ef the wigwam had stood close to the edge of the forest, it would have been comparatively easy, for once among the trees, we might have hoped to have outrun 'em, though the moon was so pesky bright; but unfortunately it was built not far from the river, and we should have to cross the hull clearing to gain the woods. The chances weren't good, I can tell you, but it was clear as we had to try them. We had purposely moved about pretty often so that our movements would not attract the attention of the Indian now. It did not take a minute to slip out of the cords, which, tight as they looked, really were not fastened at all, there being two loose double ends between our arms and our bodies. We could see the outside sentry through the open door, and we waited till he turned his back and looked out on the river; then suddenly I gripped the Red-skin sitting at the entrance by the neck with both my bands, pretty tight as you may reckon, and Jack catched his knife from his belt and buried it in his body.

"That was soon over, and not a sound made as would have startled a mouse. Then, standing up, I made a spring on to the sentry, while Jack used his knife as before. We let him drop softly down, and prepared to bolt, when of a sudden the war-whoop sounded not twenty feet away. One of the Red-skins, finding the ground hard, I suppose, was strolling up to speak to the sentry when he saw us tackle him.

"Fur a moment he wur too much surprised to holler; but when he did, he gave a yell as brought the hull tribe to their feet. Jack had taken up the sentry's rifle."

245

"'Yer had better have held yer tongue,' he said, as he levelled on the Red-skin; and before the 'whoop' was out of his lips, the bullet hit him and he went down like a log.

"It didn't need to look round to see as there was no chance of getting to the trees, fur two hundred Red-skins was between us and them.

"'We must take to the river, Jack,' I said. It wur but thirty yards away. I expected every moment, as we run, to hear the rifle bullets whistle round us, but I guess Pontiac had given orders that no gun was to be fired, lest it might be heard at the fort. Anyhow, not a shot was fired, and we got down safe to the bank."

CHAPTER XVII
THE SCOUT'S STORY

"LUCKILY enough, there was a canoe lying close at our feet. 'Shove it out, Jack,' says I, 'and then keep along the bank.' We gave it a shove with all our strength, and sent it dancing out into the river. Then we dived in and swam down close under the bank. There was bushes growing all along, and we came up each time under them. The Red-skins was some little distance behind us as we reached the river, and in course thought we had throwed ourself flat in the canoe. In a minute or two they got another and paddled off to it, and we soon heard the shout as they raised when they found it was empty. By this time we was a hundred yards below the spot where we had taken to the water, and knowing as they would be off along the bank and would find us in no time, we scrambled straight up and made for the trees.

"We was within fifty yards of the edge of the forest, and none of the Red-skins was near us, as the hull body had clustered down at the spot where we had jumped in. We hadn't fairly set foot on the bank afore they saw us, and with a whoop—which sometimes wakes me even now in my sleep, and makes me sit up with the sweat on my forehead—they started. I could run faster then than I can now, and ye may guess that I went my best. We plunged into the trees, and went as hard as we could foot it, the Red-skins being fifty or sixty yards behind.

"Our hope was to find a place with a thickish underwood. It was darker a deal under the trees than in the clearing; still, it was not dark enough to hide us from Red-skin eyes. We run straight, for we knew that they could see us, and after about four hundred yards we came upon a place where the undergrowth grew thick. Here we began to dodge them, turning now one way and now another, keeping always low in the bushes. They had lost us by

247

sight now, but there were so many of them that we pretty nigh despaired of getting through. Some of them had tried to follow us, but the best part had run straight on for a bit, and then, when sure they had headed us, scattered right and left, so that they were ahead of us now as well as on our traces, and we could hear them shouting all round us. So we did the only thing there was to be done, and made the best of our way back to the clearing, keeping low, and taking good care not to cross any patch where the moonlight through the trees fell on the ground.

"It were lucky for us that it was a camp of braves. Had it been an ordinary Red-skin encampment, there would have been squaws, and boys, and wuss still, dogs, who would have seed us the moment we got back; but being all braves on the war-path, the hull gang had started arter us, and not a soul had remained in the clearing. We did not rest there long, you may be sure, but made straight down to the water. There we picked out a canoe and crossed the river, and got into the shade of the trees the other side. Then we kept along down it till we got close to the fort of Detroit.

"We could see a good many smouldering fires out afore it, and guessed that a strong body of Red-skins, pretending to be friends, had camped there. However, we made round them, and reached the gate of the fort safe. The sentries would not let us in; but when a sergeant was fetched, it turned out as he knew us, seeing that we had been scouting out from thar in the summer. Pretty thankful we was when the gate closed arter us. Our news would keep, so we waited till morning afore we saw the major, and then told him the whole history of the matter, and how Pontiac had raised all the tribes east of the Mississippi against us.

"We found that Pontiac had been into the camp with fifty of his warriors three days afore, professing great friendship, and had said that in two or three days he would call again and pay a formal visit.

"Detroit then was but a trading post, defended by a stockade twenty feet high and 1200 yards in circumference. About 50 houses of traders and store-keepers stood within it. The garrison was composed of 120 men of the 18th Regiment and 8 officers. They had three guns, two six-pounders and a three-pounder, and three mortars, but their carriages was so old and rotten that they was of no real service. Two vessels mounting some small guns lay in the river off the fort. The governor was a good soldier, but he was naturally startled at hearing that there was something like a thousand Red-skins in the woods round; however, he said that now he had warning, he was not afraid of them. A messenger was sent off in a canoe to carry the tidings east and to ask for reinforcements and the traders was all told to get their arms ready.

"At eight o'clock in the morning, Pontiac was seen approaching with three hundred warriors. There had been no declaration of war, and the Red-skins was supposed to be friendly, so the Major did not like to be the first to commence hostilities, as folks who knew nothing of it might likely enough have raised an outcry about massacring the poor Injuns. Howsumever, he called all the troops under arms, and disposed them behind the houses. The traders, too, with their rifles, were drawn up ready. The gates was opened when Pontiac arrived, and he and his warriors entered. They had left their rifles behind them, as they pretended that their mission was a peaceful one, but they had all got their tomahawks and knives under their blankets. They advanced in a body towards where Major Gladwin and his officers was standing in front of his quarters.

"Jack and me and two or three scouts who happened to be in the fort stood just behind, careless like, with our rifles, so that in case of any sudden attack we could keep them back for a moment or two. I noticed that Pontiac carried in his hand a wampum belt. I noticed it because it was green on one side and white on the other, and it turned out arterwards that when he twisted that belt with two hands it was to be the signal for an attack.

"Pontiac spoke soft for a time. He was a fine Red-skin; that can't be denied. He was a Catawba by birth, but had been adopted into the tribe of Ottawas, and had risen to be their chief. He was a great brave, and war one of the best speakers I have ever heard. He was a wise chief, as you may guess by the way he got all the tribes to lay aside their private quarrels and make common cause against us.

I watched him close; he kept his eyes on the Major, and spoke as cool and as calm as if he had nothing on his mind, but I could see the warriors glancing about, wondering, no doubt, what had become of the soldiers. Presently the chief changed his tone, and began to pretend as he was in a rage at some grievance or other.

"The Major just put his whistle to his lips, and in a moment, from behind the houses the soldiers and traders marched out, rifle in hand. You never saw a more disgusted crew than those Red-skins. I will do Pontiac justice to say that he never so much as moved, but just went on talking as if he had not noticed the troops at all. The Major answered him in the same way, and after half an hour's talk, the Red-skins went out again without so much as a knife having been shown. Major Gladwin gave Jack and me papers testifying as how we had saved Detroit from destruction, and sent an account of it to Governor Amherst, and to this day Jack and me draws special pensions for that ere business besides what we earned as British scouts."

"That was an adventure, Peter!" Harold said. "They did not take Detroit after all, did they?"

"No; we beat them off handsome when they tried it. Then they laid siege to Fort Pitt, and tried very hard there, too, but the place held out till some troops who had come up marched out from here and raised the siege. At some of the little places they succeeded. Lots of settlers was massacred. At Fort Sandusky, Ensign Paulli and the garrison was massacred by a party of Hurons and Ottawas, who came in as friends. This was on the same day as they had intended to do for us at Detroit.

"At St. Joseph's an English ensign with fourteen soldiers were killed by the Pettawatomies, but nowhere did Pontiac obtain any real successes. The French in Illinois were preparing to leave, and he could get no assistance from them. After the siege of Fort Pitt was raised, peace was patched up again. Pontiac's confederacy, finding as they had got none of the successes he promised them, was beginning to break up, and the English saw no chance of doing any good by hunting the Red-skins among the forests, so both parties was willing for peace.

250

THE SCOUT'S STORY

"Pontiac never gave any more trouble, and some years afterwards, coming into one of the towns, he was killed by an Indian who had a private grudge agin him. And now I am longing for a quiet pipe, and you had better turn in. There's no saying whether we shall have a quiet night of it."

A fortnight passed without further incident. Then the sky became overcast, and Peter and the Indians agreed that snow would soon fall. All hands were at once set to work to make up their stores into packages. The deers' skins and blankets were tied in bundles; besides these, there were only two kegs of powder and about 200 lbs. of frozen fish.

Harold was in high glee at the thought that their imprisonment was to come to an end, although there was no doubt that the attempt would be a hazardous one, as the backwoodsmen were sure that the instant the snow began to fall, the Indians would be out in great numbers round the island to prevent the defenders taking advantage of the storm.

Several times Harold observed the two backwoodsmen talking with the Seneca chief and looking at the sky, and he thought that their countenances expressed some anxiety.

"What is it, Peter?" he asked, at length. "Don't you think we shall have a snowstorm?"

"We may have snow," Peter said, "but I think it is more than a snowstorm that is coming up. The clouds are flying past very fast, and it seems to me as ef we were in for a big gale of wind."

"But that will drift the snow and cover our footsteps almost as well as a snowstorm," Harold said.

"Yes, it would do all that," the scout answered.

"What is the objection to it, Peter?"

"In the first place, lad, ef it don't snow we may stop where we are, for there would be no chance of getting through the Injuns unless it snowed so thick that you could not see five feet away. It will be difficult enough anyhow. There will be four or five hundred of the varmint out, for they will bring even their boys with them, so as to form a pretty close line round the island. Our only chance will be for the Senecas to go first, and to silence, before they can

251

give the alarm, any they might meet on our line. That might be done in a heavy snow-storm, but without snow it would be impossible. In the next place, even if we got through them, we should have to carry our canoe."

"Why?" Harold asked, surprised. "What good could the canoe be to us, with the lake frozen hard?"

"You see the wind is on the shore here, lad, and when it does blow on these lakes, it blows fit to take the har off your head. It is as much as a man can do to make way agin it, and I doubt whether the gals could face it even with our help. As to carrying a canoe in its teeth, it could not be done."

"But why carry the canoe at all, Peter? That's what I cannot understand."

"Well, you see, lad, that the force of the wind acting on such a big sheet of ice will move it, and like enough you would see it piled up in a bank forty feet high on this side of the lake, and there will be a strip of clear water half a mile wide on the other. That's why we must take the canoe."

Harold was silent. In the face of such a probability, it was clear that they must encumber themselves with the canoe.

The prevision of the scout proved well founded. Before evening the wind was blowing with tremendous force; small flakes of snow were driven before it, inflicting stinging blows on the face and eyes of those who ventured out of shelter. As it became dark, the look-out announced that he could see large numbers of Indians starting from the shore at some distance to the right and left of them, showing that the Red-skins were fully alive to the possibility of the garrison of the island taking advantage of the storm, which would hide their trail, to effect their escape.

Every hour the fury of the gale increased, and it was unanimously agreed that until it diminished, it would be impossible for the girls, and for men carrying a canoe, to face it.

Two men were placed on watch at the mouth of the cove, where mines similar to the first had been sunk in the ice in a semicircle, some little distance outside that before exploded. This precaution had been taken on the day succeeding the great repulse of the enemy, although the scouts felt assured that the attempt would not be repeated. It was, however, thought possible that the Indians might, towards morning, if they found the Whites did not attempt to pass them, take advantage of the storm to attempt a surprise.

After it became dark, Cameron and Harold, as was their custom, went into the girls' hut to chat until it was time to turn in. The deer's skin and blankets had again been unrolled, and the covering of snow kept the interior warm in spite of the storm without.

"What is that noise?" Nelly asked, in a pause of the conversation.

"I don't know," Harold answered. "I have heard it for some time."

All were silent, intent upon listening; even above the fury of the gale a dull grinding sound with occasional crashes could be heard.

"I think it must be the ice," Harold said. "I will go out and see."

On issuing from the hut, he was for a time blinded by the force of the wind and the flying particles of snow. The din was tremendous. He made his way with difficulty in the teeth of the storm to the edge of the rocks. Then he started in surprise. A great bank of cakes and fragments of ice was heaped up against the wall of the rock, crashing and grinding against each other as they were pressed onward by fresh additions from beyond. Already the bank was nearly level with the top of the rock, and some of the vast blocks, two feet in thickness, had been thrust on to it. The surface of the lake beyond was no longer a brilliant white; every particle of snow had been swept away, and the dull gray of the rough ice lay unbroken.

He made his way at once to the hut of the men, and just as he reached the entrance, Peter (who had also been out to reconnoitre) came up, and before Harold had turned to speak, he put his head into the hut.

"Turn out," he said. "I tell yer, we are in a fix. This ain't no common gale. I don't know as ever I have been in a worse one."

"What is the use of turning out?" Pearson asked. "We can do nothing; and it is warmer here a sight than it is outside."

"I tell yer, ye have got to go. The ice is breaking up fast, and it is level with the top of the island already. Unless I am mistaken, there will be forty foot of ice piled over this island before an hour."

This was, indeed, alarming news. And in a minute the occupants of the hut were all in the open air.

"You can call in your scouts, Seneca; there ain't no fear of an attack to-night. No mortal soul—not even an Injun—could stand the force of the wind out on the lake."

A very short examination sufficed to show the truth of Peter's anticipations.

Already the upper part of the bank was sliding over the rock, and it was clear that in a very short time the whole would be covered.

"What is to be done, Peter?" Harold shouted.

"We must take to the canoe; there is clear water on the other side."

Harold crossed the island, and saw that what Peter said was correct. A broad strip of black water stretched away in the darkness towards the shore. The whole ice sheet was moving bodily before the wind, and as the island stood up in its course, the ice to windward of it was forced up over it, while under its lee the lake was clear. Not a moment was lost. The canoe was got out, carried over the rocks, and carefully lowered into the water under shelter of the island. All the stores and provisions were lowered into it. A deer's skin was spread on the bottom, and the girls, having been helped down into the boat, were told to lie down, and were then covered with blankets. The men wrapped themselves up in skins and blankets, and took their places in the canoe, the four Indians taking paddles.

Quickly as the preparations had been made, there were but a few feet of the island uncovered by the ice as the last man descended into the boat and they pushed off, and, after a couple of strokes, lay with the boat's head facing towards the island at a distance of fifty yards from it. Although somewhat sheltered from the wind, the Indians were obliged to paddle hard to maintain their position. Harold wondered at first that they had not kept closer to the island, but he soon understood their reason for keeping at a distance. The massive blocks of ice, pressed forward by the irresistible force behind, began to shoot from the top of the island into the water, gliding far on beneath the surface with the impetus of the fall, and then shooting up again with a force which would have destroyed the canoe at once had they touched it.

Soon a perfect cataract of ice was falling. Peter and Pearson took their places on each side of the bow of the canoe, with poles to push off the pieces as they drifted before the gale towards the shore. The work required the utmost strength and care. One touch from the sharp-edged blocks would have ripped open the side of the bark canoe like a knife, and in the icy-cold water encumbered by floating fragments of ice, even the best swimmer could not have gained the solid ice. The peril was great, and it needed all the strength and activity of the white men and the skill of the paddlers to avoid the danger which momentarily threatened them. So quickly did the blocks float down upon them that Pearson thought that it might be impossible to avoid them all. The skins, therefore, were hung round the boat, dropping some inches into the water, and these, although they could not have prevented the boat from being stove in by the larger fragments, yet protected its sides from the contact of the smaller ones.

For upwards of an hour the struggle continued, and Harold felt something like despair at the thought of a long night passed in such a struggle. Presently, however, sounds like the booming of cannon were heard above the gale.

"What is that?" he shouted to the Seneca chief, next to whom he was sitting.

"Ice break up," the chief replied. "Break up altogether."

This proved to be the case. As the ice was driven away from the farther side of the lake, the full force of the wind played upon the water there, and, as the streak widened, a heavy sea soon got up. The force of the swell extended under the ice, aiding the effect of the wind above, and the vast sheet began to break up. The reports redoubled in strength, and frequently the ice was seen to heave and swell. Then, with a sound like thunder, it broke, and great cakes were forced one on the top of another, and soon, instead of a level plain of ice, a chaos of blocks were tossing about on the waves.

Harold watched the change with anxiety. No longer was the channel on either side marked by regular defined lines, but floating pieces encroached upon it, and, looking towards the shore, the channel appeared to be altogether lost. The danger was overwhelming, but the Indians, paddling with increased strength, urged the boat forward until within ten yards of the island.

A few minutes before, such an approach would have assured the immediate destruction of the boat. But Harold saw with surprise that almost simultaneously with the breaking up of the ice-sheet, the fall of blocks from the island had ceased. A moment's reflection showed him the reason of this phenomenon. With the break-up of the ice-field, the pressure from behind had suddenly ceased. No longer were the blocks piled on the island pushed forward by the tremendous pressure of the ice-field. The torrent was stayed, and they could approach the island with safety. As soon as they were assured that this was so, the canoe was brought close to the rocks.

Pearson leapt ashore, climbed the rocks, and the ice piled twenty feet above them, and with his pole convinced himself that at this point there were no loose blocks likely to fall. Having satisfied himself on this head, he descended again and took his place in the boat. This was moored by a rope a few feet long to a bush growing from a fissure in the rock close to the water's edge. He and Peter remained on watch with their poles to fend off any pieces of ice which might be brought round by the waves, while the rest of the crew, wrapping themselves up in their blankets, lay down at the bottom of the boat.

The next morning, the storm still raged, and the lake presented the appearance of an angry sea. Sheltered under the lee of the island, the party were protected from its effects, although the light canoe rose and fell on the heavy swell. The ice had wholly disappeared from the lake, the pieces having been ground to atoms against each other in the storm. Along the line of shore there was a great bank of ice as high as the tree tops.

"The ways of the Lord are wonderful," Donald Cameron said. "The storm which threatened to be our destruction has proved our salvation. When it abates we shall be able to paddle down the lake without fear of interruption."

"Yes," Peter said, "the varmint are not likely to follow us. In the first place, unless they thought of taking their canoes into the forest when the storm first began, which ain't likely, as they was a thinking only of cutting off our escape, they would have been smashed into tinder. In the second place, they could not catch us if they had canoes, for as we have eight paddles, counting those we made out of the seats when we was on shore, we should be able to laugh at them. And lastly, they have had such a taste of the quality of our rifles that even if they had a dozen canoes on hand, I doubt if they would care to attack us. No, sir; when this storm is over, we have nothing to do but to paddle down to the settlements at the other end of the lake."

Towards the afternoon the storm abated, and next morning the sun was shining brilliantly, and the waves had gone down sufficiently to enable the canoe to start on her voyage.

"Now, boys," Pearson said cheerfully, " ef ye don't want to get froze up again, you had best be sharp, for I can tell yer about thirty-six hours of this weather and the lake will be solid again."

Five minutes later the canoe with its eight sturdy paddlers started on its way, speeding like an arrow from the ice-covered island which had done them such good service in their greatest need.

"Now, Jake," Peter said, "the more strength you put into that paddle of yours, the sooner you will have a piece of meat atween your jaws."

The negro grinned. "Don't talk ob him, Massa Peter; don't say a word about him until I see him. Fish bery good when der noting else to eat, but Jake never want to see him again; he hab eaten quite enough for de rest ob his life."

Cameron, who was not accustomed to the use of the paddle, sat in the stern with the two girls, but the others were all used to the exercise, and the boat literally bounded along at each stroke from the sinewy arms, and by nightfall they had reached the opposite shore. After some hours' work together, two of them had rested, and from that time they took it by turns, six paddles being kept constantly going.

Without any adventure they arrived safely at the end of the lake. The clearing where Nelly had lived so long and where her father and mother had been killed, was passed in the night, much to Harold's satisfaction, as he was afraid that she would have been terribly upset at the many sad memories which the sight of the place could not but call up. On their way down, they had seen many gaps in the forest caused by the gale, but it was not until they reached the landing-place that the full effect of its destructive force was visible. Several scows and other boats lay wrecks upon the shore, every house in the little village was levelled to the ground, the orchards were ruined, palings and fences torn down, and the whole place strewn with fragments.

A few people were moving among the ruins. They gazed with a dull apathy upon the new-comers, apparently dazed by the misfortune that had befallen them. Harold learnt on questioning them that twenty-seven persons had been killed and the majority of the survivors more or less seriously injured. With the exception of the few whom they saw about, all the survivors had been taken off to the town in boats down the river, or in waggons lent by neighbours whose villages, sheltered in the woods, had escaped the ravages of the gale. After a few hours' halt, having obtained meat and other stores, they proceeded on their way to Detroit.

Here Nelly had several friends, who had long believed her to have fallen at the massacre at the farm. By them she was gladly received, and she took up her abode in a family with some daughters of her own age. Harold found that there was a considerable sum of money in the bank in her father's name, and from this, after a consultation with her, a sum of money sufficient to provide the Seneca and his followers with blankets, powder, and Indian finery for years, was drawn and bestowed upon them.

THE SCOUT'S STORY

A day or two afterwards the Indians left for their own country, highly gratified with the success of the expedition, and proud of the numerous scalps which hung from each of their girdles.

Harold learned that there was but little fighting going on along the Canadian frontier. The winter had set in again with extreme severity. The St. Lawrence would be frozen, and he would have no means of leaving Canada. He was therefore well content to settle down until the spring at Detroit, where he received numerous and hearty invitations to stay for any time, from the various friends of his cousins. Jake, of course, remained with him. Peter went up to Montreal, where he had some relations residing, Harold promising to call for him on his way east in the spring. Pearson, after a few days' stay in Detroit, started again with a comrade on a hunting expedition. Cameron and his daughter also spent the winter at Detroit.

The months passed very pleasantly to Harold. Since the war began he had had no period of rest or quiet, and he now entered with zest into the various amusements, sleighing and dancing, which helped to while away the long winter in America. He also joined in many hunting parties, for in those days game abounded up to the very edge of the clearings. Moose were abundant, and the hunt of these grand deer was full of excitement. Except when the snow is on the ground these animals can defy their pursuers, but the latter, with their snow-shoes, go lightly over the frozen snow, in which the moose sink heavily.

There were many discussions as to the future of Nelly. Several of her friends would gladly have adopted her as a member of their family, but Harold warmly urged that she should go to England and take up her abode with his mother, who was her nearest relative, and Nelly, somewhat to the surprise of her friends, finally agreed to this proposal. A purchaser was readily found for the farm, which was an excellent one, and the proceeds of the sale with the amount of savings in the bank gave her a little fortune of some two thousand five hundred pounds.

When the spring came and the navigation of the lake was open, Harold, Nelly, the Camerons, and Jake started in a ship for

Montreal. There they were joined by Peter, and sailed down to Quebec, where Nelly and the Camerons took passage for England. Very deep was the gratitude which Donald expressed to the friends who had restored his daughter to him. He had had enough of the colonies, and intended to spend the rest of his life among his own people in Scotland. Harold, Peter, and Jake sailed to join the English army in the south.

CHAPTER XVIII
THE SIEGE OF SAVANNAH

AFTER the surrender of General Burgoyne at Saratoga, the English parliament made another effort to obtain peace, and passed an act renouncing all rights to tax the colonists, and yielding every point as to which they had been in dispute. Commissioners were sent over with full authority to treat, and had the colonists been ready nominally to submit to England, a virtual independence, similar to that possessed by Canada and the Australian Colonies at the present time, would have been granted. As a very large body of the Americans had from the first been desirous of coming to terms, and as the paralysed state of trade caused great and general distress, it is probable that these terms might have been accepted, had it not been for the intervention of France. That power had all along encouraged the rebellion. She had smarted under the loss of Canada, and although her rule in her own colonies was far more arbitrary than that of England in America, she was glad to assist in any movement which could operate to the disadvantage of this country. Hitherto, nominally, she had remained neutral, but now, fearing that the offers of the English would induce the colonists to make peace, she came forward, recognized their independence, and engaged herself to furnish a large fleet for their assistance.

The colonists joyfully accepted the offer, seeing that the intervention of France in the struggle would completely alter its conditions. Hitherto the British had been enabled to send over men and stores at will, but were they blockaded by a French fleet, their difficulties would be immensely increased.

As there had been no cause of quarrel between England and France, this agreement was an act of wanton hostility on the part of the latter. On obtaining information of the signature of the treaty between France and the colonies, the English ambassador was recalled from Paris, and both countries prepared vigorously for war.

The first result was that the English deemed it prudent to evacuate Philadelphia and retreat to New York. Washington endeavoured to cut off their retreat, and a battle took place at "Freehold Court-house," in which the Americans were worsted. Washington drew off his army, and the British army continued its march to New York without further opposition. Early in May the French sent off a fleet of twelve ships of the line and six frigates carrying a large number of troops commanded by Count D'Estaing. An English fleet, under Admiral Byron, was lying at Portsmouth, and this sailed on the 9th of June in pursuit; for it was not until that time that information was received of the intended destination of the French fleet.

D'Estaing reached the American coast upon the very day on which the English army re-entered New York, and, after making a demonstration before that town, the French fleet sailed for Rhode Island to expel the British troops, under Sir Robert Pigott, who held it.

Lord Howe sailed with the fleet from New York to give battle to that of D'Estaing. For two days the fleets manœuvred in sight of each other. Howe, being inferior in force, wished to gain the weather-gauge before fighting. Failing to do this, on the third day he offered battle, but a tremendous storm prevented the engagement and dispersed both fleets. The French vessels retired to Boston and the English to New York.

Taking advantage of the departure of the French fleet, Sir Robert Pigott attacked the American force, which had crossed to Rhode Island to act with the French, and drove them from it. The fleet under Admiral Byron had, while crossing the Atlantic, met with a tremendous storm, which had entirely dispersed it, and the vessels arrived singly at New York. When their repairs were completed, the whole set out to give battle to the French, but D'Estaing, finding that by the junction of the two English fleets he was now menaced by a superior force, sailed away to the West Indies.

THE SIEGE OF SAVANNAH

After his departure an expedition was sent down along the coast to Georgia and East Florida. This met with great success. Savannah was captured, and the greater part of South Carolina was occupied. The majority of the inhabitants joyfully welcomed the troops, and many companies of volunteers were raised.

Harold had arrived in New York early in the spring. He had been offered a commission, but he preferred remaining with his two comrades in the position of scout. In this way he had far greater independence and, while enjoying pay and rations sufficient for his maintenance, he was to a great extent master of his own movements. At an earlier period of the war he was offered by General Howe a commission in the army, and his father would have been glad had he accepted it. Harold, however, although determined to fight until the struggle between the colonists and the mother country came to an end one way or the other, had no great liking for the life of an officer in the regular army, but had resolved, at the conclusion of the war, to settle down upon a farm on the lakes—a life for which he felt far more fitted than for the strict discipline and regularity of that of an officer in the army.

As, with the exception of the attack by the French fleet and American army upon Rhode Island, both parties remained quiet all through the summer of 1778, the year passed uneventfully to him, and the duties of the scouts were little more than nominal. During the winter, fighting went on in the Carolinas and Georgia with varied success.

In the spring of 1779 Harold and his comrades were, with a party of scouts, sent down to Georgia, where constant skirmishes were going on, and the services of a body of men accustomed to outpost duty were required. They were landed in May, and joined General Prevost's force on the island of St. John, situated close to the mainland, and connected with it by a bridge of boats, at the end of which, on the mainland, a post had been erected. Shortly afterwards General Prevost left for Savannah, taking with him most of the troops, which were carried away in the sloops which had formed the bridge of boats. On the American side, General Lincoln commanded a considerable army, which had been despatched by Congress to drive the English from that state and the Carolinas.

Lieutenant-colonel Maitland, who commanded the post on the mainland, was left with only a flat boat to keep up his communication with the island. He had under his command the first battalion of the 71st Highlanders, now much weakened in numbers, part of a Hessian regiment, some provincial volunteers, and a detachment of artillery, the whole not exceeding 500 effective men. Hearing that General Lincoln was advancing against him, Colonel Maitland sent all his sick, baggage, and horses across to the island, and placed the post as far as possible in a defensive position. Most of the scouts who had come down from New York had accompanied General Prevost to Savannah; but Harold, with Peter Lambton, Jake, and three or four others, had been ordered to remain with Colonel Maitland, and were sent out to reconnoitre when the enemy were known to be approaching.

"This is something like our old work, Peter, upon Lake Champlain," Harold said, as, with his two comrades, he took his way in the direction from which the enemy were advancing.

"Aye, lad, but they have none of the Red-skins with them, and there will be no great difficulty in finding out all about them. Besides, we have got Jake with us, and just about here Jake can do better than we can. Niggers swarm all over the country, and are as ready to work for one side as the other, just as their masters go. All Jake has got to do is to dress himself as a plantation nigger, and stroll into their camp. No question will be asked him, as he will naturally be taken for a slave on some neighbouring estate. What do you say, Jake?"

Jake at once assented, and when they approached the enemy, he left his comrades and carried their plan into execution. He was away six hours, and returned saying that the enemy were 5000 strong, with eight pieces of artillery.

"We must hurry back," Peter said. "Them are big odds agin us. Ef all our troops was regulars, I don't say as they might not hold the place, but I don't put much count on the Germans, and the colonists ain't seen no fighting. However, Colonel Maitland seems a first-rate officer. He has been real sharp in putting the place into a state of defence, and I reckon ef the Yankees thinks as they are going to eat us up without trouble, they will be mistaken."

Jake reported that the enemy were on the point of marching forward, and the scouts hurried back to give Colonel Maitland news of their coming.

It was late in the afternoon when they reached the post.

"At what time do you think they will arrive here?" the Colonel asked, when Jake had made his report.

"Dey be pretty close by dark, for sure," Jake replied.

"But I don't think, sir," Peter added, "they will attack before morning. They would not be likely to try it in the dark, not knowing the nature of the place."

The commander was of the same opinion, but, to prevent the possibility of surprise, he placed pickets at some distance round the fort, the scouts being, of course, of the party.

The night passed quietly, but at seven in the morning, Peter, Harold, and Jake, who were at some distance in advance of the others, saw the enemy approaching. They fired their pieces and fell back upon the outposts. Their position was rather to the right of the line of defence. The pickets were about to fall back when seventy men, being two companies of the 71st under Captain Campbell, were sent out to feel the enemy.

"We are going to have a skirmish," Peter said. "I know these Highlanders; instead of just firing a bit and then falling back, they will be sticking here and fighting as if they thought they could lick the hull army of the Yankees."

It was as Peter predicted. The Highlanders took post behind a hedge and maintained a desperate resistance to the advance of the enemy. Harold and his comrades for some time fought with them.

"It is time for us to be out of this," Peter said presently. "Let's jest get back to the fort."

"We cannot fall back till they do, Peter."

"I don't see that," Peter said. "We are scouts, and I don't see no advantage in our chucking away our lives because these hot-headed Highlanders choose to do so. Peter Lambton is ready to do a fair share of fighting, but when he is sure that fighting ain't no good, then he goes;" and, suiting the action to the word, Peter rose from his recumbent position and began to make his way back to the camp, taking advantage of every bit of cover.

Harold could not help laughing. For an instant he remained irresolute, and then, seeing the overwhelming forces with which the enemy were approaching, he called to Jake and followed Peter's example. So obstinately did the Highlanders fight that they did not retreat until all their officers were killed or wounded, and only eleven men out of the two companies succeeded in regaining the camp.

The whole force of the enemy now advanced against the works, and, halting at a distance of 300 yards, opened a tremendous fire from their cannon on the intrenchments. The defenders replied, but so overwhelming was the force of the assailants that the Hessians abandoned the portion of the works committed to them and fell back.

The enemy pressed forward, and had already gained the foot of the abbatis when Colonel Maitland brought up a portion of the 71st upon the right, and these gallant troops drove the Americans back with slaughter. Colonel Maitland and his officers then threw themselves among the Hessians, and succeeded in rallying them and bringing them back to the front. The provincial volunteers had also fought with great bravery. They had for a time been pressed backward, but finally maintained their position.

The Americans, finding that all their efforts to carry the post were unavailing, fell back to the forest. On the English side the loss amounted to 129. The Americans fought in the open, and suffered much more heavily.

The position of matters was suddenly changed by the arrival of Count D'Estaing with a fleet of forty-one ships of war off the coast. The American general, Lincoln, at once proposed to him to undertake a combined movement to force the English to quit Georgia. The arrival of the French fleet was wholly unexpected; and the *Experiment*, a frigate of fifty guns, commanded by Sir James

"The Highlanders maintained a desperate resistance."

Wallace, having two or three ships under his convoy, fell in with them off the mouth of the Savannah river. Although the *Experiment* had been much crippled by a gale through which she had recently passed, Sir James Wallace would not haul down his flag, and opposed a desperate resistance to the whole of the French fleet, and did not surrender until the *Experiment* was completely dismasted and riddled with shot.

Upon the news that the French fleet was off the mouth of the river, Captain Henry, who commanded the little squadron of four small English ships, fell back to Savannah after removing all the buoys from the river. He landed his guns from the ships and mounted them on the batteries, and the marines and blue-jackets were also put on shore to assist in the defence. Two of the brigs of war were sunk across the channel below the town, to prevent the French frigates coming up. A boom was laid across above the town, to prevent fire-rafts from being sent down.

D'Estaing landed the French troops at the mouth of the river, and, marching to the town, summoned General Prevost to surrender. The English commander, who had sent off a messenger to Colonel Maitland, ordering him to march instantly to his assistance, with the force under him, which now amounted to 800 men, asked for twenty-four hours before giving an answer. D'Estaing, who knew that General Lincoln was close at hand, made sure that Prevost would surrender without resistance, and so granted the time asked for. Before its expiration, Colonel Maitland, after a tremendous march, arrived at the town. As the French commanded the mouth of the river, he had been obliged to transport his troops in boats through the marshes by a little creek, which for two miles was so shallow that the troops were forced to wade waist-deep, dragging the boats by main force through the mud.

Upon the arrival of this reinforcement, General Prevost returned an answer to Count D'Estaing that the town would be defended to the last. Some time was spent by the enemy in landing and bringing up the heavy artillery from the ships, and the French and Americans did not begin their works against the town until the 23d of September. The garrison had utilized the time thus afforded to them to erect new defences. The allied force of the assailants consisted of more than 10,000 Americans and 5000 French troops, while the garrison, including regulars, provincial corps, sailors, militia, and volunteers, did not exceed 2500.

Nevertheless they did not allow the enemy to carry on their work without interruption. Several sorties were made. The first of these under Major Graham of the 16th Regiment reached the lines of the enemy, and threw them into confusion. Large reinforcements came up to their assistance, and, as Graham's detachment fell back upon the town, the enemy incautiously pursued it so close up to the British lines that both artillery and musketry were brought to bear upon them, and they lost a large number of men before they could regain their works. On the morning of the fourth of October the batteries of the besiegers opened fire with fifty-three pieces of heavy artillery and fourteen mortars. General Prevost sent in a request to Count D'Estaing that the women and children might be permitted to leave the town and embark on board vessels lying in the river, there to await the issue of the fight, but the French commander refused the request in a letter couched in insulting terms.

The position of Savannah was naturally strong. The river protected one of its sides, and a deep swamp partially flooded by it covered another. The other two were open to the country, which in front of them was for several miles level and clear of wood. The works which had been thrown up on these sides were extremely strong. When the French first landed, there were but ten pieces of cannon upon the fortifications, but so incessantly did the garrison work that before the conclusion of the siege, nearly 100 pieces of artillery were mounted on the redoubts and batteries erected round the town. Upon the side of the swamp there was not much fear of attack, but three redoubts were erected to prevent a surprise from this direction. The defence on the right face of the town was conducted by Colonel Maitland. The defence on the left, consisting of two strong redoubts and several batteries, was commanded by Lieutenant-colonel Cruger. In the centre were several strong works of which General Prevost himself took the special supervision. The whole British line, except where the swamp rendered no such defence necessary, was surrounded by a thick abattis.

The French fire made no sensible impression upon the English defences, and finding that the British artillery equalled his own, D'Estaing determined to discontinue the attack by regular approaches, and to carry the place by storm. His position was a perilous one; he had already spent a long time before the place, and at any moment the English fleet might arrive from the West Indies and attack his fleet, which was weakened by the men and guns which had been landed to carry on the siege. He therefore determined to risk an assault rather than remain longer before the town. To facilitate the attack, an officer with five men on the eighth of October advanced to the abattis and set fire to it. The wood, however, was still green, and the flames were easily extinguished.

The attack was fixed for the following morning. Bodies of the American militia were to feign attacks upon the centre and left, while a strong force of the combined armies were to make a real attack in two columns upon the right. The troops composing the two columns consisted of 3500 French soldiers and 950 Americans. The principal force, commanded by Count D'Estaing in person, assisted by General Lincoln, was to attack the Springfield redoubt, which was situated at the extreme right of the British central line of defence, and close to the edge of the swamp. The other column, under the command of Count Dillon, was to move silently along the margin of the swamp, to pass the three redoubts, and get into the rear of the British lines.

The troops were in motion long before daylight. The attempt to burn the abattis had excited the suspicion of the English, that an assault might be intended; and, accordingly, pickets were thrown out in front of the intrenchments, and the scouts were ordered to keep a sharp watch among the trees which grew in and near the swamp.

Harold with his friends had accompanied Colonel Maitland's column in its march to Savannah, and had laboured vigorously at the defences, being especially occupied in felling trees and chopping wood for the abattis. Before daybreak they heard the noise made

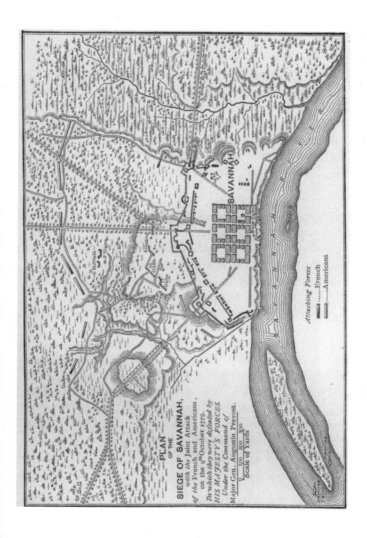

PLAN OF THE

SIEGE OF SAVANNAH,
with the Joint Attack
of the French and Americans,
on the 9th October 1779,
In which they were defeated by
HIS MAJESTY'S FORCES
Under the Command of
Major Gen. Augustin Prevost.

100 100 200 300
Scale of Yards

Attacking Forces
.....French
.....Americans

by the advance of the enemy's columns through the wood, and hurried back to the Springfield redoubt, where the garrison at once stood to arms. In this redoubt were a corps of provincial dismounted dragoons supported by the South Carolina Regiment.

Just as daylight appeared, the column led by Count D'Estaing advanced towards the Springfield redoubt; but the darkness was still so intense that it was not discovered until within a very short distance of the works. Then a blaze of musketry opened upon it, while a destructive cross-fire was poured in from the adjoining batteries. So heavy was the fire that the head of the column was almost swept away. The assailants, however, still kept on with great bravery until they reached the redoubt. Here a desperate hand-to-hand contest took place. Captain Tawse fell with many of his men, and for a moment a French and an American standard were planted upon the parapet; nevertheless, the defenders continued to cling to the place and every foot was desperately contested.

At this moment Colonel Maitland, with the grenadiers of the 60th Regiment and the marines, advanced and fell upon the enemy's column, already shaken by the obstinate resistance it had encountered and by its losses by the fire from the batteries. The movement was decisive. The assailants were driven headlong from the redoubt, and retreated, leaving behind them 637 of the French troops killed and wounded and 264 of the Americans.

In the meantime the column commanded by Count Dillon mistook its way in the darkness, and was entangled in the swamp, from which it was unable to extricate itself until it was broad daylight; and it was fully exposed to the view of the garrison and to the fire from the British batteries. This was so hot and so well directed that the column was never able even to form, far less to penetrate into the rear of the British lines.

When the main attack was repulsed, Count Dillon drew off his column also. No pursuit was ordered, as, although the besiegers had suffered greatly, they were still three times more numerous than the garrison.

A few days afterwards the French withdrew their artillery and re-embarked on board ship.

THE SIEGE OF SAVANNAH

The siege of Savannah cost the allies 1500 men, while the loss of the garrison was only 120. The pleasure of the garrison at their successful defence was marred by the death of Colonel Maitland, who died from the effects of the unhealthy climate and of the exertions he had made.

The French fleet, a few days after the raising of the siege, was dispersed by a tempest, and Count D'Estaing, with the majority of the ships under his command, returned to France.

During the course of this year there were many skirmishes round New York, but nothing of any great importance took place. Sir Henry Clinton, who was in supreme command, was unable to undertake any offensive operations on a large scale, for he had not received the reinforcements from home which he had expected. England, indeed, had her hands full, for in June Spain joined France and America in the coalition against her and declared war. Spain was at that time a formidable marine power, and it needed all the efforts that could be made by the English government to make head against the powerful fleets which the combined nations were able to send to sea against them. It was not only in Europe that the Spaniards were able to give effective aid to the allies. They were still a power on the American continent, and created a diversion, invading West Florida, and reducing and capturing the town and fort of Mobile.

In the spring of 1780 Sir Henry Clinton sent down an expedition under the command of Lord Cornwallis to capture Charlestown and reduce the province of South Carolina. This town was extremely strongly fortified. It could only be approached by land on one side, while the water, which elsewhere defended it, was covered by the fire of numerous batteries of artillery. The water of the bay was too shallow to admit of the larger men-of-war passing, and the passage was defended by Fort Moultrie, a very formidable work. Admiral Arbuthnot, with the *Renown*, *Romulus*, *Roebuck*, *Richmond*, *Blonde*, *Raleigh*, and *Virginia* frigates, with a favourable wind and tide, ran the gauntlet of Fort Moultrie, succeeded in passing up without great loss, and co-operated on the sea face with the attack of the army on the land side.

A force was landed on Sullivan's Island, on which Fort Moultrie stood, and the fort, unprepared for an attack in this direction, was obliged to surrender. The American cavalry force, which had been collected for the relief of the town, was defeated by the English under General Tarleton. The trenches were pushed forward with great vigour, and the batteries of the third parallel opened at short range on the town with great execution. The advances were pushed forward at the ditch, when the garrison, seeing that further resistance was impossible, surrendered. Five thousand prisoners were taken, 1000 American and French seamen, and 10 French and American ships of war.

With the fall of Charlestown all resistance ceased in South Carolina. The vast majority of the inhabitants made their submission to the British government, and several loyalist regiments were raised.

Colonel Tarleton, with 170 cavalry and 100 mounted infantry, was despatched against an American force under Colonel Burford, consisting of 350 infantry, a detachment of cavalry, and two guns which had taken post on the border of North Carolina. Tarleton came up with him, and after a sharp action, the Americans were entirely defeated. One hundred and thirteen were killed on the spot, and 207 made prisoners, of whom 103 were badly wounded.

For some months the irregular operations were continued, the Americans making frequent incursions into the Carolinas. The British troops suffered greatly from the extreme heat and the unhealthiness of the climate.

In August the American General Gates advanced towards Camden and Lord Cornwallis also moved out to that town, which was held by a British garrison. The position there was not hopeful. Nearly 800 were sick, and the total number of effectives was under 2000, of whom 500 were provincials. The force under General Gates amounted to 6000 men, exclusive of the corps of Colonel Sumpter, 1000 strong, which were manœuvring to cut off the English retreat. Cornwallis could not fall back on Charlestown without abandoning the sick and leaving all his magazines and stores in the hands of the enemy, besides which, a retreat would have

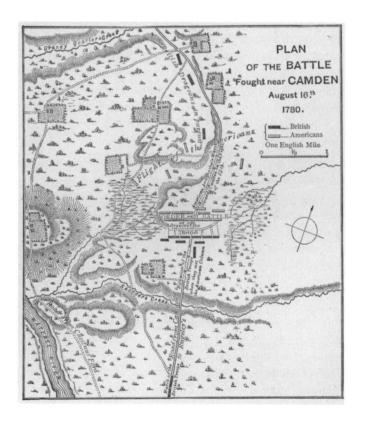

involved the abandonment of the whole province, with the exception of Charlestown. He therefore decided upon giving battle to the enemy, who were posted at Rugeley's Mills, a few miles distant, leaving the defence of Camden to Major M'Arthur, with some provincials and convalescent soldiers, and a detachment of the 63d Regiment, which was expected to arrive during the night.

The army marched in the following order:—The 1st division, commanded by Lieut.-colonel Webster, consisting of four companies of light infantry, and the 23d and 33d Regiments, preceded by an advanced guard of forty cavalry. The 2d division, consisting of provincial troops and two battalions of the 71st Regiment, followed as a reserve. The dragoons of the legion formed the rear-guard. The force marched at 10 o'clock on the night of the 16th of August, intending to attack at daybreak the next morning, but it happened that at the very same hour in which the British set out, General Gates with his force were starting from Rugeley's Mills with the intention of attacking Camden in the morning.

At 2 o'clock in the night, the advance guards of the two armies met and fired into each other. In the confusion, some prisoners were taken on both sides, and the generals, finding that the two armies were face to face, halted and waited till morning. Lord Cornwallis placed Webster's division on the right, the second division, which was under the command of Lord Rawdon, on the left. The battalion known as the Volunteers of Ireland were on the right of Lord Rawdon's division, and communicated with the 33rd Regiment on the left of Webster. In the front line were two 6-pounders and two 3-pounders under the command of Lieut. Macleod, R.A. The 71st, with two 6-pounders, was in reserve, one battalion being placed behind each wing. The dragoons were held in reserve to charge in the event of a favourable opportunity.

The flanks of the English position were covered by swamps which somewhat narrowed the ground and prevented the Americans from utilizing fully their great superiority of numbers. The Americans were also formed in two lines.

Soon after daybreak Lord Cornwallis ordered Colonel Webster to advance and charge the enemy. So fiercely did the English regiments attack that the Virginia and North Carolina troops who opposed them quickly gave way, threw down their arms, and fled. General Gates and General Casswell in vain attempted to rally them. They ran like a torrent and spread through the woods in every direction. Lord Rawdon began the action on the left with no less vigour and spirit than Lord Cornwallis on the right, but here and in the centre the contest was more obstinately maintained by the Americans. Their reserve were brought up, and the artillery did considerable execution. Their left flank was, however, exposed by the flight of the troops of Carolina and Virginia, and the light infantry and 23rd Regiments were halted in the pursuit, and, wheeling round, came upon the flank of the enemy, who, after a brave resistance of nearly three-quarters of an hour, were driven into total confusion and forced to give way on both sides. Their rout was completed by the cavalry, who continued their pursuit twenty-two miles from the field of action.

Between 800 and 900 of the enemy were killed, and about 1000, many of whom were wounded, were taken prisoners. Among these were Major-general Baron de Kalbe and Brigadier-general Rutherford. All the baggage stores and camp packages, a number of colours, and several pieces of cannon, were taken. General Gates, finding himself unable to rally the militia, fled first to Charlotte, 90 miles from the seat of action, and then to Hillsborough, 180 from Camden. General Gist alone, of all the American commanders, was able to keep together about 100 men, who, flying across the swamp on their right, through which they could not be pursued by the cavalry, made their escape in a body. The loss of the British troops amounted to 69 killed, 245 wounded, and 11 missing. The loss of the Americans in killed, wounded, and taken, exceeded the number of British regular troops engaged by at least 300. It was one of the most decisive victories ever won.

CHAPTER XIX
IN AN AMERICAN PRISON

UPON the morning after the victory of Camden, Lord Cornwallis despatched Colonel Tarleton with the light infantry and the German legion, three hundred and fifty men in all, to attack Colonel Sumpter, who, with 800 men and two pieces of cannon, had, upon hearing late at night of General Gates' defeat, marched away at all speed. Thinking himself out of danger, he halted at mid-day to rest his men. The British came upon them by surprise; 150 were killed or wounded and 300 made prisoners. The rest scattered as fugitives. Two guns and 1000 stand of arms, and all the stores and baggage, were taken; and 250 prisoners, some of the British soldiers, and the rest loyal militiamen, whom Sumpter had captured near Camden, were released.

Lord Cornwallis, after obtaining supplies for his troops and taking steps for the pacification of the province, was about to move forward into North Carolina when he received news of the destruction of a column under Major Fergusson. This officer, with a detachment of 150 British regulars and 800 provincials, was attacked by 5000 mounted partisans, most of them border men, accustomed to forest fighting. Fergusson took up a position on a hill called King's Mountain. This from its height would have been a good position for defence, but being covered with wood, it offered great opportunities for the assailants, who dismounted and fought behind trees in accordance with the tactics taught them in Indian warfare. Again and again the English charged with the bayonet, each time driving their assailants back; but these, from their shelter behind the trees, instantly recommenced their destructive fire. In little over an hour from the commencement of the fight, 150 of the defenders were killed and many more wounded. Still, they repulsed every attack until their commander fell dead; then the second in command, judging further resistance in vain, surrendered.

On the news of this misfortune, Lord Cornwallis fell back, as the western frontiers of South Carolina were now exposed to the incursions of the band which had defeated Fergusson. In the retreat the army suffered terribly. It rained for several days without intermission. The soldiers had no tents and the water was everywhere over their shoes. The continued rains filled the rivers and creeks prodigiously and rendered the roads almost impassable. The climate was most unhealthy, and for many days the troops were without rum. Sometimes the army had beef and no bread, sometimes bread and no beef. For five days it was supported on Indian corn, which was collected in the fields; five ears being served out as a daily allowance to each two soldiers. They had to cook it as they could, and this was generally done by parching it over the fire. One of the officers of the quarter-master's department found some of the loyal militia grating their corn. This was done by breaking up a canteen and punching holes in the bottom with their bayonets, thus making a kind of rasp. The idea was communicated to the adjutant-general, and afterwards adopted for the army.

The soldiers supported their hardships and privations cheerfully, as their officers were no better provided than themselves, and the fare of Lords Cornwallis and Rawdon was the same as their own.

The toilsome march came to an end at last, and the army had rest after its labours. The only other incident which occurred of importance was an action between a force under Colonel Tarleton and one of considerably superior strength under General Sumpter strongly posted on a commanding position. The British attack was repulsed, but General Sumpter, being badly wounded, was carried off the field during the night, and the force under his command at once dispersed.

No other event occurred, and the army passed its time in winter quarters till the spring of 1781. During this winter the enemies of Great Britain were reinforced by the accession of the Dutch. At this time the efforts which England was called upon to make were indeed great. In Europe, France, Spain, and Holland were banded against her; in India, our troops were waging a desperate war with Hyder Ali, while they were struggling to retain their hold on their American colonies. Here, indeed, the operations had for the last two years languished. The reinforcements which could be spared were extremely small, and although the British had almost uniformly defeated the Americans in every action in which there was any approach to equality between the forces engaged, they were unable to do more than hold the ground on which they stood. Victorious as they might be, the country beyond the reach of their rifles swarmed with their enemies, and it became increasingly clear to all impartial observers that it was impossible for an army, which in all did not amount to more than twenty thousand men, to conquer a continent in arms against them.

Harold was not present at the later events of the campaign of 1780. He and Jake had been with the column of Major Fergusson. Peter Lambton had not accompanied him, having received a bullet wound in the leg in a previous skirmish, which, although not serious, had compelled him to lay up for a time.

"Me no like the look ob dis affair, Massa Harold," Jake said, as the Americans opened fire upon the troops gathered at the top of King's Mountain. "Dese chaps no fools; dey all backwoodsmen, dey know how to fight de Red-skins; great hunters all ob dem."

"Yes," Harold agreed, "they are formidable opponents, Jake. I do not like the look of things. These men are all accustomed to fighting in the woods, while our men have no idea of it. Their rifles are infinitely superior to these army muskets, and every man of them can hit a deer behind the shoulder at the distance of one hundred and fifty yards, while at that distance most of our men would miss a haystack."

The scouts and a few of the provincials who had been accustomed to forest warfare took up their position behind trees, and fought the advancing enemy in their own way. The mass of the defenders, however, were altogether puzzled by the stealthy approach of their foes, who advanced from tree to tree, seldom showing as much as a limb to the fire of the defenders, and keeping up a deadly fire upon the crowd of soldiers.

Had there been time for Major Fergusson, before being attacked, to have felled a circle of trees and made a breast-work round the top of the hill, the result might have been different. Again and again the British gallantly charged down with the bayonets; but the assailants, as they did so, glided away among the trees after firing a shot or two into the advancing troops, and retreated a hundred yards or so, only to recommence their advance as soon as the defenders retired again to their position. The loss of the assailants was very slight, the few who fell being for the most part killed by the rifles of the scouts.

"It am no use, Massa Harold," Jake said. "Jest look how dem poor fellows am being shot down. It all up wid us this time."

When, upon the fall of Major Fergusson, his successor in command surrendered the post, the defenders were disarmed. The Kentucky men, accustomed only to warfare against Indians, had no idea of the usages of war, and treated the prisoners with great brutality. Ten of the loyalist volunteers of Carolina they hung at once upon trees. There was some discussion as to the disposal of the rest. The border men, having accomplished their object, were anxious to disperse at once to their homes. Some of them proposed that they should rid themselves of all further trouble by shooting them all. This, however, was overruled by the majority. Presently the prisoners were all bound, their hands being tied behind them, and a hundred of the border men surrounded them and ordered them to march across the country.

Jake and several other negroes who were among the captives were separated from the rest, and, being put up to a rough auction, were sold as slaves. Jake fell to the bid of a tall Kentuckian, who, without a word, fastened a rope round his neck, mounted his horse, and started for his home. The guards conducted the white prisoners to Woodville, eighty miles from the scene of the fight. This distance was accomplished in two days' march. Many of the unfortunate men, unable to support the fatigue, fell and were shot by their guards. The rest struggled on, utterly exhausted, until they arrived at Woodville, where they were handed over to a strong force of militia gathered there. They were now kindly treated, and by more easy marches were taken to Richmond, in Virginia, where they were shut up in prison. Here were many English troops, for the Americans, in spite of the terms of surrender, had still retained as prisoners the troops of General Burgoyne.

Several weeks passed without incident. The prisoners were strongly guarded, and were placed in a building originally built for a jail, and surrounded by a very high wall. Harold often discussed with some of his fellow-captives the possibility of escape. The windows were, however, all strongly barred, and even should the prisoners break through these, they would only find themselves in the court-yard. There would then be a wall thirty feet high to surmount, and at the corners of this wall, the Americans had built sentry-boxes, in each of which two men were stationed night and day. Escape, therefore, seemed next to impossible.

The sentries guarding the prison and at the gates were furnished by an American regiment stationed at Richmond. The warders in the prison were for the most part negroes. The prisoners were confined at night in separate cells; in the daytime they were allowed in parties of fifty to walk for two hours in the court-yard. There were several large rooms in which they sat and took their meals, two sentries with loaded muskets being stationed in each room. Thus, although monotonous, there was little to complain of; their food, if coarse, was plentiful, and the prisoners passed the time in talk, playing cards, and in such games as their ingenuity could invent.

One day when two of the negro warders entered with the dinners of the room to which Harold belonged, the latter was astounded at recognizing in one of them his faithful companion Jake. It was with difficulty that he suppressed an exclamation of gladness and surprise. Jake paid no attention to him, but placed the great tin dish heaped up with yams, which he was carrying, upon the table, and with an unmoved face left the room. A fortnight passed without a word being exchanged between them. Several times each day Harold saw the negro; but the guards were always present, and although, when he had his back to the latter, Jake sometimes indulged in a momentary grin or a portentous wink, no further communication passed between them.

One night at the end of that time, Harold, when on the point of going to sleep, thought he heard a noise as of his door gently opening. It was perfectly dark, and after listening for a moment he laid his head down again, thinking that he had been mistaken, when he heard close to the bed the words in a low voice:

"Am you asleep, Massa Harold?"

"No, Jake," he exclaimed directly. "Ah, my good fellow, how have you got here?"

"Dat were a bery easy affair," Jake said. "Me tell you all about it."

"Have you shut the door again, Jake? There is a sentry coming along the passage every five minutes."

"Me shut him, massa; but dere ain't no fastening on dis side, so Jake will sit down with him back against him."

Harold got up and partly dressed himself, and then sat down by the side of his follower.

"No need to whisper," Jake said. "De walls and de doors bery thick; no one hear. But de sentries on de walls hear if we talk too loud."

The windows were without glass, which was in those days an expensive article in America, and the mildness of the climate of Virginia rendered glass a luxury rather than a necessity. Confident that even the murmur of their voices would not be overheard if they spoke in their usual way, Jake and Harold were enabled to converse comfortably.

"Well, massa," Jake said, "my story am not a long one. Dat man dat bought me he rode in two days, someting like 100 miles. It war a lucky ting dat Jake had tramp on his feet de last four years, else soon enough he tumble down, and den de rope round him neck hang him. Jake awful footsore and tired when he get to de end of dat journey. De Kentuckyman he live in a clearing not far from a village. He had two oder slaves; dey hoe de ground and work for him. He got grown-up son, who look after dem while him fader away fighting. Dey not afraid of de niggers running away, because dere plenty Red-skin not far away, and nigger scalp just as good as white man's. De oder way der were plenty ob villages, and dey tink nigger get caught for sure if he try to run away. Jake make up his mind he not stop dere bery long. De Kentuckian was a bery big, strong man, but not so strong as he was ten years ago, and Jake tink he more dan a match for him. Jake pretty strong himself, massa."

"I should think you were, Jake," Harold said. "There are not many men, white or black, who can lift as great a weight as you can."

"For a week Jake work bery hard. Dat Kentucken hab a way of always carrying his rifle about on his arm, and as long as he do dat, dere no chance of a fair fight. De son he always hab a stick and he mighty free wid it. He hit Jake seberal times, and me say to him once, 'Young man, you better mind what you do.' Me suppose dat he not like de look dat I gib him. He speak to his father, and he curse and swear awful, and stand wid de rifle close by, and tell dat son of his to larrup Jake. Dat he do, massa, for some time. Jake not say noting, but he make a note ob de affair in his mind. De bery next day de son go away to de village to buy some tings dat he want. De father he come out and watch me at work. He curse and swear as usual; he call me lazy hound, and swear he cut de flesh from my back. Presently he come quite close and shake him fist in Jake's face. Dat was a foolish ting to do. So long as he keep bofe him hands on de gun, he could say what he like, quite safe; but when he got one hand up lebel wid Jake's nose, dat different ting altogether. Jake throw up his hand and close wid him. De gun tumble down, and we wrestle and fight. He strong man for sure, but Jake jest a little stronger. We roll ober and ober on de ground for some minutes. At last Jake get de upper band, and seize de white man by de throat, and he pretty quickly choke him life out. Den he pick up de gun, and wait for de son. When he come back he put a bullet trough him. Den he go to de hut and get food and powder and ball, and start into de woods. De oder niggers dey take no part in de affair. Dey look on while de skirmish lasts, but not interfere one way or other. When it ober, me ask dem if dey like to go with me, but dey too afraid of de Red-skins, so Jake start by himself. Me hab plenty of practice of de woods, and no fear of meeting Red-skins, except when dey on de war-path. De woods stretch a bery long way all over de country, and Jake trabel in dem for nigh tree weeks. He shoot deer and manage bery well; see no Red-skin from de first day to de last; den he come out into de open country again, hundreds of miles from de place where he kill dat Kentuckian. He leab his gun behind him now, and trabel for Richmond, where he hear dat de white prisoners was kept; he walk all night, and at day sleep in de woods or de plantations, and eat de ears of Indian corn. At last he get to Richmond. Den he gib out dat him massa wanted him to fight on de side of de English, and dat he run away. He go to de prison and offer to work dere. Dey think him story true, and as he had no massa to claim him, dey say he state property, and work widout wages like de other niggers here— dey all forfeited slaves whose massas had joined the English. Dese people so poor, dey can't afford to pay white man, so dey take Jake as warder, and by good luck dey put him in to carry de dinner to de bery room where Massa Harold was."

"And have you the keys to lock us up?"

"No, massa, dese niggers only cook de dinners and sweep de prison and de yard, and do dat kind of job. De white warders— dere are six of dem—dey hab de keys."

"Then how did you manage to get here, Jake?"

"Dat not bery easy matter, Massa Harold. Most of de warders drink like fish, but de head man, him dat keep de keys, he not drink. For some time Jake not see him way, but one night when he lock up de prisoners, he take Jake round wid him, and Jake carried de big bunch of keys—one key to each passage. When he lock up de doors here and hand de key to Jake to put on to de bunch again, Jake pull out a hair ob him head and twist it round de ward ob de key so as to know him again. Dat night me get a piece of bread and work him up with some oil till he quite like putty, den me steal to de chief warder's room, and dere de keys hang up close to him bed. Jake got no shoes on and he stood up bery silent. He take down de bunch ob keys and carry dem off. He get to quiet place and strike a light, and search trough de keys till he find de one with de hair round it. Den he take a deep impression ob him with de bread. Den he carry back de keys and hang dem up. Jake not allowed to leave de prison. We just as much prisoners as de white men, so he not able to go out to get a key made, but in de store-room dere are all sorts of tools, and he get hold ob a fine file. Den he look about among de keys in de doors of all de store-rooms and places which were not kept locked up. At last he find a key just de right size, and dough de wards were a little different, dey was of de right shape. Jake set to work and filed off all de knobs and points which did not agree with de shape in de bread. Dis morning when you was all out in the yard, me come up quietly and tried de key and found dat it turned de lock quite easy. With a feather and some oil, me oil de lock and de key till it turned without making de least noise. Den to-night me waited until de sentry came along de corridor, and den Jake slip along, and here he is."

"Capital, Jake! " Harold said. "And now, what is the next thing to do? Will it be possible to escape through the prison?"

"No, Massa Harold, der am tree doors from de prison into de yard, and dere is a sentry outside ob each, and de main guard ob twenty men are down dere too. No possible to get out of doors without de alarm being given."

"With the file, Jake, we might cut through the bars."

"We might cut trough de bars and get down into de court-yard; dat easy enough, massa. Jake could get plenty of rope from de store-room; but we hab de oder wall to climb."

"You must make a rope-ladder for that, Jake."

"What sort ob a ladder dat, massa?"

Harold explained to him how it should be made.

"When you have finished it, Jake, you should twist strips of any sort of stuff, cotton or woollen, round and round each of the wooden steps, so that it will make no noise touching the wall as we climb it. Then we want a grapnel."

"Me no able to make dat, massa."

"Not a regular grapnel, Jake; but you might manage something which would do."

"What sort ob ting?" Jake asked.

Harold sat for some time in thought. "If the wall were not so high it would be easy enough, Jake, for we could do it by fastening the rope within about three inches of the end of a pole six feet long and three inches thick. That would never pull over the wall; but it is too high to throw the pole over."

"Jake could trow such a stick as dat over easy enough, massa, no difficulty about dat; but me no see how a stick like dat balance massa's weight."

"It would not balance it, Jake; but the pull would be a side pull, and would not bring the stick over the wall. If it were only bamboo it would be heavy enough."

"Bery well, Massa Harold; if you say so, dat all right. Jake can get de wood easy enough; dere am plenty of pieces among de fire-wood dat would do for us."

"Roll it with strips of stuff the same way as the ladder steps, so as to prevent it making a noise when it strikes the wall. In addition to the ladder, we shall want a length of rope long enough to go from this window to the ground, and another length of thin rope more than twice the height of the wall."

"Bery well, Massa Harold, me understand exactly what am wanted, but it will take two or tree days to make de ladder, and me can only work ob a night."

"There is no hurry, Jake. Do not run any risk of being caught. We must choose a dark and windy night. Bring two files with you, so that we can work together, and some oil."

All right, massa; now me go."

"Shut the door quietly, Jake, and do not forget to lock it behind you," Harold said, as Jake stole noiselessly from the cell.

A week passed without Jake's again visiting Harold's cell. On the seventh night the wind had got up and whistled around the jail, and Harold, expecting that Jake would take advantage of the opportunity, sat down on his bed without undressing and awaited his coming. It was but half an hour after the door had been locked for the night that it quietly opened again.

"Here me am, sar, with ebery thing dat was wanted; two files and some oil, de rope-ladder, de short rope for us to slide down, and de long thin rope and de piece of wood six feet long and as thick as de wrist."

They at once set to work with the files, and in an hour had sawn through two bars, making a hole sufficiently wide for them to pass. The rope was then fastened to a bar. Harold took off his shoes and put them in his pocket and then slid down the rope into the court-yard. With the other rope Jake lowered the ladder and pole to him and then slid down himself. Harold had already tied to the pole, at four inches from one end, a piece of rope of some four feet long, so as to form a loop about half that length. The thin rope was put through the loop and drawn until the two ends came together.

Noiselessly they stole across the yard until they reached the opposite wall. The night was a very dark one, and although they could make out the outline of the wall above them against the sky-line, the sentry-boxes at the corners were invisible. Harold now took hold of the two ends of the rope, and Jake, stepping back a few yards from the wall, threw the pole over it. Then Harold drew upon the rope until there was a check, and he knew that the pole was hard up against the edge of the wall. He tied one end of the rope-ladder to an end of the double cord, and then hauled steadily upon the other. The rope running through the loop drew the ladder to the top of the wall. All this was done quickly and without noise.

"Now, Jake, do you go first," Harold said. "I will hold the rope tight below, and do you put part of your weight on it as you go up. When you get to the top, knot it to the loop, and sit on the wall until I come up."

In three minutes they were both on the wall, the ladder was hauled up and dropped on the outside, while the pole was shifted to the inside of the wall. Then they descended the ladder and made across the country.

"Which way we go, massa?" Jake asked.

IN AN AMERICAN PRISON

"I have been thinking it over," Harold replied, "and have decided on making for the James River. We shall be there before morning, and can no doubt find a boat. We can guide ourselves by the stars, and when we get into the woods, the direction of the wind will be sufficient."

The distance was about twenty miles, but although accustomed to scouting at night, they would have had difficulty in making their way through the woods by the morning, had they not struck upon a road leading in the direction in which they wanted to go.

Thus it was still some hours before daylight when they reached the James River. They had followed the road all the way, and at the point where it reached the bank there was a village of considerable size, and several fishermen's boats were moored alongside. Stepping into one of these, they unloosed the head-rope and pushed out into the stream. The boat was provided with a sail. The mast was soon stepped and the sail hoisted.

Neither Harold nor Jake had had much experience in boat sailing, but the wind was with them, and the boat ran rapidly down the river, and before daylight they were many miles from their point of starting. The banks of the James River are low and swampy, and few signs of human habitation were seen from the stream. It widened rapidly as they descended, and became rougher and rougher. They therefore steered into a sheltered spot behind a sharp bend of the river and there anchored.

In the locker they found plenty of lines and bait, and, setting to work, had soon half a dozen fine fish at the bottom of the boat. They pulled up the kedge and rowed to shore, and soon made a fire, finding flint and steel in the boat. The fish were broiled over the fire upon sticks. The boat was hauled in under some over-hanging bushes, and, stretching themselves in the bottom, Harold and Jake were soon fast asleep.

The sun was setting when they woke.

"What are you going to do, sar?" Jake asked. "Are you tinking ob trabelling by land or ob sailing to New York?"

"Neither, Jake," Harold answered. "I am thinking of sailing down the coast inside the line of keys to Charlestown. The water there is comparatively smooth, and as we shall be taken for fishermen, it is not likely that we shall be overhauled. We can land occasionally and pick a few heads of Indian corn to eat with our fish, and as there is generally a breeze night and morning, however still and hot the day, we shall be able to do it comfortably. I see that there is an iron plate here which has been used for making a fire and cooking on board, so we will lay in a stock of dry wood before we start."

The journey was made without any adventure. While the breeze lasted, they sailed; when it fell calm, they fished, and when they had obtained a sufficient supply for their wants, they lay down and slept under the shade of their sail stretched as an awning. Frequently they passed within hail of other fishing-boats, generally manned by negroes. But beyond a few words as to their success, no questions were asked. They generally kept near the shore, and when they saw any larger craft, they either hauled the boat up or ran into one of the creeks in which the coast abounds. It was with intense pleasure that at last they saw in the distance the masts of the shipping in Charlestown harbour.

Two hours later they landed. They fastened the boat to the quay, and made their way into the town unquestioned. As they were walking along the principal street, they saw a well-known figure sauntering leisurely toward them. His head was bent down, and he did not notice them until Harold hailed him with the shout of "Hallo! Peter, old fellow, how goes it?"

Peter, although not easily moved or excited, gave a yell of delight which astonished the passers-by.

"Ah, my boy!" he exclaimed. "This is a good sight for my old eyes. Here have I been a fretting and a worrying myself for the last three months, and cussing my hard luck that I was not with you in that affair on King's Mountain. At first, when I heard of it, I said to myself, 'The young 'un got out of it somehow. He ain't going to be caught asleep.' Well, I kept on hoping and hoping that you would turn up, till at last I could not deceive myself no longer, and was forced to conclude that you had either been rubbed out or taken prisoner. About a month ago we got from the Yankees a list of the names of those they had captured, and glad I was to see yours among them. However, as I thought as how you were not likely to be out as long as the war lasted, I was a thinking of giving it up and going to Montreal and settling down there. It was lonesome like without you, and I missed Jake's laugh, and altogether things didn't seem natural like. Jake, I am glad to see you. Your name was not in the list, but I thought it likely enough they might have taken you and set you to work and made no account of yer."

"That is just what they did, but he got away after settling his scores with his new master, and then made for Richmond, where I was in prison. Then he got me loose, and here we are. But it is a long story, and I must tell it you at leisure."

CHAPTER XX
THE WAR IN SOUTH CAROLINA

THE fishing-boat was disposed of for a few pounds, and Harold and Jake were again fitted out in the semi-uniform worn by the scouts. On the 13th of December, the very day after their arrival, a considerable detachment of troops, under General Leslie, arrived, and on the 19th marched, 1500 strong, to join Lord Cornwallis. Harold and his mates accompanied them, and the united army proceeded north-west, between the Roanoke river and the Catawba. Colonel Tarleton was detached with a force of 1000 men, consisting of light and German Legion infantry, a portion of the 7th Regiment, and of the 1st battalion of the 71st, 350 cavalry, and 2 field-pieces. His orders were to pursue and destroy a force of some 800 of the enemy under General Morgan. The latter, finding himself pressed, drew up his troops for action near a place called the Cow Pens. Then ensued the one action in the whole war in which the English, being superior in numbers, suffered a severe defeat.

Tarleton, confident of victory, led his troops to the attack without making any proper preparations for it. The infantry advanced bravely, and although the American infantry held the ground for a time with great obstinacy, they drove them back, and the victory appeared to be theirs. Tarleton now sent orders to his cavalry to pursue, as his infantry were too exhausted, having marched at a rapid pace all night, to do so. The order was not obeyed, and Major Washington, who commanded the American cavalry, advanced to cover his infantry. These rallied behind their shelter, and fell upon the disordered British infantry. Thus suddenly attacked when they believed that victory was in their hands, the English gave way, and were driven back. A panic seized them, and a general rout ensued. Almost the whole of them were either killed or taken prisoners.

Tarleton in vain endeavoured to induce his German Legion cavalry to charge; they stood aloof, and at last fled in a body through the woods. Their commander and fourteen officers remained with Tarleton, and with these and forty men of the 17th Regiment of dragoons, he charged the whole body of the American cavalry, and drove them back upon the infantry.

No partial advantage, however brilliant, could retrieve the misfortune of the day. All was already lost, and Tarleton retreated with his gallant little band to the main army under Lord Cornwallis, twenty-five miles from the scene of action. The British infantry were all killed, wounded, or taken prisoners, with the exception of a small detachment which had been left in the rear, and who fell back hastily as soon as the news of the result of the action reached them. The Legion Cavalry returned to camp without the loss of a man.

The defeat of Cow Pens had a serious influence on the campaign. It deprived Lord Cornwallis of the greater portion of his light infantry, who were of the greatest utility in a campaign in such a country, while the news of the action had an immense influence in raising the spirits of the colonists. Hitherto they had uniformly met with ill success when they opposed the British with forces even approaching an equality of strength. In spite of their superior arms and superior shooting, they were unable to stand the charge of the British infantry, who, indeed, had come almost to despise them as foes in the field. The unexpected success urged them to fresh exertions, and brought to their side vast numbers of waverers.

General Morgan, who was joined by General Greene, attempted to prevent Cornwallis passing the fords of the Catawba. It was not till the first of February that the river had fallen sufficiently to render a passage possible. Colonel Webster was sent with his division to one of the principal fords, with orders to open a cannonade there and make a feint of crossing, while the general himself moved towards a smaller and less known ford. General

TRUE TO THE OLD FLAG

Davidson, with 300 Americans, was watching this point; but the brigade of guards were ordered to commence the passage, and were led by their light infantry companies under Colonel Hall. The river was 500 yards across, and the stream so strong that the men, marching in fours, had to support one another to enable them to withstand its force. The ford took a sharp turn in the middle of the river.

The night being dark, the guards were not perceived until they had reached this point, when the enemy immediately opened fire upon them. The guide at once fled without his absence being noticed until it was too late to stop him. Colonel Hall, not knowing of the bend in the ford, led his men straight forward towards the opposite bank; and although their difficulties were much increased by the greater depth of water through which they had to pass, the mistake was really the means of saving them from much loss, as the Americans were assembled to meet them at the head of the ford, and would have inflicted a heavy loss upon them as they struggled in the stream. They did not perceive the change in the direction of the column's march until too late, and the guards, on landing, met them as they came on, and quickly routed and dispersed them. The British lost four killed, among whom was Colonel Hall, and thirty-six wounded.

The rest of the division then crossed. Colonel Tarleton, with the cavalry, was sent against 500 of the Americans who had fallen back from the various fords, and, burning with the desire to retrieve the defeat of Cow Pens, the Legion Horse charged the enemy with such fury that they were completely routed, fifty of them being killed.

Morgan and Greene withdrew their army through the river Roanoke, hotly pursued by the English. For a few days the British army remained at Hillsborough, but no supplies of food sufficient for its maintenance could be found there, so it again fell back. General Greene being reinforced by a considerable force, now determined to fight, and accordingly advanced and took up a position near Guildford Court-house.

THE WAR IN SOUTH CAROLINA

The American force consisted of 4243 infantry and some 3000 irregulars—for the most part backwoodsmen from the frontier;—while the British force amounted to 1445, exclusive of their cavalry, who, however, took little part in the fight. About four miles from Guildford the advanced guards of the army met, and a sharp fight ensued—the Americans, under Colonel Lee, maintaining their ground staunchly until the 23d Regiment came up to the assistance of Tarleton, who commanded the advance.

The main American force was posted in an exceedingly strong position. Their first line was on commanding ground, with open fields in front; on their flanks were woods, and a strong fence ran along in front of their line. The second line was posted in a wood 300 yards in rear of the first, while 400 yards behind were three brigades drawn up in the open ground round Guildford Court-house. Colonel Washington, with two regiments of dragoons and one of riflemen, formed a reserve for the right flank; Colonel Lee, with his command, was in reserve on the left.

As soon as the head of the British column appeared in sight, two guns upon the road opened fire upon them, and were answered by the English artillery. While the cannonade continued, the British formed in order of attack. The 71st, with a provincial regiment supported by the first battalion of the guards, formed the right; the 23d and 33d, led by Colonel Webster, with the grenadiers and 2d battalion of guards, formed the left. The light infantry of the guards and the cavalry were in reserve.

When the order was given to advance, the line moved forward in perfect steadiness, and at one hundred and fifty yards, the enemy opened fire. The English did not fire a shot till within eighty yards, when they poured in a volley and charged with the bayonet. The first line of the enemy at once fell back upon the second; here a stout resistance was made. Posted in the woods and sheltering themselves behind trees, they kept up for some time a galling fire which did considerable execution. The British, however, would not be denied. General Leslie brought up the right wing of the 1st battalion of guards into the front line, and Colonel Webster called up the 2d battalion. The enemy's second line now fell back on their third, which was composed of their best troops, and the struggle was a very obstinate one.

The Americans from their vastly superior numbers occupied so long a line of ground that the English commanders, in order to face them, were obliged to leave large gaps between the different regiments; thus it happened that Webster, who with the 33rd Regiment, the light infantry, and the second battalion of guards turned towards the left, found himself separated from the rest of the troops by the enemy, who pushed in between him and the 23rd. These again were separated from the guards. The ground was very hilly, the wood exceedingly thick, and the English line became broken up into regiments separated from each other, each fighting on its own account and ignorant of what was going on in other parts of the field.

The second battalion of guards was the first that broke through the wood into the open grounds of Guildford Court-house. They immediately attacked a considerable force drawn up there, routed them, and took their two cannon with them; but, pursuing them with too much ardour and impetuosity towards the woods in the rear, were thrown into confusion by a heavy fire from another body of troops placed there, and being instantly charged by Washington's dragoons, were driven back with great slaughter, and the cannon were retaken.

At this moment the British guns, advancing along the road through the wood, issued into the open and checked the pursuit of the Americans by a well-directed fire. The 71st and the 23d now came through the wood. The second battalion of guards rallied and again advanced, and the enemy were quickly repulsed and put to flight. The two guns were recaptured with two others.

Colonel Webster, with the 33d, returned across the ravine through which he had driven the enemy opposed to him, and rejoined the rest of the force. The Americans drew off in good order. The 23d and 21st pursued with the cavalry for a short distance, and were then recalled. The fight was now over on the centre and left; but on the right, heavy firing was still going on. Here General Leslie, with the first battalion of guards and a Hessian regiment, had been greatly impeded by the excessive thickness of the woods, which rendered it impossible to charge with the bayonet. As they struggled through the thicket, the enemy swarmed around them, so that they were at times engaged in front, flanks, and rear. The enemy were upon an exceedingly steep rise, and lying along the top of this, they poured such a heavy fire into the guards that these suffered exceedingly; nevertheless, they struggled up to the top and drove the front line back, but found another far more numerous drawn up behind. As the guards struggled up to the crest, they were received by a tremendous fire on their front and flanks, and suffered so heavily that they fell into confusion. The Hessian regiment, which had suffered but slightly, advanced in compact order to the left of the guards, and, wheeling to the right, took the enemy in the flank with a very heavy fire. Under cover of this the guards reformed and moved forward to join the Hessians and complete the repulse of the enemy opposed to them. They were, however, again attacked both in the flank and the rear; but at last they completely dispersed the troops surrounding them, and the battle came to an end.

This battle was one of the most obstinate and well contested throughout the war, and the greatest credit is due to the British, who drove the enemy, three times their own number, from the ground chosen by them and admirably adapted to their mode of warfare.

The loss, as might have been expected, was heavy, amounting to 93 killed and 413 wounded—nearly a third of the force engaged. Between 200 and 300 of the enemy's dead were found on the field of battle, and a great portion of their army disbanded. The sufferings of the wounded on the following night were great. A tremendous rain fell, and the battle had extended over so large an area that it was impossible to find and collect them. The troops had had no food during the day, and had marched several miles before they came into action; nearly 50 of the wounded died during the night.

Decisive as the victory was, its consequences were slight. Lord Cornwallis was crippled by his heavy loss, following that which the force had suffered at Cow Pens. The two battles had diminished the strength of his little force by fully half. Provisions were difficult to obtain, and the inhabitants, some of whom had suffered greatly upon previous occasions for their loyal opinions, seeing the weakness of the force and the improbability of its being enabled to maintain itself, were afraid to lend assistance or to show their sympathy, as they would be exposed on its retreat to the most cruel persecutions by the enemy.

Three days, therefore, after the battle, Lord Cornwallis retired, leaving seventy of the wounded who were unable to move, under the protection of a flag of truce. From Guildford Court-house he moved his troops to Wilmington in North Carolina, a seaport where he hoped to obtain provisions and stores, especially clothing and shoes.

General Greene, left unmolested after his defeat, reassembled his army, and receiving reinforcements, marched at full speed to attack Lord Rawdon at Camden, thinking that he would, with his greatly superior force, be able to destroy him in his isolated situation. The English commander fortified his position, and the American general drew back and encamped on Hobkirk Hill, two miles distant, to await the coming of his heavy baggage and cannon, together with some reinforcements. Lord Rawdon determined to take the initiative, and, marching out with his whole force of 900 men, advanced to the attack. The hill was covered at its foot by a deep swamp, but the English marched round this and stormed the position. The Americans made an obstinate resistance, but the English climbed the hill with such impetuosity, in spite of the musketry and grape-shot of the enemy, that they were forced to give way. Several times they returned to the attack, but were finally driven off in confusion; 100 prisoners were taken, and Lord Rawdon estimated that 400 of the enemy were killed and wounded. The American estimate was considerably lower, and as the Americans fought with all the advantage of position, while the English were exposed during their ascent to a terrible fire, which they were unable to return effectively, it is probable that the American loss, including the wounded, was inferior to that of the English, whose casualties amounted to 258.

THE WAR IN SOUTH CAROLINA

Harold and his companions did not take part either in the battle of Guildford Court-house or in that of Hobkirk Hill, having been attached to the fort known as Ninety-six, because a milestone with these figures upon it stood in the village. The force here was under the command of Lieutenant-colonel Cruger, who had with him 150 men of a provincial corps known as Delancey's, 200 of the second battalion of the New Jersey volunteers, and 200 local loyalists. The post was far advanced; but so long as Lord Rawdon remained at Camden, its position was not considered to be dangerous. The English general, however, after winning the battle of Hobkirk Hill, received news of the retirement of Lord Cornwallis towards Wilmington, and seeing that he would thereby be exposed to the whole of the American forces in South Carolina, and would infallibly be cut off from Charleston, he determined to retire upon that port. Before falling back he sent several messengers to Colonel Cruger, acquainting him of his intention. So well, however, were the roads guarded by the enemy that none of the messengers reached Ninety-six.

Colonel Cruger, being uneasy at the length of time which had elapsed since he had received any communication, sent Harold and the two scouts out with instructions to make their way towards the enemy's lines, and, if possible, to bring in a prisoner. This they had not much difficulty in doing. Finding out the position of two parties of the Americans, they placed themselves on the road between them. No long time elapsed before an American officer came along. A shot from Peter's rifle killed his horse, and before the officer could recover his feet, he was seized by the scouts. They remained hidden in the wood during the day, and at night returned with their prisoner to Ninety-six, thirty miles distant, avoiding all villages where resistance could be offered by hostile inhabitants.

From the prisoner Colonel Cruger learnt that Lord Rawdon had retreated from Camden, and that he was therefore entirely isolated. The position was desperate, but he determined to defend the post to the last, confident that Lord Rawdon would, as soon as possible, undertake an expedition for his release.

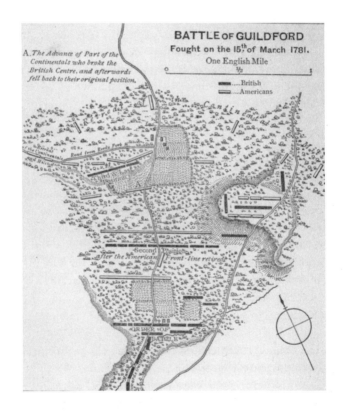

BATTLE OF GUILDFORD
Fought on the 15th of March 1781.
One English Mile

A. The Advance of Part of the
Continentals who broke the
British Centre, and afterwards
fell back to their original position.

British
Americans

THE WAR IN SOUTH CAROLINA

The whole garrison was at once set to work: stockades were erected, earthworks thrown up, a redoubt formed of casks filled with earth constructed, and the whole strengthened by ditches and abattis. Block-houses were erected in the village to enable the troops to fire over the stockades, and covered communications made between the various works. The right of the village was defended by a regular work called the Star. To the left was a work commanding a rivulet from which the place drew its supply of water.

Colonel Cruger offered the volunteers, who were a mounted corps, permission to return to Charleston, but they refused to accept the offer, and, turning their horses into the woods, determined to share the fate of the garrison. In making this offer the colonel was influenced partly by motives of policy, as the stock of provisions was exceedingly scanty, and he feared that they would not last if the siege should be a long one. Besides this, he feared that, as had already too often happened, should the place fall, even the solemn engagement of the terms of the surrender would not be sufficient to protect the loyalists against the vengeance of their countrymen.

On the 21st of May, General Greene with his army appeared in sight of the place and encamped in a wood within cannon-shot of the village. He lost no time, and in the course of the night threw up two works within seventy paces of the fortifications. The English commander did not suffer so rash and disdainful a step to pass unpunished. The scouts, who were outside the works, brought in news of what was being done, and also that the working parties were protected by a strong force.

The three guns, which constituted the entire artillery of the defenders, were moved noiselessly to the salient angle of the Star opposite the works, and at eleven o'clock in the morning these suddenly opened fire, aided by musketry from the parapets. The covering force precipitately retreated, and thirty men sallied out from the fort, carried the intrenchments, and bayoneted their defenders. Other troops followed, the works were destroyed, and the intrenching tools carried into the fort. General Greene, advancing with his whole army, arrived only in time to see the last of the sallying party re-enter the village.

"I call that a right-down good beginning," Peter Lambton said, in great exultation. "There is nothing like hitting a hard blow at the beginning of the fight; it raises your spirits, and makes t'other chap mighty cautious. You will see next time they will begin their works at a much more respectful distance."

Peter was right. The blow checked the impetuosity of the American general, and on the night of the 23d he opened his trenches at a distance of 400 yards. Having so large a force, he was able to push forward with great rapidity, although the garrison made several gallant sorties to interfere with the work.

On the 3d of June the second parallel was completed. A formal summons was sent to the British commander to surrender. This document was couched in the most insolent language, and contained the most unsoldierlike threats of the consequences which would befall the garrison and its commander if he offered further resistance. Colonel Cruger sent back a verbal answer that he was not frightened by General Greene's menaces, and that he should defend the post until the last.

The American batteries now opened with a heavy cross-fire, which enfiladed several of the works. They also pushed forward a sap against the Star fort, and erected a battery composed of gabions, thirty-six yards only from the abattis, and raised forty feet high so as to overlook the works of the garrison. The riflemen posted on its top did considerable execution, and prevented the British guns being worked during the day.

The garrison tried to burn the battery by firing heated shot into it, but from want of proper furnaces they were unable to heat the shot sufficiently, and the attempt failed. They then protected their parapets as well as they could by sand-bags with loopholes, through which the defenders did considerable execution with their rifles.

Harold and his two comrades, whose skill with their weapons was notorious, had their post behind some sand-bags immediately facing the battery, and were able completely to silence the fire of its riflemen, as it was certain death to show a head above its parapet.

THE WAR IN SOUTH CAROLINA

The enemy attempted to set fire to the houses of the village by shooting blazing arrows into them, a heavy musketry and artillery fire being kept up to prevent the defenders from quenching the flames. These succeeded, however, in preventing any serious conflagration, but Colonel Cruger ordered at once that the whole of the houses should be unroofed. Thus the garrison were for the rest of the siege without protection from the rain and night air; but all risk of a fire, which might have caused the consumption of their stores, was avoided.

While the siege had been going on, the town of Augusta had fallen, and Lieutenant-colonel Lee, marching thence to reinforce General Greene, brought with him the British prisoners taken there. With a scandalous want of honourable feeling he marched these prisoners along in full sight of the garrison, with all the parade of martial music and preceded by a British standard reversed.

If the intention was to discourage the garrison, it failed entirely in its effect. Fired with indignation at so shameful a sight, they determined to encounter every danger and endure every hardship rather than fall into the hands of an enemy capable of disgracing their success by so wanton an insult to their prisoners.

The Americans, strengthened by the junction of the troops who had reduced Augusta, began to make approaches against the stockaded fort on the left of the village, which kept open the communication of the garrison with their water supply. The operations on this side were intrusted to Colonel Lee, while General Greene continued to direct those against the Star.

On the night of the 9th of June a sortie was made by two strong parties of the defenders. That to the right entered the enemy's trenches and penetrated to a battery of four guns, which nothing but the want of spikes and hammers prevented them from destroying. Here they discovered the mouth of a mine intended to be carried under one of the defences of the Star.

The division on the left fell in with the covering party of the Americans, killed a number of them, and made their commanding officer a prisoner.

On the 12th Colonel Lee determined to attempt a storm of the stockade on the left, and sent forward a sergeant and six men with lighted combustibles to set fire to the abattis. The whole of them were killed before effecting their purpose. A number of additional cannon now arrived from Augusta, and so heavy and incessant a fire was opened upon the stockade from three batteries that on the 17th it was no longer tenable, and the garrison evacuated it in the night.

The suffering of the garrison for want of water now became extreme. With great labour a well had been dug in the fort, but no water was found, and none could be procured except from the rivulet within pistol-shot of the enemy. In the day nothing could be done, but at night negroes, whose bodies in the darkness were not easily distinguished from the tree-stumps which surrounded them, went out and at great risk brought in a scanty supply. The position of the garrison became desperate. Colonel Cruger, however, was not discouraged, and did his best to sustain the spirits of his troops by assurances that Lord Rawdon was certain to attempt to relieve the place as soon as he possibly could do so.

At length, one day, to the delight of the garrison, an American royalist rode right through the piquets under the fire of the enemy and delivered a verbal message from Lord Rawdon to the effect that he had passed Orangeburgh and was on his march to raise the siege.

Lord Rawdon had been forced to remain at Charleston until the arrival of three fresh regiments from Ireland enabled him to leave that place in safety and march to the relief of Ninety-six. His force amounted to 1800 infantry and 150 cavalry. General Greene had also received news of Lord Rawdon's movements, and finding from his progress that it would be impossible to reduce the fort by regular approaches before his arrival, he determined to hazard an assault.

The American works had been pushed up close to the forts; the third parallel had been completed, and a mine and two trenches extended within a few feet of the ditch. On the morning of the 18th of June a heavy cannonade was begun from all the American batteries. The whole of the batteries and trenches were lined with riflemen, whose fire prevented the British from showing their heads above the parapets. At noon two parties of the enemy advanced under cover of their trenches and made a lodgment in the ditch. These were followed by other parties with hooks to drag down the sand-bags, and tools to overthrow the parapet. They were, however, exposed to the fire of the block-houses in the village, and Major Green, the English officer who commanded the Star fort, had his detachment in readiness behind the parapet to receive the enemy when they attempted to storm.

As the main body of Americans did not advance beyond the third parallel and contented themselves with supporting the parties in the ditch with their fire, the commander of the fort resolved to inflict a heavy blow. Two parties, each 30 strong, under the command of Captains Campbell and French, issued from the sally-port in the rear, entered the ditch, and taking opposite directions charged the Americans who had made the lodgment with such impetuosity that they drove everything before them until they met. The bayonet alone was used and the carnage was great—two-thirds of those who entered the trenches were either killed or wounded.

General Greene, finding it useless any longer to continue the attempt, called off his troops, and on the following day raised the siege, and marched away with all speed, having lost at least 300 men in the siege. Of the garrison 27 were killed and 58 wounded.

On the 21st Lord Rawdon arrived at Ninety-six, and finding that it would be hopeless for him to attempt to overtake the retreating enemy, who were marching with great speed, he drew off the garrison of Ninety-six and fell back towards the coast.

A short time afterwards a sharp fight ensued between a force under Col. Stewart and the army of General Greene. The English were taken by surprise and were at first driven back, but they recovered from their confusion and renewed the fight with great spirit, and after a desperate conflict the Americans were repulsed. Two cannon and 60 prisoners were taken—among the latter, Col. Washington, who commanded the reserve. The loss on both sides was about equal, as 250 of the British troops were taken prisoners at the first outset. The American killed considerably exceeded our own. Both parties claimed the victory: the Americans because they had forced the British to retreat, the British because they had ultimately driven the Americans from the field and obliged them to retire to a strong position seven miles in the rear. This was the last action of the war in South Carolina.

CHAPTER XXI
THE END OF THE STRUGGLE

BEING unable to obtain any supplies at Wilmington, Lord Cornwallis determined to march on into Virginia, and to effect a junction with the British force, under General Arnold, operating there. Arnold advanced to Petersburgh, and Cornwallis effected a junction with him on the 20th of May. The Marquis de La Fayette, who commanded the colonial forces here, fell back. Just at this time the Count de Grasse, with a large French fleet, arrived off the coast, and after some consultation with General Washington, determined that the French fleet and the whole American army should operate together to crush the forces under Lord Cornwallis.

The English were hoodwinked by reports that the French fleet was intended to operate against New York, and it was not until they learned that the Count de Grasse had arrived with twenty-eight ships of the line at Chesapeake that the true object of the expedition was seen. A portion of the English fleet encountered them, but after irregular actions, lasting over five days, the English drew off and retired to New York. The commander-in-chief then attempted to effect a diversion, in order to draw off some of the enemy who were surrounding Cornwallis. The Fort of New London was stormed after some desperate fighting, and great quantities of ammunition and stores, and fifty pieces of cannon, taken. General Washington, however, did not allow his attention to be distracted. Matters were in a most critical condition, for although to the English the prospect of ultimate success appeared slight indeed, the Americans were in a desperate condition. Their immense and long-continued efforts had been unattended with any material success. It was true that the British troops held no more ground now than they did at the end of the first year of the war, but no efforts of the colonists had succeeded in wresting that ground from them. The people were exhausted and utterly disheartened. Business of all sorts was at a standstill. Money had ceased to circulate, and the credit of Congress stood so low that its bonds had ceased to have any value whatever. The soldiers were unpaid, ill fed, and mutinous. If on the English side it seemed that the task of conquering was beyond them, the Americans were ready to abandon the defence from sheer exhaustion. It was then of paramount necessity to General Washington that a great and striking success should be obtained to animate the spirits of the people.

Cornwallis, seeing the formidable combination which the French and Americans were making to crush him, sent message after message to New York to ask for aid from the commander-in-chief, and received assurances from him that he would at once sail with 4000 troops to join him. Accordingly, in obedience to his orders, Lord Cornwallis fortified himself at York Town.

On the 28th of September the combined army of French and Americans, consisting of 7000 of the former, 12,000 of the latter, appeared before York Town and the post at Gloucester. Lord Cornwallis had 5960 men, but so great had been the effects of the deadly climate in the autumn months that only 4017 men were reported as fit for duty.

The enemy at once invested the town and opened their trenches against it. From their fleet they had drawn an abundance of heavy artillery, and, on the 9th of October, their batteries opened a tremendous fire upon the works. Each day they pushed their trenches closer, and the British force was too weak, in comparison with the number of its assailants, to venture upon sorties. The fire from the works was completely overpowered by that of the enemy, and the ammunition was nearly exhausted. Day after day passed and still the promised reinforcements did not arrive. Lord Cornwallis was told positively that the fleet would sail on the 8th of October, but it came not, nor indeed did it leave the port until the 19th, the day on which Lord Cornwallis surrendered.

On the 16th, finding that he must either surrender or break through, he determined to cross the river and fall on the French rear with his whole force, and then turn northward and force his way through Maryland, Pennsylvania, and the Jerseys. In the night the light infantry, the greater part of the guards, and part of the 23d were embarked in boats, and crossed to the Gloucester side of the river before midnight. At this critical moment a violent storm arose which prevented the boats returning. The enemy's fire reopened at daybreak, and the engineer and principal officers of the army gave it as their opinion that it was impossible to resist longer. Only one 8-inch shell and a hundred small ones remained. The defences had in many places tumbled to ruins, and no effectual resistance could be opposed to an assault.

Accordingly, Lord Cornwallis sent out a flag of truce, and arranged terms of surrender. On the 24th the fleet and reinforcements arrived off the mouth of the Chesapeake. Had they left New York at the time promised, the result of the campaign would have been different.

The army surrendered as prisoners of war until exchanged, the officers with liberty to proceed on parole to Europe and not to serve until exchanged. The loyal Americans were embarked on the *Bonito* sloop of war and sent to New York in safety, Lord Cornwallis having obtained permission to send off the ship without her being searched, with as many soldiers on board as he should think fit, so that they were accounted for in any further exchange. He was thus enabled to send off such of the inhabitants and loyalist troops as would have suffered from the vengeance of the Americans.

The surrender of Lord Cornwallis's army virtually ended the war. The burden entailed on the people in England by the great struggle against France, Spain, Holland, and America united in arms against her was enormous. So long as there appeared any chance of recovering the colony, the English people made the sacrifices required of them, but the conviction that it was impossible for them to wage a war with half Europe and at the same time to conquer a continent had been gaining more and more in strength. Even the most sanguine were silenced by the surrender of York Town, and a cry arose throughout the country that peace should at once be made.

As usual, under the circumstances, a change of ministry took place. Negotiations for peace were at once commenced, and the war terminated in the acknowledgment of the entire independence of the United States of America.

Harold, with his companions, had fallen back to Charleston with Lord Rawdon after the relief of Ninety-six, and remained there until the news arrived that the negotiations were on foot and that peace was now certain. Then he took his discharge, and sailed at once for England, accompanied by Jake—Peter Lambton taking a passage to Canada to carry out his intention of settling at Montreal.

Harold was now past two-and-twenty, and his father and mother did not recognize him, when, without warning, he arrived at their residence in Devonshire. It was six years since his mother had seen him, when she sailed from Boston before its surrender in 1776.

For a year he remained quiet at home, and then carried out his plan of returning to the American continent and settling in Canada.

Accompanied by Jake, he sailed for the St. Lawrence, and purchased a snug farm on its banks, near the spot where it flows from Lake Ontario.

He greatly improved it, built a comfortable house upon it, and two years later returned to England, whence he brought back his cousin Nelly as his wife.

Her little fortune was used in adding to the farm, and it became one of the largest and best managed in the country.

Peter Lambton found Montreal too crowded for him, and settled down on the estate, supplying it with fish and game so long as his strength enabled him to go about, and enjoying the society of Jack Pearson, who had married and established himself on a farm close by.

As years went on and the population increased, the property became very valuable, and Harold, before he died, was one of the wealthiest and most respected men in the colony. So long as his mother lived, he and his wife paid occasional visits to England, but after her death his family and farm had so increased that it was inconvenient to leave them. His father therefore returned with him to Canada, and ended his life there. Jake lived to a good old age, and was Harold's faithful friend and right-hand man to the last.

THE END

PrestonSpeed Publications 51 Ridge Road Mill Hall, PA 17751
(570) 726-7844
www.prestonspeed.com

Historiae Dona Repertum

Books by G. A. Henty

For The Temple
The Dragon & The Raven
In Freedom's Cause
By Pike & Dyke
Beric The Briton
St. Bartholomew's Eve
With Lee in Virginia
By Right of Conquest
The Young Carthaginian
Winning His Spurs
Under Drake's Flag
The Cat of Bubastes
Wulf The Saxon
A Knight of the White Cross
St. George for England
With Wolfe in Canada
By England's Aid
The Dash for Khartoum
The Lion of the North
Won by the Sword
Facing Death
The Lion of St. Mark
Bonnie Prince Charlie
In the Reign of Terror
The Tiger of Mysore
A March on London

Under Wellington's Command
At Agincourt
Orange and Green
With Moore at Corunna
To Herat and Cabul
For Name and Fame
With Clive in India
Both Sides The Border
No Surrender
True to the Old Flag

Other Publications

The Captain (A Magazine)
By Right of Conquest (unit study guide)
By Pike and Dyke (unit study guide)
The Cat of Bubastes (unit study guide)
A Journey of Souls
The List
The Henty Companion

Audio Books

The Cat of Bubastes
Wulf The Saxon
The Young Carthaginian

PrestonSpeed Publications takes great pride in re-printing the complete works of G. A. Henty. New titles are released regularly. Both our hardcover and tradepaper printings include the complete text of the original edition, as well as all maps and illustrations.

For a free catalog call 570-726-7844
or write to us and request your free catalog at:
PrestonSpeed Publications
51 Ridge Road
Mill Hall, PA 17751
USA
A catalog may also be obtained at our web site:
www. prestonspeed.com